"I'm not paying the scrawny little bastard anymore," Julie whispered to her reflection. "It's over."

She opened her purse and yanked out a compact. She wouldn't give him the satisfaction of knowing he'd made her cry. *No one* made her cry. Hell, *she* was the one who made people weep. On the air, in front of the entire city.

The doorknob of the hotel bathroom jiggled. "Keep your pants on, Harry. I'll be out by the time room service gets here with your celebratory champagne."

Footsteps moved rapidly away.

She flung open the door and stepped into the suite. "You've pushed me too far, Harry. You're not getting another nickel from me. You can do whatever you want with the evidence. If it goes public, you'll go to prison. I'll see to it. Nobody threatens my daughter and gets away with it."

She turned slowly to face Harry. He sat in the chair, just as he had before. Only now the white dress shirt he wore was completely soaked in blood.

Her body began to shake. She was alone in the room, and Harry Blackwood was dead.

MAGGIE SHAYNE

THICKER THAN WATER

MIRA®

ISBN 1-55166-737-1

THICKER THAN WATER

Visit us at www.mirabooks.com

Printed in U.S.A.

This book would not have happened if not for the assistance of some very special people, and I wish to acknowledge and thank them. I dedicate this book to the following wonderful, talented people. I feel lucky to share the planet with every one of them.

To Gayle Wilson, whose words of wisdom broke the dam! I was stuck fast, but you inspired me at NJRW, 2002.

To Molly Herwood, who went above and beyond to help me find the information I needed.

To WTVH-5's Maureen Greene and Melissa Medalie, who helped me get inside the head of a news anchor. To photojournalists John and Al, who changed my entire concept of this book's hero. And to everyone else in the newsroom at WTVH-5 Syracuse, for your invaluable assistance and inspiration.

To David O. Norris, veteran cop, skilled P.I. and captain of the Genesee Belle for unwavering support and tireless advice, and for helping me get the "cop stuff" right.

To my precious husband, Rick, who stands between me and the world like a suit of armor. Without you, I'd be done for.

I'd also like to thank those I think of as "my team." My agent, Eileen Fallon, for her solid guidance, wise advice and for her steady hands at the helm of my career. My editors: Leslie Wainger, who has been in my corner, supporting me and believing in me from the very start, and Dianne Moggy and Amy Moore-Benson, who had the faith to embrace both sides of this writer's split personality by welcoming both my vampires and my suspense novels into the MIRA family. My editors deserve sainthood for putting up with an author who changes the story *while* the back cover copy is being written—and never once flinching or complaining.

Thank you, all. My life is richer (and my books are better) because of you.

Prologue

"Can't you see that we'll die if we don't get the hell out of here?"

"We won't, Jewel," Lizzie whispered. "Mordecai would never let anything happen to us. Not to us." Her voice changed to a singsong kind of coo. "No, he wouldn't. Not to his own baby, would he, Sunshine? No." She sat cuddling her newborn daughter in the rocking chair Mordecai Young, "the reverend," had brought into their quarters.

They no longer had to room in the barracks with the other so-called Young Believers. Mordecai Young had moved his special girls into the spacious attic of the main house, where he could be closer to them.

"Lizzie, you're being stupid. You're forgetting the plan." Jewel paced the length of the large room, growing more and more agitated. "And it was working so damn well."

Lizzie looked at her and for a moment Jewel thought she saw the sharp mind and clear eyes of the girl her friend had been six months ago. "It was," Lizzie said. "We made him believe we loved him, didn't we? And it worked."

It *had* worked. Mordecai had made them his right hands. They had access to the house. They ate better. He never hit them anymore.

"But, Jewel, I'm not acting anymore. I love him."

"He's a criminal. Jesus, Lizzie, he takes in runaways and makes us into slaves. He has armed guards and those dogs of his patrolling the compound in case any of us try to leave. We're fenced in, fed all the drugs he can slip into our food to keep us complacent while we listen to his sermons and cultivate his crops. And you've seen the weapons room. He's got more firepower than the freaking National Guard down there!''

Unmoved by Jewel's impassioned speech, Lizzie stroked a forefinger along her baby's whisper-soft cheek. "He's my daughter's father."

"He's a drug dealer with a Messiah complex, Lizzie. And this is no place for a baby." She moved closer, ran a palm over Sunny's silken baby hair. "We have to get out—for *her* sake."

Lizzie closed her eyes. A tear squeezed through her lashes. "I know. I know you're right. I just…I don't think he means to be…I think he really believes the things he tells us."

Maybe he did, Jewel thought. Maybe he really did believe he was more enlightened than the rest of the world, or that he'd been chosen by God to be his new messenger and ordered to create this compound. And that the marijuana crop didn't do much real harm, and that it was the good he could do with the money it brought in that made it all right in the eyes of the Almighty.

Yeah, maybe he really did believe all that. Which made him insane, and even more dangerous.

"He loves her. It'll kill him to lose her."

"He wants to control her," Jewel insisted. "He named her. He sets her schedule. When she eats, when she sleeps, when she's bathed, how often you get to hold her. He sees her as something he owns, just like us."

"It's just his way."

Jewel thinned her lips. "Tonight," she said. "I made a special snack for the dogs. It ought to put them out of commission. We'll tell the guard at the gate that Sunshine is sick and that Mordecai ordered us to get her to a hospital. If he gives us any trouble—" She took the paring knife out of her jeans pocket. "I snatched this from the kitchen tonight."

"My God, Jewel!" Lizzie's eyes widened. "Why can't we try to go out through the tunnels?"

"How, when he keeps the only key on a chain around his neck?" Jewel put a firm hand on Lizzie's shoulder. "I'm seventeen years old, Lizzie. I am *not* going to spend the rest of my life in this prison. And neither is she," she added with a nod at Sunshine. "I love her, too, you know."

"I know you do." Lizzie sighed, lifting her eyes. "What about Sirona and Tessa?"

"I don't know. Since he moved them into the main house, he's been visiting us less and less at night. I think he's going to get tired of us soon, anyway. We lose favor, we end up back out in the barracks. And you know that wouldn't be good for the baby."

"I know." She looked more sad, though, than afraid. Sad that her lover was spending time with other women. She'd never minded sharing him with Jewel. But that was different. They were like sisters, the two of them.

"I'd like to take Sirona and Tessa with us, but I'm not sure we can trust them not to run straight to Mordecai if we tell them our plan."

"I don't like them, anyway," Lizzie said.

She was pale and far too thin. She'd been bleeding heavily since giving birth—too heavily, in Jewel's opinion, but then again, what did she know? It had been seven weeks. She thought it should have stopped by now. Lizzie wasn't the same spunky, fun-loving girl she'd been when Jewel had met her on the streets. They'd heard rumors of this place, that it was a dream come true for runaways.

It wasn't a dream, it was a nightmare.

They both looked up quickly as they heard his unmistakable footsteps, coming up the stairs. The door opened, and he stood there, with his warm brown eyes, long, mink hair, and neatly trimmed beard. He wore white robes and sandals, and he looked for all the world like Jesus. But when he spoke, the illusion was shattered by his soft Southern twang.

"I need to take li'l Sunshine now. Bedtime." He smiled as he looked at the baby.

Lizzie kissed her child's forehead and hurried to hand her over to her father. "Good night, my sweet baby."

Jewel watched him take the baby. He stared down at the child adoringly, his brown eyes softer than ever. "You're a special li'l girl, you know that? The daughter of the Son. You're blessed, my Sunshine. You're blessed." Then, as he turned and carried the baby away, he began to sing. "You are my sunshine, my only sunshine…"

"Mordecai," Jewel said, knowing he would be angry at her interruption, but daring it all the same.

He turned, scowling at her.

"I'm worried about Sunny. Do you really think it's safe for her here, with the drugs and the weapons and all?"

"Do you think I'd risk my only child?" he asked.

She licked her lips. "I just—I overheard you talking to one of the guards today. You said there had been some kind of…government men asking questions in town."

He walked closer to her, his face gentle—right up until his fist connected with her jaw, knocking her backward to the floor. Lizzie shot to her feet, rushing to where Jewel landed.

"Let that be a lesson to you about eavesdroppin'," Mordecai said. "Haven't I taught you better?"

"I'm sorry," she whispered, a hand on her face, not daring to get to her feet. Lizzie was leaning over her, hands on her shoulders, but she turned now to the man who stood nearby, cradling the baby in his arms.

"You didn't answer her question, Mordecai. What happens if these government men try to come in here? What we're doing isn't exactly legal. And you have all those guns—"

Sighing, he gazed down adoringly on his child. "It's as I've always told all of you, mankind is not ready for a soul like mine. They may very well try to kill me, in the end. And if they do—well, now, what better place for my only child than with her daddy?"

"You—you mean…?"

"Death is nothing to fear, you know. Haven't I taught you as much? Haven't you learned a thing in your time here?" He shook his head slowly, then turned and carried the baby out of the room, pulling the door closed behind him.

Lizzie hurled herself after him, only to collide with the door. When she went to tear it open, it had been locked from the outside. She pounded on it uselessly, then collapsed against the wood, sobbing.

Jewel got to her feet and went to her friend, sliding her arms around her and pulling her close.

"Oh, God, you were right, Jewel. You were right. He doesn't care if Sunny lives or dies!"

"It's all right. It's going to be all right. We'll get out of here, and we'll take her with us. Everything will be okay."

"I thought he loved her," Lizzie sobbed. "I thought he loved *us!*"

"He only loves his own crazy ideas. He loves the power he has over all of us. He loves being in control and this God complex of his. And he loves money. God, he's got scads of it down there somewhere."

Lizzie lifted her head. "I know where he keeps it. It's in the escape tunnel." She stared hard at Jewel. "It's almost as if he knows something horrible is going to happen. It's like he's…preparing for it."

"Yeah, well, we won't be here when it does. And neither will *our* baby."

As it turned out, she couldn't have been more wrong.

They awoke to the sound of gunfire, rapid and loud.

Jewel leaped out of bed and ran for the door. "It's coming from inside the house!" The knob wouldn't turn in her hand, though.

Lizzie was at the window, looking out. "From outside, too! There are soldiers!" Her entire body jerked backward when the glass shattered, and she hit the floor.

"Lizzie!" Jewel ran to her, sliding across the floor on her knees when she got close. "Lizzie, my God." There was blood on the front of her nightgown.

Lizzie sat up, pushing Jewel's hands away from her belly. "It's okay. Just a little cut. The glass."

Jewel shook her head, terrified her friend had been hit by a bullet. "Are you sure? Let me see."

"I'm fine, Jewel." Lizzie pressed her palm to the bloody spot on her nightgown. Jewel tried to shift it aside to see the damage, but Lizzie pushed her away. "We have to get the baby out of here!"

"I know, I know." Jewel helped her friend to her feet, watching her face, worried.

Lizzie went to the locked door. The gunshots were ringing out faster, louder, than before. Then something even louder than a gunshot shook the entire house, and Jewel thought she smelled smoke. Lizzie gave up twisting the knob, stood back, and kicked the door. It was an old door, and the wood began to split under the pressure of her foot. She kicked again, and then Jewel was beside her with a small metal chair in her hands. Using the chair as a battering ram, she slammed it against the door. The two took turns attacking the door, until it finally gave way under the assault. The smoke smell was stronger now, as they raced down the stairs to the second floor nursery.

But Sunny's crib was empty. "Oh, God. Oh, God, where is she?" Lizzie moaned.

"Mordecai must have her!"

Jewel gripped her friend's arm and tugged her out of the nursery. They ran together down to the ground floor. Fire and smoke were everywhere. The front door was open, but instead of running out of the house, people were running into it, bullets chasing them down. Some lay on the floor, dead or dying. Others stood at the windows, firing shots at the army of men outside. The front of the house was completely engulfed in flames.

"He couldn't have got out that way!" Jewel cried.

"The basement. He must have taken her to the tunnel."

As they ran for the basement, Jewel tripped over someone, turned to look, and saw Sirona, cowering in a corner, sobbing. Tessa was nearby, sitting on the floor looking shocky, her face blank, her body rocking.

"Come on, come with us," Jewel said, bending to grip Tessa's upper arm, jerking her to her feet. Sirona followed wordlessly. Lizzie was several steps ahead of them by then. The fire was spreading—chasing them it seemed. "Hurry!"

They made it to the basement stairs, then down them. It was dark, but Jewel saw Lizzie come to a sudden stop ahead of them and heard her as she shouted, "How could you? How could you try to save yourself and leave the rest of us to die?"

Jewel raced closer, shocked into stillness when she saw Mordecai there, cradling little Sunny in his arms.

"Go back to your room!" he shouted. "You have no idea what's happening here!"

"I know exactly what's happening." Lizzie's voice was weaker than before. The red stain on the front of her nightgown was larger now, spreading. There was an explosion from somewhere close. It was deafening, and it shook them physically. A loud roar followed, and Jewel felt the heat.

"Give me my daughter," Lizzie said.

Mordecai lifted one hand, and Jewel stiffened when she saw the gun he held. "Go back or die right here."

Jewel ran at him. He was so focused on Lizzie that he didn't see her fast enough to fire, and she hit him with every ounce of strength she possessed, knocking him right off his feet and wrestling the baby from his arms as she fell on top of him. The gun skittered across the concrete floor. Jewel tore herself and little Sunny from Mordecai's arms, and then it seemed like the end of the world as the beams and boards above them came crashing down like some fiery avalanche.

She was knocked to her knees, and when she managed to get up again, holding the screaming baby close, choking on the smoke and heat, she saw Lizzie on her knees. Sirona and Tessa hovered two feet away, looking terrified in the dancing light of the flaming beams that littered the floor now. And beneath one of those beams, Mordecai lay, trapped.

He held out a hand toward Lizzie. "Help me. Help me, and I'll get you out of here."

Lizzie got slowly to her feet and edged closer to him. She stepped carefully over and around the burning beams that crisscrossed his torso. Then she knelt beside Mordecai. "I loved you," she told him.

"You still do, you know you do. It'll be like I promised, Lizzie. You and me and Sunny, the plantation house in Virginia. A real family."

"Just like you promised," she whispered. Then she reached out...and snatched the chain with the key dangling at its end from around his neck. She looked past him then, at the other girls. "Come on."

The flames blazed higher. Soon they would all be trapped. They hurried forward, and the four women ran as Mordecai cried out to them to save him. Then the rest of the ceiling came crashing down, and he was silent, buried under flaming debris.

"Hurry!" They made it to the secret door that was hidden behind a set of false shelving, and Lizzie took the baby from Jewel's arms and handed her the key. Then she leaned back against the wall, as if she could barely stand on her own.

"Lizzie?"

"Just get the door."

Jewel nodded, hurrying to fit the key to the lock, taking off the padlock, opening the door onto a pitch-dark tunnel. The air that wafted from it smelled of earth and cool dampness but, blessedly, not of smoke. "It's open. Come on."

She turned back to Lizzie, who had slumped to a sitting position on the floor. Lizzie leaned close to her baby, kissed her cheek. Then she lifted her gaze to Jewel's again. "Take her," she said, her voice so hoarse and weak that Jewel could barely hear her over the fire.

Jewel dropped the key, taking the baby from Lizzie's arms, tucking her into one of her own and reaching down with her other hand to help Lizzie. Lizzie only shook her head from side to side and let her upper body fall backward to the floor.

"Lizzie!" Jewel leaned over her.

"Take her. Take her, Jewel. She's yours now."

"Get up, Lizzie. Come on, I'll help you."

"Take the money. There's so much of it, there in the tunnel. Duffel bags full of it. Take it and make a good life for my Sunny."

"I'm not leaving you!"

Lizzie smiled gently. "No. I'm leaving you." She pressed her hand to her belly again. "It wasn't glass, honey. It wasn't glass at all." Her eyes fell closed.

Jewel shook her, but there was no response.

Someone tugged Jewel away. Sirona. Tessa was already moving past them into the tunnel. "You have to go. You have to get the baby out," Sirona said gently.

"I can't leave her!"

"She's gone, Jewel. She's gone."

The fire surged closer, brighter and hotter. Jewel got up and handed the baby to Sirona; then she took Lizzie by the wrists and dragged her limp body into the tunnel. She couldn't bear the thought of her being burned, or ending her life so close to Mordecai Young. She pushed the door closed behind them, then turned to take the baby from Sirona again.

As she moved through the seemingly endless tunnel, she wondered how her life had managed to change so drastically over the course of one short summer. First her drunken, abusive father had hit her mother one too many times and wound up in prison for murder. Then the streets, where Jewel had fled to avoid ending up a ward of the state. Then this place, this supposed underground haven for runaway teens.

And now? What now?

She made her way through the tunnel, Sirona and Tessa flanking her. Eventually it grew lighter, and she spotted the duffel bags resting on the ground along the wall. She said, "Grab those and bring them. We'll split up what's inside once we get out of here. *If* we get out of here. And then we'll go our separate ways." She looked sternly at the two girls. "None of us can tell what happened here. Not ever, do you understand? If we do, little Sunny will end up a ward of the state—just like I almost was—or worse yet, with Lizzie's family, whoever they are. And that couldn't have been good, or Lizzie wouldn't be…" She swallowed hard, lowered her head. "She never even told me her last name."

"I was in the system," Sirona said. "It's no place for Sunny. It's okay. We'll never tell."

"There's enough money in those bags for all of us to start fresh, start new lives. We can never look back from here. Never. It's a pact. Understand?"

They both nodded.

"Good. Then let's go."

Sirona and Tessa each grabbed a bag and followed Jewel along the last leg of the tunnel. It angled slowly upward from deep in the earth, growing lighter and lighter, until finally it opened into sunlight.

They climbed out, helping each other. "It's morning," Sirona whispered.

Jewel turned to look back at the flames and smoke rising in the distance from what had been the Young Believers' compound. Every building on the place must be burning, she thought. And everyone left behind must be dead.

But that was behind her. She turned her back on all of it and faced the slowly rising sun that shone its red-orange light onto her and onto the baby.

Her baby now.

''It's Dawn,'' she whispered.

1

Sixteen Years Later
Syracuse, NY

Mascara tears were so far beneath her that she could barely believe they would dare skim down her face. She speed-yanked a half-dozen tissues from the hotel-issue dispenser and wiped the trespassers off. Then she cranked on the cold water, splashed her face and went still, staring at her reflection as the water dripped from her chin.

What would Dawn think of her if she saw her mom like this? Was this the way she was raising her daughter to be? Weak? Compliant? Afraid?

No.

"I'm not paying the scrawny little bastard anymore," she whispered to her reflection. She stood a little straighter, lifted her chin a little higher. "No more. It's over. One way or another, it's finished."

She opened her purse and yanked out a compact. She wouldn't give the bastard the satisfaction of knowing he'd made her cry. *No one* made her cry. Hell, *she* was the one who was known for making other people weep. On the air, in front of the entire city. This idiot had jerked her around long enough. The fact that he'd dared to even try—the fact that she had let him get away with it, even for a little while—it was beyond the pale.

"What the hell was I thinking?" she asked her reflection, while her hands moved to automatically and expertly return her face to a state of near perfection. "I'm not some little nobody. I'm Julie Fucking Jones."

The doorknob of the hotel's bathroom jiggled. She sent it a burning glance. "Keep your pants on, Harry. I'll be out by the time room service gets here with your goddamn celebratory champagne."

Footsteps moved rapidly away from the bathroom door.

She paused, glanced down at the mascara she'd just pulled out of the handbag, and grimaced at it. "Waterproof, my ass." She flung it at the wastebasket, then snapped the bag shut and turned on her heel to return to the other room—to end this thing, as she should have done six months ago.

She flung open the door and stepped through it. "I don't know why it took so long," she said, her voice as firm and strong as it was when she was on the air. "But you've finally pushed me too far. It's finished, Harry. You're not getting another nickel from me. You can drop this now, or I'm going to go to your brother and tell him everything."

He sat in the small armchair, right where he'd been when she'd excused herself to go to the bathroom and gather her courage. As if he'd never moved. His back was to her. She could only see the top of his head. The little pink patch where his black hair was starting to thin. He said nothing, probably too surprised. She couldn't imagine why he hadn't been expecting this. Did he really think she would let him keep pushing?

"You can do whatever you want with the evidence, I don't care," she lied. She *did* care. "If it goes public, Harry, you'll go to prison. I'll see to it, even it means losing everything. Nobody wrongs me like this, much less threatens my daughter, and gets away with it. Nobody."

She strode straight past him to the nightstand, wondering at the metallic smell in the air. He always brought copies of the damning evidence to these meetings. Always promised they were the last copies in existence as he sold them to her for large amounts of cash. Always insisted on closing the deal with a glass of champagne. And a month later, he always showed up with another set of demands. She looked down at the table. But the envelope was gone.

She turned slowly to face Harry. "All right, what did you do with the…"

Her voice tripped over a heartbeat when she faced him fully. He sat in the chair, just as he had before. Only now he was dead. The white dress shirt he wore was completely soaked in blood. So were his hands, and the chair itself, his shoes and the beige carpet underneath them.

Her gaze slid to his face again. The slightly open mouth. The wide, sightless eyes. The dark, gaping, bloody crescent in his long, skinny neck. Her body began to shake. A tremor formed somewhere down deep and worked its way outward to her hands and knees and even her head, lips, eyes. Fear gripped her heart like an icy fist as her gaze danced around the room. But no one else was there. Not now. She checked the tiny closet just to be sure, but it was empty. She was alone in the room, and Harry Blackwood was dead.

A wave of nausea rose up in her stomach as she lunged toward the door to turn the dead bolt. She barely got it done before she had to run for the bathroom again, and while she leaned over the toilet, she got so dizzy she nearly fell in.

When she could finally stop retching, she braced one hand on the tank to hold herself upright, knocked the lid down, flushed. Then she turned weakly to the sink to rinse her mouth.

It was as she turned the taps off again that she found herself blinking down at her hands on the knobs. And slowly a line of news copy printed itself across her mind.

Respected News Anchor Sole Suspect in Brutal Murder. Fingerprints Found at Scene. Blackmail Plot and Scandalous Past Uncovered.

"Details at eleven," she whispered softly. She was swimming in motive. And standing in the middle of a visit that spelled opportunity in 30-point type. She closed her eyes. "No. No, goddammit." Yanking tissues again, she used them to wipe the faucet and valves, the toilet tank, its handle and anything else she had touched in the bathroom. She tossed the used tissues into the wastebasket, and then grabbed a washcloth from the stack, wet it and wiped down the counter, the doorknob, everything. She removed the plastic bag from the wastebasket and carried it with her back into the main part of the hotel room. When she bent to wipe off the nightstand she had touched moments ago, an icy chill whispered along her spine. The envelope. Where was the envelope? What if the killer had taken it?

"Jesus. What is this? How could anyone know what was in that envelope? And why would they take it if they didn't know, and…"

No time, not now, her mind whispered, and she found herself nodding in agreement. She had to move; she had to be smart, eliminate any hint of her presence and get the hell out of here, all unseen. She could not afford to panic.

Moving silently and quickly, her entire body still trembling, she wiped down the dead bolt, the doorknob, every surface and door frame in the room, anything she had even been close to, just in case she had rested her hand on any surface. She was careful, and she was thorough. She searched as she wiped. Every cupboard and drawer. She found a stack of self-help books by self-proclaimed psychics on the nightstand: John Andrews and Sylvia Brown and Nathan Z. But the envelope wasn't there. It wasn't under the bed. It wasn't in Harry's coat pockets or his shaving kit, and those were the only things in the entire room that belonged to him.

When she finished her search and her wiping, she dropped the washcloth into the wastepaper bag and looked around the room. There were two glasses on the table.

Her eyes were drawn back to the dead man in the chair. Her shaking intensified, and her breath began to rush in and out too quickly.

"Focus, dammit!" She barked the words aloud, forcing her attention to the job at hand, told herself to hurry before room service brought the champagne. She focused again on the two glasses. One nearly empty, one half full of whiskey. She picked up the fuller one, which had been hers. It had her prints on it, and maybe her lipstick. She downed the whiskey fast, grating her teeth against the burn and welcoming the warmth that spread outward from her belly when it landed. Then she added the glass to her bag of rubbish and backed toward the door. She yanked her tan trenchcoat from the back of the desk chair where she'd left it, hurriedly put it on, and used the sleeve to wipe off the back of the chair, where it had been hanging. Then, on the edge of panic again, she checked the large inside pocket. But the bundle of cash was still there. A sigh of relief tumbled from her lungs. She took the scarf and oversize sunglasses from another of the deep pockets and put them on. No one had recognized her coming in. She'd always done her best not to be noticed or recognized when meeting with her blackmailer to pay him off. She had become adept at that over the last six months. Thanks to Harry.

She took her small handbag, then pulled her coat sleeve over her hand to open the door and close it behind her, wiping the outer knob clean. At the elevator, she used that same coat sleeve to push the button. The car came to a stop. She tucked her little bag of rubbish underneath her coat as the doors slid open.

A short, round woman of Hispanic descent, wearing a teal designer knockoff dress, glanced at her, then looked away. A tall, thin man with skin so pale he seemed colorless stood beside her in a cheap suit. He didn't make eye contact at all. Julie stepped into the elevator, then went stiff from head to toe when a loud rattling sound came along the hall. As the elevator doors slid closed, she saw the young man, pushing the room service cart along the hall. Along for the ride were a champagne bottle in an ice bucket and two glasses. He stopped in front of Harry's room.

Sickening fear choked Julie as the elevator doors closed and the car began to drop. That man. He would be opening Harry's door about now. Finding his body. Shouting in horror. Jesus, she had to get out of here—fast.

The couple got off at the lobby. The moment they did, Julie reached out to wipe the button marked 12 clean of any prints she might have left on it on her way up earlier. She kept her back to the security camera, using her body to block her hands from its all-seeing gaze as she worked. She rode the elevator down to the lower level parking garage, and then she got off and hurried to her car. Her heels were loud in the darkness, clicking over the concrete. They sounded like gunshots to her raw senses.

She dipped in her pocket for her keys. Pushed aside the ever-present notebook, the mini-cassette recorder, the pen... *Goddammit,* where were her keys?

She stood where she was, ten feet from her Mercedes, closed her eyes and prayed as she slowly, methodically, searched every single pocket, without luck. She searched the small handbag, as well, but the keys were not there.

God, please, tell me I didn't leave them in Harry's room.
She couldn't have. She couldn't—

"Calm. Slow. Just think."

Drawing a calming breath, she hit her mental rewind and then tried to replay the events of the last hour.

She knocked once. Harry opened the door and stood there smirking at her as she pushed past him to go inside. "I thought that twenty grand I paid you a month ago bought me the last copies."

"I know," he said, having the good sense to look guilty. "I lied. But this time, I swear, I brought the originals." He turned and pointed toward the nightstand where the envelope rested. *"Look for yourself, if you don't believe me. I mean it, Jewel, this is the last time you'll ever hear from me."*

She shook her head slowly, not looking at the items in the envelope. She knew well enough what it contained. The photographs of her at the compound. Proof that her daughter's birth certificate was a fake. "No. No, you're lying, just like you've been lying all along. This is never going to end, is it, Harry? You'll keep on bleeding me until there's nothing left, and then you'll sell the evidence to the highest bidder anyway. Won't you?"

"Come on, you know I won't do that. I promise. This is the last time." He walked away from her, sat in the chair and poured whiskey into two glasses. *"Have a drink. You're so damn tense you're making me nervous, and the customary champagne isn't here yet. Damn slow room service."*

She moved forward, slapped her keys onto the coffee table and picked up one of the glasses. After taking a slug, she set the glass down again.

"People trust you, you know. They respect your opinions. They count on you to be practical and levelheaded and

reliable. That's why you're so good at what you do, Jewel.''

"It's Julie."

"Sure. Now. You're good, and you know it. That's why the networks have started sniffing around you."

She looked at him sharply. "How the hell do you know about that?"

He shrugged, drank his whiskey. "I hear things. What, you think I don't keep track of you? I probably know more about your life than you do. You know your station's been talking to male news anchors?"

"What do you know about any of that?"

He smiled. "I know your ratings have been falling since your former coanchor retired. I know you prefer to keep the spotlight all to yourself. I know—"

"You just keep your nose out of my career, Harry. None of it has anything to do with you."

He shook his head as if she were being ridiculous, then faced her squarely. "I need fifty thousand this time. Cash."

Her throat tried to close, and she felt tears burn her eyes. Angry tears. Outraged tears. "You're *fucked*, then, because I only brought twenty." She yanked a fat wad of cash, bound in a rubber band, from the inside pocket of her coat, showed it to him.

"You're *fucked*, then, 'cause I can start the rag sheets' bidding at seventy-five, and it'll only go up from there. Come on, what happened to all that cash you stole from Mordecai?"

"It's gone, Harry. I bought a house, a new identity, got an education. All I have now is what I earn at the station—"

"Which you'll lose—if I share your secret with the world."

"You wouldn't dare…"

The look on his face told her that he would *dare. God,
she had to stop him. She held the cash out to him, silently
pleading with him to take it and leave her alone. But he
only looked at it as if it were something that smelled bad
and then looked away. Julie stuffed the money back into
her coat pocket and began to shake. She'd already paid
him more than two hundred thousand dollars over the last
six months. Her 401K was drained, and she'd had to sell
stocks at a loss to get this additional twenty thousand for
him.*

*"Well? Can you get another thirty or do I place a call
to* The Exposer?*"*

*"I...don't know. I...I don't know how I can get another
thirty. I don't know." She got up, paced back and forth.
She was hot, sweating with it, so she peeled off her coat
and hung it over a chair near the door. She needed to think,
to clear her head. "I need to use the rest room," she told
him.*

*He shrugged. "It's over there," he said, nodding toward
the door on the far side of the room. "Don't be long. Time
is money, babe."*

So she went into the bathroom....

"And when I came out, he was dead," she whispered.

Blinking back to the present, she gave her head a firm
shake. "The keys were on the coffee table. Dammit, why
didn't I see them when I was cleaning up?"

*Because there were a dead man and a pool of blood in
the room with you, some cynical voice inside her taunted.
You may have been a little distracted.*

"No. That's not it. Maybe they got knocked off the table.
Onto the floor. They must have. They were probably right
there, on the floor, or maybe under the edge of a chair,
or..." She shivered as her mind raced on. Maybe they were
under that blood-soaked chair where she'd left Harry.

Maybe they were on the blood-soaked carpet. "Oh God, oh Jesus."

She had to go back.

The idea of walking back into that room sent her heart racing. Her knees felt weak, and she leaned on a support column to keep from falling over. This was idiotic. She didn't hyperventilate, and she didn't faint. It wasn't *in her* to faint. But she felt goddamn close to it right now.

Just figure out what to do. Think, *dammit!*

Dawn. She could call Dawn. Have her bring the spare keys from the rack in the kitchen. She shouldn't really be driving on her own. She only had her learner's permit. But in an emergency…

Yeah, that's the answer, Julie. Bring your daughter into this mess.

No. She couldn't call Dawn. She didn't want Dawn within a million miles of this nightmare. Dawn needed to be protected at all costs. Dawn was everything to her.

So think of something else, then.

But there was nothing else to think of. If the police found her keys in that room, that put her there. She had to go back. She wanted to argue with the calm, cool voice in her head. The news anchor voice. But she couldn't. It was right.

She took a steadying breath, straightened her spine and took another. She'd been standing here, fighting panic and racking her brain, for twenty minutes. She could stand here all night, and it wouldn't change the facts. She had to find a way to get back inside that room and get her keys before the police did. There wasn't really a choice here. Turning, she walked firmly, steadily, to the elevator, stuffing the small garbage bag from Harry's room into a large overfilled Dumpster on the way. Once again she used her coat sleeve to hit the elevator button.

The elevator went up, but not far. It stopped on the lobby

level. The doors opened, and two men in police uniforms got on. "What floor did he say?" one was asking.

"Twelve. The manager who called it in is up there with the fellow who found him."

Like a flash, Julie's hand shot out to hit a button. Any button besides 12, because these two were cops, and they would damn well notice if 12 was the only button lit, and then they'd want to know why she was going there.

The doors slid closed, and one of the cops, a solid looking man with a face like a road map, hit the button marked 12, noticed it was already lit and glanced her way. The other one stood back. He was taller, leaner and younger. But if anything, he looked even meaner than his partner. Neither was familiar to her, and she considered that a lucky break. But the shorter one glanced at her briefly, then, with a frown, looked at her again.

The car stopped on the third floor, and the doors slid open. She left the elevator as if her feet were on fire, acting as if she were looking for her room key as she did.

When the doors closed again, she stopped, braced her hand on a wall and tried to stop shaking. The police were here already. Now what the hell was she going to do?

A door opened somewhere further down the hall, so she moved in the opposite direction, spotted the stair door ahead of her and headed toward it as if it were a haven.

It was cool and dark in the stairwell. Every breath echoed. But at least she was alone. She could think. She had to get back into that room before the cops found her keys. But how?

Sean MacKenzie didn't like looking at dead people. You never really got used to it, he supposed. According to his police scanner, there was one waiting for him at the Armory Square Hotel. He'd been up. Lately, sleep was not an option. And trying to sleep when he couldn't was sheer hell. So he spent a lot of time cruising the city, scanner on, looking for stories.

He had no idea how much it had paid off until he stood outside the door to room 1207, staring in at the body in the chair. His throat was slashed, and there was blood everywhere, and it was goddamn creepy the way the eyes stayed open and seemed to stare right at him. And then he recognized the stiff, and his heart skipped a beat.

"Jesus Christ, isn't that Harry Blackwood?" he whispered to himself.

"My God, I think it is."

He damn near jumped right out of his skin when that answering whisper came from so close beside him. He jerked his gaze to the side and saw his nemesis standing right beside him. Julie Jones.

"What the hell are *you* doing here?"

"Getting a story, just like you," she told him.

"You don't *get* stories. You *read* them."

The two police officers had moved from the main room into the bathroom, checking it out. Other cops, homicide detectives, would be arriving any second to help secure the crime scene, and the two journalists would be tossed out on their asses.

"Have they found anything?" she asked him.

"You think I'd tell you if they had?"

She shrugged. "Don't tell me you're going to try to scoop me on the hard facts, MacKenzie. We both know you make them up as you go along."

"At least I got my job based on my talent and not on my cleavage."

She shot him a hate-filled glance. He mirrored it back at her. Then he yanked his camera out of the case that hung from his shoulder and snapped several photos of the dead man. The camera was the quietest one he owned, and he didn't use the flash. It was a tacky and cheap thing to do, and he would probably be barred from selling the photos, Harry being who he had been, black sheep of a political family that rivaled royalty in New York State. But the photos would be worth some nice cash if he could get away with it.

She said, "You're a ghoul, MacKenzie." Then she shouldered him aside. "I'm going in there." And she walked right into the room.

He reached out to grab her arm, to stop her, but his reaction wasn't fast enough. She walked right into the crime scene. Granted, there was no yellow tape across the door just yet, but she still knew better. What the hell was she *thinking?*

She stood near the glass-topped coffee table, her back to him, a notebook in her hand, scribbling rapidly. Only it was odd, because she wasn't really looking at the notepad as she wrote on it. She was scanning the room, craning her neck, looking at the floor, peering underneath the table. Sean didn't see all that much of interest besides the body. What was she looking for?

The two cops came from the bathroom, one of them carrying a small zippered plastic evidence bag in his hand. Mac shoved the camera back into the case and backed off just a little, out of the line of fire, but still close enough to see. He was going to relish watching Julie Jones get her ass toasted for this temporary bout of idiocy or whatever had made her walk into that room. He didn't really think she'd been sitting at the anchor desk long enough to have forgotten the procedure for crime scene reporting. The press did not trample crime scenes. Even *he* knew that much.

The cops froze in their tracks at the sight of her.

"Just what the hell do you think you're doing in here? This is a crime scene!"

She jerked her head up sharply, and Sean saw the moment the cop recognized her. The most famous news anchor in Central NY. "I'm reporting. That's what I do," she said. She tucked the pencil behind her ear and started to open the little handbag she carried. "I have ID, if you—"

"Get your fucking ass out of here before I haul you in on an unlawful entry charge!"

It must have startled her, because she dropped the bag. Several items spilled out of it when it hit the floor.

"Jesus, you're contaminating the hell out of my crime scene," the second cop said, pushing past the first one toward her. He dropped to his knees on the floor, scooping up her items and shoving them back into her bag, then rising and pushing it into her hands even while shoving her bodily out the door. "You saw her drop that shit, didn't you, Klein?"

"Yeah, yeah, it's fine. There was nothing on the floor when we came in. It's fine, just get her the fuck out before we end up explaining to the lieutenant how she got by us, all right? Jax will have us doing paperwork for a freaking month if she hears about this."

Julie was pawing through the open bag as the cop shoved her out into the hallway. He caught sight of Sean. "You with her?"

"I'm just waiting for a statement." Sean held up both hands, backing off.

"Stay out here." The cop glanced at the camera bag. "And no photos."

"Yes, sir."

Julie was still digging through the purse. "Hey, hey, wait a minute. Where are my keys?"

Both cops turned. They did not look amused. Probably

had visions of that paperwork mountain and an unpleasant session with their superiors dancing in their heads, Sean thought. He knew Lieutenant Jackson, and they were right. She would have them buried in paperwork for this.

Jones went through the items in the purse, taking them out one by one. A cell phone, a pack of gum, a business card case, an earring. "I can't find my keys," she said again.

"Jesus, lady, are you saying you lost 'em in here?"

She searched all of her pockets. Made a big production about it, Sean thought. "I had them. And now I don't. That's all I know."

One cop closed his eyes, sighing and shaking his head.

The other one was talking fast. "What do they look like?"

"The key ring is silver, in the shape of my initials. *J.J.* It's got several keys on it. House, office, garage, file cabinet, my car, my daughter's Jeep."

As she kept talking, the other cop got back on the floor, looking underneath the chairs, shaking his head in disgust when he found nothing.

The other one said, "Look, if we find your keys, we'll get 'em to you, okay? That's the best we can do for you, lady, and lemme tell you right now, if you breathe a word to anyone about this, I'll see to it you never get any kind of cooperation from our department again. No tips, no exclusives, no press releases, and we'll keep you so far away from crime scenes from now on that you'll have watch someone else's news show to get the details." He glanced at Sean. "That goes for both of you. Understand?"

"Yes. Yes, of course I do," Julie said quickly. "Thank you, Officer. I don't know what I was thinking. I'm so sorry." She yanked the card case from her purse again, took out a card and handed it to him. "When you find the keys, just call me, all right?"

He muttered something unintelligible.

The other cop came forward. "Look, go wait in the lobby. Homicide and Forensics are on the way. I want you two out of here."

"Can't we at least get a statement?" Sean asked. And he couldn't figure out why she hadn't asked it first. Was she that rusty when it came to actual reporting? The elevator pinged and opened, and several plainclothes cops got out, including the one Sean thought of as the sexiest cop on the force—and maybe also the scariest—blond-haired, blue-eyed Lieutenant Cassandra Jackson.

"You want a statement?" she asked, honing in on the conversation as she strode toward the room. "Here's your statement. 'An unidentified man was found dead in the Armory Hotel. Police suspect foul play and an investigation is underway.'"

Sean had started to write, then lifted his head. "That's *it?*"

"That's it."

"Oh, come on, Jax. It's Senator Blackwood's lowlife brother, and his throat's been cut!"

"That's Lieutenant Jackson to you." She took his camera bag from his hand, took out the camera and easily popped open the back. A second later his film was hanging from her hands like crepe paper. She stuffed it into the deep pockets of her olive drab trench coat. "Cause of death will be determined at the autopsy. The identity is unofficial until next of kin are notified and come in to verify it."

"We won't release his name until we get the okay," Julie Jones offered. "Just so long as you give us the okay before you tell anyone else."

"Uh—both of us, that is. Not just her," Sean put in,

sensing that Jones was trying to scoop him, as usual. He had to admit, though, he was a little relieved that she was finally acting like the professional he reluctantly knew her to be. He tugged a card from a pocket. "My beeper number is on that."

Jax took it and nodded. "As if I don't have ten of these?"

"Yeah, but you never call." He gave her his most charming smile.

She returned a wink. "I'm way more than you could handle, MacKenzie." Then she rolled her eyes. "Fine, fine, you two get the scoop. But only if you get out of here right now and let my people do their job."

"Deal." Sean turned to head to the elevator, surprised when the normally aggressive Julie Jones turned around and followed him. Something was up with her. He wanted to know what.

He got into the elevator; she got in beside him. The doors slid closed. She sighed audibly, and he swore her body sagged.

"Do you have another set of keys?" he asked.

"Not on me."

"So then…you need a ride home?"

"I can get a cab."

He shrugged. "I could drive you."

She narrowed her eyes on him. "Why?"

"Why not?"

Frowning as if she trusted him about as far as she could throw him—a sentiment he understood well, since he felt the same way about her—she finally shrugged. "What the hell. Okay, fine. Drive me home."

2

Sean walked Julie Jones out of the hotel to his Porsche Carerra GT, which he figured would have impressed the socks off most women. With her, though, he wasn't expecting a hell of a lot.

She looked at the shiny black car, then at him. "Midlife crisis?"

Ignoring her, he depressed the button on his electronic key ring. The door locks popped open, the headlights came on, and the engine started. He opened her door for her.

"Am I supposed to take off my shoes or just sprinkle myself with holy water first?"

"Just get in, would you?"

She did. He closed the door and went around to his side. She was making with the sarcasm, yes, but not in her usual way. It was almost automatic. Almost as if she were speaking with her mouth while her mind was somewhere else. The zings were hardly worthy of her and nowhere near up to her usual standards. She'd been zinging him for so long, she could probably do it in a coma.

He shifted into gear and pulled the car away from the curb. "So what was with the little crime-scene-trampling demonstration back there?" he asked.

She blinked at him. "I don't know what you mean."

"What, do you think I'm as gullible as those cops are? I know you, Jones. You're a pro. You knew better than to walk in there like that."

Her eyes were huge and dark, and she blinked them now, using them to their full potential as proof of innocence. "I was just so stunned at seeing a New York State Senator's brother like that."

"Bullshit." He shifted, told himself to keep his eyes on the road. It wasn't easy, because she was wearing a skirt, and her legs were a longtime weakness of his. She had this skin... It was the first thing he'd noticed about her. Her skin. Smooth, almost luminous, bronze satin. The color didn't fade, even in the winter months. He had often wondered about her ethnic background, but how did you ask someone a question like that in the age of political correctness?

"Turn here," she said. "Take 92."

"Huh? Oh!" He got his mind back on his driving and took the turn she indicated. "I forgot you live all the way out in Cazenovia."

"Caz is only twenty minutes away from downtown."

"Yeah, by air." She sent him a look. He ignored it. "We got off the subject. Why were you so determined to get into that room?"

"I just wanted a closer look at Blackwood. I wasn't sure it was him."

"Uh-huh." She was lying through her teeth. "And what was up with emptying your purse onto the floor?"

She looked at him fast, almond-shaped brown eyes beaming purity, almost willing him to buy into it. "It was an accident."

"The hell it was."

Once she realized innocence had struck out, arrogance arrived to take its turn at bat. She folded her arms across her chest, straightened in her seat and faced him squarely, chin pulled in and slightly downward to give the illusion she was looking down her nose at him. She reminded him of royalty when she copped that attitude. Like some kind of queen who would have your head if you pissed her off much more than you already had. "If I *say* it was an accident," she assured him, "then it was an accident."

It was really too bad he hated her guts. He lifted his brows and tipped his head to one side. "If you *say* it was an accident, then you're lying through your pretty teeth, because *that* was no accident."

She rolled her eyes. "Your powers of observation stink, MacKenzie. No wonder you got passed over for the anchor seat I won."

"They passed me over for that job because you're easier on the eyes than I am, sweetie, and because your boss was narrow-minded enough to think he needed a male-female team. Don't even think for a minute it had to do with talent. It was those big brown eyes and that sexy little body." And that skin, he thought to himself.

"Right." She tossed her head, shook her hair a little. "You honestly think the viewing public watches the evening news just to ogle me?"

"Hell, *I* watch the evening news just to ogle you. And I don't even *like* you. Much less your presanitized, government-approved idea of news."

"You're an animal."

He shrugged. "I'm also the guy whose beeper is going to go off when they release the name of the victim. So if I were you, I'd be nice to me."

"I gave the lieutenant my number, and I have no doubt she'll call me first."

"Yeah, well, I gave her my beeper number, and that's way easier and quicker for her. So I have no doubt she'll call *me* first."

She sniffed. "For a date, maybe."

He lifted his brows. "She always seems to look me over

pretty thoroughly, now that you mention it. Gotta be that MacKenzie magic.''

She pursed her lips, looking as if she would like to strangle him. "Guess I must be immune." Then she focused on the road ahead. "Turn left here."

He did. Then he drove along a tree-lined lane, with rich, gorgeous homes scattered a half acre apart from each other and fifty yards away from the road, to be closer to the lake.

"Right there." She was pointing out her place, a brown cobblestone split-level, with a lawn and gardens that were manicured to perfection, and with the midnight-blue of Cazenovia Lake as a backdrop. He almost gaped as he pulled into the long paved driveway.

"You, uh, live here?"

"Yeah."

"The station pays that well?"

"Not quite. I bought it with some money I inherited a long time ago."

"Uh-huh."

She got out of his car. He shut it off and got out, as well, though she hadn't invited him in. She sent him a frown, but he pretended not to see it.

"You gonna be able to get in without your keys?"

"Of course." She walked over the flagstone path, up the front steps to the door and poked the doorbell.

Oh, so that was it. She didn't live alone. He racked his brain for tidbits about Jones. Getting dirt on her would make his freaking year. But there was never much to find. She guarded her privacy like a goddamn pitbull. She wasn't married, he knew that much. Maybe she had some stud living with her. He expected someone too young, too skinny and probably unshaven to open the door when he heard footsteps approaching. It would be just like Jones to go for some underfed, left-wing Bohemian type.

"It's me, hon," Jones called. And her tough as nails newswoman voice had gone all sugary sweet. It was enough to make him puke.

The door opened.

The teenager on the other side was pale and blond and cuter than hell. She smiled as if she really meant it. "Hi, Mom. Forget your key?" Then she caught sight of him and smiled even wider. "Hey, you brought home a date? Wow, we should declare a national holiday. And he's cute, too. You wanna come in?" she asked him.

"Sure," he said, at the same time Jones said, "No."

The girl smiled wider. She could have been a supermodel with a smile like that. "I'm Dawn."

"Sean MacKenzie."

"So are you coming in or what?" She stepped back. Julie rolled her eyes but walked in and didn't blow a gasket when he walked in behind her.

"You want coffee or soda or anything?" Dawn asked.

"Coffee would be great, thanks." The living room was two steps up, and it resembled, Sean thought, a woodland paradise. Hanging plants everywhere, dark wood furniture and a small bubbling fountain full of tumbled stones in the far corner were what produced the effect, he realized. The colors were earth tones, greens and browns, with touches of russet and mustard in the throw rugs and pillows. It was a great room, though it was dim, lit at the moment only by the TV, the screen of which was frozen in place.

Dawn hurried through the room, under an archway into the kitchen, flicking on the light as she did. "Go on in and sit. Help yourself to popcorn," Dawn called. "I was just watching *Nathan Z's Power Hour*."

"You taped that thing again today?" Julie asked.

"Oh, come on, Mom. It's Ms. Marcum's favorite show,

you know, though I personally think Van Praagh is better. He's on right after—I taped them both.''

''Efficient of you.''

''I think he really helps some of those people.'' She shrugged. ''Besides, he's about to go big time. I read his cable show's going into syndication.''

Julie rolled her eyes and headed for the sofa. Sean followed, leaned over her shoulder. ''I didn't know you had a daughter,'' he whispered.

''Now you do.''

''She's a doll. She looks nothing like you.''

Jones sent him a scowl. ''Gee, thanks.''

''What is she, fifteen?''

''Sixteen,'' she said. ''Barely. Just got her driving permit.''

He frowned. ''Sixteen? Hell, Jones, what did you do, give birth at the age of ten?''

''Trying to flatter me now?''

''Here we go.'' Dawn came in with a mug in each hand, handing one to her mother and the other to Sean. Jones sat in a nearby chair, so Sean took a seat on the sofa and glanced at the hottest New Age guru of the season in freeze-frame on the television screen. Dawn plopped down beside him, folded her legs under her and picked up the remote. Then she paused and looked at him, frowning. ''Wait a minute. Are you *the* Sean MacKenzie? From the radio?''

''Yep. That's me.''

''Oh, God, I *love* your show. I listen to it all the time.''

That put a smile on his face. ''Really?''

''Oh, yeah. Mom does, too.''

''Does she really?'' He slanted Julie an amused look.

''What's not to love?'' Dawn went on. ''You're totally irreverent. I never know what you'll say next.'' She pursed her lips. "I don't always agree with your politics, but your taste in music is awesome. Especially for someone your age."

He had sipped coffee, beaming at her praise, but the last line had him damn near spitting hot java out his nostrils. Jones wasn't so reserved. She laughed out loud, smiling at her daughter.

He swallowed, cleared his throat. "Thank you."

"You're welcome. Sometimes Ms. Marcum tapes your morning broadcast and lets us listen to it during study hall. You know, after she's edited out all the swearwords and stuff."

He leaned toward Julie. "Ms. Marcum?"

"Favorite teacher, English Eleven."

"Got it."

"She says you're relevant and thought provoking."

"Ms. Marcum has excellent taste."

"Don't let it go to your head, MacKenzie," Julie said with a nod toward the TV. "She just told you the woman's favorite show is *Nathan Z's Hour of Wasted Air Time*."

He frowned, then returned his attention to the teenager beside him. "So do you like my show better than your mom's?" he asked, just to wipe the smug look from Jones's face.

Dawn frowned in thought, then sighed. "I guess I can't really compare. I mean, Mom does news."

He blinked as if she'd hit him between the eyes. "Ouch."

"Oh, crap, that's not the way I meant—" Dawn looked from her mother to Sean and back again. "I didn't mean you *don't* do news. I mean you *do,* sort of, it's just…different. It's like comparing Howard Stern to Barbara Walters, you know? You run this irreverent, wild commentary on the most notorious events and people, with your opinions right out there. Exposé stuff, mixed in with music and guests. And she just reports the news, sensational or otherwise, from an unbiased point of view. It's totally different.''

"He entertains and I inform," Jones clarified.

"I enlighten. You enable," he said.

"I report and you sensationalize," she countered.

"You report what the powers that be want you to report. I pull the curtain away and expose the little man at the controls behind it."

They glared at each other.

Dawn said, "This wasn't a date, was it?"

He slugged back his coffee. "Nope. It was just a nice guy giving a colleague a ride home."

"Colleague," Jones muttered, shaking her head.

Sean put his cup down and got to his feet. "It was nice meeting you, Dawn. Thanks for the coffee."

"Nice meeting you, too, Sean. Play some Stroke Nine for me tomorrow, will you?"

"You got it." He started for the door.

Jones strode along beside him, and opened it when he reached it.

"Nice kid," he said. "Amazing, with a barracuda like you for a mom. Who was her father? Ghandi?"

"Go to hell, MacKenzie."

He rolled his eyes, sighed, forced himself to turn back. "You really listen to my show every day?"

"Yeah. So I know how *not* to report the news."

His temper heated.

"You really watch my show every night?" she asked.

"Yeah. It's the best sleep aid I've ever tried."

She pursed her lips.

He smiled at her. He didn't think he had ever enjoyed fighting with anyone the way he enjoyed fighting with her.

"This is great," he told her. "It's been too long since we had a good sparring match. Not since that tornado hit the state fair."

"I figured you finally realized you'd never win one and just gave up."

He held her eyes for a long moment and noticed that the shadow from earlier in the evening was still there, hiding behind her make-believe smile. Something was wrong with his favorite enemy, and knowing it made his own smile fade. "So are you gonna tell me what you were up to in that hotel room tonight, or do I have to go digging for it?"

The color left her face in a rush. "I told you, I just had an off night. Will you let it go?"

"No way in hell." If looks could kill, he would be a dead man, he thought. He sighed. "So are you gonna call me if you get word they've released the stiff's name for public consumption?"

"Probably not."

"That's good, 'cause I'm not calling you when Jax beeps me."

"Fine."

"Good night, Jones."

"'Night, MacKenzie."

She closed the door on the pain in the ass, pseudophoto-journalist turned tabloid radio jockey. But the second she did, everything she'd been through tonight came rushing back. For a little while sparring with MacKenzie had taken her mind off it all. Now that he was gone, there was nothing to keep the horror at bay.

She told herself she'd done nothing unethical. It wasn't as if she had killed Harry. She had only taken precautions to see to it that no one else might think she had. So she'd wiped away a few fingerprints and sneaked out of the room.

So what? And lied to the police, her mind added. And contaminated a crime scene.

Hell. It occurred to her that she just might have inadvertently wiped away the fingerprints of the real killer.

"Mom, come here!"

She turned to see Dawn leaning over to peer out the window. "What, hon?"

"Look at his car. God, it's a Carerra!"

Julie moved toward her, frowning. "He's such a liar. He told me it was a Porsche."

"It *is* a Porsche! That is so cool!"

Smiling, Julie locked the door and walked back to the living room. She heard MacKenzie's muscle car roar away, and then Dawn rejoined her. "Did you actually ride home in that?" she asked.

"Mmm-hmm." She shrugged. "If I'd known how much it would impress you, I would've made him let me drive. Think he would've let me?"

"Not if he's ever *seen* you drive."

Julie grabbed a handful of popcorn and threw it at her daughter. Dawn caught a few kernels and tossed them back, laughing. "It's true, Mom. You're a terrible driver, and you know it."

"I get by."

"You don't even buckle up."

"I do when I remember." Julie leaned back on the sofa, and Dawn sank down beside her, close to her. Julie picked up the remote. "So can we ditch the Z-man here and watch a movie or what?"

Dawn nodded, curled her legs beneath her and leaned against her mother. Julie slid an arm around her daughter's shoulders, held her close and hit the buttons, killing the video and surfing the channels instead.

"Are you okay, Mom?" Dawn asked suddenly, staring up into her mother's face, searching it with her eyes.

"Of course I'm okay. Why? Have I done something to make you think otherwise?"

Dawn shrugged. "I got the feeling something's been wrong...lately, you know? As if maybe someone were—I don't know, bothering you, I guess."

Dawn's perceptiveness never ceased to amaze. They were as tuned in to each other as any mother and daughter had ever been. "Well, there was a bit of a problem, and work's been giving me headaches. Ratings are down. I'm probably going to end up with a new partner within a couple of weeks. But things are calmer now. And there's nothing for you to worry about."

"I got the feeling it was something besides work and ratings."

Julie nodded. "Too sharp for me. It was, but it's okay. It's over."

"Did it have anything to do with him?"

"Who? MacKenzie?"

Dawn nodded. "Was he the one giving you a hard time?"

"No. He's got the moral values of an earthworm, but he would never do anything like that." Or she hoped in hell he wouldn't, Julie thought. Because if he started digging and he found out the truth—but no. He wouldn't find anything.

"That's a relief."

"Why?"

Dawn shrugged. "I like him, Mom."

"Blech. Honey, you have *terrible* taste in men." Julie ate a handful of popcorn and looked at her beautiful, precious daughter. God, how would Dawn feel if that evidence of Harry's ever went public? She lowered her eyes, pretended to watch TV. It didn't matter what she had done today. She would do whatever she had to do to protect Dawn from anything that might threaten her happiness. Especially the secrets of their past.

She would do whatever she had to. Always.

3

An hour after collapsing in her bed, Julie sat up, her eyes flying open wide and her heart hammering in her chest as the thought that had jolted her awake echoed endlessly in her mind.

"His apartment," she whispered. "God, the police will go to Harry's apartment. They'll search his place for clues, and that damned Detective Jackson won't miss a thing. She'll find everything Harry had on me and Dawn. Oh, God."

She flung back her covers, put her feet on the floor and fought to catch her breath. There had never been any love lost between Julie and Cassandra Jackson. Julie hadn't worked with the woman often, but whenever she'd been compelled to seek out Lieutenant Jackson for information, she'd hit a brick wall. She didn't know why "Jax" disliked her. Maybe it was the natural enmity that tended to form between the police and the press, but she didn't think so. The woman didn't seem to have the same attitude toward MacKenzie.

She was going to have to stop Jackson from getting her hands on that evidence. It wasn't too late, she told herself. The cops wouldn't have gone there tonight, would they? No, not in the middle of the night like this. They would want to clear it with the senator. Discuss it with him, make sure it was handled with finesse. And they would need a search warrant, too. They would want to make sure it was all done legally. Hell, Harry was the victim in this, not the suspect. They had no reason to go charging in like bulls, offending a New York State senator in the process.

"Okay, good, then." She got to her feet, yanked open a dresser drawer and dug for a pair of jeans, then hopped on one foot while pulling them over the other. "They might have put a cop on Harry's place, just to watch it. Maybe not, though. But even if they did, that's okay. I can handle one cop. Maybe two. It'll be fine. Hell, they'll probably be sleeping in their car at this hour."

She pulled on a sweatshirt, white socks and a pair of running shoes from underneath the foot of her bed. Harry's condo was in one of the renovated old buildings downtown, within walking distance of the War Memorial at the Oncenter and City Hall. She hoped to God the security was as lax as it had been the one time he had insisted she meet him there. Even so, getting into the building would be the hard part. She tied her shoes, her mind racing. You needed a key card, or to have someone inside buzz you in from upstairs. She wouldn't be likely to catch someone else going in at this time of the night and be able to slip in with them.

She hurried out of her bedroom, into the upstairs hall, and thought of her car, still parked in the hotel's garage. She was going to have to take Dawn's Jeep. Not that Dawn would mind, really, although she would pretend to, and probably gripe about her mother's notoriously poor driving skills being turned loose on an innocent Jeep.

Julie paused at her daughter's bedroom door and peeked in. Dawn was sound asleep, her back to her mother, nothing visible but the shape of her body underneath the blankets. The radio was playing softly beside the bed. She always fell asleep with her music playing. All the better, Julie thought, and she pulled the door closed and tiptoed to the stairs, down them and out to the garage.

Sean hadn't gone home at all. He'd driven around for a little while, wondering who, among all the man's known enemies, would have had the best motive to murder Harry Blackwood. The senator's brother had a less than stellar reputation. He drank. A lot. He gambled. And it was widely known that he liked his women. In fact, the big scandal of the last election had involved allegations from a prostitute who claimed Harry was one of her best customers. The guy was a lowlife.

But now he was a dead lowlife, and Sean wanted to know why. In fact, he wanted to know a lot more than he already did about Harry Blackwood and his sleazy side. A guy like that must have more than a few skeletons in his closet. And the public would want to know. Within twenty-four hours this was going to be the biggest story in the state. People would be clamoring for inside dirt, and he was just the man to provide it. His value as a reporter, he thought with a slow smile, was about to sail through the roof. And that new job he'd been thinking he didn't stand a chance of landing might just be in the bag. He could use this.

Meanwhile Channel Four's ratings were sinking, had been ever since Julie Jones's former coanchor had retired and she'd begun sitting alone at the evening news desk. She was good, he thought. But he was better. People liked the dynamics of a male-female anchor team. She couldn't give them that. People also liked dirt, and she wouldn't give them that, either.

He was about to leave her in the dust.

People's dirt, he knew from experience, turned up in people's garbage. So he used his cell phone and directory assistance to get the exact address, minus the apartment number, and he drove to Harry's building. He parked his car where it seemed relatively safe and took what he needed from the glove compartment. The Dumpster Diving Kit, he called it. He always carried one. He'd thought once or twice that he ought to patent it and sell it to journalists the world over.

Harry had lived in a good neighborhood; he had to give the guy that much, Sean thought as he locked his car and walked casually toward the alley beside the building. The building was a century-old brick structure that had been in pretty decent shape up until the city's recent downtown restoration efforts. Now it was like new again, sound, clean and safe, even while keeping its original look.

He used a small penlight to guide his feet. No rats scurried out of its beam, and there were no homeless old men to trip over. Yep, a nice neighborhood. Toward the far end of the alley, he found what he needed. The Dumpster. The lid was raised, and the garbage chute angled into it from the side of the building.

Digging through garbage was never a pleasant job but almost always a profitable one. Sean opened the gallon-size zipper-seal freezer bag and took out a pair of yellow rubber gloves. He had found some of his very best material in the garbage. He'd learned of extramarital affairs, celebrity pregnancies, addictions, nose jobs and political corruption from various piles of refuse. Occasionally he found stuff that was too lowbrow even for his radio show. Stuff that would be considered beneath him, though granted, according to most of the respected press, that was a very narrow area. When he found stuff like that, he never used it for his show. He had to preserve what little journalistic integrity he had. So he would simply sell it to the tabloids, which were always more than willing to keep his name out of it.

It was a tidy little side business. Hell, it had paid for his Porsche.

At worst, this Dumpster should provide something kinky enough to bring a good price at the tabloids. At best, it would provide a motive for Harry Blackwood's murder and enough leverage to move him up a few rungs on the journalistic ladder.

He pulled on the yellow rubber gloves, then took out the white surgical face mask and tied it around his head. Then he found a small broken crate lying on the ground, and he flipped it upside down beside the Dumpster to use as a makeshift stepladder. It was dark. He put his penlight in his mouth and peered down into the depths of trash.

Most of the garbage was bagged. People were neater these days than they'd been ten years ago. He reached for a plastic trash bag, picked it up by its knotted top and let it dangle and turn in slow-mo, shining his light and peering through the transparent sides until he spotted a name on a discarded envelope or sheet of paper. He repeated this process over and over, tossing the bags aside when he found any name other than Harold R. Blackwood. Harry had lived alone, as far as Sean knew. He wouldn't likely have anything addressed to anyone else. There! Harold Blackwood. Apartment 624.

He tossed the bag to the ground to be examined later and kept on digging for more, stopping only when headlights spilled into the alley from the street beyond and he heard a car pulling to a stop out in front of the building. The engine shut off. The lights went out.

He glanced at his watch. 2:00 a.m.

Okay, it was probably nothing, but he had a little nerve at the base of his skull that tingled when there was a story nearby, and it was tingling now. Maybe he'd better check it out, just in case....

He jumped down from the crate and picked up the bag he'd retrieved, peeled off his gloves and face mask, tossing them into the trash, and then he walked back up the alley to the street.

A powder-blue Jeep Wrangler had stopped there, and the woman who got out of it was... He had to blink and look again. There was no mistake. She was none other than Julie Jones.

"Well, I'll be," he muttered. Licking his lips, he set his trash bag down and pressed himself closer to the wall so he could peer around it and watch her without being seen. "What the hell is she up to now?"

She walked up the broad stone steps of Harry's building, then paused at the front door, biting her lip and squinting at the security panel. Finally she pushed a button. She was only three yards away from Sean. She kept her finger on the button until a groggy, angry voice came over the intercom in reply. "Who the hell is this?" it demanded. "Do you have any idea what time it is?"

"I'm sorry to wake you, but I forgot my key. Could you just buzz me in?"

"Fuck off, lady," the man said.

She waited a couple seconds, then hit the same button again. The voice returned. "You want me to call a cop?"

"You want me to keep my finger on this button until they get here?"

"All right, all right. Jesus."

The guy buzzed her in. Sean heard the deep drone of the buzzer and the door lock disengaging, and shook his head in amazement, both at her brass and at the fact that her ploy had actually worked. Jones opened the door and walked through. Swearing under his breath, Sean lunged out of his spot, running in three long strides to the stairs. The door was already swinging closed and Jones was striding toward the elevators, her back to him. He flung himself bodily, landing chest first on the stairs, arms stretching doorward. He just managed to thrust his fingertips into the opening before the door slammed on them.

Clenching his teeth and swearing under his breath, he pulled himself forward, grabbed the door with his free hand and pulled it open. Then he got to his feet and stepped inside. His fingers throbbed. Shit. He rubbed them and shook his hand as the door fell closed behind him. Then he heard the elevator ping and looked ahead to see its doors closing, as well.

Crossing into the lobby, he dug through his memory for the number he'd seen on that envelope—624, that was it. Sixth floor. There was only one elevator, and he didn't want Jones getting too goddamn far ahead of him. Nor did he relish the thought of being caught there in plain sight should the irate neighbor Jones had bothered with the buzzer decide to call the cops after all.

He looked around, found the stair door and took that way up. Five flights. He hurried, because he didn't want Jones out of his sight long enough to do anything he would regret not seeing. He figured it took him a minute or so before he made it to the sixth floor landing, opened the stair door and stepped quietly into the hall. Or as quietly as he could manage while panting for breath. His heart was pounding hard enough to wake the residents of the entire floor, and he told himself he was too old for this kind of cloak-and-dagger bullshit.

Then he shook his head. *Getting* too old, maybe. But he wasn't there yet—he'd managed to catch up to her. Jones was walking down the hall, peering at the numbers on the doors of the condos on this floor. He walked forward, stepping just as softly as he could manage. She was wearing jeans now. Her hair was a mess, and her sweatshirt was baggy. This was not a Julie Jones too many people would recognize.

Then she stopped suddenly and just stood there, staring at one of the doors. And when he got a little closer, Sean realized why. It was Harry's apartment door, and it was standing wide-open.

Someone had been there first, and even as he wondered whether they might still be around, Julie Jones walked inside.

Swearing under his breath, Sean rushed ahead and paused momentarily outside the door to look in at Jones as she tiptoed through the apartment like some kind of goddamn cat burglar. He knew it was freaking insane, but he had to find out what she was up to. My God, he didn't have *dreams* this good. Oh, he'd fantasized lots of scenarios involving Julie Jones over the years, getting the best of her being his second favorite. But this was better than anything he could have made up. So he crept in after her.

Harry's living room looked like some dated idea of a playboy's love nest. Black leather furniture, white shag carpet, wall-size stereo system, wet bar. Jones moved through it into a hallway and went through a door about halfway down. God, he hoped she wasn't heading for the bedroom. He could only imagine what *that* would look like.

She wasn't. He moved quietly to the door she'd entered. She'd left it open, so he could look inside. It was a study or library. Desk, chair, file cabinet and a big-screen TV that would have seemed out of place if not for the wall of videos.

He thought they were books at first, in the muted light. But no. VHS tapes. One entire wall housed a built-in cabinet that must have been full of them. Right now, its doors were flung open wide, and video cassettes lay toppled on the shelves and strewn over the floor. The file cabinet nearby was open wide, too. File folders and papers were thrown everywhere.

Jones stood there, looking at the mess, shaking her head from side to side as if the sight rendered her unable to move or speak. She pressed her hands to either side of her head, fingers digging in her own hair. "Oh, Jesus, look at all this," she whispered.

"Jones."

She whirled when Sean said her name, one hand clenched in a fist and the other pressing to her chest as if to keep her heart from busting out.

"Easy, easy, it's just me."

"MacKenzie. What the hell are you doing here? Are you *following* me?"

"Hell, no. I was getting some background for my story."

She tipped her head to one side and lowered the fist. "How?"

He opened his mouth, closed it again.

"Well, you sure as hell couldn't be interviewing neighbors at this hour. What were you doing, digging through the trash?"

It was supposed to be a sarcastic little barb, and he would be damned before he admitted that it was dead-on target. There was nothing *wrong* with digging through the trash. "You're the one breaking and entering," he reminded her.

"The door was open."

Arguing in whispers was an interesting concept, he thought. Each of them tried to whisper more forcefully than the other.

"It *was*," she said, apparently mistaking his silence for doubt.

"I know, I know, I saw." He took her arm. "Let's get out of here before both our asses wind up behind bars."

She tugged her arm free. "You go on. I have to look

around some more." Her eyes were on the scattered files, scanning them as if trying to read the labels.

"Jones, someone broke in here tonight."

"Obviously."

"Well, has it occurred to you that it might have been the killer?"

"Gee, no, I hadn't thought of that," she said, her voice dripping with sarcasm.

"He might still be around here somewhere, Jones. Did you think of *that?*"

That brought her head up. Her eyes leveled on his, widening a little. Her body went so still that he didn't think she was breathing for a second. The idea of someone else in the apartment frightened her. Good. She *should* be frightened. But after a second, she seemed to decide her reasons for being there outweighed her fear.

"Maybe you should go check out the rest of the place," she suggested. "Make sure no one else is around." Then she turned away from him, dropping to her knees to scan the file folders littering the floor.

"Right, and leave you here alone to abscond with whatever evidence you find." He knelt right beside her, checking the videocassettes. Some were commercially made, with printed labels, films that sounded like porn, with titles like *Mistress Mary's Discipline* and *Dungeon Lover.* Others had white labels on them with handwritten titles. Sean pulled out his penlight for a better look, because the handwritten ones were harder to read in the dark. He flicked the light on and read them aloud in a whisper. "*Vanessa. Marianne. Barb & Sally.*" He looked at Jones. She was still pawing frantically through the files that carpeted the floor. "Just what is it you're looking for?"

"I'm not looking *for* anything. I'm just looking." She took his light from his hand, shining it on papers with an air of impatience, then stopping the beam on something that lay on the floor, something that reflected the light with its glossy surface. Photographs, Sean thought, but as soon as he thought it, she dropped an empty folder on top of them.

"What was that? Was that something?"

"No. Nothing." She shone the light elsewhere; then, getting to her feet, she scanned the few files still in the open drawers.

"What is it you expect to find in the files, Jones?" He got up, too, brushing off his pantlegs, waiting for a chance to see what it was she had covered up.

"How would I know?"

"Then why do I get the feeling you're looking for one that says *Julie Jones* on it?" Then he lifted his brows. "Or should I be looking for a tape with that label instead?"

She turned toward him, probably about to tear him a new one, he thought, but then she went still at the sound of a bell—just one single ping. "What's that?"

"The elevator." He grabbed the light from her, shut it off and ran back through the apartment to the still-open door. He peered out into the hall. She came up behind him a couple of seconds later. "Is it…?"

Lieutenant Jax was striding down the hall toward them, flanked by the same two cops from the hotel room. Sean ducked back inside. "Police," he whispered. "Come on."

The two of them ran through the apartment, ducked back into the study and closed the door behind them. Sean went to the window and parted the curtains, looking for a balcony. What he found was even better. Thank God this was an old building. He yanked open the window, turned and held out a hand to Jones. "Come here."

"What the hell are you doing?" she whisper-shouted at him.

"Fire escape. Come on. Hurry." Taking her hand in one

of his, holding the curtains for her with the other, he helped her out first, then climbed out after her. As he did, he glanced back into the room, at the floor. And, yes, it was dark, and his light was in his pocket now—but he didn't see the file folder covering up the photographs anymore. It had been kicked aside, and he didn't see the photos at all. Maybe they'd been kicked aside, too, but he didn't think so.

He had an inkling that those photos were in Jones's pocket by now. Sighing, he closed the window behind them and turned to where she stood on the black metal landing, looking down at the skeletal flights of iron stairs and the street below. "You all right?"

The wind blew none too gently, and it carried a bite of autumn chill with it. She nodded but didn't speak. She kept looking down, and he thought maybe heights were not her favorite thing in the world. He had no idea why, but he squeezed past her, so he was in front, then reached behind him and caught her wrist in his hands.

"What the hell are you doing?"

"Relax, Jones. This is strictly business." He pulled her hand up, pressed it onto his shoulder. "Just hold on to me, okay?" And then he started down the fire escape's zigzagging stairs.

She stayed right behind him, her hand closing tight on his shoulder, the second one quickly following suit on the other side. The fire escape was a good one, as fire escapes went, but even the best of them tended to sway and jiggle. Every time this one did, her nails dug into his flesh, right through his clothes. He moved slowly, carefully, because the thing was noisy. He figured he had maybe five minutes, maximum, before the cops noticed the window unlocked and came outside to check. It might be far sooner. Jax was sharp; she didn't miss much. If he'd been alone, he could have taken it twice as fast and been gone by now, despite the noise.

He told himself he ought to do it and leave Jones to face the music. But instead he kept to the slow pace all the way to the bottom, where the fire escape ended with a good ten feet left between it and the ground.

"Put the ladder down," Jones whispered, pointing urgently at the folded up ladder that would extend almost to the ground, when released.

"No way. You think Jax would miss something like that?"

"Then how are we—"

"We jump."

She shook her head side to side, backing up a step.

"Come on, Jones, it's not that far."

She met his eyes. "You go first."

If he did, he thought, she wouldn't go at all. And for some reason, the idea of her getting caught wasn't one he relished as much as he thought he should. "We'll go together." He slid his arm around her waist, pulled her to the edge. She resisted, but he said, "Trust me, Jones. I won't let you get hurt."

She looked up at him—surprised, maybe—but just when she opened her mouth to argue, he tightened his grip on her waist and jumped. She clutched him as they fell, even though it was only a second until they hit the ground, falling apart. He got to his feet first, reaching down to help her up. "You okay?"

"Fine."

"Told you so."

She released his hand and brushed herself off. Sean could barely believe they'd made it undetected. He took Jones by the arm and led her around the building, via the alley he'd been in earlier. His bag of rescued garbage still sat right where he'd left it, near the front corner of the building. Her Jeep was just beyond it, parked by the curb. There were plenty of other vehicles parked the same way up and down the street, so he figured the cops wouldn't have had any reason to note her plate number. He looked at some of the cars more closely. The dark sedan in front of the building hadn't been there before he'd gone inside. It was, he assumed, what the cops had driven here, and it was empty. He strained his eyes for a closer look. Yep. Crown Victoria.

Quickly he led Jones to the Jeep, opened the driver's door. Hell, she hadn't even locked it, and the keys were dangling from the switch.

He glanced back at her. "Go on, get in and get the hell out of here."

She nodded, but she didn't get in. She gripped his eyes with hers instead. Big, brown and scared right now. It almost knocked the wind out of him. He had never seen Julie Jones look like that. Never.

"You're not going to tell anyone about this, are you?" she asked him.

Shit, for a second he thought she was going to thank him for helping her out. He was an idiot. "Not until I know what's going on, Jones. But believe me, I *will* find out."

"Don't," she whispered. "This has nothing to do with you."

"But it does have something to do with *you,* doesn't it?"

She pursed her lips, then turned away and got into her Jeep. He closed the door as she started it up. Then he yanked the door open again. "Put on your seat belt, Jones."

Pursing her lips, she pulled the belt around her, yanked her door closed and popped the clutch. The Jeep jerked, nearly stalled, but managed to take off. He heard her grinding gears and winced. Poor freaking car. If the transmission survived long enough for the kid to get her license, it would be a miracle.

When her taillights were out of sight, Sean jogged into the alley, grabbed his bag of garbage and then ran a block to where he'd left his car. He didn't relax until he got home, safe and sound. And even then, the questions kept going round and round in his mind. What was Julie Jones hiding? And what did she have to do with the murder of Harry Blackwood?

Julie pounded the steering wheel with a fist. She hadn't found the documents. There hadn't been anything there with her name on it, but that didn't mean a thing. Any one of those dozens of folders and reams of papers could have been the one she was looking for, but she hadn't had time to check them out.

What if the police found the truth in that mess? What if they found out about Dawn?

God, if it hadn't been for that bastard MacKenzie showing up, she could have scooped them all up, thrown them into a trash bag from Harry's kitchen and carried them home.

If it hadn't been for MacKenzie showing up, I'd have been caught there, red-handed, an inner voice whispered. *I never would have found that fire escape in time to avoid the police, much less had the gumption to go down it in the dark.*

Oh, God, the police. She imagined them—the two officers, and that bitch Detective Jackson—were gathering up the papers and documents and videotapes one by one, even now. They would probably sit in a roomful of cops and go over all of them. If they found out the truth, her life would be destroyed. They would take Dawn away from her. Track down her birth mother's relatives—the very same people

Lizzie had been compelled to run away from all those years ago—and hand her over to them.

Dawn.

Shivering all over, Julie kept steering the Jeep with one hand, dipping into her jacket pocket with the other. She pulled out the two photographs she had found on the floor, both of them taken in a place so jarringly familiar that the sight of them had almost floored her. They'd been taken at Young Believers' compound.

She looked at them now, tried to make out the faces in the group shots. And finally she realized why one of those faces seemed so familiar. The young man with the three-piece suit and the automatic rifle was Harry Blackwood.

"He was there," she whispered. Not as one of the inmates, though. Those who lived at the place didn't wear suits but plain, functional clothes more suited to working in the greenhouses and gardens. No, Harry must have been one of Mordecai's visiting dignitaries. The men who brought large sums of money in exchange for some of Mordecai's crops.

Julie lowered the photos toward her pocket, glanced up at the road and saw the glowing orange eyes and red-brown coat in her headlights' beam. Startled, the deer froze in the middle of the road. Equally startled, Julie jerked the wheel hard to the left and jammed her foot on the brake. The Jeep's rear end skidded right, so she jerked the wheel right, overcorrected, and sent it skidding the other way. Her body jerked hard against the car's motions, but the seat belt kept her from being whipped across the seat. She thought she was going into the brush at the side of the road for sure, but somehow she pulled out of the skid, and the back end's fishtailing slowed and finally stopped. She forgot about the clutch, and the car bucked and then stalled.

She sat there, the car at a cockeyed angle on the shoulder,

watching the deer bound merrily away into the woods, and she thought how right her daughter was about her driving skills. Damn deer anyway. Thank God she hadn't wrecked Dawnie's sixteenth-birthday present or she would never have heard the end of it, even though her insurance would have covered the damage.

She told herself it didn't matter. She hadn't wrecked the Jeep, or hit the deer or anything else. She hadn't been hurt, and she supposed that might have turned out differently if Sean hadn't reminded her to buckle up. Though she would be damned before she admitted that to him.

Pulling herself together, she pushed down the clutch, re-started the engine, pulled back onto the pavement and drove slowly the rest of the way home, her full attention on the road the entire time. She pulled the Jeep into the garage, closed the door and crept into the house as quietly as she could. She checked all the locks, shut off all the lights. God, it was 3:30 a.m. She had to get up again in a little more than three hours.

She tiptoed up the stairs and paused outside her daughter's bedroom door to peek inside. Dawn was lying in the bed, exactly the way she had been before. She hadn't so much as moved in her sleep.

What had at first seemed reassuring changed in an instant as Julie stared in at the bed and realized what she was seeing.

She pushed the door open further and stepped inside. "Dawn?"

Dawn said nothing. Julie moved closer to the bed, reached down to touch Dawn's shoulder. "Dawnie?"

Still nothing. She pulled the covers back.

Pillows lay beneath them, lined up to resemble the form

of a sleeping sixteen-year-old covered in blankets. Lifting her head, Julie saw the curtains floating on a breeze coming in through the open window.

"Oh my God," Julie whispered. "Dawn!"

4

Dawn crouched in the bushes on the front lawn as the Jeep's headlights shone on the slowly rising garage door. The Jeep rolled inside. Dawn's mother got out of the car in a pair of old jeans and a sweatshirt, half her hair hanging loose from what looked like a haphazard pony tail. The garage door lowered slowly.

"Was that your mom?" Kayla asked in an overly loud whisper.

"Yeah."

"Why's she driving your Jeep?"

Dawn shrugged. "Left her car keys someplace today and had to catch a ride home with, uh…a friend, I guess."

"Good thing we left the party early."

"Not early enough." Dawn rubbed her arms, the possibility of getting caught adding to the chill of the crisp October night air. Wondering where her mom had been in the wee hours of the morning gave her an even deeper chill. She'd overheard part of a phone call earlier tonight, before her mom had left for her first late-night meeting or whatever. Dawn had picked up the upstairs extension and heard her mother say, "You won't quit until you destroy me utterly, will you, Harry?" and a man reply, "Not utterly, Jewel. I don't want to kill the golden goose, you know." Her mother's reply to that had been, "Fine, eleven, then." And then she'd hung up the phone.

Dawn knew her mother had secrets. She'd always had

secrets, things that Dawn knew were best not asked about. She didn't ask about her father, for instance. Julie would only say they'd both been teens, and that he'd been killed in a car accident before Julie had even realized she was pregnant. His family were devoutly religious, and telling them of Dawn's existence would only have added to their pain. To push for more information only wound up with one or both of them getting angry, the same result that came of asking too many questions about Julie's side of the family.

Dawn often thought she was probably adopted. It would explain her mom's secrets, and it would explain how Julie could be so dark that she must have Latin blood, while Dawn herself was as pale as a daisy. She was going to ask about it someday, but privately she thought it wasn't half as important as Julie seemed to think it was. It wouldn't change anything.

Dawn loved her mother, secrets and all. But this was the first time she'd had this sickening feeling that one of her mom's secrets might be dangerous, or that she might be in trouble because of them.

"Where do you suppose she went?" Kayla asked softly.

Dawn shook herself out of her thoughts, focused on the present situation and shrugged. "There was probably breaking news somewhere," she lied. She knew better, though. Her mom didn't go out to cover breaking news in jeans and a sweatshirt. It was a running joke how fast she could make herself ready to go on the air. Five minutes with a makeup mirror and a compact would be plenty, in a pinch.

"You'd better get back in there, Dawnie, before she realizes you're gone."

Dawn saw her bedroom light come on and swallowed hard. "Too late," she said, her heart falling to somewhere in the region of her stomach. "You might as well go home. There's no sense in both of us getting caught. Your dad would kill you."

Kayla nodded. "My dad's a cop, and he's not as good a snoop as your mother is." She sighed. "Call me in the morning," she said, then she ran off into the darkness.

Dawn squared her shoulders and walked toward the house. She thought about going around to the back and climbing in through her bedroom window but decided against it. It would only make her mother angrier. Instead she went to the front door and used her spare key to let herself in.

Before she'd even closed and locked the door behind her, her mother's steps came rapidly down the stairs. "Dawnie?"

"Yeah, it's me, Mom."

Julie appeared in the foyer, then lunged at Dawn and wrapped her in a fierce bear hug that squeezed the breath from her lungs. "My God, I was so worried," she said, her voice quivering with relief and love.

Then, just as suddenly, she released Dawn from the mamma-bear-hug and stepped back to stare at her. The motherly relief in her eyes faded fast, and her voice took on a firmer, sharper tone. "Just where have you been, young lady?"

Dawn took a breath, lifted her chin. Her mother detested lies above all things, which was kind of ironic, considering, Dawn thought a little rebelliously. Still, she knew it would be best to just get the truth out and face the music. "Okay," she said. "I snuck out. I'm sorry. It was wrong, and it'll never happen again."

"Snuck out where? And with whom?"

Heaven help the sixteen-year-old with a reporter for a mom, she thought. Julie Jones didn't know how to accept anything less than who, what, where, when, why and how from anyone. Especially her own kid.

"Come on, Mom, it was a mistake. I'm sixteen. I'm not a little kid anymore, and I said I was sorry."

"Dawn." There was that warning tone in her voice, the one Dawn knew not to mess with.

"All right," she said with a heavy sigh. "If you must know every detail, there was a party on the lakeshore, down by the landing. A bunch of kids, a little bonfire, a boom box and a pile of CDs. I left after you went to bed and walked down there with a friend. A *female* friend, but I'm not going to tell you which one, because if I do, you'll call her mom and get *her* into trouble, too. Consider it protecting a source."

Her mother lifted her perfectly shaped eyebrows and gave two slow blinks of her pretty brown eyes that told Dawn she was treading on thin ice. "Was there alcohol at this party?"

"Not at first. About an hour ago a carload of kids from F.M. high showed up with a couple of cases. Things started getting a little crazy, so my friend and I decided to leave."

"It was Kayla Matthews, wasn't it?"

Dawn didn't answer. "I didn't drink, Mom. Smell." She blew toward her mother's face.

Her mother actually took her up on the offer and sniffed her breath, then seemed only slightly relieved. "What else? Were there drugs?"

Dawn licked her lips, lowered her eyes. "I thought I caught a whiff of weed just before we took off, but I didn't see it."

"I see."

"Mom, it was just harmless fun. I didn't do anything wrong. I mean, aside from the sneaking out without asking.'' She lifted her head, thinking fast. ''Besides, you snuck out tonight, too. In my Jeep.''

Her mother's eyes widened just enough to tell Dawn she wasn't supposed to know about her little midnight run. ''Dawnie, you were on foot, in the dark, without me even knowing you'd left. Suppose, on your way down to that party, you and Kayla had encountered a predator?''

''I never said Kayla was with me!'' Her mom didn't even pause.

''Suppose some fiftysomething pervert with a taste for teenage girls had happened by? Would there have been any harm then? My God, I wouldn't even have known you were missing until morning!''

''Oh, come on, you knew I was missing the second you came home from wherever you were tonight. You don't miss a thing. Besides, I wasn't alone, and nothing happened.''

''Don't you even *watch* the news I have to read every night, Dawnie? Don't you realize what kind of risk you were taking?'' Sighing, shaking her head, she turned and walked back into the living room, reaching for the telephone.

Dawn raced after her. ''What are you doing? Who are you calling?''

''The police, of course.''

''Mom, you can't!''

She paused in dialing, the phone in her hand. ''Dawnie, how am I going to feel if I go in to work tomorrow and someone hands me some copy about a carload of Fayetteville-Manlius students who crashed on their way home from a party? You said yourself they brought beer. Did they have a designated driver?''

Dawn swallowed the lie that leaped to her throat, lowered her head, shook it slowly. "No. They were all drinking."

"Then maybe a patrol car will get there before they leave, and maybe they'll get home alive tonight." She finished dialing.

Dawn sighed hard enough to make her mother fully aware of her feelings about this, then stalked through to the stairs and up them.

"We're not finished here, Dawn. You're grounded. Two weeks. No arguments."

"Whatever," Dawn muttered. God, everyone was going to know who had ratted them out. She and Kayla were the only two who'd left the party early. She closed her bedroom door with a bang and flopped facefirst onto her bed. She would be the most hated junior in Cazenovia High School tomorrow.

It wasn't fair. Her mom was keeping secrets, too. Big ones. But it was okay for *her* to sneak around and hide things. Just not for Dawn. It was such a double standard.

She punched her pillow, buried her face in it and wished for a solution.

A pebble hit her window. Then another. She scrambled off the bed, yanked the curtains wide and stared through the open window. Kayla stood on the back lawn, in the spill of light from her bedroom. "I thought you went home."

Kayla rubbed her arms, glanced behind her. "Something creeped me out. You get in trouble?"

"Yeah, some."

"Grounded?"

"Two weeks."

"Bummer."

The bushes that formed the boundary between the neat back lawn and the untamed field that sloped downhill to the lake shore moved, as if something were creeping through them. Dawn frowned, and Kayla turned her head quickly. There was nothing there. Just the wind, Dawn thought. "My mom's on the phone, narc-ing out the party."

Kayla shivered. "I should go back down to the landing and tell everyone before I head home."

"I wouldn't. She might just call your mom next. I didn't say your name, but she's not stupid."

Again the bushes moved. This time Dawn swore she saw a shape, a dark shadow, moving with them. Someone was out there, watching.

"Jesus, Kayla, get in here!"

Kayla moved a few steps closer to the house. "I gotta get home. My parents will kill me if they go to check my room and find me gone."

The shadow moved again, looking so much like a dark, menacing human shape this time that Dawn opened her mouth to scream.

But before the sound escaped, there was a sudden, brighter pool of light flooding the back lawn, and the shadow vanished in its glow. A second later, Dawn realized the light was coming from her own house's open back door when she heard her mother say, "You might as well come on in, Kayla."

Kayla grimaced but hurried inside, seeming almost as relieved as she was upset at being caught. Dawn went downstairs to do damage control, telling herself all the way that she probably hadn't seen a damn thing, other than maybe a stray deer or a nightbird. Her mother's paranoid tendencies were finally starting to rub off on her.

Every person in the newsroom looked up when Julie burst in the next morning, ten minutes late.

Bryan, her assistant, who'd been on her heels from the front entrance all the way to the newsroom, talking all the way, finally managed to thrust the cup of coffee he was carrying into her hands.

"Rough night?" the news director, Allan Westcott asked.

"No sleep. Did you get my fax?"

"Yeah. It came in at 5:00 a.m." Westcott shuffled the pages in front of him. "Your report says the body was discovered around midnight?"

She nodded.

"So why the delay?"

She had to say something, and admitting that she'd been out rifling through the dead man's apartment in the wee hours was out of the question, nor were Dawn's antics any of the man's business. By the time she'd phoned the police about the party, called Kayla's parents, lectured the girls while awaiting Mr. and Mrs. Matthewses' arrival, seen Kayla safely off, double-checked the locks and gotten Dawn back into bed, it had been four-thirty. She'd barely had time to type up the details, reread them to be sure she hadn't included anything she wasn't supposed to know and fax the report to the station.

There'd been no point in trying to sleep by then.

"Julie?"

She blinked and sipped her coffee. Perfect, just enough cream and sugar. Bryan was learning fast. "Yes," she finally answered. "Rough night. Long, rough, sleepless night. Have the police released the identity of the victim yet?" She took another sip, trying to hide her nerves as she hoped the cops hadn't mentioned her missing car keys or her behavior at the crime scene to her boss.

"No. We've been checking every half hour. I, uh, I understand Sean MacKenzie was on the scene with you last night.''

Julie felt her eyes widen but hid her surprise behind a bright smile. ''Which makes it even more vital that we stay on this. I couldn't bear to have that snake in the grass scoop me.''

Westcott cleared his throat and glanced at the producer, who was chewing her lower lip. Other glances were being exchanged around the table.

''What?'' Julie asked, looking from one face to the next. ''What's going on?''

No one looked her in the eye, until Allan shrugged and cleared his throat. ''Sit down, Julie. Drink your coffee.''

Frowning, suddenly very worried, she sat. There was a folder in front of her customary chair. She pretended to look through it, while knowing, deep in her gut, that she was about to be fired. They knew about her walking into that crime scene last night. The cops had told—or more likely that rat bastard Sean MacKenzie…

…whose face was smiling up at her from an eight-by-ten glossy. It sat inside the folder, opposite his professional bio.

Lifting her head slowly, she speared Allan Westcott with a look that should have set his hair on fire. ''You didn't—you *wouldn't*…''

The door opened, and a man walked in. She felt him before she even turned to look at him, standing there, looking fresh and handsome and smug. ''Hope I'm not so late I get fired on my first day,'' he said. Then he met her eyes. ''Morning, partner.''

She rose slowly from her chair, not smiling, not speaking, not quite able to process anything she was seeing.

Allan Westcott cleared his throat. ''Julie, meet your new coanchor.''

Sean, still smiling, extended a hand. She took it automatically, without even thinking, and he pulled her close, as if to give her a friendly embrace, and whispered close to her ear, "Breathe, Jones, before your head explodes."

Then he released her. She turned around and sank into her chair, feeling as if someone had just hit her with a stun gun.

"Welcome to WSNY, Sean." Allan had come around the table now and was pumping MacKenzie's hand as if they were best friends.

"When did all this happen?" Julie asked. "I haven't even tested with him. I thought we had another two weeks before we had to decide who would replace Jim." She blinked and shot a glance at MacKenzie. "I didn't even know you'd sent an audition tape."

"Julie," Westcott said, "I know this comes as a surprise, and I wanted more time to break it to you. The truth is, Sean's the best man we've interviewed for the job. We'd planned to see a few more applicants before making any decisions, but since you and he were both on the scene of the murder last night, we thought it best to move fast."

"I didn't give them much of a choice, Jones," MacKenzie said quickly. "If they hadn't hired me, I'd have taken the story elsewhere."

Bryan vacated his seat beside Julie, pulling it out for Sean and waving him into it. MacKenzie took it.

"You blackmailed yourself into a job," she interpreted.

Sean shrugged. "At least now I won't scoop you."

She blinked at him. "They call you at the last minute with a job offer based solely on their desire to stop your show from scooping ours, and you accept?"

He shrugged. "Actually, I called them. They made an offer only an idiot would have turned down."

She was certain her eyes must have been flashing fire by then. "What about your radio show?"

"I've been trying to land this job for a month, Jones. It's not like I didn't plan ahead, just in case hell froze over, and I got it." MacKenzie smiled at her. "The radio station's playing a taped show today. I'm under contract for ten more shows, which translates to another two weeks, but I can make arrangements to go in and tape the new stuff when I'm not busy here. Don't worry, Jones, I'll have plenty of time to work with you on this."

She looked from him to Allan, who was still standing. The look he returned told her this was a done deal. Not to argue. So she didn't, not right then, anyway. Allan returned to his seat and started with the daily briefing. She sat there, using the stoic face she had to put on when reading news that made her want to cry, barely hearing him, glad Bryan was there rapidly taking notes so she could catch up later.

Finally the meeting ended, and she got up, went to her office, turned to close the door behind her—and bumped it against the body that stood there, blocking the way.

"We should probably talk," MacKenzie said. He pushed the door wider, waltzed inside as if he owned the place and then closed it behind him. As he did, she saw a crowd of co-workers looking on curiously, but they all scattered as soon as they saw her looking.

Then the door was closed, and it was just the two of them.

"You have an office." He sounded impressed. "I figured a cubicle in the newsroom."

She shrugged. "You figured right, up until two months ago. This was Jim's office. He was a legend, you know. There's a street named after him. He'd been here twenty years. He rated an office of his own."

"So...when he retired?"

"I asked for it and got it." She shrugged. "I was as surprised as anyone when they said yes. You wanna take notes on this or...?"

"Photographic memory," he said, tapping his skull with a forefinger. She would have preferred a sledgehammer.

"So why are you in here?"

He pursed his lips. "Up until last night, I didn't really think I had a chance in hell of landing this job. I'd have given you a heads-up when I first applied, if I had. Thought you ought to know that."

She didn't think a reply was called for, so she didn't give one.

"Hell, I applied here ten years ago, as a photojournalist. That's how I started, you know. Behind the camera. But then I got ambitious. You know I applied for your spot, three years ago, same time you did. I wasn't 'on air' material, they said. Besides, they wanted a woman." He pursed his lips. "Funny thing is, I haven't changed a thing. Not my style, not my look. The only difference is that now my radio show is a hit. My name is known as well as yours is, and I'm your polar opposite. To be honest, I think we could be dynamite together."

She blinked, not missing the double entendre. "On the air, you mean."

"Of course. What else would I mean?" Then he smiled slowly. "Oh, that. Gee, Jones, you don't waste any time, do you?"

She rolled her eyes.

"Don't panic, Jones. I probably won't last a week."

"Why not?"

He smiled, holding his arms out to his sides. "Look at me. Your boss was right the first time. I'm *not* anchor material."

She did look at him. He was wearing faded jeans that looked sinfully good on him, a khaki polo shirt with a Syracuse Orangemen logo patch on one side of the chest, a baseball cap and an olive drab jacket that looked like army surplus. He hadn't shaved this morning, so there was a sexy whisper of prickly stubble on his face. He did look more like one of the photojournalists than an on-air reporter— and she had already known that was where he'd started, behind the camera, not in front of it.

He was right. He didn't look like an anchor. What the hell could Allan have been thinking, hiring him for an on-air spot?

"I figured you'd blackball me if you could," he said finally.

It made her realize that she'd been looking him over pretty thoroughly for several seconds now, and that he was fully aware of it. Maybe even enjoying it.

"I would have, if I'd had a clue they were even thinking of hiring you," she said. Then she sighed and moved behind her desk, sinking into her chair, hugging her coffee mug between her hands, even though it was nearly empty. "Might still try it, though I think Allan's mind is made up."

He sat down in one of the chairs in front of her desk, pulling it closer as he did. "Assuming they don't fire me in short order, I meant what I said before. I think we could make this work for both of us."

"Yeah?"

"Yeah. And look, if it's last night that has you worried, you can relax. I'm not going to say anything about your little snafu at that crime scene. I'm not out to get you fired."

She lifted her brows. "Why not? Wouldn't that give you the anchor seat all to yourself?"

He probed her eyes with his. "Don't trust me as far as you can throw me, do you, Jones?"

"Less than that, even."

His jaw tightened. "Okay, we'll put this on terms you might believe. I want to succeed."

"So?"

"So every marketing study out there shows that viewers prefer news shows with male-female coanchors. Your boss was right about that when he hired you as Jim's partner three years ago. If I get you fired, they'll just hire someone else. I already know you're good. And for some inexplicable reason, you're popular. The viewers love you. The fact that your ratings have dropped since Jim retired isn't because of you, it's because he's gone. The other shows have coanchors, and they're picking up your audience because of it."

She lifted her chin. "My ratings haven't dropped that much."

"You were number one in Central N.Y. Now you're number three."

"The difference between one and three is only a few points."

"The difference between one and three is the difference between winning and being the second runner-up, kid. WSNY wants that number one slot. And now that I'm on board, we're going to give it to them."

She lowered her head, shook it. "Maybe I'll just quit."

He pursed his lips. "No, you won't. That would be unprofessional, and you might be a whole lot of things, Jones, but you are not unprofessional."

She pursed her lips.

"Why do you hate me so much, anyway?"

"I don't hate you, MacKenzie. I couldn't care less about

you. Don't flatter yourself by taking it personally. I'd feel the same way about anyone who was after my job."

"Yeah?"

"Yeah."

"Prove it."

"How?"

"Name one other journalist who went up against you for that anchor chair three years ago. Just one."

She frowned, looking around the room as she searched her memory for names and found none. MacKenzie drummed his fingers on the arm of his chair, glanced at his watch, whistled an uneven tune.

"Well?"

"That doesn't prove anything."

"Proves one thing," he said, getting to his feet. "Proves it *is* personal. Hell, Jones, if I didn't know better, I'd say you're working so hard to hate me just to hide what you really feel."

"Oh, please. This I've gotta hear. What does your warped little imagination tell you I *really* feel?"

He smiled at her. "You want me."

She stared at him for a long moment—at his smoky gray eyes and full lips. And she said, "You're right. I do want you—in so many ways."

"Yeah?" He looked surprised, and maybe a little bit turned on. "God, tell me more."

She began counting on her fingers. "I want you drawn, quartered, gelded without anesthetic, beheaded and spit-roasted. But for now, I just want you out of my office."

His smile didn't disguise the look of relief that flooded him. "*Damn,* I'm gonna love working here," he said, and he turned, whistling off-key, and walked with a spring in his step out of her office.

But not, she feared, out of her life.

5

When Sean returned to the newsroom, he noticed three things. First, the early-morning bustle of the place had slowed to a hum. Reporters were making calls from their partition-separated desks, and several had already left to cover stories. Second, his office door was marked for him by the handful of foil balloons tied to the knob. It was just past the newsroom on the right. An office hadn't been part of the initial offer, but he'd insisted on one as part of the deal, then been surprised that WSNY had agreed readily to that and everything else he'd asked for. Jones would probably be livid when she found out.

The third thing he noticed, after walking into his new digs, was the new suit hanging from a hook in the wall. A red tie, white shirt, navy jacket. They'd even included the pants. He pursed his lips and leaned back into the hallway, glancing toward the glass-enclosed office attached to the newsroom. The news director was inside at his desk, the phone to his ear. He gave Sean a smile and a thumbs-up.

Sean took two steps in that direction before his beeper went off. "Hell." He took it out, glanced at it and read the text message. Then he sighed and hurried across the hall to Jones's office, reminding himself that now that they were partners, scooping her was no longer the goal. Getting dirt on her would still be fun, but it would be purely for entertainment purposes. He walked in without knocking.

She looked up from her computer as if irritated. "What now?"

"Blackwood's name is being released. We got the go. They're holding a press conference in..." He glanced at his watch. "Forty minutes."

"Call them, get the details and meet me in the studio." She was already around the desk, pushing past him into the hall and running for the newsroom, shouting Allan's name.

Five minutes later, Sean headed into the studio with a sheet of scribbled notes.

Jones was at the anchor desk, a hand mirror propped in front of her, wielding a hairbrush with one hand and a makeup brush with the other. She dropped the brushes and dug in her bag. "Where the hell is my mascara?"

Amazing. A few minutes ago she'd looked scattered, sleep deprived and a little wild. Now she looked smooth, composed and flawless. She'd tamed her hair into a respectable bun and slapped on a coat of makeup so fast it made his head spin.

He handed her the sheet of notes and sat down in the chair next to her.

"Sean, you need to change!" called a fresh-faced kid he didn't know, the one who'd given up his seat at that morning's meeting and now stood nearby with the blue suit in his hand. "Just from the waist up. Hurry."

From the control booth, a tinny voice announced, *"Thirty seconds."*

Sean glanced at the kid, licked his lips. Might as well get fired now as later, he thought. "Look, you guys need to get used to this. I don't do the suit thing. I'm not that kind of newsman." As he spoke, he stuck a tiny microphone up underneath his shirt, out the neck and clipped it to his collar.

"Doesn't matter," Jones said, scowling at him. "You don't need to be here at all."

"Standby one."

"I'm here, and I'm staying," he said. "You just read the report and don't sweat it."

She frowned so hard he thought her face would break.

"Roll one!"

The transformation was instant and nothing less than amazing. Her frown vanished as she lifted her eyes to the camera in front of her. The monitor, which Sean could see off to the left, switched from a "News-Four Special Report" screen to her poised, elegant, no-nonsense face—a face that said "You can trust me" without a single word. She began to read almost without glancing down.

"This is a News-Channel Four Exclusive Special Report. Police have just confirmed the identity of the man found lying dead in an Armory Square hotel room last night as Harry Blackwood, brother of New York's own Senator Martin Blackwood. The death is listed as suspicious and is under investigation. I was on the scene of this story last night," she read, "with invaluable assistance from Team Four's newest member, and my new partner, Sean Mac-Kenzie. Sean?"

"Roll Two!" the control room announced.

The red light on camera one blinked out, and the one on camera two came on. Sean knew the monitor now showed both of them, and he tried to look serious as he recited the lines he'd planned on the way down the hall. "Thanks, partner," he said. He saw sparks flying from her eyes, knew they were invisible to everyone but him and deflected them with a smug half smile. Then, facing the camera, "Team Four will have full coverage and late-breaking details of this tragedy as they unfold. Keep it here, folks. This is where you'll get the inside stuff. Until then, this is Sean MacKenzie…'' He looked her way.

"And Julie Jones for News Channel Four," she said, not missing a beat.

The light went out.

"You're clear."

Jones yanked the microphone from her lapel, tugged it out from the back of her blouse—he hadn't thought of running the wire up his back, good tip—and got to her feet. "Invaluable assistance?" she asked.

He shrugged.

"That was not necessary," she told him.

"No, but it was perfect."

"What the hell was that 'inside stuff' comment, anyway? I hope you don't think you can bring your tabloid techniques here with you, MacKenzie, because we won't tolerate that at this station."

"Bullshit. Viewers are twice as intrigued now, and you can bet they'll be tuning in later. As for my techniques, I'm pretty sure they're what got me hired."

She didn't growl at him, but he thought it was close. Then she swung her gaze away, pinning the news director to the floor with her eyes.

Allan returned a slow smile while rubbing his hands. "You two are dynamite together. Now, grab a cameraman and get to that press conference, pronto."

"Both of us?" Jones asked.

"Julie, from now on everything you do, you do together. You follow?"

She closed her eyes, clenched her fists and left the studio.

Sean had to give her credit for speed. She didn't mess around—just dashed into her office, grabbed her jacket and a larger bag, and then joined him in the white SUV in the parking lot, sliding into the passenger seat, then turning to look at him as if he shouldn't be there.

"You keep frowning every time you look at me and you're gonna get wrinkles, Jones."

"The photographers usually drive," she said. "You're going to piss off whoever is coming with us."

"No chance of that." He started the car, put it in reverse, backed out of the parking space. "No one was available. All out on assignment, and we haven't got time to wait. Allan told me to handle it."

She lifted her brows. "Sean MacKenzie saves the day, huh?"

He pulled into traffic. "You wanna hold the camera and let me do the report, I'll be more than happy to let you." He glanced her way. "Buckle up, Jones."

She pulled on her seat belt as he drove. "Where's the press conference? And who will be there?"

"Outside City Hall. Chief Strong, Senator Blackwood naturally, I don't know who else."

"Those cops from last night, I hope."

He glanced at her. "No word on your keys yet?"

She shook her head.

"You ever get your car outta there?"

"Allan said he'd send one of the interns for it this afternoon. I left my spare set of keys with him."

"So it doesn't matter so much—about the other set, I mean."

It did, he could see it did, but he didn't know why. "No," she told him, and he knew it was a lie. "Doesn't matter at all."

They arrived at City Hall. Several other news stations had reporters on the scene, setting up to cover the press conference, but none, he was pleased to see, had sent their evening anchors. To them, it had been just another murder in a year that had already broken the record for violent crime in Central New York. They hadn't been prepared, and the press conference was being given on very short notice.

"Perfect," he whispered, pulling the Jeep into a parking spot at an odd angle and jumping out. He opened the back door, yanked out the camera and balanced it on his shoulder. With his free hand, he snapped on the headphone.

"You just stay behind the camera where you belong," Jones said, adjusting her earphone, picking up the microphone case and getting out, as well.

She took the lead, shouldering her way through the other reporters, most of whom were, he guessed, a little too starstruck to call her on her rudeness. There was no question who was top dog among those present. No other local celebs stood around. None. The sea of bodies parted, grudgingly, to let them pass. Jones commandeered a spot near the podium that had been set up on the front stairs, then turned to face him and almost bumped into the camera.

He backed up two paces, looked through the lens at her, wondered who the hell had ever sculpted a face that perfect or eyes that full of mystery. He saw secrets in those eyes and wondered how the hell he'd missed them up to now.

"How do I look?" she asked, and he knew she wasn't fishing for compliments. She wanted him to tell her if there was spinach in her teeth or a hair standing up straight on top of her head. There wasn't.

"You'll do."

She narrowed her eyes on him, brought the microphone to her lips, adjusted her own nearly invisible earpiece. "You ready back there?"

"Going live in thirty. Stand by."

She cleared her throat, licked her lips.

"Ten seconds, Julie."

She lifted her chin, faced the camera.

"Roll Live-Eye."

"This is Julie Jones, coming to you live outside City Hall, where Senator Blackwood and Syracuse Police Chief Strong are expected to deliver a press conference any minute now. As some of you may already know, late last night, News-Channel Four had the only team on the scene when a man was found dead in an Armory Square hotel room. In a News-Four Exclusive, just under an hour ago, we were the first to report his name—Harry Blackwood, brother of Senator Martin Blackwood."

Sean knew she was watching him, waiting for him to signal her as soon as anyone appeared at that podium up the stairs at her back, but no one had. He thought she was running out of things to say and worried about how she would fill the time if the press conference started late.

"Most Central New Yorkers know Harry Blackwood as a controversial figure, one who had numerous scrapes with the law and a less than stellar reputation. This leaves many of us to speculate on whether his lifestyle and known underworld associates could have any connection to his untimely death, a death police are calling suspicious, though I suspect we'll be hearing more on that shortly. Officially, I can say only that having been at the crime scene before Blackwood's body was removed, there was little doubt in my mind as to the cause of death. Without official permission, I cannot tell you much beyond that, except that the scene was a disturbing one that I'll see in my mind's eye for a long time to come."

Sean lifted his eyes from the camera to look at her directly and gave her a slow nod of approval. Sell it, he thought. For someone who claimed to dislike sensationalism, she sure was a master at it.

"News-Four will continue to bring you complete coverage of this investigation as the day unfolds, and—"

The doors behind her opened, and Sean lifted a hand, finger pointed in that direction.

"And now it looks as if the press conference is about to begin."

Sean turned the camera's eye on the podium, as Julie said, "Senator Martin Blackwood."

Blackwood cleared his throat. He looked as if he'd had a long night without much sleep, but he'd shaved and slicked up for the event. "Good afternoon. It grieves me to have to be here to tell you that my brother, Harold Blackwood, was killed last night. The police have told me that they do suspect foul play, but I'll let them comment on that. I only want to say that this is a difficult time for my family. No matter what people may have thought about my brother, he remained just that—my brother. I would be very grateful to all of the members of the press if you would allow me and my family the time and privacy to grieve the loss of a man we loved very much. That's all I have for you today."

Immediately reporters began shouting questions. Jones, though, had the advantage of being dead center of the senator's line of sight, and probably, Sean added silently, the advantage of being stunning enough to stop any man's eyes from looking past her. Besides, her face was a familiar one.

"Senator, can you tell us anything about the funeral arrangements?"

The senator sighed, nodded once. "We're having a private ceremony, Julie, and we've chosen not to disclose the particulars, as I'm sure you understand."

While she had his full attention, she said, "Of course. Who do you think is responsible for this, Senator?"

He was surprised. She'd slid the real question right on

the heels of the mundane, boring one and nailed him with it. He replied before he could censure himself. "I only wish I knew."

Then, licking his lips, he let one of his aides hustle him away from the microphone, with the press still shouting questions.

Chief Strong, a burly man with a salt-and-pepper crew cut and a face like granite, stepped up to the podium, holding up his hands for silence. "The Syracuse Police Department have several strong leads in this investigation, which is being headed up by Lieutenant Cassandra Jackson. We are not releasing any details regarding cause of death at this time. To do so could impede and hamper the investigation. We will keep the press fully informed, so long as you all cooperate with us in our efforts. Thank you."

"Do you have any suspects?" someone shouted.

He turned to give a reply that was not an answer. Sean kept taping, but as he did, he noticed one of the uniformed cops from last night sidling up to Julie, tapping her shoulder, and speaking near her ear. She nodded at him, then glanced back at Sean and crooked her finger. He put the camera back on her.

"There you have it, the official statement from Senator Blackwood, requesting privacy for his family to grieve this tragic loss. Chief Strong is playing this one very close to the vest—but if doing so will help catch a killer, then News-Four applauds him in that decision."

Sean scowled over the camera at her and then made kissing-up lips at her.

"One thing is obvious from what Chief Strong had to say here, and that is that this case is being treated as a homicide investigation. Lieutenant Jackson, named by the chief as the detective heading up this investigation, is one of the Syracuse P.D.'s top homicide detectives. We'll have more on this as the story develops. This is Julie Jones for News-Channel Four.''

Sean flicked off the camera and lowered it from his shoulder. ''Not kissing up to the Police Department or anything, are we?''

She said, ''I figured it couldn't hurt. They want to see us both inside.''

''Now?''

She nodded, turned and led the way back through the crowd, around to a side entrance, where a uniformed cop waited to take them inside. He paused at a reception desk. ''You can leave the camera here,'' he told Sean.

Sean lifted his brows but complied. Then they were taken into an interrogation room, where Lieutenant Jackson waited. She sat at a table, wearing a pair of shapeless navy-blue slacks and a white button-down blouse. A blazer hung over the back of the wooden chair, and she got up when they walked in. Her hair, long and butterscotch-blond, was pulled back into a ponytail, and she wore no makeup. How the hell a woman could dress that blandly and look that good was beyond Sean, but he did enjoy her. She was a good cop, an honest one, and she didn't hate his guts, always a quality he admired in a woman.

Jax smiled very slightly at Sean; then her eyes met Julie's and turned chilly. She cleared her throat. ''Sit. This won't take long.''

Jones sat. So did Jax. Sean stayed standing, interested in the slight animosity he sensed between the two women. He hadn't noticed it before and wondered about it.

''I assume you can both make a pretty fair guess at the cause of death in the Blackwood case, being that you were there when it happened,'' Jax said.

''After it happened,'' Jones corrected, maybe a little too quickly.

"That's what I meant."

Sean didn't think that was what she'd meant at all. Especially if the way she'd been watching Jones's face as she'd said it was any indication.

"Just what is it you want, Lieutenant Jackson?" Jones asked.

The cop frowned. "Your cooperation. I want you to keep the cause of death to yourselves. Say nothing about the crime scene. Not even little hints like the one you just dropped on the air, Ms. Jones, about how gruesome it was."

Julie seemed to be thinking that over. "Can I ask why?"

"Because only a handful of people outside the police know the details. You two, the hotel employee who found the body—and the killer."

Sean nodded. "I get it. You'll be able to rule out false confessions by nutcases who don't guess right on how Blackwood was killed. I think my partner and I would be glad to make you that promise, Jax, but we'd really like something in return."

He saw Jones flinch and grimace a little when he called the woman by her nickname.

"Why am I not surprised? You always want something in return, Sean."

"Oh, come on, I'm not demanding a date."

"Not this time, anyway." The lieutenant, smiling a little, lowered her sky-blue eyes, and shook her head. "There's nothing I can release just yet, Sean."

"You have any suspects?" Sean asked.

"Everyone Harry knew is a suspect."

"But you've narrowed it down."

The lieutenant nodded. "Yes."

"To?"

Jax looked from one of them to the other. "You didn't

release the name last night, even though you knew who he was. You haven't mentioned the cause of death. So far, you've kept your word. You can't release this tidbit, either, not until I give you the okay. Agreed?''

''Agreed,'' Sean said. He glanced at Julie, but instead of sitting on the edge of her seat in glee, she looked pale, a little pinched around the mouth. Almost scared.

''We think it was a woman.''

Sean was still looking at Julie when Jax said that, but he could see both women, and he knew Jax was watching Jones like a hawk watching a wounded rabbit. He thought Jones flinched and hoped the hell the lieutenant hadn't noticed.

''What makes you think so?'' he asked Jackson.

''We found some makeup in the bathroom. I can't say any more than that.''

Jones closed her eyes, but only very briefly. To Sean, her body language said ''Oh, shit,'' but aloud she said nothing, and he doubted Jax was picking up her subtle signals as clearly as he was—and then wondered why he was so tuned in.

''Keep your promise,'' Jax warned. ''Quite frankly, News-Four is the only station in town that hasn't burned us. We'll work with you if you keep it that way.''

''Not so much because you like us as to teach the others a lesson?''

''You're a sharp one, MacKenzie. Just don't let it go to your head.'' Jax glanced at Jones. ''You all right? You look a little pale.''

''Yeah. I just— It was quite a scene last night. I'm still not over it.''

''Understandable.'' The lieutenant got to her feet. ''Best get her out of here, MacKenzie. And remember what you agreed to here.''

"Will do." Sean slid a protective arm around Julie, drawing her to her feet as if she were the poor, traumatized little female and he the big strong protective male.

That was all it took. Her head came up fast, and she snapped right the hell out of her little daze. "I'm fine," she snapped. "And not in need of help, Lieutenant, though your concern is touching."

With that, she headed for the door under her own steam, yanked it open and started down the hall. Sean caught up to her after retrieving the camera from the reception desk. "Hey, someone set your shoes on fire or what?"

"I just want to get out of here." She stalked to the SUV and didn't even try to get behind the wheel.

Sean set the camera in the back seat, then got in beside her. "What's wrong? What did she say in there that knocked you on your ass like that?"

"Nothing. Nothing knocked me anywhere. I'm fine."

"To hell you are. You didn't even remember to pop in on Officer Friendly to ask if he found your car keys."

She dug in her blazer pocket, pulled out a gold key-ring shaped like a pair of *J*'s and let the keys dangle from it. They were labeled. There was the magnetic strip that unlocked the doors at the station, a key marked "car," another marked "office," another marked "files."

"He gave them to me when he told me about our invitation to see the token female," she said.

"Me-*ow*." She scowled, but Sean wasn't going to let that remark go. "Jax is no token, she's a damn good cop. And it wouldn't hurt you any to treat her a little better. She can be a reporter's best friend."

"Oh, is that what she is? Your best friend?"

He gaped, totally thrown by this side of Jones and at a loss for words.

"Screw it," she said. "At least I got my keys back. The

officer said someone turned them in at the hotel's front desk. Which doesn't make a hell of a lot of sense, but at least they're—oh, shit!''

''What?'' He glanced at her, saw her staring at the keys, her eyes wider than they had been two seconds ago. *''What?''*

She swallowed hard. ''The keys to my house. They're missing.''

Cassie Jackson frowned at the note she found on the windshield of her unmarked Crown Victoria when she came out of the Dinosaur Bar-b-que Grille. She'd left work after the press conference for lunch with some of the guys from the homicide division. Not that they were goofing off, just that they knew damned well they would be heading right back for a long day's work on this damned Blackwood murder and might very well miss dinner. They all said they would work better on full stomachs, and the chief hadn't argued. The Dinosaur was a local favorite, as noted for its long lines as for its mouthwatering ribs. For the local peace officers, though, the owners were willing to work a little harder. She and the boys managed to get in, get served and get out again in under an hour, so it was only around one when she hit the parking lot and saw from a distance the note under the windshield wiper of her car.

The sight of it, one corner flapping like the wing of a marooned dove, kicked Cassie into full cop mode without passing go. She stopped in her tracks and scanned the parking lot, looking for stragglers, watchers, anyone who shouldn't be there. But there was no one standing around, and all the cars she saw were either coming, going or empty. No one was sitting in a parked vehicle to observe her.

She walked carefully to the car, one hand on the nine

millimeter's grip, though she didn't pull it from its shoulder holster. She bent to look underneath, checked inside, the back seat, around and behind the car. No one. Finally she leaned over without touching the hood, nipped the corner of the sheet with the very tips of her fingernails and used her free hand, covered by the edge of her sleeve, to lift the wiper blade. The sheet came free without smudging any prints that might be on it. She scanned it, read the words written in pencil, in carefully formed block letters.

YOU'LL FIND THE BLADE USED TO SLIT HARRY BLACK-WOOD'S THROAT AT THE HOME OF HIS KILLER: 108 LAKE ROAD, CAZENOVIA.

Jax sighed, then caught sight of one of her colleagues, Detective Hennesey, just getting into his car across the parking lot. She shouted his name. He glanced her way and frowned. She said, "Bring an evidence bag over here." He nodded, and a second later came jogging across the lot.

"Got an anonymous tip telling us where to find the murder weapon," she said, holding up the note.

His thick red eyebrows rose, and he looked at the sheet she still held by one corner. Quickly he opened the evidence bag and held it while she lowered the note into it. "You think it's legit?" he asked as he sealed and labeled the bag.

"Got the cause of death right." She glanced at her car. "We should keep the car clean until it can be dusted for prints, though I doubt this joker was stupid enough to leave any. Still, you never know."

"I can stay with it. You can take mine back."

She nodded. "Thanks, Hennesey. The team should be here in fifteen, tops."

He nodded. "No problem. I got a doggy bag, in case I

get bored.'' He patted his coat pocket and wiggled his eyebrows. Then he tossed her his keys.

Cassie called in the moment she was behind the wheel
of Hennesey's car and had the seat adjusted for her considerably shorter legs, and asked for a team to come out
and go over her car, then read off the address from the note
and asked for a trace. It took only a couple of seconds
before the reply came back.

"108 Lake Road is the residence of one Julie Jones,
Lieutenant.''

Cassie blinked slowly. "Well, I'll be damned.'' Not only
had she been at the scene of the crime, where a female had
left a tube of mascara behind, but she had given someone
a reason to implicate her. She keyed the mic. "Do we have
the elevator surveillance tapes yet?''

"Yes, ma'am.''

"Have someone get them cued up and ready to view for
me, will you? And I'd like a look at Julie Jones's bank
records, while we're at it.''

"I'll pass it along.''

She pursed her lips and drove Hennesey's car back to
the station.

6

A_S Sean drove them back to the station, Julie replayed Lieutenant Jackson's words about the killer being a woman—the makeup left behind at the crime scene. She recalled vividly those moments in the hotel bathroom—the way the tears had made her mascara run. The way she'd angrily thrown the tube into the wastebasket. No, not *into* it, but *at* it, like a spoiled child having a temper tantrum. She'd missed her target. Her fingerprints were on that mascara tube. Maybe even an eyelash or two. Could they extract DNA from an eyelash?

She'd been so careful to remove every trace of her presence from that room, yet like a rank amateur, she'd left the mascara for the police to find. And her key ring. Let's not forget the damned key ring.

She'd gotten it back, true enough, but her house keys were missing. Nothing else. Just the keys to her house.

"Hey, it's not that big a deal," Sean said, pulling into the station parking lot. "If it worries you that much, just have the locks changed."

She shook herself out of the fear that had gripped her, glanced his way, tried to hide it. "Who said I was worried?"

He lifted his brows. "Your face says it, Jones. You look like you just saw a ghost."

She shrugged, going for nonchalant. "I'm in the public

eye. I'm less than thrilled with the idea that some lunatic might have the keys to my house.''

''You sure they were on that key ring?''

She nodded.

He frowned. ''Could you have dropped them anywhere else in the hotel?''

She racked her memory. She'd gone straight from the parking garage to Harry's room, then straight back down to the parking garage. She hadn't set foot in the hotel—lobby or anywhere else, for that matter—until after she'd discovered the keys missing. ''I suppose there's a slim chance I could have dropped them in the elevator.''

''That's probably it, then. Someone picked them up and left them at the front desk.''

''And removed my house keys on the way?'' She shook her head.

''They could have fallen off.''

''Back door *and* front? I don't think so, MacKenzie. That would be a damn big coincidence.''

''You're right, it would.'' He sighed, pulling the SUV into its assigned spot in the station parking lot. ''Call a locksmith. Hell, at least Dawn's in school all day. You don't have to worry about her.''

She swallowed hard, getting out of the car and hurrying into the building, Sean keeping pace. Then, halfway down the hall, she went still as her blood chilled. ''Staff development meeting,'' she croaked.

Sean frowned at her. ''What?''

''That's what it says on the school calendar. Staff development meeting. Jesus, there's only a half-day of school today. Dawn will be home in—'' She twisted her wrist to look at her watch. ''She's home now.'' And someone—maybe the same someone who'd slit Harry Blackwood's throat—had the keys to her house.

She opened her purse, rummaged for her cell phone, but her hands were shaking, and she thought she might vomit.

"Julie, get in here, pronto!"

She lifted her head fast, saw Allan Westcott's head poking out from the newsroom door. "I can't—I have to go get my daughter. She's—"

"She'll have to wait. We've got an anonymous caller who'll only talk to you. Move it!"

Her breath came too fast, and she opened her mouth to argue, but a solid hand on her shoulder made her pause and look up. Sean gave her a nod, a reassuring squeeze, so reassuring that she didn't take the time to analyze how ridiculous that was.

"Easy," he told her. "You go take the call. I'll go get your kid."

She blinked in surprise. Surprise that he would offer, and surprised that no objection flew to her lips. She didn't like Sean MacKenzie, but she *did* trust him—where Dawn was concerned, at least. She hadn't realized it until that very moment. But the knowledge was there, deep down in that intuitive place that grows in the soul of a mother throughout the lifetime of her children. Sean was no threat to her daughter. In fact, he would probably go out of his way to protect Dawnie. It was a stunning revelation that unfolded in the space of a single heartbeat. Swallowing against the dryness in her throat, she nodded and said, "Hurry, Sean."

He frowned, maybe a little puzzled at the urgency in her eyes. "I'll take my car—it's faster. Give her a call when you get a minute. Tell her I'm coming, or she might refuse to come back with me."

Julie nodded even as Sean turned and rushed back out the doors they'd just entered through. She hoped Dawnie would be wise enough to refuse to go with a man she barely knew without prior word from her mom—but part of her figured that if Sean showed up in the Porsche, parental consent wouldn't be an issue.

"Jones, let's go!" Westcott barked.

She swallowed hard and walked into the newsroom.

Dawn got off the school bus, rolling her eyes and mentally counting the days before her road test appointment. Eight, not counting today. After that, the bus would be a thing of the past. Unless her overprotective mother thought the roads were bad due to a passing snowflake or errant raindrop. She smiled, shaking her head as she fumbled for her house key and reached for the door.

It opened when she touched it, wasn't even closed all the way, much less locked.

"Gee, for supermom, she sure messed up this time," she muttered, pocketing her key and walking inside. Then she felt a little guilty. It wasn't like her mom to be this forgetful. She'd been really upset last night. Partly, Dawn suspected, because of her own antics. Getting caught had been really irresponsible of her. She knew how her mother worried. Should have been sneakier.

But there had been something else bothering her mom last night, too. That phone call Dawn had overheard. Her mother had been upset when she'd come downstairs a couple of minutes later. Pale and shaky. Distracted. Not at all herself, though she'd done a hell of a job of trying to hide it. It probably would have fooled anyone else. Anyone but Dawn.

Dawn was pretty sure her mom was in some kind of trouble, but as many times as she'd asked if everything was okay, if anything was wrong, her mother had denied it. Protecting her just like always.

Dawn wished she could return the favor. She'd never quite understood her mother's lionesslike attitude when it came to watching over her, but she thought maybe she got it now—at least a little bit. If she ever found out who was causing her mother so much anguish, Dawn thought she would be capable of doing some major damage.

Sighing, she slung her backpack onto the sofa, snatched up the remote and flicked on the TV. It was tuned to her mom's station, as always. Dawn started to flick it to MTV-2, then paused as she saw her mom's face on the screen.

It made her smile. Her mother was such a pro, and gorgeous to boot. Most of the time Dawn was the envy of her classmates for having a local celebrity for a mother. She thumbed up the volume, reading the line at the bottom of the screen that said this piece had been taped earlier; then she tossed the remote and headed into the kitchen for a soda.

But her ears perked up when she heard what her mother was saying. Harry Blackwood, the senator's brother, had been murdered last night.

Harry.

A little knot formed in Dawn's stomach. Harry—that was what her mother had called the man on the phone last night. Just before she'd gone out.

Dawn licked her lips and gave her head a little shake. She was being silly. Of course her mom had gone out; she'd probably gotten called to cover that very story.

She wandered back into the living room, watching what the senator and the chief of police had to say at the press conference her mom had been covering. Then the cameras were back in the studio, aimed at the midday report anchor, a blonde who wasn't nearly as good as her mom. She said, "The police department says the preliminary medical examiner's report puts the time of death at around midnight last night. Cause of death has not yet been released, though the case has now been labeled a homicide, Syracuse's twenty-third of the year.''

Midnight. Her mom had been out *before* midnight. She'd left a little before eleven. Then she'd come back with that nice-looking MacKenzie guy and gone out again sometime later—in jeans and a sweatshirt that time.

Hell.

Sighing, Dawn left the channel where it was, turning the volume up a little higher, but they'd moved on to traffic and weather. She headed back to the kitchen for a snack. She reached up to the cupboard above the sink for a box of her favorite granola bars, took one out, left the box on the counter and the cupboard door open, then peeled off the wrapper and dropped it into the wastebasket on the way by.

Then she stopped, because the paper hit the top of the mound of garbage and slid onto the floor, and her mom's voice echoed in her mind. ''I shouldn't have to tell you to take the garbage out when it's so full it's falling to the floor, Dawn. It should be obvious. It's one of the few jobs I ask you to do around this place, so the least you could do is—''

''All right, all right,'' Dawn muttered to the imaginary voice. She wondered if anyone had ever researched whether it was possible for parents to bitch at their kids psychically and thought she might write to Nathan Z and ask him, since it was the kind of thing that ought to be right up his psychic, new age alley.

She set her granola bar on the counter, gathered the edges of the overflowing garbage bag together, knotted them and then tugged the bag from the wastebasket. She carried it through the door at the back of the kitchen, into the adjoining garage, and walked to the three neat, shiny aluminum trash cans in the back. She yanked the lid off the first one, but it was full already, so she slammed it back on and moved to the next.

Only one bag of garbage was in the second can. It was what lay on top of that bag that made her go still while her heart tripped over itself and then struggled to regain its rhythm.

A large knife lay on top of the trash bag. It was coated in something—something that looked an awful lot like blood.

Her mind was racing, jumping from the feeling that her mom was in trouble to her conversation with someone she called "Harry" to her out of character late night wanderings to the report of the murdered man on the news. What if...

The sound of a car pulling into her driveway made her snap her head toward the windows in the overhead garage door. Sean MacKenzie's Porsche pulled to a stop out front. God, what if he—or anyone else, for that matter—came in and saw this?

Dawn didn't even think twice. She had to protect her mother, and that meant getting rid of the bloody knife. She reached into the wastebasket, yanked out the knife and shoved the trash bag into the can. Then she slammed on the lid and ran into the kitchen, snatching a small kitchen towel from the rack and wrapping the knife inside it. She took the disgusting thing to the living room and crammed it into the bottom of her backpack.

When she straightened and looked at her hands, there were dried pieces of the red stuff clinging to her fingers and palms. Her stomach lurched.

She heard the doorbell, then Sean MacKenzie's voice. "Hello, anybody home?"

"Uh—yeah, just a sec," she called. Swallowing bile, she forced herself to move, hurried to the kitchen again, scrubbed her hands with soap, wiped them dry on her jeans and gathered up her wits. This didn't mean anything. Certainly not that her mother had somehow been involved in the death of Senator Blackwood's brother.

Never that. Her mother wouldn't hurt a fly—unless she thought that fly was a threat to Dawn. In which case, all bets were off.

But Dawn didn't even know the senator's brother.

She turned to answer the door, just as the telephone rang.

The girl opened the door with the phoniest smile Sean thought he had ever seen. "Hi, Sean. Mom's not here." He heard the phone ringing and nodded toward it.

"I know. If you haven't heard from her yet, that'll be her on the phone. Go ahead, grab it."

She frowned at him, but veered left into the kitchen, taking the phone off the wall mount. She leaned in the doorway, watching him as she said, "Hello?" Then she nodded at him. "You're right, it's her. Hey, Mom, what's up?" She listened to her mother, and her frown grew deeper. "But I don't see why I can't just go to Kayla's." Then she rolled her eyes at Sean, as if to tell him how irrational mothers could be. "Right. I forgot, I'm grounded. Mom, are you okay? You don't sound— Yes, he's here right now. Okay. All right. Gee, Mom, ease up already. I'll see you in a few."

She turned a little away from him as she hung up the phone and stayed that way for a second, as if gathering her thoughts or something. When she faced him again, she'd done her best to hide whatever was bothering her, but it wasn't a good enough job to fool him.

She seemed to search his face for a long moment.

"What?" he asked.

"Nothing." She sighed as she came through the living

room, yanking her backpack from the sofa and slinging it over one shoulder.

He opened the door for her, stood there. ''There's something,'' he said. ''I can see there's something bothering you.'' Then he shrugged. ''If I can help...''

''You can't. You and Mom are rivals.''

''So?''

''So...'' She narrowed her eyes on him. They were perceptive eyes, intelligent ones. ''So if you found out she was in trouble—really serious trouble—what would you do? Help her out—or write an exposé about it?''

He studied her face for a moment. Her eyes were full of turmoil, and it hit him where he lived. He liked the kid, he realized. No matter who her mother was.

''Didn't your mom tell you on the phone?'' he asked.

''Tell me what?''

''They hired me over at WSNY. I'm her new coanchor.''

Dawn just blinked at him. ''You're kidding me.''

''Nope.''

''I'll bet she's...overjoyed.''

He smiled at the sarcasm in her voice and the insight behind it. ''Practically had kittens in delight.''

Dawn smiled, and he thought it was genuine this time. ''I can imagine.'' But the smile died too soon. ''So does that mean you two are friends now?''

''I wouldn't go that far.'' He shrugged. ''Doesn't matter, though. I wouldn't stab her in the back.'' He waited, watching Dawn struggle with a decision. ''Come on, Dawn. If your mom is in some kind of trouble, maybe I can help.''

Dawn faced him squarely, licked her lips. ''Maybe,'' she said. ''If she trusts you with me, that's saying a lot.''

''Is it?''

''Oh yeah. The old man next door, Rodney White, lived

there four years before she stopped being suspicious of him, and he must be in his seventies.''

''You're saying she's a little overprotective?''

''A little? I was twenty minutes late one night and she was dialing 9-1-1 when I walked in.''

He lifted his brows. Then he tipped his head to one side. Jones had trusted him to come fetch her daughter. Dawn was right; it did tell him something. Julie Jones didn't hate him quite as much as she pretended. ''So what's this terrible trouble you think she's in?'' he asked.

Dawn shrugged and walked out the door. He followed, closing and locking it behind her. ''I'm not sure yet,'' she said, and the serious, worried tone and look had returned. He hated seeing a sixteen-year-old bearing troubles that looked to be beyond adult-size. And he couldn't even ease her mind by telling her that he thought her mom was just fine, because he didn't. He'd been picking up the same feelings—that Julie Jones was in some kind of trouble.

Damn. He felt for the kid. So he did the unthinkable.

He took his keys from his pocket, tossed them to her. ''You up for a driving lesson on a real car?''

Her eyes widened, shifting from him to the Porsche in the driveway. ''You're kidding me!''

''What, you don't think you can handle it?''

Her smile widened. ''You just watch me.'' She opened the driver's door, slung her backpack in and got behind the wheel.

He'd succeeded in distracting her from whatever had been worrying her—for now, at least. He just wondered, when she started the car and revved the engine, if he was going to live to regret it.

When she backed out of the driveway without even grinding the gears and came to an only slightly jerky stop before pulling out into the road, he nodded in approval. "Your mom must be a pretty good teacher."

She released a bark that might have been laughter. "No way. I take driver's ed. My mother's the worst driver in the history of the world, Sean. Don't ever let her behind the wheel of this car, okay? Trust me on this."

He nodded. "Thanks for the tip."

"Thanks for letting me drive." She slid the car into First, eased it into motion and relaxed back in the seat.

She was a gorgeous little thing, a fledgling woman testing out her fragile wings. Jones had done all right with her. And that, he figured, was a point in her favor. You couldn't hate a woman who could raise a kid like Dawn. Not entirely, anyway.

"I tried to do this more privately," the voice on the phone whispered. It was a female voice, and obviously disguised. "But I kept getting your voice mail, or your daughter at home. And you had your cell phone turned off."

Julie held the phone to her ear. "Who is this?"

"It doesn't matter. You don't need to know that. All you need to know is—he's alive, Jewel. He's alive, and he knows."

Shivering down deep in her soul, Julie told herself those words couldn't mean what every cell in her body feared they meant. It couldn't be—it couldn't be *that.*

She looked up, searching for words, and saw Allan Westcott standing there, staring at her from beneath deeply bent brows, an extension phone pressed to his ear. He gestured with his free hand, a circular motion, telling Julie to say something, to keep the conversation going.

She cleared her throat. "Who's alive?" she asked. God, she could barely speak.

"You know. The Reverend. Mordecai Young."

His eyes shooting wider, Westcott scribbled on a sheet of paper and shoved it at Julie. Swallowing hard, she read the words he'd written, looked at him, shook her head.

Her boss glared at her, thumping an insistent forefinger on the sheet.

Licking her lips, Julie shook her head. "And you wanted to tell me this privately. Not here at the station, where others might be listening in?"

"Yes. But it's more important that you know."

She prayed whoever it was got the message even as she saw her boss's angry frown. He was shaking the paper at her now. Swallowing hard, she read the words aloud. "What do you mean when you say, 'He knows'? _What_ does he know?"

"It's a sunny day, isn't it? So sunny." The phone call ended with an abrupt click.

Julie moved the receiver slowly away from her ear, but she was shaking all the way to her toes. "She hung up," she said. She put the telephone back into its cradle.

The news director clapped his hands together once, then rubbed them rapidly. "Jesus, this is incredible. Mordecai Young? Alive? Jesus." He dashed into the hall, shouted into the newsroom, "Did we get the number?"

"It was blocked," someone called. "We got nothing."

Julie's shaking intensified. Sunny, the caller had said. That was what Dawn had been called for the first few weeks of her life. Sunny. Oh, God, it couldn't be true! Mordecai Young. Alive. And he knew—he knew about... Dawn.

"She called you 'Jule,'" Allan said. "What do you make of that?"

She shrugged. "People call me all sorts of things. Jule, Jules..."

"You think it's someone you know?"

She thought of Sirona, of Tessa—the only two people alive who might think of her as Jewel. Had it been one of them? Her boss nudged her. She said, "I'm in everyone's living room five nights a week, Allan. Everyone feels like they know me."

"Jones, you have to get on this," Westcott said.

She lifted her head, met his eyes only briefly, shook her head. "There's nothing to get on. It was probably just a crank."

"What was probably a crank?" Sean's gravelly voice preceded him into Julie's office.

Julie surged to her feet, opened her mouth to ask about Dawn, and then saw her. She came in right behind Sean. "Sean let me drive his car, Mom. Man, we have *got* to get a Porsche."

Julie was around the desk, clutching her daughter to her chest in an embrace so fierce and involuntary she couldn't have prevented it if she'd wanted to. She held Dawn hard, one hand on her slender back and the other stroking her butter-blond hair, which was just as smooth as satin. She smelled the green-apple shampoo Dawn preferred and felt tears burn in her eyes.

And then she realized that both Westcott and MacKenzie were staring, and she forced herself to let go.

Dawn stared up into her mother's eyes, her own worried. "Mom, what is it? What's wrong?"

She tried to find words. Failed. She tried not to let the fear show in her eyes, but she was afraid she failed at that, as well.

"Hey, you know your mom, kiddo," MacKenzie said. "A teeny bit overprotective, right? The thought of you driving a car that'll do one-eighty in fourth gear is probably more than she can stand." He winked at the two of them.

"Don't worry, Jones, I didn't let her go over forty-five, and I had one hand ready to grab the wheel the entire time."

Julie met his eyes and knew he was covering for her. Why? What was he up to? She looked at Dawn again, knew her daughter wasn't fooled at all. She was too perceptive, and they were too close, for her to be fooled that easily.

"You have homework?" she managed to say.

"Yeah. Tons." Dawn reached out to smooth a strand of hair off her mother's forehead, as if she were the parent. "Tough day, huh?"

"Yeah. Better now, though." She managed to smile, and Dawn smiled back.

"Don't worry, Mom. Everything's gonna be okay." Julie frowned a little, wondering what Dawn meant by that, but Dawn rushed on. "So whose office do I get to commandeer? I'm gonna need a computer, modem, phone, TV and plenty of junk food."

"Tell you what, kiddo," MacKenzie said. "They have an office all set up for me, but I've barely even been inside it."

"You got an office?" Julie asked, then glanced at her boss. "He got an office?" Allan opened his mouth to answer, but Julie held up a hand. "It doesn't matter. I don't care."

Sean frowned, puzzled, maybe, by her not objecting or arguing.

"Why don't you check out my new digs, Dawn?" he asked. "Let me know what it lacks so you can tell me what to ask for."

She nodded. "Thanks, Sean."

"It's the one that used to be my office, before we put the new newsroom in, Dawn," Westcott told her. "You remember where it is, just down the hall on the right?" She nodded. "Help yourself to snacks from the green room on your way, hon."

"Will do. Thanks, Mr. Westcott." She hitched her backpack up a little higher, then leaned up and kissed her mother on the cheek before leaving them.

Julie watched her go, breathing a sigh of relief, telling herself Dawn was safe here. No one could get in without a magnetic keycard, there were cameras monitoring every entrance, and even if someone were to come looking for her, Allan Westcott's old office would be the last place they would expect to find her.

"We've got a breaking story here, MacKenzie. You ever hear of Mordecai Young?"

Sean had been studying Julie's face—a little too closely, in her opinion—but he looked away fast when Allan said the name. "The so-called *Reverend* Young?"

"That's the one."

Julie sank into her chair again. She was shaken, and fighting to get herself under control. This was not the first time she'd had this nightmare. It was, however, the first time it had been real.

She didn't want to listen to Allan Westcott recap the story, but she couldn't seem to help herself. Nor to stop the visions—the memories—from unfolding in her mind as he spoke.

"Mordecai Young was a self-proclaimed minister, leader of a group he called the Young Believers who lived on a hundred-acre compound down in Chenango County," Westcott said. "Most of his followers were young and female, though there were a dozen or so young men with him, as well. Word was the place was lousy with illegal weapons and drugs. He was apparently growing huge crops of marijuana and opium, partly in greenhouses. When the feds went in to raid the place, all hell broke loose. The entire place burned to the ground. Young and his followers died rather than surrender.''

Julie remembered. The smoke, the heat, the bodies. She remembered her best friend, Lizzie, with her golden-blond hair and her bright green eyes pressing her newborn daughter into Julie's arms as her life seeped onto the floor.

Take her, Jewel. She's yours now.

Julie swallowed back the tears that were trying so hard to spill over.

Westcott, oblivious to the turmoil going on inside Julie, rushed on. "That anonymous caller of Julie's was a woman claiming that Mordecai Young is still alive."

"You're shitting me." MacKenzie slid his penetrating gaze to Julie, then frowned deeply and kept his eyes on her, probing, even when she looked away. "What else did she say?" he asked.

Julie shook her head, unable to meet his eyes. "Nothing that made any sense. Something about the weather. It was probably a crank call. God knows we get enough of them."

"The caller said, 'He knows,'" Westcott explained. "'He's alive, and he knows,' whatever the hell that means."

Julie shook her head. "We *have* a story. A good solid story—the biggest murder investigation to hit the state in ten years. That's where we should be focusing our attention, not on some crank caller telling ghost stories."

"Well yeah, if it *was* a crank," Westcott said. "But, Julie, what if it wasn't? What if Mordecai Young really is still alive?"

If Mordecai Young is still alive, Julie thought, turning her back on both men and clenching her fists so hard her nails cut smiles into her palms, then he's coming. He's coming…for Dawn.

Aloud, she said only, "He can't be."

7

When the news director left her office, Sean stayed behind, closing the door, turning to face her. She was sitting in her chair, elbows braced on her desk, forehead resting in her palms. He said, "Okay, he's gone. You can quit pretending you're not about to burst into flames over this anonymous tip."

"Why are you still here?"

She said it without looking up. Sean took it as further evidence that Dawn's notion that her mother was in some kind of trouble and his own gut instincts were dead-on target. Just what the hell was she hiding? If her performance at the scene of Harry Blackwood's murder, her breaking and entering at Harry's apartment and her disappearing house keys and panicked reaction to them hadn't been enough to convince him of that, then this was. The way she looked right now. She looked drained. She looked... scared.

"Dawn's worried about you." He knew that would get a reaction, and he was right.

Her head came up fast. "What did she say?"

"Not much. She doesn't trust me a hell of a lot more than you do. Yet. Though, uh, I guess you must trust me a little. You trusted me to bring her to you."

The frown lines between her brows eased. "Don't let it go to your head, MacKenzie. Don't think for one minute I'm not on to your game."

"You're gonna have to be more specific, Jones. I have a dozen games going at any given time. Which one are you 'on to'?"

She pressed her lips together, gave him a smug look that was a little more Jones-like than the one she'd been wearing earlier. "The one where you kiss up to my daughter, pretend to be her friend and then pick her brain for dirt on her mother." She shrugged. "Or the one where you convince me you really do like her, so that I let my guard down and trust you with the blade that can slit my throat."

He frowned at her. "Now *that* is an *interesting* choice of words."

She averted her eyes.

"I like your kid, Jones."

"Why, MacKenzie?"

He shrugged. "Why not? She's smart, and she's sharp, she's got good taste in music and radio-shock jocks, and she knows as much about cars as I do."

Julie sighed. "She subscribes to a half-dozen car magazines. *Moto-trend, Car and Driver...*"

"Besides all that, she's nothing like her mom. So what's not to like?" He met her eyes. "And you're a liar if you say you don't believe that, or you'd never have let me go get her."

"Don't flatter yourself. I was worried enough that I'd have asked *anyone* go get her at that point."

"You didn't ask anyone. You asked me. There were twenty other people around the newsroom you could have asked. But you asked me."

"I didn't ask. You offered."

"You took me up on it. And now that you mention it, I completed the mission in spades, and I haven't heard a word of thanks, other than from the kid herself."

She glared at him. "You're gonna milk this for all it's worth, aren't you?"

"Yep." He crossed his arms over his chest and tipped his head to one side. "Well?"

Julie pursed her lips, rolled her eyes and, finally, nodded. "Thank you, Sean."

"You're welcome. Now, see? Was that so hard?"

She sighed. "I really am grateful, you know. Probably more than you can imagine."

"Yeah. I picked up on that."

She lifted her brows in question.

"You were as glad to see her as if I'd delivered her from the jaws of a hungry shark, instead of just from an empty house."

Jones looked him squarely in the eye. "I was worried. Don't forget, my house keys and Harry's killer vanished in the same place."

"Oh, come on. The murderer was long gone by the time you got there." She looked away so fast he couldn't mistake it. He'd hit on something, some clue as to what she was hiding. He came around her desk, then crouched in front of her chair and spun it to face him, keeping his hands on either arm so she would stay put. From there, he tried to study her more closely. "Just what time *did* you arrive at that hotel, Jones?"

"About a minute and a half before you did," she snapped. "I told you last night, I heard the call on my scanner, just like you did."

"The one at your house."

"Right."

"But I was at your house, and I didn't see any scanner."

She hesitated just long enough to give away the lie. "I keep it in my bedroom."

If he could read her eyes—and he was pretty sure he

could—she would have a scanner in that bedroom before she slept tonight, just in case he checked. But he didn't believe for a minute that she had one there now. "There's still the distance," he said. "I live twenty minutes closer than you, Jones. And I left the second the call went out. There's no way you could have beaten me there from Caz if you left at the same time."

She lifted her head again, met his eyes, and hers were steady, level and determined. "Then I guess I must have heard it on the scanner in my car. And I guess I must have been closer to that hotel than you were when I did."

He narrowed his eyes on her. "I guess that must be it."

She nodded. "Then we should let it go, shouldn't we?"

Jesus, what the hell was this? "Yeah. I guess we should." Bullshit. He was just getting started. "So what do you want to do with the tip on Mordecai Young?"

She shook her head slowly. "Nothing. I think it's a hoax."

"It probably is," he said. "But I want to follow up on it anyway."

"Of course you do. This is right up your alley, after all, along with Elvis sightings and alien abductions."

He pressed a hand to his heart. "I'm wounded! I have never covered an alien abduction story in my life."

She rolled her eyes.

"Come on, Jones. If there's any chance, even a slight one, that he didn't die in that raid, don't you think there are people who have a right to know? The families of the kids who died there, maybe?"

She was staring at some unseen spot, beyond the walls that surrounded them. "You're right," she said. "We need to make sure." She seemed to shake herself then, bringing her focus back to his face. "You know, for a second there, you actually sounded compassionate. As if you were thinking beyond sensationalism and ratings.''

He fought down the anger. ''You think I'm that heartless?''

She shrugged, and it made him even madder.

''I was there, Jones.''

When her head came up, her dark brown eyes locked on him, looking way more stunned than they ought to, and he wished to God he could take the words back. She didn't need to see the one and only chink in his defenses. His only soft spot. Dammit, what had he been thinking?

''You were—you were there?''

He shrugged as if it were no big deal. ''Yeah. Me and my cameras. It was a colossal fuckup. Dead kids everywhere. Mordecai Young, too, they said, when they got around to identifying the bodies.''

''You have footage?'' she asked.

He licked his lips, formed his words carefully. ''The feds confiscated the tapes. Hit me with a gag order. If I'd written the story, my career would have been over right there.''

She was searching his face, shaking her head slowly. ''I can't believe it,'' she said softly. ''I can't believe Sean MacKenzie ever let the government tell him what he could and couldn't report.''

He had to look away from those eyes. ''It's not something I'm proud of, Jones. But I was a kid, just starting out. I didn't have any clout at all in the biz. I'd have lost my job, probably my whole career.'' He shook his head slowly.

''You've felt guilty ever since, haven't you? That's why you're such a rogue reporter, with your exposés and your inside dirt. It's all backlash.''

''You see right through me, Jones. I'm just a tortured soul, in search of redemption.'' He sent her a look. ''So you wanna have sex with me now?''

The look on her face went from one of sympathetic understanding to one of disgust faster than his Porsche could go from zero to sixty. "You are such an asshole."

"Ah, come on, I'm sure with the love of a good woman I could be whole again."

"Go to hell, MacKenzie."

He grinned at her. "Been there. They threw me out 'cause I made the devil look good." He turned, starting for the door. "Tell you what. I'm going to milk my sources on this Mordecai Young sighting, you milk yours, and we'll meet after the evening broadcast to compare notes."

"Okay."

He stopped with his hand on the doorknob, glancing back at her, surprised by her easy agreement. "Okay? Just like that?"

"Yeah. Just like that." She shrugged. "I'm not stupid, MacKenzie, and I'm not blind. I can't deny you're good at digging up dirt. In this case, my need to know outweighs my concerns about your sleazy methods and shady sources."

He tipped his head to one side. "Damn. You keep flattering me like that and I'll start thinking you have a crush on me."

"Oh, I'll crush you all right—by showing you up so badly on the air tonight."

"That's the lamest comeback you've ever thrown at me. You're off your game, Jones."

"And still kicking your ass, MacKenzie. Even on my worst day."

He studied her face for a moment longer, waxing serious in spite of himself. "So what makes today your worst day?"

She looked back at him, just as serious. "It's the day they hired you."

He smiled. "Much better." Then he left her office.

Dawn spent the afternoon doing homework and digging through computer files, including Sean MacKenzie's notes on the Harry Blackwood murder. She got a little queasy when she read that the man's throat had been cut "practically from ear to ear." Sean's notes were extremely detailed. Of course, they were for his eyes only. None of this stuff could be shared with the general public without the police department's okay. He also mentioned in his notes that her mother had been there either just before or just after he had arrived at a little after midnight. In parentheses he'd made a note to himself: "details in private files."

Frowning, Dawn searched for the files marked Private, but they were password protected, every last one of them.

Sighing, she exited the program and shut down his computer. Then she started loading her homework and textbooks into her backpack, but she paused in the process, staring down at the towel-wrapped shape in the bottom.

She had to get rid of that thing. But where?

"Dawn?"

She looked up fast. Sean stood in the office doorway.

"How's it going?" he asked.

She stuffed her books into the bag on top of the weapon. "Got the homework all done."

"Great. Listen, your mom and I are about to go on the air. You wanna go for pizza after?"

"Pizza's always good."

He nodded. "An hour, then. You gonna watch us?" He nodded toward the TV-VCR mounted high on the office wall.

"Sure. You gonna wear that?"

He glanced down at himself. He was wearing faded blue jeans and a skintight black T-shirt. "Hell, I forgot." He came the rest of the way inside, yanked a short-sleeved black button-down from where it lay on top of a pile of boxes and pulled it on. He had a layer of five-o'clock shadow, but Dawn had the feeling it was staying put. The shirt was the only concession. He was a nonconformist. A rebel.

Her approval of him moved up another notch.

"An hour," he told her.

"See you then. Break a leg, huh? And make my mom look good."

"She doesn't need me for that, kid."

Dawn's brows went up as he ducked back out of the office. "Well, now," she muttered to herself. "That's... interesting."

Dawn flicked on the television set to watch the evening broadcast. While the opening credits rolled, she opened one of the boxes that were stacked in the corner of the office and began taking things out of it, placing them around Sean's office.

She watched the two of them on the screen. Her mother seemed distracted, not her usual polished, professional self. Sean, on the other hand, was ultra-attentive. And sometimes, when he looked her mom's way, it was almost as if...

"Almost nothing," she muttered, smiling a little as she stared at the TV screen. "He *likes* her."

"Our top story tonight," Julie said, reading the teleprompter, "is the apparent murder of Harry Blackwood. Blackwood was found in an Armory Square hotel room last night, and police are now placing the time of death around midnight. Cause of death has still not been released, and the police are reporting no suspects or leads at this time."

It was Sean's turn, but instead of reading his lines, he

ad-libbed a few, surprising her. "The police may not be reporting any leads, Julie, but my gut instinct tells me they're up to their badges in them. Suspects, too."

"Gee, Sean, it's too bad we report facts rather than gut instincts," she said, and she knew the sarcasm came through in her voice. She almost bit her lip as she glimpsed Allan from the corner of her eye. But he wasn't scowling at her for her slip. He was nodding, smiling, giving her a thumbs-up.

"Harry Blackwood had no shortage of enemies," Sean said. "The women he played, their husbands. Some of them were underworld figures, according to the word on the street."

"Isn't 'word on the street' just another term for *rumor?*"

"Yeah, but rumors point the way to the facts." He sent her a wink. "Stick with me, kid. We'll get to the bottom of this thing together."

She looked directly at the camera and said, "If I don't kill you first."

Smiling, Sean launched into the scripted portion of the broadcast. "As you know by now, your News-Four team were the first on the scene at the Armory Square Hotel last night, and we brought you exclusive coverage. We'll continue to keep you informed as this case unfolds."

"That's right," Julie cut in. "And now that we've got Sean MacKenzie on our team, you can count on getting the gossip as well as the news."

It was meant to be a barb. Instead it made him smile. "You'd better believe it. And as long as we have Julie Jones to keep me in check, you'll always know which is which." He smiled at her; she scowled at him. "And now your first look at the weather with TV Four meteorologist Danny Kellogg. Danny?"

"Roll four!"

Danny Kellogg, a big redhead in a nice suit, stood in front of a green screen, grinning. "From the looks of things at the news desk, I'd say the forecast calls for stormy weather. Are those fireworks going off over there, or just lightning?"

"Don't make me come over there, Kellogg," Sean said with a grin.

Danny smiled back. "Hey, I wasn't complaining. It's about time someone put you in line, and our Julie's just the newswoman to do it."

"Ha, she can try."

"Watch me," Julie quipped. And for a moment, she felt a little lighter, joining in the fun banter. Even Danny Kellogg's usually lame puns and jokes were funny tonight. Just for that hour, she let Sean's teasing and baiting lure her away from the darkness and fear that had been gathering around her all day. She rose to the challenge and gave as good as she got.

When they finished the broadcast and went clear, the crew burst into spontaneous applause. Bewildered, Julie stared out at them. "Hell," she whispered. "*That's* never happened before."

"We kicked ass," Sean said, leaning close and keeping his voice low. "You're really good at this, Jones."

She would have considered returning the compliment, but by then Allan was striding across the room toward them, smiling broadly. He clasped Sean's hand as if to shake it, but yanked him closer and slammed his back with the other palm. Then he released Sean and hugged Julie.

"I had no idea you two would be this good together!" He was all but shouting. "By God, talk about chemistry. You were perfect. Perfect!"

Julie removed her microphone, dropped it on the desk.

"Glad you enjoyed it, Allan," she said to her boss. "But I have to go."

"Go. You've earned it. See you bright and early tomorrow."

Nodding, she turned and hurried out of the studio. She was striding down the hall toward her office when the door to Sean's office—God, but it still burned her that he got an office his first day, when it had taken her three years to earn one—opened. Dawn stood in the doorway and said, "You guys rock! Pizza now?"

Julie smiled at her daughter without effort. "You have been the picture of patience this afternoon, hon. Pizza it is."

"Great." She slung her backpack onto her shoulder, looking past her mother. "Hey, Sean, you ready?"

Was he ready? Julie turned to see Sean standing two steps behind her. What was Dawn talking about?

"Just gotta grab some notes," Sean said. Moving past Julie, he stepped into his office. Dawn moved aside to let him in, and Julie, wondering what the hell was going on, followed.

"Hey," Sean said, looking around his office and nodding in approval. "You didn't have to do all this, Dawn."

There were books on his shelves, and paper clips, stapler and blotter on the desk, along with pencil holders and paperweights. Artwork—mostly framed shots of extreme sports—lined the walls.

"Got bored," Dawn said. "So what's with the photo?"

Julie followed her daughter's nod to the old, worn-looking snapshot on the desk, and then she thought she stopped breathing.

It was a shot of the burned-out rubble that had been the Young Believers' compound. There were sheet-draped bodies littering the ground, a brilliant orange sun in a cerulean-blue sky backing the scene. A crow sat on the top of a bent, broken section of woven wire fence.

Sean's eyes lowered just a little, and his jaw flexed tight beneath the skin as he snatched the photo off the desk and jammed it into a desk drawer. "I thought I put that away."

"It's like some of those pictures of Auschwitz in my World History textbook," Dawn said.

He shook his head. "Hey, come on, I'm not *that* old."

Julie studied him, and she knew, when he glanced into her eyes and looked away quickly, that he knew what she was thinking. He'd told her that the feds had confiscated everything he had from the raid on the Young Believers' compound. But he'd lied. He still had that photo, and who knew what else? She tried to ask him with her eyes, but he pretended not to see the question and changed the subject.

"Since we have to compare notes on this Young tip anyway, I told Dawn we could do it over pizza. That okay with you?"

It took her a moment to shake off her questions and focus on his actual words. When she did, she said, "So long as it's takeout and we eat it at my place. The locksmiths are coming to change the locks at seven. I don't want to miss them."

"Fine by me," Dawn said. "I already called Joe's and ordered. Should be ready by the time we get there." She sent her mother a sweet smile. "Mom, since we're all going the same way, is it all right if I ride with Sean again?"

Julie sent Sean a questioning glance.

"Oh, sure. Would you even ask if I were driving a Chevy?"

"Nope," she said. "Can I drive again?"

"Halfway," he said. "From here to the pizza joint, or from the pizza joint to your place."

"From the pizza joint to our place," Julie said before Dawn could answer. "Less traffic and a shorter distance."

Dawn rolled her eyes but softened the expression with a wink. "Told you she worries too much."

Julie got into her daughter's Jeep, which she'd driven in to work that morning, and led the way. After stopping to pick up the pizza—Dawn had ordered two small pizzas, two dozen hot wings, garlic bread and dipping sauce—Julie continued a little more slowly, watching the rearview constantly. She had to admit, Dawn did pretty well.

Still, she paid more attention to her daughter driving that powerful car behind her than she did to the traffic ahead of her. In fact, she was so focused on Dawn and the Porsche that she didn't notice the other cars in her driveway at first.

But then she did. There was a police squad car with two officers leaning on it, and a plainer-looking, dark blue Ford with a third person. Pale blond hair shone like sunlight, and she recognized Lieutenant Jackson. All three cops were apparently waiting for her. She tried to look unconcerned as she sent them a wave, hit the button for the overhead garage door and pulled the Jeep into the two-car garage. Her Mercedes was already inside, delivered, as promised, by one of the station's interns earlier in the day.

Dawn brought the Porsche to a squeaking halt in the street, then started grinding gears as she tried to get it to move again. Julie frowned at her daughter as she walked out of the garage. She saw Sean leaning over her, guiding her through pulling the car into the driveway, and she wondered why Dawn, who had done so well up until then, was messing up suddenly.

Dawn shut the car off, and Sean got out, coming to join Julie as she approached the officers. Dawn didn't, though. Instead she hovered close to Sean's car, looking nervous.

Julie forced her attention to the cops, though Dawn was acting off-kilter.

"Officers, Lieutenant," she said in greeting. "What brings you out here?"

"This does," one of the uniforms said, handing Julie a piece of paper.

She frowned at it, then frowned more deeply. When she lifted her questioning gaze, she fixed it on Jackson, not the cop who'd handed her the sheet. "Is this a *search warrant?*" She was so surprised she thought she sounded mildly amused. She wasn't.

"I'm sorry about this, Ms. Jones," Jackson said, sounding all business. "We're just doing our jobs."

"But...why?"

Lieutenant Jackson nodded at the two cops. "You want to give them your keys, so we can get started, Ms. Jones?"

She swallowed hard. "I don't...I don't have my house key. It was lost."

"When?"

"At the hotel, when I was there covering the murder." She nodded toward Dawn. "Give the officer your key, Dawn," she called.

Dawn frowned, but complied as one of the officers went to get it from her.

Julie felt shaky, but Sean put his hand on her shoulder, and somehow just that touch helped her to steady herself. She drew strength from his hand, from his presence, and no matter how little sense it made, she was grateful that he was with her.

"Tell us what grounds you have to search Julie's house, Jax," he said. "Come on, give us a break here."

Jackson sighed. "It's just a precaution. We got an anonymous tip we'd find the murder weapon here."

Julie sucked in a sharp breath, her eyes widening. "And you took it seriously?"

"Well, you *were* at the scene of the crime, Ms. Jones. One witness puts your car in the hotel's parking garage an hour before the time you told us you arrived at the hotel. Combined with your little accident at the crime scene—" When Julie jerked in surprise, she added, "Yeah, I know about that. Walking into the room, spilling your purse, losing your keys. Is that when your house keys disappeared?"

She nodded. "When I got the key ring back, they were gone."

"Which means," Sean said, "that whoever took them was also at the crime scene. Maybe it was even the killer— who would have had access to the murder weapon. How do you know this anonymous tip of yours isn't just an elaborate frame-up, Jax?"

She shrugged. "We don't. We just know that what we have so far was enough to convince a judge we ought to take a look around Ms. Jones's house."

Julie stiffened her spine, gathered her courage. "Do you have any proof my car was there at the time this so-called witness says it was?"

Jax licked her lips. "To be honest, no. The garage surveillance tapes are too fuzzy to get the plate number, and the witness didn't get it."

"So it could have been any silver Mercedes," Sean said.

Julie rolled her eyes. "Any one except mine, because mine wasn't there." She met Jackson's eyes and waved an arm toward the house. "Be my guest. Search to your heart's content. I've got nothing to hide." Except the photographs of Harry at the Young Believers' compound, which were safely tucked away in her purse, she reminded herself. Though it might be best if she burned them at the very next opportunity.

* * *

Dawn leaned back into Sean's Carrera and shoved her backpack down onto the floor. She would have crammed it under the seat if it would have fit. But as it was, the floor was the best she could do.

Her mom led the police into the house, talking too fast—she did that when she was nervous. Sean hung back, waiting for Dawn to join him before going inside.

He turned to search her face, as if he were worried or something. She gave him a reassuring nod. "It's okay. They're not going to find anything."

That made him frown even harder, she thought, wishing she could snap the words back.

One of the cops had gone straight up the stairs with Julie right on his heels. The other one was in the living room, perusing the plants, lifting up cushions and looking underneath, only to replace them carefully. And the woman Sean had called "Jax" was in the kitchen, looking through the cupboards.

Dawn went into the kitchen and sat down at the table. "Why are you doing this?" she asked.

The woman glanced at Dawn, then actually looked a little bit sorry. "Hey, don't look so worried. This is just a formality. Really. It's not as if I expect to find anything."

"It's a stupid formality," Dawn said. "All anyone has to do is ask me if they want to know what happened last night. Why are young people always discounted, as if what we have to say doesn't even matter?"

The blond woman lifted her eyebrows. "That's not true. I'd love to hear what you have to say, Dawn. By all means, speak freely."

Dawn shrugged. "Well, for one thing, I can tell you exactly what time my mom left the house last night. It was a few minutes after midnight.'' From the corner of her eye, she saw Sean in the next room, frowning at her.

Lieutenant Jackson's perfectly arched eyebrows rose. ''Are you sure?''

''Sure I'm sure. I heard the car and looked at my clock.''

The woman nodded slowly. ''Okay. That helps, it helps a lot. Thank you, Dawn.''

''Whatever.''

Jackson left the kitchen and headed into the garage. Dawn got a soda and paced, wondering if there were any traces of blood or whatever still visible in the trash can, and if there were, whether the sharp-eyed lieutenant would find them. She wandered upstairs, ignoring Sean's eyes on her, and saw the cops going through her mom's bedroom. They must have already finished with her own, and it felt dirty and contaminated when she walked in and saw her drawers open, her bedcovers askew, her closet door standing wide. Had they been elbow deep in her underwear? she wondered, disgusted.

She closed herself in her room, turned on her stereo and hiked the volume up to a level high enough to drown out any sounds coming from the rest of the house. Then she lay on her bed, closed her eyes and pretended to be alone.

Sean hadn't missed a thing. Not from the second Dawn had hit his Porsche's brakes but not the clutch and damn near stalled his car in front of her driveway. He hadn't missed the widening of her expressive eyes, and he hadn't missed the way she'd shoved her backpack onto the floor when she thought he wasn't looking.

The cops had missed it, though. He was glad of that.

He had a bad feeling, and he didn't like what he was thinking. He didn't want to think it, but hell, he couldn't help it. Dawn flat out lied to Jax about what time her mother had left the house. He knew damn good and well Julie couldn't have left the house at a few minutes past midnight and been at the door of Harry Blackwood's room fifteen minutes later. No way in hell.

So Dawn had lied.

Or maybe she'd just gotten the time confused. If she'd been half-asleep, he supposed she might have been hazy on the time.

Later, after Jax relayed what Dawn had told her, Jones seemed pissed. As if maybe Dawn had lied and her mother knew it. The police had finished their search and left the house. As soon as they were gone, Julie went stomping up the stairs to her kid's bedroom, rapped on the bedroom door and shouted above the throbbing music, "Open up this door, young lady. We need to talk."

Sean sighed, sensing the kid's angst. She thought her mother was in trouble. That was what was driving her. Hell, he didn't know what the hell Dawn thought she was protecting her mother from, but he was pretty convinced that was exactly what she was doing.

The music stopped. Dawn came out of her bedroom, glanced past her mom down to the foot of the stairs and caught Sean's eyes. He saw the appeal she was sending. God, the kid had eyes that could melt solid granite.

He responded in spite of himself, moving up the stairs to stand beside Jones, even though he knew he was overstepping, big-time. He slid what he hoped was a calming hand over Julie's shoulder.

"Man," he said. "That was traumatic for *me*. I can't imagine how upsetting it must have been for you two. Having your privacy invaded like that."

Jones sent him a glare. "Since when are you Mr. Empathy?"

He shrugged. "Empathy, hell. I just hope to hell it's not going to interfere with dinner."

Julie widened her eyes. *"What?"*

"Hey, all I know is I was promised pizza."

"Me, too," Dawn said quickly. "It's still in the car. I'll go get it." Latching on to the excuse, she ran past them both, down the stairs and out the front door.

Jones was looking at Sean as if he'd grown another head.

"I know, I know," he said. "She lied to the cops."

She opened her mouth to deny it, but he held up a hand. "Come on, I know what time you were at that hotel. I was there, too, don't forget. And I know you need to call her on it. But not now, not as pissed off and upset as you are. Besides, it's not like she's the only one who's lying, here."

She held his gaze. "You telling me how to raise my kid now, MacKenzie?"

"She thinks she's protecting her mother."

"From what, for God's sake?"

"I don't know." He shrugged. "I think it's kind of sweet, though God knows she didn't come by *that* from the maternal line."

"No, no sweetness here."

"So then her father was sweet?"

"Her father is none of your business. And that wasn't even a very good try."

He shrugged. "You know, if she loves you that much, you must be doing something right."

"Flattery won't work, either. I'm not telling you anything. As for Dawn, she lied to a homicide detective."

"Yeah." He smiled a little, made his voice wistful. "She's a hell of a kid."

Jones tried to keep her angry expression and failed. "She is, isn't she?"

He slid an arm around Julie's shoulders and started back

down the stairs. Halfway down, he realized what he was doing, walking close to her, their bodies touching, holding her to his side in a way that was more than casually friendly. And she was letting him. It shocked him into stillness, and he jerked his arm away and barely resisted the urge to wipe it on something.

When they reached the bottom, the front door swung open and Dawn came in bearing pizzas. She carried them straight through to the kitchen and dropped them on the table. Sean and Julie followed, and Sean noticed that Dawn's backpack was hanging from one shoulder.

"It's probably cold by now," Jones complained, reaching into a cupboard for plates.

"Just like your heart, Jones." Sean winked at Dawn, opened a pizza box and tugged out a slice, ignoring the plates Julie set on the table.

Dawn slung her bag over the back of a chair, then sat down and helped herself to a slice.

"So what did you find on Young today?" he asked Julie in between bites.

Jones wasn't eating. She'd opened a cola and put a slice of pizza onto her plate but hadn't taken a bite yet. "I had Bryan go through the archives and pull everything we had from the original story. Haven't had a chance to go through it yet. You?"

"Got the original autopsy report and the dental records they used to identify him."

She blinked at him. "How the hell did you—"

"Friends in the right places. Contacts who owe me favors. I collect 'em like stamps, Jones. I'd give my right arm for a DNA sample, one known to belong to Mordecai Young, to compare with one from the body."

She thinned her lips, and he knew damn well she had contacts of her own. Not like his, though. Nobody had contacts like his. She was quiet for a moment; then she said, "So they identified him through dental records."

"Yeah." He flipped open a folder, running a finger over the text. "Never even figured out his real name. He'd seen a dentist near the compound a few years before the raid. But there was never DNA confirmation."

"We had DNA testing in eighty-five," Jones said. "What the hell were they thinking?"

She was as angry as if it were personal, he thought, surprised. "Jones, there was no known sample of Young's DNA for comparison," he said. "No known relatives, either. If we had a mom, a sibling, we could run a mitochondrial screen, but no such luck."

She pulled his file folder across the table, flipping pages. "He was burned beyond recognition."

"I remember thinking it was pretty goddamn convenient."

"So what do we do with this? Our tip was anonymous. We have no actual source."

"We talk to the dentist."

She held his gaze for a long moment. "You really think Mordecai Young could still be alive?"

He pursed his lips. "I think it's possible, though not very likely."

A heavy hand knocked on the door, and Jones damn near jumped out of her chair.

"I got it!" Dawn said, jumping up and heading for the door. Julie ran after her, right on her heels.

Sean moved fast, sliding out of his seat, to stand behind Dawn's chair. He quickly unzipped Dawn's backpack and pawed through it, feeling as guilty as hell and yet compelled. The kid was hiding something; he knew it. The way she'd shoved the pack down low and only brought it into the house after the cops left told him that whatever it was, he would find it inside. He kept glancing up, but by now Jones was talking with the guy at the door—the locksmith, he realized from the conversation.

His hand closed around something heavy that was wrapped in a towel. He looked down fast, moving the towel aside to get a look at what it hid. Then he saw it: the dark-stained blade of a knife.

"Jesus," he muttered. Looking up again, he knew he had to decide what to do, and decide fast. He was out of time.

He closed his hand around the towel-shrouded weapon and pulled it out, turning quickly to tuck it into his own briefcase.

8

Men in gray work suits, their names embroidered on pocket patches, were wielding screwdrivers and power drills. Dawn had scurried off to her bedroom with her backpack over her shoulder and a slice of cold pizza in hand, probably to escape the noise. Julie wanted to question Sean some more about his information on Mordecai Young, the ghost from her past, but it seemed fate was conspiring against her. He was already on his feet, saying he had to leave. Julie found herself wanting him to stay and needing to justify that to herself.

"I know it's noisy here, MacKenzie," she said at the door. "But we haven't finished discussing the Young story."

"It's not much of a story yet. We still don't know if he's alive. When we do, *then* we'll have a story." He chucked her under the chin. "Hey, don't look so worried. If he's alive, I'll find out."

She didn't have a single doubt in her mind that he would. He was good, good at digging into people's pasts, unearthing their most deeply buried secrets. It was a gift that could destroy her—and yet it was also one she needed right now. If there were any chance in hell Mordecai Young was alive, she had to know. She had to. And she knew Sean MacKenzie would find the truth even if no one else could.

The challenge would be to keep him from finding out too much.

"Don't look so sad, Jones. You'll get to see me again tomorrow."

She looked up fast, caught on and smirked at him. "That's way too soon, MacKenzie."

"Oh, please. Don't try to pretend you aren't wishing I'd stay." He kept the teasing expression as he headed for the door, but there was something behind it. Something probing and searching, questions and speculation, behind those dark eyes.

"In your dreams." He was a little too close to the truth. Though certainly not for the reasons his teasing suggested.

"That's a distinct possibility, Jones." For a second their eyes locked, but then he dragged his gaze away and cleared his throat. "I oughtta say good-night to the kid before I go."

"You'd never get past the homework, headphones, telephone and Instant Messenger. But I'll pass it along."

Nodding, he stepped through the open front door, avoiding the man who knelt on the floor working on it. Julie went outside with him, walked with him to his car.

He opened the driver's door and slid his briefcase into the passenger seat.

"It was nice, what you did for Dawn today. Not just picking her up for me, but…letting her drive your car."

He turned to face her, standing beside the car, its open door between them. "I know it's a shock to your system, Jones, but I'm a nice guy."

"Well, you're nice to Dawnie, anyway. I appreciate it."

"De nada." He got behind the wheel, started to close the door.

"You, um…you did all right today. On the air, I mean."

He looked up at her. "And the shocks just keep on coming," he said. "You expected me to stink on ice, right?"

"Frankly, yeah. I did. But…you were right. This can work for us. We seem to have some kind of…chemistry."

"She finally admits it."

"I think it's more you than me, really. You seem to work well with women."

"Women love me. You're the exception, not the rule, Jones. In case you haven't noticed, I'm charming as hell."

She laughed a little. "Charming? That's what they call it?" He made a face, but she quickly steered the conversation back to the subject at hand. "I don't know, maybe I'm a fluke. Dawn seems to like you. So does Lieutenant Jackson, for that matter."

He waited, watching her, saying nothing, damn him. And he had to know what she was getting at here. Nope, he wouldn't give. Not an inch. He was going to make her come out and ask.

She cleared her throat. "Are you and she…is it just a working relationship?"

He pursed his lips, put on his sunglasses. "I'll see you tomorrow at work, Jones." He closed the door, vanishing behind the darkly tinted glass. The engine roared, and the little car backed out of the driveway, turned forty-five degrees, then rolled forward again, its motions short and sharp and fast.

She stood there for a moment, watching him go. So he didn't want her poking around in his private life? Well, good, then it shouldn't be too much of a surprise to him when she refused to let him poke around in hers.

"Evening, Julie!"

She turned at the friendly, familiar voice from next door and spotted Rodney White standing near his mailbox. He wore tan dress pants that were a size too big, hitched up high on his waist and held in place by a belt. His plaid flannel shirt was tucked in, and he wore a denim jacket, unbuttoned, over it. No hat, and his white hair was like a crop of overripe cattails in the fall—out of control, white tufts. He sent her a wave, and she waved back. "Evening, Rodney."

"Everything all right?" he asked. He was pushing seventy, and lately his body seemed to be shrinking away from underneath his skin. He'd been her neighbor for five years now, and he'd sort of adopted her and Dawnie as his unofficial family. "I saw the police there earlier, and now the locksmiths. You didn't have a break-in, did you?"

"Nothing so dramatic as that," she said. "The police came about a story I'm working on, and I'm having the locks changed because I lost my keys."

He smiled, seemingly relieved. "That's good. I gotta tell you, my imagination has been working overtime, what with seeing Dawnie leave in that fancy car earlier, with your friend there. Then I saw you on the air tonight and recognized him. MacKenzie, right?"

"Yeah. What did you think?"

He grinned and shook his head. "You two are like gasoline and a book of matches."

"Is that a good thing?"

"So far." He shrugged. "Who was that other fella hanging around before MacKenzie came and picked up Dawn?

"Other fella?"

"He was at your door, noontime or so. Just a bit before Dawnie came home. Don't know why anyone would expect to find you home that time of day. Probably a salesman."

She walked closer to Rodney. "Probably," she agreed. "Did you get a look at him?"

He pursed his lips, shook his head. "Wore a hat, sunglasses. You know, men don't wear hats the way they used to. There was a time a man didn't consider himself fully dressed without a nice hat. Women, too." He sighed deeply. "I miss that."

"I love a good hat," she said, agreeing, forcing herself not to bark out a series of questions and scare the old man half to death. It was probably nothing, just a salesman or someone taking a survey, some nonsense like that. "Did you happen to see what kind of car he was driving?"

"Well now, that's odd, now that I think of it."

"What is?"

Rodney rubbed his chin thoughtfully. "I didn't see a car. Not in the driveway, not parked alongside the road, either. Hmm." He scratched his head.

"And he didn't come to your house?"

"No, but that don't mean much. Salesmen take one look at my place and know I'd make a poor target. Your place, on the other hand…"

"You have a perfectly beautiful home, Rodney." Julie found his tiny cottage charming, even if its builders had intended it as a weekend camp rather than a year-round residence.

"That's sweet of you to say," he said. "It's home, that's what matters." He turned and started back up the driveway as he said it. "Tell Dawnie I'm making a big batch of peanut butter chocolate chip tonight. I'll save a dozen aside for you."

"Oh, God, Rodney, you're going to make us fat."

He glanced back at her. "Well, if you'd rather I didn't…"

"Are you kidding? We'll smell them from next door and come knock your door down if you hold out on us."

He smiled broadly. "Then I'll save you some. You have a nice evening, now, Julie. Give Dawnie a hug for me."

"I will. Good night, Rodney."

* * *

"I know it's short notice," Sean said, handing the towel-wrapped item to his friend, Freddy Drummond, who looked like more like a surfer dude than a scientist. Sun-bleached hair and a dark tan, pale brows and lashes. The guy tended to make woman look past Sean as if he wasn't there, which was why Sean preferred not to socialize with him too often.

"Hey, don't think I won't be charging my short-notice rates," Freddy said. He took the item, peeling away the towel to look at the blade. Then he lifted his gaze to Sean's again. "Is that blood?"

"That's what you're supposed to tell me."

He nodded. "What else?"

Sean almost backed down. The goddamn guilt—an emotion he was unused to—was swamping him. He hadn't had a chance to tip Dawn off that he'd taken the knife from her bag before he'd left. He'd tried calling ten times since, but the line had been busy. Kids and the freaking Internet were a menace. He could have tried the cell, but Julie would have answered that for sure, and she would be damn suspicious of him if he told her he wanted to speak to her sixteen-year-old daughter. He would just have to keep trying. Too bad he didn't know the kid's e-mail address.

He tried to force down the guilt. He was a reporter. Finding the truth was what he did best, and it wasn't as if he could stop himself from digging. Dammit, he was allergic to secrets—when he saw one, it was almost a compulsion to dig until he found the truth. It was Jones's own fault for forcing this. She should know better than to try to keep secrets from him. "I need to know whose blood it is," he told his friend. "Whose prints are on the knife, anything else you can find."

Freddy frowned. "You know I won't be able to tell you much—not without blood and prints for comparison."

"Yeah, I know the drill. I don't have anything on the probable victim yet. I'll get that to you by tomorrow. Meanwhile…" He pulled a gallon-size zipper bag from his briefcase. Inside it two were smaller bags, containing the two soft drink cans he'd taken from Julie's kitchen table tonight. Each was labeled with a number. Not a name in sight.

Freddy took the larger bag. "These are samples from the suspects, I take it?"

"These are samples from two people I hope to rule out as suspects. There should be a good set of prints on each can to compare to any you might find on the knife. I need to know what the cops are going to find on this blade before I decide whether to turn it in. And I need this fast, pal."

Freddy's brows rose. "Sounds like this one's personal, MacKenzie. These two nonsuspects friends of yours?"

He thought on that for a moment. "The kid's starting to be, I think. Her mother can't stand me. And it's mutual. She's my goddamned worst enemy. But she's *my* enemy, you know? I don't like some other SOB messing with her." He sighed. "Listen, Fred, this is—"

"Strictly confidential. Jesus, MacKenzie, you hand me a bloody knife, that kind of goes without saying."

Sean nodded. His jaw was tight, and he kept fighting the urge to reach out and snatch the blade and the zipper bag back. But he had to know. He had to know what the hell Julie Jones and her daughter were trying so hard to hide.

Dawn didn't stash the backpack in her locker. Hell, it would be just her luck there would be an unannounced locker search if she did. She kept it with her, and she wrestled with what to do with that bloody knife. The walk home would have been perfect—if her mother hadn't suddenly decided she needed to be dropped off at school in the morning and picked up again in the afternoon. She'd phoned

Kayla's mom last night and asked her to pick Dawn up after school today. Which would give Dawn no time to ditch the weapon.

"I have to give your mom the slip tonight," she told her friend as they hurried from American History to Biology Lab. "I need to walk home."

"How come?"

Dawn glanced quickly at Kayla. She trusted her friend more than anyone in the world. And yet…something made her keep quiet. "I need to get rid of something. In the lake. And I can't tell you what it is. I need you to trust me on this."

Kayla started to smile, but it died when she saw that Dawn wasn't doing the same. "Jesus, you're scaring me."

"I'm scaring myself. But I gotta do this. You gonna help me?"

Kayla nodded. "Sure. I can tell my mom you got sick and went home early. But she'll probably check with your mom." She tipped her head. "Besides, maybe you shouldn't walk home alone."

"I've been walking home alone forever."

"Yeah, but all of the sudden your mom wants you riding with someone." She narrowed her eyes. "What's up with that, Dawn?"

"I don't know. Something. I know it's something."

"Then maybe you shouldn't go alone."

"I don't know what else to do. Mom isn't gonna let me out of her sight once she gets home. Not the way she's been acting lately."

"That bad?"

"She came in to check on me so many times last night I barely got any sleep. She was on the phone with your mom before eight this morning, making sure I would have a ride home, and then she drove me to school this morning.'' She shook her head. ''She's got poor Mr. White next door on red alert, too. I heard her on the phone with him when I got out of the shower this morning. Said she doesn't plan to let me beat her home, but just in case I do, he's playing backup.'' She shook her head. ''I swear, she's gone off the deep end.''

''Maybe.''

''Maybe?''

''Well…Dawn, have you stopped to wonder if she might have a real reason to be this hyper all of the sudden?''

Dawn thought of the blade hidden deep in her backpack. She refused to look at it again until she could hurl it into the lake. She drew a breath, sighed. ''I'm trying not to.''

''Well, maybe you shouldn't be walking alone. Look, we'll call my mom, tell her we're staying after school—for a review class or something. We'll go to the lake together, then get back here and be out front when my mom arrives to pick us up. Okay?''

Dawn thinned her lips; then she hugged Kayla. ''You're my best friend.''

''You're mine, too. So it's a plan, then?''

''Yeah, it's a plan.''

''Everything all right, girls?''

Ms. Marcum stood in the hallway, arms crossed over her chest, one brow arched a little higher than the other behind her glasses. Dawn realized all of the sudden that aside from Kayla and herself, the hall was empty. ''Uh, no, no problem, Ms. Marcum. We're just on our way to Bio Lab.''

''You've got ten seconds to the late bell. You'll never make it.''

Dawn groaned. The bell sounded. Ms. Marcum smiled. ''Come on, I'll cover for you. But next time, don't dawdle.''

The girls headed toward class with their favorite teacher in between them. ''You're the best, Ms. Marcum.''

"You know it. Anything you need to talk about? You seemed a little upset back there."

"Nah, just the usual teen angst," Dawn said.

The teacher smiled a little brighter at that. "Teen angst is serious stuff." She glanced at Kayla. "But having good friends helps, I'll bet."

"It sure does."

There was a tap on the dressing room door before it opened a mere crack. From beyond it, MacKenzie's voice called, "Morning, Jones. Is it safe to come in?"

She looked up, frowning at herself in the large mirror. "I'm decent, if that's what you're asking."

The door opened further. "Damn, well hell, maybe next time." He walked in, balancing a cardboard takeout tray with two foam coffee cups in one hand and a large white box in the other. "I brought offerings from Dunkin' Donuts."

"Then it's *way* safe to come in." She got up from her chair, took the box from his hands and set it on the long, narrow counter that stretched along the mirrored wall. Opening the lid, she examined a dozen confections of various sizes, shapes and fillings.

MacKenzie took the two coffees from the tray, setting one in front of her. "You have on-air stuff to do already this morning?"

She'd settled back into her chair, bitten into a doughnut and returned to her task of trying to erase the dark circles of sleeplessness from under her eyes. "Westcott wants us to tape a couple of promo spots this morning. Didn't he tell you?"

"I just got in." He helped himself to a doughnut, sipped his coffee. "Did you sleep at all?"

"Not really." She smeared a little more tinted base underneath her eyes, dabbing it gently with a cotton ball. Then she tossed the ball toward the wastebasket and leaned back in her chair, drawing the hot coffee cup with her. "I give up. That's as good as it gets."

He was staring at her in the mirror. "You look great, Jones. You always look great."

She turned toward him, setting her cup down. "You could use a little touch-up yourself."

"I don't do makeup."

"Oh, come on. If I have to do it, you have to do it. Sit."

She was surprised when he popped the last of his doughnut into his mouth, took a swig of coffee and sat in the chair beside her. She grabbed a compact and a brush, then, holding his slightly bristly chin in one hand, dusted his forehead and nose with a bit of translucent powder. "This keeps you from looking shiny on camera."

"God forbid I look shiny."

She smiled a little, setting the brush and powder aside, smoothing a little smudge from his cheek with her thumb. He opened his eyes, staring into hers. And there was this *thing* between them, just for an instant. It was like a power surge.

She swallowed hard, averted her eyes and wondered just where the hell that had come from.

"So can you do anything with my hair?"

She glanced back at him. His eyes were teasing now, the tension broken. She ran a hand over his extremely short though not quite crew-cut hair. "Only if you're open to extensions."

"I'm not." He glanced toward the door. "And I shouldn't be in here. This is the women's dressing room. What would people think?"

"Since when have you cared?"

He shrugged. "I was thinking of you." Then he muttered

something that sounded like, "Been doing that a lot lately."

"What?"

He was on his feet, though, turning for the door, running one of his own hands over his short-cropped dark bristles. "Let's get this promo thing over with, huh? I've got something in my office I want to go over with you."

"Involving the Blackwood murder?"

"No. The Young case."

"The dentist?" she asked, trying to think of what he might have.

"Better than that. Don't be long, okay?"

Her attention was piqued. She nodded as he left the dressing room, and then she scooped the makeup that belonged to her into a basket and shoved it to the rear of the counter, leaving it there.

Ten minutes later, she and MacKenzie were in an empty spot in the newsroom, three feet from the face of a camera. Julie perched on the edge of a very tall wooden stool, and Sean stood just behind and beside her, so close his chest brushed against her back now and then.

"Hey, I like this. We look good, Jones."

"We'd look better if you would shave."

"I shave a couple of times a week. Besides, some women think a little shadow is sexy." He slid his arms around her waist and leaned close to rub his cheek against hers. "Come on, admit you like it."

Her stomach knotted, and a little bolt of raw desire shot through her as if she'd touched a live outlet. It was so unexpected that she jumped right off her stool.

He stared at her oddly, and she averted her face, pretended to adjust her microphone and slid back onto the stool again. "Oh, yeah," she said. "That was about as sexy as rubbing sandpaper over my face would be. Get real, would you, MacKenzie?''

"Okay, okay." He stood at attention, his hands at his sides. Just before they went live, he whispered, "Jones, what the hell are you wearing?''

"What do you mean?''

"You smell good enough to eat. How am I supposed to concentrate?''

"How about you focus on something like, oh, I don't know. Defining the term sexual harassment?''

"Oh, please," he muttered.

"We're rolling!" someone said.

Julie smiled at the camera. "Coming up on News-Channel Four at five, we'll have the latest on the murder of Harry Blackwood," she read from the teleprompter. "Police sources now say there are several potential suspects in this developing case." She threw to Sean with a glance.

"And we'll take a look back at the raid on the Young Believers' compound in 1987, and the latest claims that cult leader Mordecai Young might still be alive.''

"He's been sighted more times than Elvis, Sean.''

"If Elvis is sighted in Central New York, you can bet I'll investigate that, too, Julie.''

She gave an exaggerated eye roll to the camera. "No doubt UFO sightings, as well.''

"If only to debunk them," he said with a grin. "Tune in tonight at five for all this and weather with Danny Kellogg.''

"News-Channel Four," Julie said. "Always first, always best.''

The light on the camera went out, and beyond it, Allan Westcott gave them a thumbs-up sign. "Perfect, first time out." He squinted at Sean. "Except your forehead's a little shiny, MacKenzie. You should have Julie put some of that powder on you.''

Julie turned to him, frowning. Then her brows rose. ''You wiped it off!''

''Guilty,'' he admitted.

''Well, hell, Sean, why did you even bother letting me put it on you if you were just going to wipe it off?''

He sighed. ''To tell you the truth, Jones, I never turn down a woman who offers to put her hands on me, for whatever reason.''

She shook her head as if disgusted and slid off the stool. ''Hey, who wrote that copy?'' she asked.

''I did,'' Westcott said, coming across the room. ''Viewers responded to the banter between you two last night. And they liked it. Take a look at this.'' He offered a copy of the morning newspaper, folded into a small rectangle, with a section circled.

Julie took it and read aloud. '''WSNY's latest move, the pairing of trash radio jockey Sean MacKenzie with their anchor, the straitlaced, clean-cut Julie Jones, is sheer brilliance. These two come alive on the air as the sparks fly. We love this new team and predict the viewers will, too.'''

''Trash radio jockey?'' Sean repeated, sounding wounded.

''At least you're interesting. I sound like I'm straight out of a convent. Straitlaced and clean-cut?''

''Yeah, but 'trash'?''

''You two are missing the bigger picture here,'' Westcott cut in. ''You're a hit. Don't you get that?''

Julie rolled her eyes. ''One columnist saw the show and liked it. I hardly think—''

''The focus group loved it, too,'' Westcott said.

''We had a focus group?'' Julie shot Sean a look. ''Did you know about this?''

He held up both hands in a "don't shoot" gesture. "Not a clue."

"I didn't want you to know. Wanted you natural on the air. Anyway, the tension between the two of you, the perception of you being polar opposites and that almost sexual chemistry, is a gold mine."

"Sexual?"

They both echoed the word together, then glanced at each other, and quickly away.

"Exactly. We want to play that up by putting you on opposite sides of the news from time to time."

"I've got no problem with that," MacKenzie said.

Julie crossed her arms over her chest. "Well, I do. We're supposed to be objective and unbiased, not taking either side of an issue, just reporting the news."

"Right. We'll be sure not to lose sight of that," Westcott said, and, turning, he hurried away to his office.

Julie glanced at Sean, sighed helplessly.

He shrugged, took her arm. "Come on, I've got something that'll cheer you up in my office."

She lifted her brows, sending him a questioning look.

He smiled at her. "You wish," he said with an evil grin. "This is work related, hon. Sorry to disappoint."

"This is relief on my face, MacKenzie."

"Sure it is." He gave her a wink and led her into the hall.

In his office, he closed the door, turned the lock, drew the miniblinds tight.

"MacKenzie?" She was getting a little nervous. It was dim in here, and small. But he didn't come toward where she stood stiffly near the door. He turned, instead, toward the TV-VCR mounted on a high rack in the corner and slid a VHS tape into the slot. He moved across the room then, nodding at her to sit.

She did, taking the comfortable chair in front of his desk. He pulled his own out from behind the desk, moving it beside hers and then sitting. "I've been thinking hard on this, Jones. This isn't something I do lightly. But…hell, we're partners right? It's only fair I let you see what I have on this. I don't really think you'll rat me out to the feds." Lifting the remote, he aimed and thumbed a button.

The screen lit, and she saw the last thing she would have expected to see on that screen. The Young Believers' compound. The numerous outbuildings, made of prefab metal nailed to wooden frames. The greenhouses. The barracks. The main building, which had been an oversize Georgian farmhouse, made of red brick. The grassless, barren ground and worn dirt tracks between the buildings, and the rolling wooded hills beyond them. The young men, dressed in army surplus green fatigues, walking around with automatic rifles in their hands. The tall chain-link fence with rings of barbed-wire looping along the top that completely surrounded the place. And the girls, all those girls, working in the gardens, hanging the laundry, sweeping the porch, walking around with dazed eyes and smiling faces. Long hair blowing in the dusty wind, feet bare, wearing worn jeans or loose-fitting sundresses.

She saw Lizzie pass by carrying a tiny newborn baby girl in her arms. And nearby, as she had always been, she saw herself, seventeen and lost. "Oh, God!" The words were ripped from her chest as she leaped to her feet.

"What?" Sean asked. "What's wrong?"

Julie snatched the remote from MacKenzie's hand and stopped the tape, returning the TV screen to gray-and-white snow. "I thought you said the feds confiscated all your footage of the compound?" She fought to make her tone calm, objective, and tried to keep the tears of shock from surfacing in her eyes.

He was watching her, probing her eyes so deeply that she had to look away. "I made copies before I complied. Figured they might come in handy someday."

He paused, there, as if waiting for her to speak. She didn't; she couldn't think of a damn thing to say.

"Why the overblown reaction, Jones?"

She closed her eyes, gave her head a shake. "You could get into a lot of trouble for having those tapes. I was...I was shocked to see them, that's all."

He shook his head slowly. "So you're worried about me?"

"And me. You're my partner, and now I've seen them. I'm as guilty as you are."

He narrowed his eyes, and she knew he wasn't buying it.

"No one else can know you have this footage, Sean. No one."

"You think I want them to? No one's going to know, Jones. This is for our eyes only."

She lifted her chin. "Is there just the one tape?"

"I dubbed all the footage onto one, yeah. I have the raid, the fire, and just a little bit I took that day before all hell broke loose."

"And that's the only copy?"

He frowned at her, tilting his head to the side. "Why?"

"Just...curious." She walked to the VCR, hit the eject button, took the tape in her hand. "I'd like to take it home, review it myself."

"How is that better than watching it with me?"

"I can concentrate better if I'm alone."

He smiled just a little, but she got the feeling it was forced. "Should I take that as a compliment?"

"Take it any way you want." She hugged the tape to her chest. "So is it okay with you?"

"Why do I get the feeling you're gonna take it either way?"

She shrugged.

"Go ahead, Jones. Knock yourself out."

She nodded and left his office without another word.

9

"Got a real coup for you, Sean," Allan Westcott said, leaning into Sean's office.

Sean looked up fast, startled out of his thoughts. He'd been sitting at his desk, wondering just why the hell the sight of that tape had upset Jones so much.

"Do tell," he said, trying to work up a little enthusiasm.

Allan came the rest of the way inside. "Got a list here of celebs and dignitaries planning to pass through our fair city in the next two weeks. Some heavy hitters. Figured I'd let you and Julie take your pick on who to cover." He handed a sheet to Sean.

Sean skimmed the list. The governor was going to be in town, a former first lady and current U.S. Senator, two authors, a soap star doing his hunk routine at the Carousel Mall, and the hottest psychic on the circuit, Nathan Z.

"What's the guru promoting?" he asked. "He release a new line of crystal balls or something?"

"Press release says his cable show's about to go network."

"Really?" Sean's eyebrows rose. "Our network?"

"Yup. He'll be touring the country, taping in a different location every week with a live audience, just the way he's done in the past. Turns out Syracuse is the first stop. He's in town now, will be here all week."

"So do they sell snake oil at the door?"

"Yeah, I knew you'd be a skeptic." He tilted his head.

"We could have Julie take the more open-minded angle, and you two could go at it over the whole New Age movement. The two of you could have a ball with this."

"I think she'd rather play the skeptic in this case. Speaking of which, where is Jones, anyway? Shouldn't she be in here for this discussion?"

"She didn't tell you?"

"Tell me what?"

"She was feeling ill, so she decided to go home. Said she'd be back in time for the evening broadcast, though." Allan shook his head slowly. "She hasn't been herself lately, Sean. Frankly, I'm worried about her."

Sean almost said, "So am I," but bit his lip in time. Instead he looked his boss squarely in the eye. "You don't have to worry about Jones. It's nothing more than a passing head cold. She's a professional. She's not gonna let it interfere with her work."

"Oh, I know that. So should I book the interview with Nathan Z?"

Sean nodded. "Yeah, I think it'll make for good television. As for the rest, I'll check with Jones first. Just leave the list, all right?"

"Sure. What are you working on now, Sean? The undead Mordecai Young or the Harry Blackwood murder?"

"A little bit of both." He yanked his jacket off the hook. "I have to go out—got a source to check on—but I'll be back later."

"Great." The boss followed him out of the room and said goodbye in the hall.

So Julie had pled sick and gone home. If Sean had thought she actually was sick, he might even have spared her a get-well wish, but he knew damn well she wasn't. He knew exactly what she was doing. She'd taken that tape home for a closer look. He didn't know what she would be looking for when she did, but there was something on that tape that had sent her into a tailspin.

He hadn't answered her directly when she'd asked if it was his only copy. It wasn't, of course. It was contraband, which meant it was valuable, which meant only an idiot would keep just one copy. He had the footage dubbed onto DVD at home, and he was going to watch it as many times as it took to find whatever had hit Jones so hard. So hard that she felt she had to take the tape and leave work. So hard that she'd been hoping it was his only copy; he'd seen that clearly when she'd asked.

His gut was telling him that he wouldn't see that tape again. He hoped he was wrong. He hoped she wouldn't destroy it on him, but his instincts told him that was exactly what she planned to do.

Sean drove back to his apartment, took his DVD copy out of its locked drawer, stuck it into his VCR/DVD combo and lowered himself to the edge of his favorite leather chair to watch.

He let the footage run from its beginning forward to the point where, as best he could remember, Jones had jumped out of her skin.

He shivered, then, as the action rolled and he remembered.

He'd had to get into position just before dawn. It was the only time he could have gotten as close as he had without being seen. It had been cold that early in the morning, a wet, heavy kind of cold that seemed to seep into his bones.

One of his contacts in the ATF had tipped him off that something big would be going down at the Young Believers' compound that day. He'd gambled on that tip being a good one, and braved the cold and the dark, the mesh fence and the armed guards and the dogs, to get what would turn out to be a the story of a lifetime, one he would never be allowed to tell.

He'd found himself a spot just outside the compound's fence, where the few trees left standing became his cover. He'd been all of twenty-two years old, and ambitious as hell. So he stayed there. He stayed there all day long, and nothing happened. He taped the apparently peaceful, mundane daily lives of the kids—and that was all they were, just kids, from the boys in fatigues patrolling the perimeter with automatic rifles to the placid-faced girls who walked around in bare feet, tending gardens and hanging laundry.

All day he'd watched them. All day he'd taped. And into the night, when the battle erupted and all hell broke loose. The explosions and gunfire, the inferno that house became. And after that, the smouldering rubble. And the bodies.

He'd taped it all. He'd *witnessed* it all.

He'd coated himself in scent-block, a concoction deer hunters used to keep the animals from catching wind of them in the woods. It kept the guard dogs from picking up his scent. He'd brought along water. No food, and he regretted that by day's end, but he stuck it out all the same.

It got dark again. It got cold again. The pretty young girls went inside, and the boys changed shifts. He'd kept crouching there in the brush, unable to move more than slightly without running the risk of being seen. The trees were thin, small, offering only minimal cover, and he'd been surprised as hell when the dogs hadn't started barking in his direction. He'd ended up with a lot of footage, hours and hours of footage—but it had been this segment, the one he was looking at right now, that had elicited the powerful reaction from Julie Jones.

He squinted at the television screen. He searched the hollow eyes of the young women who walked around like inmates in a prison. Not much older than Dawn, he thought. Dead now. All of them.

When it finally all went down, he'd been in position to capture the raid, though it had been tough to hold on to the camera and keep taping when things exploded. Government agents and police had swarmed, dressed in riot gear. Young's boys—frightened and panic-stricken—fired at the soldiers, and that seemed to break the dam of government restraint. From then on, it was nothing but a storm of gunfire, grenades, smoke and people running, shouting and falling facedown in the dirt. Everyone still able ran into the main house. Within seconds there was an explosion and the house burst into flames.

He'd thought it was over then. He'd expected to see the dazed followers of Mordecai Young come out of the house, hands behind their heads, surrendering to the troops. He'd focused his lens on the front door, waiting.

But none of them came out. None of them. No one.

He'd been twenty-two years old and certain he could handle anything. But that...

He'd stayed into the morning, when fire trucks were finally allowed to lumber onto the scene and douse the smoldering ruins with water. Even when Sean had been ordered to stop taping, even when they'd confiscated his camera, minus the tapes he'd stashed in his backpack and shoved under a bush, he'd stayed. When the rubble cooled, they'd started pulling out bodies, or what was left of them. Charred and gnarled lumps that had been beautiful young people. Misguided, yeah. But kids, just kids.

He'd left that place finally, exhausted and sick to his soul. He'd managed to make copies of his footage before the feds got around to coming to him with a subpoena and a search warrant. But mostly he'd gone home and asked himself again and again how he was ever going to live with the fact that he had known the raid was coming and had hidden in the bushes waiting to get it on tape, when a single word of warning to any one of those young kids he'd seen earlier in the day might have saved them.

It was still with him, that weight on his shoulders. Still with him, and he didn't think he would ever be able to shake it.

If Mordecai Young were still alive, then Sean Mac-Kenzie would bring his ass down.

Sighing, focusing again on the TV, he realized he'd become too lost in his memories to pay attention. He hit the remote's back button and began viewing that opening sequence again. He let it play, then watched it again, each time trying to narrow it down a bit closer to the very frames that had caused Julie to lose it. He'd better find it soon, he was due to go on the air in a short while.

He watched as two girls walked from the house to the gardens in back and knew he was close to the right spot. One of the girls carried a baby in one of those sling-type baby carriers that slid over her shoulders. Another girl walked along beside her. As he watched, she said something, smiled and tipped her head in a certain familiar way.

Sean stopped the DVD, freezing on that frame as he studied her face. He used the remote to isolate that section and enlarge it.

He got off the chair, moving closer to the screen, narrowing his eyes on her, tracing the shape of her jaw, the line of her nose, the wide set, almond eyes and the deep, rich color of her skin.

"Jesus," he said softly. "She was there. Julie Jones was there."

And that, he knew in that moment, changed everything.

* * *

Dawn and Kayla walked along the roadside, backpacks slung over their shoulders. They took the trail that led off the road and around to the lakeshore. The lake gleamed crystal blue in the late-afternoon sun, and the hills around it blazed with color. The poplars had gone yellow-gold, and the sugar maples orange, scarlet and russet, while the pines held stubbornly to their deep green hue. "We really do live in a beautiful place," Dawn remarked. It was the first time either of them had spoken. They'd been silent and serious since leaving school, and Dawn thought that Kayla sensed just how important this mission was, even though she didn't know the details.

"Yeah. The lake looks like a postcard today." Kayla sighed, eyeing Dawn. "So you're really not gonna tell me what this is about?"

"I can't." Dawn paused in walking, glancing at the worn path ahead, which twisted away from the road. "In fact, you should wait here. I'll go a few more yards, do what I need to do and come right back. Okay?"

A car passed on the road behind Kayla. The girls automatically perused it as it approached, just enough to be sure it wasn't one of their parents or someone who knew them. Dawn grimaced a little. It was a sleek black Jaguar with tinted windows and custom hubcaps. "Glorified Ford," she muttered. She'd never liked Jags.

Kayla sighed. "You care way too much about cars." Then she gave Dawn a nod. "Go on. Get it over with. I'll wait here." She glanced at her watch. "But make it quick. It's past five now, and we have to be back at school for Mom to pick us up from that review class we told her didn't end until six."

"Thanks, Kayla. I know you hated lying to your mom for me."

She shrugged. "It wasn't a lie, exactly. I just added an hour to the class." She pursed her lips. "And that's not saying I like any of this, Dawn. I don't."

"I don't like it much, either." Dawn turned and trudged along the path until she rounded a bend and was out of Kayla's sight. She glanced out over the water. It was deep here. There was a steep drop-off not far from shore. She should be able to hurl the knife that far without too much trouble. And no one would ever find it again.

She shucked her backpack, set it on the ground and hunkered over it, opening it and reaching down deep for the gross thing. Her mind was working overtime as she pawed through the bag, digging beneath the heavy books. She could wipe the fingerprints off with the towel, she thought. But she wouldn't throw the towel into the lake. No sense leaving anything with the knife that might connect it to her house or her mom. She would have to smuggle the towel back into the house and run it through the washing machine—maybe a few times, just to make sure. Or maybe she should burn it, just to be safe.

She stopped digging in the bag, frowning down into it instead. Slowly she began taking things out, textbooks, a binder, a stack of notebooks, her assignment pad…. There was nothing else. Just a handful of pens and pencils resting at the bottom of her bag.

"Oh, no!" She clapped a hand over her mouth after the exclamation burst from her.

Sudden movement made her spin around almost guiltily, but it was only Kayla, racing toward her. "What? What happened?"

Dawn pushed her hair back, staring helplessly into the empty bag. "It's gone. The thing I had to get rid of is gone. God, where could it be?"

Kayla ran closer, looking at the items on the ground, then peering into the bag. "If I knew what it was..."

"It doesn't matter. It's gone." Dawn rose to her feet, kicked the backpack and shoved a hand through her hair. "Someone must have taken it. Oh, God, this is terrible."

"But, Dawnie, you haven't let that backpack out of your sight all day. I mean, you had it with you every time I saw you."

Dawn racked her brain, mentally moving backward through her day. "It sat on the cafeteria bench right next to me during lunch." She licked her lips. "I went back for more milk. Maybe that's when it happened. Or in the girls' room. I set it on the windowsill and faced the mirror to fix my hair." She kept thinking. "Or last night, at the house. God, there were people in and out all night. Those lock guys, and my mom, and Sean."

"Who's Sean?" Kayla furrowed her brows, then lifted them. "Oh, Porsche guy, your mom's new partner, right?"

"Yeah."

"I saw them last night. They were great together." Kayla tipped her head. "Dawn, you look really awful. Is it that bad?"

"It could be. I was trying to help my mom, but I think I might have made things worse."

"Come on," Kayla said. "Let's get back to school before my mom shows up."

Dawn closed her eyes and tried to think of some scenario where this might end up being all right, but she couldn't imagine one. Someone had taken that knife. And God only knew what they would do with it.

She repacked her bag, zipped it up and slung it over her shoulder, then followed Kayla along the path back to the road.

A car passed, and they both looked up.

Dawn frowned. "Hey, isn't that the same Jag that went by us once already?"

"Twice," Kayla said. "Not that I know one black car from another, but I think it passed by again while you were down by the lake."

They watched the car approach. As it did, it slowed to a crawl. Dawn couldn't see much through the tinted windows, but she was pretty sure the head she saw silhouetted there was turned her way. She thought about Sean Googin, the fifteen-year-old boy who'd been murdered here years ago, his body found in the lake at her back, a hundred and fifty yards from shore, weighted down with rocks. It took the cops ten years to catch the guy who did it. It was a famous case in this town, because it had been the first murder in Cazenovia's two-hundred-year history. Everyone remembered it. They still talked about it.

The car slowed some more. "Shit," Dawn muttered.

"It's stopping," Kayla said.

"Let's get out of here!" Dawn gripped Kayla's hand and tugged until she turned and ran with her, back along the path. She heard a sound, like the opening and closing of a car door, and knew Kayla heard it, too, when she ran even faster.

"So you made it back," Sean said softly, rising from the sofa in the reception area with a fresh cup of coffee in one hand.

Julie looked at Sean and got the feeling he'd been waiting for her. She felt guilty as hell for what she'd done to him, but she hadn't had a choice. She had to protect Dawn. "Yeah, I'm back."

"Feeling better?"

"Mmm-hmm."

"You get a chance to view the tape?"

She licked her lips, glancing nervously at the receptionist, Penny, who pretended not to be listening. "Yeah. Uh...about the tape."

Sean lifted his brows, waited.

She pulled the cassette out of her bag, the tape hanging out of it in an impossible tangle. "My machine kind of ate it."

He closed his eyes slowly.

"I'm really sorry, Sean. I know this must have been the biggest story of your career, and if I could make it right, I would, but—"

"I don't give a damn about the tape." He took it from her, turning as if to toss it into the wastebasket beside the reception desk, but then he stopped himself, shaking his head.

"I really am sorry," she repeated.

He lifted his eyes to lock them on hers, started to speak, then seemed to think better of it. "Your office is closer. Come on."

Swallowing hard, wondering what on earth he was going to say to her, she followed. Not that he gave her much choice, with the grip he had on her elbow. He had every right to be angry—furious—with her for what she'd done. She'd expected it, and she would deal with it.

He entered her office first, closing the door after she came in behind him. He didn't hesitate or offer any preamble. "You're not sorry at all. You destroyed the tape on purpose, probably hoping it was my only copy. It wasn't, Jones."

She stared at him, her eyes growing wider.

"I had a feeling that's what you would do. I just hoped to God I was wrong. You really let me down, you know."

"You don't under—"

"I understand more than you think, because I went home

and watched that footage, just like you probably did. And I saw what got you so upset. I saw *you*. You were there.''

''No!'' She turned away so fast she nearly wrenched her neck. ''There might have been someone who looked like me. But it wasn't me. I was never there.''

''Don't.''

''It wasn't—''

''Jones.'' He moved in front of her, caught her shoulders to prevent her turning away and held her eyes with his. ''Don't. Don't lie to me, please, not about this. I was there, too, goddammit.''

She had to close her eyes; she couldn't look at him.

His hands on her shoulders tightened, guiding her to her chair, easing her into it. ''Look, I know what you're thinking. That I've finally got the dirt on you that I've always wanted. And you're right, I do. You should have known I would. Jesus, Jones, I'm too good not to find out about something this big.''

''Not so big when compared to the size of your ego,'' she said, automatically, though her heart wasn't in it.

''I'm not going to tell anyone about this.''

She shook her head. ''Yes, you will. Maybe not today, but eventually, you will. It's what you do.''

''Not this time. It's different this time.''

She opened her eyes, dared to peer up into his. ''Why?''

His lips thinned; he seemed to swallow. ''Let's just say—I owe you.'' Straightening away from her even as she frowned, he turned his back, pressing a hand to the nape of his neck and rubbing there, as if it ached. ''I thought everyone in that compound died. How the hell did you get out alive?''

She sighed. ''I...can't. I can't talk to you about this, MacKenzie.'' She got up, heading for the door.

But he stopped her, his hands clutching her arms almost

too tightly, and the look in his eyes was something she'd never seen there before. He seemed almost desperate.

"You *have* to talk to me about it, Jones."

"Why?"

"Because I have to know."

Two quick taps on the office door preceded its opening. Bryan stuck his head in. "You two are on the air in five, you know. Holler if you need anything."

The door closed again. Neither of them had blinked; they were still staring at each other. She didn't like this—this serious, life-and-death kind of tension hanging between the two of them. She wanted the old banter back, the fun of hating his guts. Not this. This was too real.

Finally, she looked away. "We have to go."

"This isn't over," he warned.

"I'm sorry, Sean, but it is."

He lifted his brows. "I'll force it if you make me, Jones. You know I can. Don't make me do that to you. You'll end up hating me more than you already do."

"I don't think that's possible."

"You're a liar, and we both know it." His grip on her shoulders eased, but he didn't let go. She felt his hands change, soften, and then begin to tug her closer to him, just a little. His gaze focused on her lips, and something stole her breath.

She wrenched herself away and fled the office so fast she nearly tripped over her own feet on her way out.

Sean's stomach was queasy, and he kept having to force his hands steady as he and Jones read the news to the cameras that evening. His attempts at baiting her were lame, her reactions barely there and way below her usual standards. They wouldn't be winning any public praise for tonight's broadcast, he thought. The crew loved it, but he knew they could be so much better.

Their hour was nearly up, and they were just coming back from commercial when Allan Westcott rushed in, handed Sean a sheet of news copy and ducked back out of camera range just as the red light came on.

Westcott stood beside camera one, pointed at Sean and gave him a nod.

"This just in," Sean read. "The Syracuse police are seeking the public's help in the Harry Blackwood murder investigation. They are looking for a woman in connection with the case. She is described as approximately five-five, slender, with very dark hair." He was aware of the photo being flashed on the monitor to his left, caught it just from the corner of his eye. Black and white, grainy, unidentifiable, it showed a woman who was all but concealed beneath a trench coat, huge sunglasses, a scarf. The handbag, though, was one he'd seen before.

He had to clear his throat to convince his voice box to keep on working. "The police want to stress that the woman is not a suspect at this time. If anyone saw this woman at the Armory Square Hotel between 11:00 p.m. and midnight Monday night, or can identify her, they are asked to call the SPD Tipline at 800-555-TIPS. Now, here's TV-Four Meteorologist Danny Kellogg with your final look at the weather."

"Roll three!"

Danny Kellogg was in the third chair behind the desk, smiling into camera three, which was giving a wide shot that included all three of them. "Hey, that photo could have been anyone, even our own Julie, don't you think, Sean?" He was joking, trying to give some life to an otherwise dead broadcast.

Sean glanced at Jones, who looked pale and shaken. He

put a teasing expression on his face. "It's probably the first and only time she can be glad she got stuck with me tagging along on a story, Danny. She was never outta my sight. Which is more than I can say for the sun this week, up until this afternoon. Any more of this fabulous sunshine in the forecast?"

"*Roll four!*"

The light on camera three went out, and camera four focused solely on Danny, following him as he moved to the weatherboard. "You're right, Sean, things cleared up nicely for a couple of hours this afternoon, but it looks like the clouds are due to roll back in. Let's take a look at the radar."

He went on. Sean glanced at Jones. She was studying him as if she'd never seen him before. They were both still miked. He couldn't say anything, didn't know what the hell he would say if he could. He had just become, publicly, her alibi. He'd lied to protect his worst enemy, and he knew damn well why, and he hated it.

He *hated* it.

Lieutenant Cassie Jackson sat in a small room with two televisions running. One was tuned to Channel Four's evening news. She just couldn't get enough of watching Julie Jones coming undone. Oh, no one else might see it. But Cassie did.

She was pretty sure she'd been looking for a woman for this Blackwood killing from the moment she'd gone over the evidence from the scene and spotted that tube of mascara. When she'd heard about Jones's little purse-dumping incident in the room, she'd become suspicious. The witness placing Jones's silver Mercedes in the parking garage an hour earlier than she would admit added weight to the theory, and the anonymous note on her car tipped the scales even more, even though the search of the house had turned up nothing. Then there were the massive withdrawals from Jones's retirement accounts over the past six months. More than two hundred grand. She hadn't matched it up yet with deposits into any of Blackwood's accounts, but she was working on that.

She'd gone over the damned surveillance camera footage from the hotel elevators for hours, countless hours, and the only suspicious female she'd found on those tapes was the one in the silk scarf and raincoat, who kept her face averted from the camera like a goddamn pro.

Her height and build fit Jones, though. So did that single lock of dark hair that had escaped the scarf. She'd ridden from the parking garage to the 12th floor at 11:22 p.m.

The mascara tube was still being analyzed. So far they'd only lifted one partial print from it, and it was smudged to hell and gone. They were still working on trying to extract some DNA from the brush. A couple of eyelashes had been retrieved, but it would be a few days before she knew if a sample had been extracted.

Meanwhile, she had the kid as her mom's alibi to contend with. It didn't surprise her that the girl would lie to protect her mother. She couldn't even hate the kid for it. But it was really throwing a monkey wrench into her own investigation. A jury would want to believe a girl like Dawn Jones.

The second television screen was running the Armory Square Hotel's elevator surveillance tapes. She'd been praying for another shot of the mystery woman, maybe as she left the building, but so far she hadn't found it.

Then, suddenly, she saw something on the tape that grabbed her interest. She quickly reached for the control button, stopped and rewound the tape, and let it play again. The person in the elevator was not the mysterious woman with the obvious disguise. It was Sean MacKenzie, arriving on the scene.

"Hey, that photo could have been anyone, even our own Julie, don't you think, Sean?"

The tinny voice of Channel Four's meteorologist drew Cassie's gaze to the first television set, the one airing the evening news. She paused the surveillance tape with one remote, turned up the volume of the news show with another. Just in time to hear Sean MacKenzie say, "It's probably the first and only time she can be glad she got stuck with me tagging along on a story, Danny. She was never outta my sight."

Cassie Jackson glanced back at the first TV, frozen on an unfocused image of Sean MacKenzie standing in the hotel elevator—alone. Smiling slowly, she pointed her forefinger at the television screen and cocked her thumb. "Gotcha."

Dawn and Kayla emerged from the brushy path into Dawn's backyard, breathless and frightened. They had opted not to try to run back toward the school. It was further away, and they would have had to go over open road to get there. Dawn's house had been closer, and the shortcut along the lake let them keep under cover as they ran. Dawn fumbled in her jeans pocket for her new set of house keys, found them and then paused to look around. "I don't see anyone. Do you?"

"No." Kayla shot a look behind them. "Let's just get inside, okay?"

Nodding, Dawn jogged across the lawn, unlocked the back door and opened it. The two girls crowded into the house, clutching each other. Kayla closed the door and locked it, while Dawn released her grip on her friend's arm to run through to the living room and check the lock on the front door. Then she peered out the window.

Her heart almost jumped out of her chest when she saw the car parked on the side of the road, across from the house next door.

"Kayla!"

Kayla came running, then followed Dawn's gaze. "Oh, God. It's the same car. Isn't it?"

Dawn nodded.

"What do we do?"

"I don't know." Dawn spun to look at the clock. "Mom will be home soon."

"Dawnie, can you see anyone in that car?"

"No. The glass is too dark."

Kayla's voice came out softer and tight. "What if he's not out there? What if he's already in the house?"

Dawn went cold at those words. It felt as if her blood turned into ice. She grabbed the phone, hit the speed dial, then put her free arm around Kayla and backed into a corner, eyes on the front door and the stairway, ears straining to catch any sound.

"Who are you calling?" Kayla whispered.

"Mr. White, next door."

A solid knock sounded on the front door. Both girls jumped. "He's not answering," Dawn said.

"Hang up and dial 9-1-1."

10

The knocking came again. "Dawnie? You home?"

Dawn's muscles all seemed to go limp. "Mr. White?" She hurried to the door, peeking through the window, then rapidly unlocking and opening it. "Come on in." She looked past him as she ushered him inside, up the road and down it. The black car was gone.

"I made your favorite," Mr. White was saying as Dawn closed and locked the door, mouthing "He's gone" to Kayla. "Peanut butter chocolate chip cookies! Thought you might enjoy some. Hello, Kayla."

"Hi, Mr. White. It's really good to see you." She moved forward as he peeled the plastic wrap from the plate of cookies, helping herself to one and taking the phone from Dawn. "I'd better call my mom. She'll be at school looking for us by now."

"Right." Dawn hadn't thought about the lie they'd told ever since the car had stopped by the lake. That little problem had been frightened right out of her head.

The old neighbor carried the cookies into the kitchen, setting them on the table, looking around the place. "You girls home alone?"

"Mom should be here any time now." Dawn said, taking a cookie from the plate. "You want some coffee or anything?"

"Oh, no. That caffeine…" He shook his head side to side. "Milk, now, that would be a different matter."

Dawn got three glasses, filled them all with ice-cold milk and took a seat at the table, waving Mr. White to take one, too. He did, methodically dipping a cookie into his glass of milk, then biting off the moistened bit.

Kayla joined them in the kitchen, sipping her milk, as well.

"I noticed a strange car outside earlier," Mr. White said. "Just sort of sitting there, across from my place. You see it?" He dipped again, bit again.

Dawn and Kayla exchanged glances. "Yeah, we did. It made us nervous. In fact, I was just calling you when you knocked on the door."

He lifted his brows, then smiled. "Well, that makes me feel pretty good, Dawnie. I hope you never hesitate to call if you feel scared over here alone."

"I think you scared him away. The car was gone when I opened the door to let you in."

Rodney nodded. "Yeah, I saw that. He pulled away when I got halfway here. Probably took one look at me and ran." He grinned when he said it and made a fist as if to flex his bicep. He was wearing a long-sleeved flannel shirt with a windbreaker over it. But Dawnie didn't need to see his arm to know there wasn't much muscle there. Her mother often joked that a strong wind would blow Mr. White away if he wasn't careful, despite the fact that he apparently existed on his own homemade cookies, brownies and fudge.

"Probably best to tell your mom about it, Dawnie. She'd want to know."

Dawn looked at him. "She told you to keep an eye on me, didn't she?"

"I've always got my eye on you, missy. But, yes, your mother has seemed a little bit more nervous than usual, these past couple of days.'' He tipped his head sideways. ''You wouldn't know why that is, would you?''

''No idea.'' Dawn heard a car pulling in. ''That's probably her now, though.''

Mr. White finished his cookie, drained his milk. ''Well, I only came to deliver the cookies and put the fear of the aged into that lurker outside. You two be careful, now.''

''We will. Thank you, Mr. White.''

''Yeah, thanks a bunch for coming over.''

''Anytime.'' He headed for the front door and let himself out.

Kayla and Dawn followed him to the living room, and watched him go. He met Dawn's mom halfway across the driveway.

''I'm gonna have to tell her we walked home,'' Dawn said. ''Even though that was exactly what she told me not to do. What did you tell your mom?''

''I told her the review class let out early and that we were so glad the sun finally came out that we decided to walk.''

''Did you mention the car?''

''Figured I'd wait until I got home. But we have to tell them. I mean, if this is some sicko looking to pick up kids...''

''Yeah. We have to tell them.''

Kayla licked her lips. ''You gonna say anything to your mom about the rest—the thing that was missing from your bag?''

Dawn sighed. ''I think maybe I have to. I mean, if I made it worse, she deserves to know.'' She closed her eyes, shook her head. ''I've got to think some more, first.''

''I think you should tell her.'' Kayla shrugged. ''Then again, I don't even know what this is about, so don't go by me.''

The two adults finished talking. Dawn's mother gave the
old man a gentle hug and hurried inside. Dawn braced her
shoulders and prepared herself to face the music.

"What have you got?"

Sean sat on a bar stool, nursing a Guinness. Beside him,
Freddy Drummond sipped his seven-seven. Sean had
bought.

"Did you get me a sample from the victim?"

"No, but I learned his blood type." Sean glanced around
the place. The bartender was at the other end, deep in conversation with one of the regulars. Others milled around,
but not close enough to listen in. Still, he kept his voice
low. "O negative."

"Interestingly, that's the same type that was all over the
blade."

Sean closed his eyes. "I was afraid of that."

"We got some prints off the handle. Two very clear
ones. They matched the prints on cola can number two."

Frowning, Sean said, "I was afraid of that." Can number
two had been Dawn's soda can. He'd hoped the kid had
had more sense than to get her fingerprints on the murder
weapon. "Any other prints?"

"None."

Sean swallowed hard, relieved there was no evidence
Jones had been the one to wield that blade. Still, Dawn's
fingerprints were on it. Dammit to hell. He didn't for a
minute think the kid was capable of murder, but that didn't
mean the police wouldn't. He'd seen kids younger than her
tried as adults. Hell.

"What else do you need?"

He managed to shake the dust from his head long enough
to think. "Nothing. Nothing, that's all I need to know."
God knew what Jax and the D.A.'s office would do with

this evidence if they got hold of it. He wouldn't be surprised if they used it to wring a confession out of Jones. She would give it, too. She would do anything to protect her daughter. "I need the item back," he said at length. He'd made up his mind. He had to get rid of it.

Freddy nodded. "Finish your Guinness, then, and follow me. It's at the lab."

Sean nodded, drained his glass and left his money on the gleaming oak bar. "Let's do it." He glanced at his watch. "And let's make it quick." He still hadn't managed to let Dawn know he was the one who'd taken the blade from her bag. She hadn't answered the phone after school. He wasn't worried—he knew her mother had people watching her like hawks—but he was concerned that she would freak out when she found the blade missing, which she must have by now. He would have to speak to her just as soon as he could.

Freddy drove a Ford Taurus. A new one, but still, Sean thought he could have afforded something a little pricier. His private lab brought in good bucks. Excellent bucks. He was hired by lawyers and district attorneys all the time, and he was a PI's dream come true. By the book, but completely discreet. Nothing entrusted to him went any further. It was how he stayed in business.

His place was downtown, not far away. A one story brick rectangle, it housed laboratory facilities, offices and a reception area always stocked with coffee and tea. The red Taurus wagon pulled into the paved driveway, and Sean pulled his Porsche in right beside it. By the time he shut his car off and got out, Freddy was swearing a blue streak and yanking out his cell phone.

Sean rushed forward, but Fred held up a hand to stop him.

That was when Sean saw the double doors. They'd been

made of glass. Now they were made of air, mostly, aside from the few broken spears that still glimmered in the frames. "Jesus."

Fred was speaking into his cell phone, rattling off the address, saying he didn't know if the person was still on the premises, giving details.

Sean moved past him, stepping through the broken doors, shards of glass crackling under his feet.

"Sean, don't! They might still be inside." Fred folded his phone and stuck it into his pocket. "Just be patient. The police are on their way."

"That's why I can't be patient. I need the knife, Fred, and the report and the cans. Everything. Now."

Fred held his gaze for one moment, then nodded and followed him inside. They moved slowly, but it was clear within a few moments that no one was inside but them. Sean followed his friend through the place and into his private office. The refrigerator door stood open, its padlock bent and broken on the floor. Gasping, Fred ran to the fridge. "Oh, Jesus. Sean, it's gone. The knife you brought—it's gone."

Sean snapped his head around. "It can't be—" He ran to the cooler, where he knew Fred would have stored the blade to keep the blood from deteriorating. But the knife wasn't inside, confirming the knot he'd felt in his gut from the first moment he'd seen the broken doors. Somewhere, deep down, he'd known. What other thing could Fred have been working on that was as big as the murder of a state senator's brother?

He stood there, staring into the open refrigerator, and slowly let his head fall forward. "Dammit."

"I'm sorry, Sean. They must have disabled the alarm somehow. I can't believe—look, this is my responsibility. I know that."

Sean shook his head slowly. "You had no way of knowing. I should have thought…"

"How do you want it handled? With the police, I mean?"

Sean stared at him for a long moment. "It was never here. *I* was never here. Forget you ever saw that blade. Can you do that for me?"

Freddy's tongue darted out to moisten his lips. "Just tell me one thing. Has this got anything to do with the murder of Harry Blackwood?"

"It's got to do with protecting an innocent kid, Fred. That's all I can tell you. You're gonna have to trust me on this."

Fred held Sean's eyes, then sighed, lowering his head. "Get your report out of the files, assuming it's still there."

Sean opened the file drawer, located his folder and took it out, while Freddy turned to a cabinet, unlocked it and fished out the large plastic bag containing the soda cans from Jones's house. He tossed it to Sean.

"Now get out of here before the cops arrive."

"Thanks, Fred. You're a decent guy."

"You're a good customer."

"We need to talk."

Julie stood in her open front door, staring at Sean MacKenzie and wondering just how much it was going to take to get him to drop his snooping and leave her alone. She had enough to worry about without him poking around. God, why the hell had fate conspired to tangle him up in her life? And yet, part of her was glad to see him. Part of her knew he'd pulled her from the path of destruction by giving her an alibi tonight, on the air, in front of the entire viewing audience. And part of her just wanted to hug him for that.

"Sean, not tonight, please. It's just not a good time."

"Why, what's happened?"

"Hi, Sean," Dawn called from behind her mother. "Coffee or cocoa?"

"Sean can't stay," Julie said, making her voice firm. "And stop with the delaying tactics. We're going to discuss what you did tonight."

"Cocoa," Sean said, coming inside anyway, walking past Julie and focusing on her daughter instead. "What'd you do, Dawnie?"

"I promised to ride home with Kayla's mom, but we decided to walk instead."

"Dawn," Julie said, using a warning tone.

"There was this car that kind of—I don't know, followed us, I think."

Sean stopped where he was, and Julie thought the shock in his eyes was real. He seemed to go tight all over, and a muscle worked in his jaw. "Are you okay?"

Dawn nodded. "It was scary. He passed by us three times, and the third time he slowed down, and I think he stopped. We took off, used the shortcut by the lake, and came in the back door. But when we got here, he was parked across the street."

"Did you get a plate number?"

Dawn shook her head side to side. Sean shot Julie a look. "Have you called the police?"

"Not yet."

His lips thinned. He lowered his head, pushed a hand through his hair. He seemed as upset as Julie had been.

"I learned my lesson, I'll tell you that," Dawn said. She was moving around the kitchen, putting water on to heat and pouring packets of cocoa mix into three mugs. "I know you're mad, Mom, but I swear to God, it won't happen again."

Sean drew a breath, sighed heavily, started to speak, then stopped himself.

Julie frowned at him. "What, Sean? What is it?"

He met her eyes, then looked at Dawn. "Considering what's happened, kiddo, don't you think you ought to tell your mom about what you had in your backpack yesterday?"

She blinked at him, clearly unsure what he knew. Then Dawn's face seemed surprised and relieved at once. "You mean it was you?"

"Yeah," Sean said. "Sorry I didn't tell you sooner, kid. I tried, but…" He just shook his head.

Julie fought a chill. What could MacKenzie possibly know about her daughter that she didn't? No one was closer to Dawn than she was. "Dawn, what is this all about?"

Dawn's lips thinned. "Okay. I…there are a couple of things I haven't told you. First…the other night, the night of that party, when Kayla came over?" Julie nodded. "When she was out on the lawn, there was—I thought I saw something. Someone, I mean."

"Someone?"

Dawn nodded. "In the bushes. Kind of watching. But then you opened the back door and told her to come inside, and he was gone, and I thought it was all in my head." She shrugged. "It was probably nothing."

My God, someone was stalking her daughter. Julie went to the telephone.

"What are you doing?" Dawn asked.

"Calling the police."

Dawn moved closer, put her hand over her mother's on the phone. "Don't, Mom. There's more."

Julie put the phone down and searched Dawn's face.

Dawn licked her lips, then glanced toward Sean. He gave her an encouraging nod. "I messed up, Mom, but I was only trying to help." She lowered her eyes. "When I came home yesterday, I took out the trash. And there was... something in the trash can out in the garage."

Julie frowned. "What?"

"A knife. It was a knife, and it had something on it that looked like...like blood."

Julie's eyes widened. She shot a look at Sean, but he only shrugged and shook his head.

"I didn't know what to think. You were on the news talking about that man who'd been murdered. And I thought—I thought—"

Julie frowned. "You thought I might have had something to do with it?"

Dawn looked up slowly, tears brimming in her eyes. "I didn't know what to think. I just wanted to get rid of that thing until I could find out. I grabbed it out of the trash, wrapped it in a dish towel and crammed it into the bottom of my backpack." She sniffed. "That's why I decided to walk home. I planned to throw it into the lake on the way. But...but when I looked in my bag, it was gone."

"But, Dawnie, how could you think..." Julie shook her head slowly, then shifted her attention to Sean. "How did you know about this?"

"What do I look like, an amateur?" He walked into the kitchen, where the teakettle was whistling insistently, turned off the burner and calmly filled the three cups. "When we arrived to find the cops here, I noticed Dawn shove the backpack onto the floor of my car, out of sight. She went back out to get it after the police left. I knew there was something in there she didn't want them to see, so I took a look while you two were distracted by the lock guys."

"It was none of your business, Sean."

He lowered his head. "I know."

"Then why did you do it?"

He shrugged. "I can't stand secrets."

"So you were digging, just like always. Looking for dirt."

He nodded. "Yeah. At first, that's exactly what I was doing. But now, I want to help."

"You want to help," she repeated. "My worst enemy wants to help me out of a bind."

"I don't exactly see anyone else lining up and offering."

"And I'm supposed to believe you've got no ulterior motive here? No angle to play?"

"If I did, I'd have written the story by now. I haven't. Hell, I covered for you on the air tonight. If that's not enough to convince you, I don't know what is. You want an oath signed in blood or what?"

She pursed her lips, turning and pacing away from him. If it were anyone but him offering to help her, she might have taken them up on it. But him? God.

"Dawn thinks you're in trouble, Jones, and so do I."

"He's right," Dawn said. "Mom, I...I heard you on the phone that night. I heard that man giving you a hard time. And I heard you call him Harry. Then you left, in the middle of the night like that...."

"I did *not* kill Harry Blackwood," Julie said. "My God, I can't believe you ever thought for one minute that I could be capable of murder." She closed her eyes, fought for calm.

"I don't," Dawn denied. "I believe you, Mom."

"For what it's worth, I believe you, too."

Julie shot Sean a look. "Right. Sure you do."

"I do. I figure, if you were capable of murder, I'd be six feet under by now."

"You'd be dust by now."

He smiled a little. She took some small comfort in the brief, familiar sniping.

Sean said, "So what we deduce from this, is that someone planted the knife in your garage. That's the only other answer. Julie, your house keys were missing, remember? They must have used them to get in. The blade was planted here before the locks were changed."

Dawn looked up fast. "The door was unlocked when I got home! I thought it was odd at the time, but I forgot, with everything else. God, Mom, do you think someone's trying to frame you for murder?"

Julie's head was spinning. "Stop, just stop." She paced into the living room. "Dawn, this isn't the kind of thing you should be worrying about at your age. Trying to protect me, lying to the police, hiding what might be a murder weapon—no. No, this is not going to happen." She paced, talking to herself. "I'm going to have to find somewhere safe for you, Dawn. To hide you until this is over. A private school maybe, or—"

"No!"

Dawn shouted the word so loudly that it stopped Julie in her tracks. She turned and saw her daughter standing in the kitchen doorway, tears brimming in her eyes, a cup of cocoa in one trembling hand. Sean gently took the mug from her.

"Baby, I have to protect you. That's got to be my first priority."

"Mom, I'm sixteen years old. I'm tired of you always trying so hard to protect me from everything in the world. I'm not going anywhere, and if you try to send me away, I'll just leave and come right back. I swear I will."

"Dawnie…"

"I can help," she said. "Stop sheltering me as if I were

a two-year-old. Let me help you, Mom. I'm not useless, and I'm not a child.''

Julie went to Dawn, wrapped her arms around her and pulled her close. "I know you're not useless, honey. And I know you're not a child. But, my God, someone is following you now. You're not safe here. Baby, I have to do whatever is necessary to keep you safe, even if it breaks my heart.''

Dawn wrenched herself free of her mother's arms, turned and fled up the stairs. Julie heard the bedroom door slam and flinched bodily.

She pressed her hands to her head. "God, oh, God, why is this happening?''

She started when she realized Sean was standing close to her, having all but forgotten his presence in her anguish over seeing her daughter in so much pain. When he slid his arms around her shoulders, pulling her against his chest, she went rigid in surprise. What the hell was this?

But he only held her there, his hands gentle. "It'll be okay,'' he said.

He was actually comforting her. It wasn't a come-on, and it wasn't a joke. He was actually trying to reassure her.

"Th-thank you.''

He released her, and she looked up, searching his face. He honestly seemed as worried as she was. She shook her head slowly. "So what did you do with the knife?''

"I took it to a private lab for analysis.''

She blinked at him. "You did what?''

"Like it or not, Jones, knowledge is power. We needed to know whose blood was on that blade, and whose fingerprints. We can't fight this thing unless we know what it is we're fighting.''

"What the hell do you mean, *we?*'' She stared at him.

"I want it back. You had no business doing this, Mac-Kenzie."

His sympathetic expression hardened slightly. "I can't give it back, Jones. There was a break-in at the lab. It was taken."

The blood rushed from her head so rapidly she felt dizzy. She actually swayed a little, but he caught her shoulders.

"I know you could probably kill me right now. I can't say I blame you, but Jesus Christ, Jones, if you'd come clean with me from the beginning..."

"It's none of your goddamn business!" She shouted it, furious at him.

He kept his own voice level and low. "I'm making it my business."

Tears welled in her eyes. "Why? For the love of God, Sean, why are you so determined to dig around in my life?"

He held her gaze, and she saw something there, just briefly, before he lowered his head. He released her shoulders, turned and paced a few steps away. "Look, I don't like this any more than you do, but I'm compelled to help. And I don't need a shrink to tell me why. You were at that goddamn compound during the raid I still have nightmares about, and somehow you survived. I was there. I watched it happen, and I did nothing. Then I let them silence me when I could have told the story. It's guilt, all right? I'm using you to ease my own guilty conscience."

She shook her head slowly. "And that's it? That's why you've suddenly become the only person in the goddamn universe who's on my side?"

He shrugged. "That's most of it. It might also be the fact that Dawn's prints are on that knife, not yours, and that I'm nuts about the kid." He lifted his head again, met her eyes. "Or maybe it's something else entirely."

"Like that you could finally get enough dirt on me to write the exposé of a lifetime?"

His eyes clouded, darkened. "Hell, Jones, if that's all I wanted, I could quit now and go home. I think I know what Harry had on you."

Time seemed to stop for an instant. Julie went icy cold. "Wh-what?"

"He was a blackmailer. He was good at it. It's pretty common knowledge that he slept around, taped his escapades and then took payoffs from the women in the tapes. If he was calling you, harassing you, and you went to meet him, it stands to reason he was blackmailing you, too."

She sighed, a little bit of relief daring to seep into her mind. "I never slept with Harry Blackwood."

"I know. What he had on you was considerably more volatile than that. He must have known about Dawn."

Her voice a mere whisper, she asked, "What about her?"

"She was born at that compound, wasn't she, Jones?" He said it very softly, carefully, so there was no chance Dawn might overhear.

"You're insane." She averted her eyes, pacing away from him as she said it.

"Maybe. Hell, I must be, or I wouldn't be here. But there was another young woman with you in that snippet of tape. She was carrying a baby. It was Dawn, wasn't it?"

"No."

"Then where was she? She'll turn seventeen this summer, she told me. She was either already born when I got that footage or you would have been obviously pregnant. And you weren't. You were thin as a rail."

She shook her head rapidly. "You're wrong about this, Sean. Just let it go."

"I can't let it go. I have a gut feeling this all ties in together somehow. That compound, the raid, the murder of

Harry Blackwood and, somehow, you and Dawn. Now you
can let me help you, or you can be stubborn and try to go
it alone. But I'm gonna get to the truth either way.''

"Why? Why the hell do you even care about any of
this?''

"I told you why. Because I was there, goddammmit! I
was there, and I knew that raid was coming, and I kept my
mouth shut so I could get a story.'' He spun away from
her, but she saw the anguish cross his face before he closed
his eyes as if to blot it out. "I let them all die. I need to
know what happened in that house. I need to know how
you survived and whether anyone else did.'' Swallowing
hard, he opened his eyes again, faced her once more. "I
may be the only guy in this city who can help you get out
of this mess you've landed in, and for some reason, that's
what I want to do.''

She stared at him, searching and probing the depths of
his eyes until he averted them with a frustrated sigh.

"Sleep on it,'' he said. "Let me know what you decide.''
Then he turned and walked out.

11

Julie didn't go to her own bedroom after Sean left. She went to Dawn's, slid into bed beside her and wrapped her arms around her.

Dawn was awake, her body rigid, her face wet with tears. "Don't send me away, Mom. Don't."

Julie smoothed the tear-damp hair from Dawn's forehead. "I love you, honey."

"You always say we can get through anything as long as we're together. You know you do."

"I know, but—"

"There's nowhere I could go, anyway. No one else would watch out for me the way you do. You know that."

Pursing her lips, Julie admitted, silently, at least, that her daughter had a point. There was no one. It had been the two of them against the world since Julie was only slightly older than Dawn was now. She'd never depended on anyone else. Julie had no family aside from a father who was, as far as she knew, still in prison. She hadn't spoken a word to him since the day she'd found her own mother lying in her bed, just as she'd found her on so many other mornings. Her face had been bruised, her body battered and tucked in as if it were just another ordinary morning when she slept late because it hurt too much to wake up. But that last time, she never woke up at all.

"I just need to be sure you're safe," Julie told Dawn,

holding her close. The thought of being away from her daughter, even for a little while, made her heart bleed.

"I swear, I'll be more careful, Mom. No more sneaking out, no more walking home from school. I'll do whatever you want. But I want to stay here with you."

Julie nodded slowly. "No more trying to protect me. No more keeping secrets, Dawn. It's important."

"I know. I'm sorry, Mom. But…"

"But?"

Dawn sat up in the bed, pushing her hair out of her eyes. "You've been keeping secrets, too, Mom."

Julie sat up, too, faced her daughter, held her steady, intelligent gaze. "You're right. Dawnie, I need you to trust me right now. There are some things I have to tell you, things you need to know. But I don't want to put you in a position where you feel you have to lie to protect me." She sighed, knowing she must sound as if she were making excuses, and maybe she was. "I promise, I'm going to tell you everything. Everything, Dawn. Just as soon as we get through this."

She looked into her daughter's eyes again. They were full of questions, and Julie knew her daughter deserved the answers. She hadn't done her any favors, keeping the truth from her all this time.

"I didn't kill Harry Blackwood. And I don't know who did. That's the truth."

Dawn nodded. "I believe you."

Relief sagged Julie's shoulders. "That means everything to me." She drew a breath. "As for the rest—let me see what I can work out, okay?"

"You won't send me away?"

"Let me see what I can work out," she repeated, making no promises.

Dawn closed her eyes. "Sean will help. I think he wants to, if you'll let him."

"I'm not sure I trust him."

"You do, you just don't want to."

Julie sighed. "You're too smart for me." She rolled to her feet, taking a pillow with her, then tossed it at Dawn's head. "Shower up. I'll make us some dinner."

Dawn got up, but it pained Julie to see the red tear streaks marking her perfect, pale cheeks.

"Let's bunk together tonight," Julie said. "We'll make popcorn, watch some movies."

Dawn paused to stare at her mother, and Julie sensed she knew the truth. A couple of times in the past few months, Dawn had hinted that she thought she might be adopted. She hadn't come right out and asked, but she'd left huge openings for Julie to tell her. Julie had chosen not to. She just hadn't been ready then, but she knew that was wrong of her. Her own readiness had nothing to do with it. If Dawn was ready to ask the questions, then she was ready to hear the answers. Julie had been selfish and afraid.

She was going to have to tell her everything soon.

But not until she made sure Dawn was safe. The fact was, Julie was still afraid, afraid the boogeyman in the dark car would come back here tonight—would come after her kid.

Dawn painted a brave expression over the frightened one on her face and forced a smile. "We'll make it a slumber party, just like we used to when I was little," she said. "It'll be fun."

When it got light outside, Sean released the parking brake and let the car roll quietly down the slightly sloped driveway into the road. It coasted backward several yards. Then he started the Porsche and drove back toward the city, figuring he would just about have time to take a shower and head in to work.

He asked himself all morning long what the hell he was doing, why he'd felt compelled to sit in Julie Jones's driveway all night long, watching over her house as if he were some kind of goddamn superhero protecting an innocent, and he came up with plenty of answers. He felt responsible for the missing blade—as well he should. And he was still shouldering a lot of guilt over his inaction the day of the raid on the Young Believers' compound. He felt compelled to help Julie and Dawn because they had survived. It was like a second chance, an opportunity to do penance for that old mistake. To make it right.

But all of that was just a bunch of psychoanalytical bullshit and rationalization. There was more. A lot more. There was something happening between him and Julie Jones. He didn't think she would admit it—maybe she hadn't even figured it out yet, but he had. He didn't like it, but he couldn't ignore it, either.

When he arrived at the station and went inside, Lieutenant Jackson was waiting for him in his office. He hadn't noticed her car outside but supposed she would have parked in the back, anyway. She got to her feet, her smile bright, her handshake warm and firm. "The receptionist said I could wait in here. Hope you don't mind."

He glanced at his desk, doing a mental rundown and vowing to give that receptionist hell before he left this building again. Had he left any notes that might be incriminating to Julie? Any evidence of his contraband tapes and photos lying around?

"I wouldn't go through your things without a warrant, MacKenzie."

He shrugged. "You'd be bored to tears if you did, Jax."

"I'll bet."

He walked past her. She returned to her former position, sitting in one of the chairs in front of his desk. He went behind the desk and sat down. "You want anything? Coffee, tea?"

"Answers, MacKenzie. I want answers."

He held up his hands. "I'm an open book. What do you want to know?"

"I caught your broadcast last night," she said.

"Yeah? How'd I do?"

"Great. I thought Julie was a little off, though."

He shrugged. "Really?"

"Didn't you?"

"I thought she was perfect."

Her smile was slow, knowing. She was a beautiful woman, in a clean, crisp, efficient way. Strawberry-blond, shoulder-length hair, parted to one side and smooth as satin. Big blue eyes that were deceptively innocent. "You two have great chemistry. Are you close?"

He knew what she was asking. "Not the way you mean."

"You, uh—you said you were with her that night at the hotel, the night of the murder. 'Never out of her sight,' wasn't that how you put it on the air last night?"

"That's close enough."

"But you didn't arrive together?"

"She had her car, I had mine."

"How was it you heard about the body being found in the hotel?"

"What do you mean?"

"Well, you didn't just happen by there. It wasn't an accident."

He took a slow breath, chose his words with care. "I heard it on my scanner."

"I see. So, uh, Julie heard about it the same way? Or did you call her and tip her off?"

"She heard about it the same way." He knew where she was going now. He would give her the same story Julie had given him, even though he knew it was a lie. "Julie has a scanner in her car. Normally I'd have beaten her to the scene, being that I live closer, but she was already on her way into the city when the call went out. So we arrived at the same time."

Jax nodded slowly, but he could see the intelligence behind her eyes and thought she was up to something. "Where was she going at that time of night?"

He shrugged. "That you'd have to ask her."

"Uh-huh. So you met…where? In the lobby?"

He narrowed his eyes. She was trying to trip him up; he just wasn't certain how. "I'm not sure I remember. Why?"

"Just that we've been going over those elevator surveillance tapes, trying to get a second glimpse of that mystery woman—the one in the photo we distributed to the press. I found the section of tape where you went up to the twelfth floor. No one was in the elevator with you, though. So I guess Julie actually *was* out of your sight at some point that night."

He forced a charming smile while he groped around in his mind for a plausible answer and came up with one. Jax was good, he thought. But he was better. "Yeah, Jones would have taken the stairs. She generally takes the stairs."

Her brows went up. "Claustrophobic?"

He shrugged. "We've never discussed it. But if I had to guess, I'd say it was for the extra steps."

"Extra steps?"

"Yeah. Haven't you heard? The camera adds ten pounds."

She lowered her head, poking her cheek with her tongue

from the inside. She knew he had her. "I *have* heard that. But twelve floors is a little excessive isn't it?"

"Not as excessive as what other women in the public eye do. Bulimia, anyone?" He shrugged. "Anything else?"

She hesitated, and he thought she was thinking about her words, planning them in advance. "So you both arrived at the dead man's room around the same time."

"I beat her. The elevator is faster."

"I understand from the station manager that you weren't even hired here until the next day. How is it you and Julie were working together on this?"

"We weren't exactly working together. More like trying to scoop each other. We're longtime rivals, you know. Or were, until now. I wasn't going to let her out of my sight, in case she snagged some clue I might have missed. And the feeling was mutual."

She nodded slowly, made a note on a pad he hadn't even noticed in her hand.

"My turn," he said. She looked up, brows raised. "Hey, I'm in the news biz. You had to know I'd want to ask a few questions of my own."

"I probably won't be able to answer them."

He shrugged. "Ah, come on. At least hear them first."

"Shoot."

"Why are you so interested in Julie Jones on this?"

She pursed her lips. "We're just checking out everyone who was there that night. That's all."

"I heard you were looking at blackmail as a motive."

She frowned at him. "Where did you hear that?"

"You know I can't reveal a source."

She pursed her lips. "Well, I won't confirm or deny it. And you can't report it."

"I didn't plan to."

"That would be a switch."

He pressed a hand to his chest. "I'm wounded. I've been completely cooperative with your department since coming to work here at WSNY."

"And with Julie Jones, too."

"She's my partner."

Jax looked angry for a moment, but she covered it quickly. "I'm done." She got to her feet, headed for the door. "If you're lying to provide her with an alibi, MacKenzie, I *will* find out. And I *will* charge you with obstruction."

"I wouldn't lie to the police, Jax."

She sent him a look from the doorway, half in and half out of his office. "Thank you for your *cooperation*, Mr. MacKenzie."

"Anytime, Lieutenant."

"I've already spoken to the principal, as well as to Kayla's parents. Her father's a policeman, you know," Julie said into her cell phone as she pulled into her parking space at WSNY, twenty minutes late. "But I wanted to talk to you personally about this, Ms. Marcum. I know how highly Dawn thinks of you."

"I think pretty highly of her, too. She's a special girl."

"I couldn't agree with you more."

"Do you know…anything about this man the girls saw following them?"

Julie hesitated, licking her lips as thoughts swam through her mind. She did. She knew a lot about him—if he was who that anonymous caller had suggested he was. But he couldn't be. That was impossible. She'd seen Mordecai Young die in that fire, seen him buried under a mountain of flaming debris. No one could have survived that.

"No. I don't. He was driving a dark sedan with tinted windows. Dawn said it was a Jaguar." Julie got out of her car and hit the lock button on the key ring, hiking her leather shoulder bag higher on her shoulder.

"Dawn really knows her cars," Ms. Marcum said, sounding amused. "If she says it was a Jaguar, it probably was. I'll be extremely vigilant, Ms. Jones. I promise you that. Dawn is very special to me."

"I know that, and I can't tell you how grateful I am. You're special to her, too. Her favorite teacher. She says so on almost a daily basis."

"That's so sweet." The woman sounded a little choked up, the words emerging tightly in a voice gone hoarse.

"I really have been wanting to get together with you," Julie went on. "It's not a lack of interest on my part, just that my life has been so busy lately."

"Please don't apologize. I'm the one who had to miss last month's parent-teacher day, after all."

"You couldn't be expected to show up with the flu."

"Still…"

Julie had paused near the entry doors but got moving again now. "I'll be dropping Dawn off in the morning and picking her up after school from now on. She's under strict orders not to leave the building until I arrive."

"Good. And if there are days when you're running late to pick her up, feel free to call me. Dawn can keep me company in my classroom until you arrive. Let me give you the number of my cell, so you can call me directly without having to go through the office."

She rattled off the number as Julie dug into her shoulder bag for a pen while walking along the hallway toward her office. She scribbled the number on the back of a gas receipt, then paused outside Sean MacKenzie's office door, because it was standing open and Lieutenant Cassie Jackson was standing in the doorway.

"Thank you for your *cooperation*, Mr. MacKenzie," she

said. The emphasis she put on the word made Julie wonder just how *cooperative* MacKenzie had been.

"Anytime, Lieutenant."

Julie swallowed hard and hurried past them while the cop's back was still facing her, ducking into her own office and quietly closing the door before she could be seen. "Thank you, Ms. Marcum," she said into the telephone. "I appreciate your help with this."

"No problem. Be sure to call if there's anything else I can do." The woman hung up, and Julie hit the cutoff button on her cell and dropped it into her bag. Then she turned to open her door just enough to peer outside, so she could watch Lieutenant Jackson heading back down the hall.

The last thing she felt like doing was talking to that cop today. The woman was dangerous, because she had something to prove. She was one of the few women to have achieved the rank and status she had with the Syracuse Police Department. She had to solve cases, make arrests, come off as being as tough and efficient as any of the male detectives, if not more so, in order to keep the approval of her superiors, and she had to do even better than that to earn the respect of the men and women who served under her.

And besides all of that, she was beautiful. It might serve as a detriment to her on the job, but it had certainly earned her some notice from MacKenzie.

The man in question had come out of his office, and he now stood there in the hallway, watching the woman as she walked away, apparently mesmerized by the sway of her hips. Julie looked at him, eyes narrowing; then she looked down the hall at Cassie Jackson again, trying to see her this time through MacKenzie's eyes.

She was beautiful, yes. She also exuded sex appeal like

a scent. It wasn't intentional, Julie thought. She didn't dress provocatively or flirt, or toss her hair or wear a lot of makeup. No, she did the opposite, in fact. She dressed down, starched button-down shirts and shapeless pants and blazers. She kept her hair in buns or ponytails, and wore barely any makeup at all.

She would appeal to a man like Sean MacKenzie, though. Cassie Jackson was sexy, smart, independent and tough as nails. What was not to like? If she were a man, Julie thought, she would date the woman herself. How could MacKenzie help but be attracted to her?

A woman like Jackson was smart enough to know that, and to use it to her advantage. She could probably get any information she wanted out of MacKenzie, including the fact that he had no idea whatsoever what time Julie had arrived at the hotel that night. No, that was wrong. He did have *some* idea.

What if he'd talked to Lieutenant Jackson? He never took his eyes off the woman as she left. If he hadn't spilled his guts yet, Julie worried that he would very soon.

She closed her eyes and her office door at the same time. He'd offered to help her. And while she hadn't exactly thrown his offer back in his face, she hadn't taken him up on it, either. God, what the hell had she been thinking?

She lowered her forehead against the cool surface of her office door. Someone knocked on the other side, and she jerked her head up fast, then stepped back and opened it.

Sean MacKenzie stood there, looked her up and down, and frowned. She looked like hell, and she knew it. "They're waiting for us in the newsroom."

She nodded, turning her back and wishing for a makeup mirror. "I'll be there in a sec."

"Didn't sleep, huh?" He came in, closed the door behind him.

"Not a lot, no."

"Worry will do that to you."

She paced across the office. "Why didn't you come into the house when you came back by this morning?" she asked him. When he only frowned, she went on. "I saw your car go by around six-thirty."

"Oh. Um. Yeah. Well, I didn't want to wake you." He rubbed the back of his neck, and she noticed how tired he looked—almost as if he hadn't slept any more than she had. It occurred to her that she'd never actually seen his car leave last night. She'd only assumed, when she saw it pulling slowly away this morning, that he had left and come back, maybe just to check on them. But now she wondered.

"Sean, did you spend the night in your car?" She knew by the look on his face that he had. "You did. You slept in your car outside our house all night."

He looked at the floor. "Guilty," he said. "I was afraid Dawn's stalker might come back."

She blinked in stark disbelief. He'd posted himself outside her house like a guard on duty. Sean MacKenzie, the antihero, had stayed up all night to protect her daughter. My God.

She licked her lips, unsure just what the hell to say to such a startling revelation. "I want to talk to you, Sean. But…later."

"Yeah?" He lifted his brows. "You finally decide to let me help you, Jones?"

She pursed her lips, lowered her head. "I don't see that I have much choice."

When she looked up again, he was frowning. "You sound like you're agreeing to make a deal with the devil."

"Isn't that what I *am* doing?"

He smiled a little. "Quit with the flattery, would you?"

She swallowed hard. "We'll talk later."

"One thing you should know first, Jones. When we both arrived at the Armory Square Hotel that night, at the same time, you took the stairs and I took the elevator."

She frowned at him. "Why did I do that?"

"Because you usually take the stairs. I'm not sure why, but my guess is that it has something to do with keeping your butt as cute as it is now."

She blinked in confusion.

"And because Jax has the elevator surveillance tapes that show me going up alone."

The light dawned. "Oh." She lifted her brows. "You... you told her all that, just now?"

"Only because she asked nicely."

Julie didn't know whether to laugh or cry. Now her nemesis and arch enemy had joined her daughter in lying to the police to protect her. When had the world tilted off its axis?

"We'll talk more later," he said. "At lunch, all right?"

"All right."

"For now, let's get to work. And try to wipe the shocked expression off your face, Jones. It's downright insulting. It's as if you've never seen me do anything nice before."

He turned and left her office. And Julie stood there, stunned to her toes. Sean MacKenzie had spent the night in his car, watching over her and Dawn. He had lied on the air, making himself her alibi in front of the entire viewing audience, and then he had lied to a lady cop who looked like a swimsuit model.

He was either up to something—or he was not the man she'd always believed him to be. Or maybe the guilt he'd been bearing in the years since he'd witnessed the raid on the Young Believers was far, far heavier a burden than she had realized.

That had to be it. But that MacKenzie was capable of remorse that ran this deep, of hiding it so well and for so long, of being willing to help even his worst enemy to make reparations...those were revelations she had never expected.

Sean knew damn well that the last thing Julie Jones wanted to do was trust him with her secrets. It seemed the morning dragged on forever, and he felt both nervous and disgusted with himself for feeling that way.

But finally he and Jones were sitting in a secluded booth at a diner around the corner from the station. She was on the edge of her seat, folding her napkin into an accordion while the waitress poured their coffee, took their sandwich orders and got out of the way. And still she said nothing.

"Well?"

She looked up at him, blinking. "I don't *want* to need your help, Sean," she said, not quite meeting his eyes. "But I guess I do."

He nodded, watching her, weighing her every expression, every breath. She'd called him "Sean." He didn't think he remembered her ever calling him that. "I want something in return, Jones. I'm not gonna help you if you won't return the favor."

She lifted her eyes to his, waited.

"You have to tell me about the compound. What it was like there. How you survived. Who else made it out."

She licked her lips. "I ran away just before the raid. It was dumb luck."

She was lying. She didn't lie well, or maybe she did, but not to him. He could see through her like a freshly washed windowpane. "Then there's no reason to believe there could have been other survivors?"

She shook her head firmly, side to side. Then stopped. "No reason, aside from that anonymous telephone call. We have to find out if Mordecai Young somehow got out alive,'' she told him. "That's the main thing."

He nodded. "Then it makes some kind of sense to you that he would come after you and Dawn?"

She blinked in surprise. "We survived the raid. That would be reason enough."

We survived. He frowned at her. "We? So you're admitting Dawn was there with you?"

She closed her eyes, bit her lip, and he knew she was wishing she could take the words back. But it was too late. "Yes. She was there with me."

"She was born there, wasn't she?"

"That's got nothing to do with any of this." Jones had picked up another napkin and was folding it into a paper hat this time, her hands unsteady. "The point is, the authorities think Mordecai Young died in that fire. If he's alive and they find out, he'll be arrested and prosecuted for what he did."

He watched her hands, mesmerized by them. The quick, jerky motions. She was pouring her nerves into her hands and into the napkin, so they wouldn't show on her face or in her voice.

"So your theory is that he's been alive all this time but is only coming after you now?"

She nodded.

"Why would he wait so long?"

"Maybe he didn't know I was alive until now."

"And he wants to silence you."

"Maybe."

"Harry Blackwood knew you and Dawn were there, didn't he? He was blackmailing you. That's why you were at the hotel the night he was killed."

She stopped folding. Her eyes shot to Sean's, and she

seemed to give his words careful thought before finally nodding. ''Yes, but I didn't kill him.''

''I know that, Jones.''

She sighed, lowering her head.

''You think it was Young, don't you? That he murdered your blackmailer and planted the weapon in your house to frame you for the crime.'' Again she nodded. ''It doesn't make any sense, Jones,'' Sean said.

''Why not? If I'm in prison for murder, I won't be any threat to him.''

''You could testify just as easily from inside a prison cell as you could from anywhere else.''

''But I'd have a lot less credibility as a convicted murderer.''

He didn't agree with her, but he didn't press it. She wasn't telling him everything. It was that simple. This would all make sense, but only when he had all the pieces.

''The first thing is to find out if he's alive,'' Julie said. ''That's all I need you to help me do. That's all.''

He nodded. She wanted him to help her, but she wasn't willing to give him the whole truth, and that would make it more difficult. ''Jones, there's more. I know there's more. How long were you there?''

''Eleven months, two weeks and three days,'' she whispered, almost involuntarily, her voice sounding haunted. Her hand crushed the napkin into a tiny ball, and then she dropped it. Swallowing hard, she slid her hand across the table, covering his with it. He almost fell out of his seat, he was so surprised by that. She was touching him. Holding his hand, for the love of Christ!

''I need your help, Sean. Please, don't press this. Just help me find out if he could still be alive.''

Her hand was warm, her eyes, soft and pleading. And even though he knew it was all just an act, he nodded.

"Sure. I'll help." He cursed himself and all his sex for being so easily influenced by big brown eyes and feminine pleas. He was a sap.

No, he wasn't. Because he *would* find out the rest. All of it.

She nodded. "Thank you, Sean."

The waitress brought their sandwiches, and Jones dug into hers. They didn't discuss the case anymore. Sean had a theory, though, percolating in his mind. If she'd been there as long as she said, then Dawn had not only been born on the compound but conceived there, as well. Which meant someone else in the compound had to have fathered her.

What if it wasn't Julie this guy was after at all? What if was Dawn?

Julie returned from lunch feeling good about the way things had gone with MacKenzie. She thought she'd won him over—that he would continue to take her side over Lieutenant Jackson's. He had to, to ease his guilt. It was lousy of her to use that knowledge to manipulate him, but she had only done what she had to do to protect Dawn.

And she'd done it without giving away too much information. If anyone could find out the truth about Mordecai Young's fate, it would be Sean MacKenzie.

Now if she could only keep him from finding out the rest in the process.

She and Sean parted in the hall, and she headed for her own office, then paused at the large manila envelope that was in the mail bin on the outside of her door.

Frowning, she picked it up, went into the office and, after closing the door behind her, tore it open.

Two tiny newspaper clippings were all the large envelope contained. Julie shivered a little as she realized they were obituaries, each one including a black-and-white photo of a vaguely familiar female face.

Teresa Sinclair. Sharon Beckwith. The names were different, but the faces...

She looked closer, and the information clicked into place. When it did, she dropped the entire package from suddenly numb fingers. Tessa and Sirona. They were dead. Both of them!

"Oh, God, oh God, no..."

Julie bit her lip until she tasted blood and ordered herself to calm down. Take a breath. She didn't have time to panic. Dawn didn't need her panic-stricken, but strong and capable and sharp.

She took a couple of breaths, forced herself to pick up the envelope and clippings, and to read the obituaries carefully. Neither of them listed the cause of death, just the polite rendering of the victim's age and surviving family members. They'd died only a couple of days apart, both within the last two weeks. One in Rochester, one in Albany. Sirona had left children behind, for God's sake.

She thought of Dawnie, waking one morning to find her mother dead.

She thought of herself, waking one morning to find her mother dead.

Tears burned paths down her face.

"Stop it, goddammit. Think."

Blinking her eyes clear again, if not entirely dry, she turned the envelope over. It was addressed to her here at the office. It was marked Private. And it was postmarked...

"Cazenovia," she whispered.

Jesus, it had been mailed from her own town.

12

She had to go home. She had to get to the bottom of this. Find out how they'd died and who the hell had sent her this envelope, and she didn't want to do it from here. Not with MacKenzie watching her every move and suffering from this hero-delusion, all just to ease his own guilty conscience.

Cramming the clippings into a pocket, she hurried out to her car and drove home. There were still twenty minutes before she had to pick up Dawn from school. Close enough so anyone who noticed her absence would assume that was where she had gone. She went into her house, up to her bedroom and into the closet. It took her a few minutes to find the false board in the back. She hadn't needed to open it in a very long time. Not since she and Dawn had moved into this place. She took the metal security box out and turned the combination padlock to the four numbers of Dawn's birthday. Then she opened the box and removed the tiny address book from inside.

Her eyes strayed to the photographs in the bottom of the box. Their edges were starting to curl and yellow. They'd been tucked into the pockets of one of Mordecai's duffel bags full of ill-gotten cash. Somehow Julie hadn't been able to make herself throw them away.

The best friend she'd ever had in her life, Lizzie, smiled up at her from the bed where she'd just given birth. Her blond hair was untidy and her striking blue eyes damp. She was holding her baby daughter cradled in her pale arms. Julie remembered when Mordecai had snapped that photo. It had been only a short time after Julie had helped Lizzie through the delivery, as soon as she'd cleaned everyone up and changed the bedding. God, Lizzie had been so happy.

But the image in the photo was replaced by another in Julie's mind. The memory of Lizzie lying limp on the basement floor while the house burned down around them. The blood that stained her clothes, and the way she'd used the last of her strength to push her most precious possession into Julie's arms and to mutter a barely coherent plea.

Julie blinked out of the memory and moved the photo aside. Beneath it were two others. Sirona, with her olive skin and black eyes. Tessa, the green-eyed redhead.

Julie lowered the lid of the metal box, clinging to the address book. They couldn't exchange addresses before they had gone their separate ways, because those were apt to change. So they'd only shared the names they would use and the cities in which they would stay, promising to keep their numbers listed. They'd made a pact, back then, three teenage girls scared to death of being found out, never to contact each other again unless it was absolutely necessary. It was necessary now.

Hands trembling, Julie checked the clock. Fifteen minutes until she had to pick Dawn up from school. She flipped open the book. Tessa had been planning to go by Teresa Smith and to live in Rochester. Sirona was using the name Sharon Brown and living in Albany. They'd all agreed to keep their numbers listed under the names they had chosen, even if they were to marry or change them. Just so they would be able to get in touch.

Julie dialed Information and asked for both listings, scribbling the numbers and the date in her little book. Then she dialed the first number.

"Hello?"

"Hello. I'm calling for Teresa Smith. Is she there?" She closed her eyes, praying Tessa would come to the telephone, that the woman in the obituary hadn't been her at all.

There was a pause. Then, "Do you mean Teresa Sinclair?"

Her throat went dry. "It was Smith when I knew her."

"Yes, that was her maiden name." The woman on the other end cleared her throat. "Who's calling?"

Julie sighed, swallowed her fear. "I'm an old friend of hers. I actually knew her when we were both in our teens. My name is Julie."

"I'm sorry, Miss. Teresa…is—she's passed away."

Julie felt her heart sink. "I'm sorry," she said, but her throat had closed tight, and the words emerged in a coarse whisper. Her eyes welled. She cleared her throat forcibly, willed words to emerge again. "I know I shouldn't ask, but…can you tell me what happened to her?"

The voice of the woman on the other end sounded equally taut when it delivered the one-word reply. "No." Then the connection was broken.

Closing her eyes, fearing with everything in her what she would find, she dialed the second number, the one listed under Sharon Brown, but she held little hope that the dead woman, Sharon Beckwith, was anyone other than her own Sirona.

"Beckwith residence," a voice said.

Julie didn't bother speaking. The greeting confirmed what she'd already known, sensed. Sirona aka Sharon Brown, had been living as Sharon Beckwith. And she was dead. She wouldn't offend this family by asking questions. Leave them in peace. She hung up the phone.

For a long moment she sat on the bed, her head lowered,

her chest feeling hollow, as if her heart had been removed. Sirona and Tessa. They hadn't been close at the compound, but during those hours of hell, they'd shared something powerful, something that bonded them more closely than sisters. Together they'd seen Lizzie die. Together they'd rescued her tiny daughter from the flames. Together they'd descended into darkness and emerged into the rising sun.

That was when they'd chosen the baby's new name, the three of them. Dawn.

They'd hidden out together in a warm, hay-scented barn. Sirona had sneaked away for a few hours and then come back with some clothes she said she'd stolen from an un-attended dryer in a nearby town's only Laundromat. They cleaned up as best they could, divided up the money, bought some bottles and formula for the baby, and bus tickets for themselves.

There had been tears and fierce embraces when they'd said goodbye at the station. Julie had missed those two women to the point of pain, as much as she'd missed her own mother. The only person she'd grieved more deeply had been Lizzie.

She had never ever trusted anyone else with the truth about Dawn. She never would.

Lowering her head, Julie whispered a prayer for the two women who had become her sisters. Then she opened her eyes and told herself she didn't have time for emotions and sentiment. She had to find out what had happened to them.

She would just have to find another source for the information. It shouldn't be too difficult for a reporter. She reached for the telephone again but stopped when she noticed the glowing numbers on the digital alarm clock beside her bed. Time to pick up Dawn. This would have to wait.

She went into the bathroom to rinse the tear tracks from

her face with cold water. Then she went to pick up her
daughter and hoped Dawn wouldn't see that her mother was
in mourning.

"Hey, Jones, where you been?" MacKenzie asked when
she walked into the studio. He was sitting in the dark, at
the news desk, mentally rehearsing for the evening broadcast, just over a half hour from now. The place was aban-
doned, though soon it would be bustling.

"I just picked up my kid."

"That I know. I was munching snacks with her in the
green room while you were holed up in your office for the
past hour."

She shrugged. "Since when am I not allowed to spend
some quality time in my office chasing down a few leads?"

"Leads on what?"

"Nothing I'm ready to talk about with you."

"I thought we were partners?" He gave her his most
innocent expression.

She only shrugged.

There was something going on with her. He could see
it. And if he wasn't mistaken, and he didn't think he was,
she'd been crying recently. "Is everything okay?" he
asked. Dawn had seemed fine, but Jones looked as if she'd
been hit with a brick.

"Fine." She slid into her own chair, pulled open the
drawer hidden on her side of the desk and set up the small
round mirror. She flipped a switch, and the mirror lit up.
Then she reached for the makeup she kept with it.

MacKenzie was still watching her, still searching her
face for clues. She sighed, looking up from the mirror, a
compact at the ready in her hands.

"Do I have spinach in my teeth or what?"

"You look like a nervous breakdown waiting to happen, Jones."

"Gee, thanks. You sure do know how to charm a girl."

"Only girls who are willing to be charmed, which excludes you entirely. Give me that thing." He snatched the compact from her hands, flipped it open and removed the soft circular pad.

"What are you doing?"

"Aw, come on. I let you do me. Now you have to let me do you." He gave her an evil wink and was pleased when her lips pulled into an unwilling smile even as she shook her head in disapproval.

"You are a master of subtlety, MacKenzie."

"Close your eyes, Jones."

She closed her eyes and leaned slightly forward. Sean rubbed the little pad around on the hard surface of the pressed powder, then touched her face with it, brushing it over the slightly reddened areas around and beneath her eyes. He smoothed it over her too-pale cheeks, then dropped the pad back into the compact and closed it.

She was still sitting there, still leaning forward, eyes closed. As if waiting to be kissed, he thought, and then he thought how funny it would be if he did that. Kissed her.

But instead of laughter, he felt something else bubbling up inside him as that idea crossed his mind. Something hot and really uncomfortable. And he realized he would *like* kissing Julie Jones. He would like it quite a lot. In fact, once born, the idea didn't seem willing to go away.

"Are you done?"

"I haven't decided."

She opened her eyes. "I have. You're done." She turned back to the mirror, reaching for tubes and pencils and brushes, wielding them as if she had eight arms instead of two.

"We got an interview with Nathan Z, you know." He only said it to change the subject.

"I didn't even know that was in the works."

"Yeah, well, you've been a little...distracted."

Sighing, pausing with a lipstick in her hand, she looked his way. "I know I have. I'm sorry about that, MacKenzie."

"Hell, it's not your fault. Any red-blooded woman would be distracted with a gorgeous partner like me around all the time. It's really no wonder you can't focus on your work."

She smiled slightly. "Yeah, that must be it."

"Of course that's it. You're not the first female to fall victim to my allure."

"Nor the last, I'll bet."

He sent her a wink. "Maybe. If you play your cards right."

She actually laughed, then, a soft, less-than-full-body chuckle, but still... "Better get a shovel. The bullshit's getting pretty deep in here."

He grinned at her. "Allan's setting up an appointment for the interview tomorrow or the day after. Z's people had his press kit sent over today so we'd have plenty of background."

"Yeah? Anything interesting?"

"A signed copy of his new book." He reached for it and slid it across the desk to her. It was a hardcover volume with a starry night dust jacket and the words *Messages From God* by Nathan Z splashed across the top.

"I thought Dawn might like it," Sean said. "Just wanted to check with you first."

"She'll love it. What did he write?"

"I haven't looked. Doesn't matter, Dawn's gonna love this even more." Sean dipped into a pocket and brought out four paper rectangles, holding them up in a fan pattern.

"Four tickets to a taping of his show. Right here in the city. Tonight. Dawn can bring a friend. You up for it?"

Julie swallowed hard. "I don't know."

"Come on, it'll get your mind off things. Besides, we'll be more prepared to interview him if we get to see him in action."

"I suppose that's true. It's just with so much else going on, I don't think I can possibly..." She turned the book over, and stopped talking. Her eyes seemed to narrow, her brows drew together.

Sean glanced at her. "What?"

"Nothing. I...I changed my mind. Let's go to that taping tonight."

"Great. I'm gonna tell Dawn before we go on the air. Is she still in the green room?"

Julie nodded, and Sean hurried out of the studio, calling. "Back in five."

The studio was empty now. Dark, with the hot stage lights turned off. Cameras stood like space-age robots, heads nodding in temporary slumber. Cables snaked over the floor in every possible direction.

Julie thought she heard movement behind her. She came out of her seat so sharply she almost lost her balance. She saw nothing in the shadowy room. And yet she felt something. Something dark. She shivered, rubbed her arms. She was just letting all this go to her head. That was all.

Swallowing hard, she returned her attention to the book on the news desk and the author photo on the back of the jacket that had so captivated her. No wonder. The man was striking, but it wasn't as if she hadn't seen him before, on his television show the few times she'd glanced at it while Dawn was watching. He kept his head cleanly shaved, and he had the most penetrating brown eyes. But it was none of those things that had caught her attention. It was the knowing smile he wore. There was something about it that made her mind itch.

She flipped the book over once more and opened its front cover to look at the autograph, curious to see what pearls of wisdom a renowned psychic used when inscribing a book to the press.

Then her cell phone bleated, distracting her.

Sighing, she reached into the bag, tugged the cell phone from its pocket and brought it to her ear. "Julie Jones," she said.

"Julie? It's Melanie Wright, from WKLL in Albany. I got that information you wanted."

Julie blinked and thought for sure her heart skipped a few beats. She'd spent an hour in her office, making calls, calling in favors, looking for someone in the Albany or Rochester press who would be willing to tell her how Sirona and Tessa had died. She'd all but given up on anyone coming through with the information.

Clearing her throat, she said, "Thanks. I'm glad you called me back. What did you find out?"

"Sharon Brown's death was ruled a suicide. She hanged herself."

The air seemed to seep from Julie's lungs against her will.

"The funny thing is, I did a little digging on that other death you were asking about. The one in Rochester? My sister works for one of the newspapers out there."

"And?" Julie asked.

"Same thing," the reporter told her. "Death by hanging, ruled a suicide."

"Oh, my God." The whisper issued from her lips without her permission. Both dead by the same method within such a short period of time? It couldn't be coincidence. God, someone had killed them. Someone had *hanged* them.

"I smell a story here, Ms. Jones. Do you think we could have a serial killer on our hands?"

"No." She blurted the answer quickly, sharply.

"What's the connection between those two women? I haven't been able to find any, but you seem to—"

"There's no connection." But there was. The connection was her…and Dawn. "There's no story here. Just leave it alone."

Julie hung up the phone while the ambitious young newswoman was still asking questions and pressed a hand to her forehead, wishing she'd gone to the police instead of the press. She lowered her head, battling tears. God, they'd been murdered. Both of them.

Her gaze found the open book lying on the desk and the elegant scrawl on the title page.

The darkness seemed to close in around her. Julie ran out of the studio, tripped over a cable, caught herself on a camera, and made it to the door and into the lighter hallway. And still she didn't slow down. She ran as if the devil were on her tail, until damn near colliding with Sean as he stepped out of his own office.

He caught her shoulders, steadying her. "Whoa, whoa, where're you going in such a hurry? You miss me that much already?"

She looked past him, saw Dawn sitting behind Mac-Kenzie's desk, rapidly clicking keys on his computer. Dawn looked up, smiling. "Isn't it great that we get to go to that taping tonight?" she asked. "And there's an extra ticket! Can we take Kayla?"

Julie forced a smile she was far from feeling. "I—I guess."

"We should grab dinner on the way," Dawn rushed on.

"I'm starved already, and by the time you do the evening broadcast, I'll be gnawing on the desk."

"Tacos?" MacKenzie asked, grinning at Dawn's dramatic analogy.

"Sounds good to me. Mom?"

Julie blinked from Dawn's hopeful eyes to MacKenzie's probing ones. He saw right through her. He was too damned insightful for his own good—for *her* own good. But including him in the dinner invitation was a good idea. She needed his help; she had to remember that. And besides, she didn't want to be alone tonight. She was scared, and she knew she had good reason to be. Someone, it seemed, was systematically killing the survivors of the raid on the Young Believers. She and Dawn could be next on the killer's to-do list.

She was terrified.

It would be a very public event, with cameras rolling. With MacKenzie by her side, she should be able to keep Dawn safe.

She mustered up a smile and tried to keep the terror from her face. "Tacos sound great. Maybe Kayla can meet us at the restaurant. Are we taking two cars or one?"

MacKenzie shrugged. "We can drop my car at your place and leave from there in yours. More room. But, uh— I want to drive."

"You want to drive?"

He exchanged a secret glance with Dawn. "Yeah. Hey, it's only fair. I let Dawn drive my car. So I get to drive yours."

"Excuse me? The correct answer to that equation is that she has to let you drive her Jeep. Not my Mercedes."

"From what I understand, your Mercedes will be a lot safer in my hands."

She shot Dawn a scowl. "You've been spreading that

horrible gossip again, haven't you? About what a bad driver I am?''

Dawn laughed. "Gossip? C'mon, Mom. You hold the county record for most orange construction cones destroyed in a single season.''

"I heard the DMV was making her a trophy," Mac-Kenzie said. "A little orange cone with a sign on it that reads 'Not A Target.'"

Dawn covered her mouth and kept laughing anyway.

"You two will pay for ganging up on me," Julie promised. But she felt better. The trembling had stopped, and she wasn't freezing cold anymore. A few minutes basking in the glow of her beautiful Dawn always made her feel better. And verbal duels with MacKenzie tended to have a tonic effect, as well.

"Fine, you can drive," she told him haughtily. She turned to Dawn. "You call Kayla and see if her dad can bring her to meet us for dinner. Just to keep you from starving to death, we'll head to the taco place right after we wrap, speaking of which…''

She glanced at her watch.

"That's right, we'd better get on it." MacKenzie put a hand on her shoulder, turned her and hustled her down the hall, calling, "See you in a half hour, Dawnie."

When they'd gone several feet, he looked at her again. "You don't fool me for a minute, you know."

She glanced up at him, almost argued, then gave up. She was tired. "I know," she said.

"You gonna tell me what has you so on edge today?"

She lowered her head. "I haven't decided."

"But you're gonna let me hang around anyway. What's up with that, Jones?"

She lifted her head, looked him right in the eye. "I'm scared half to death."

He stopped walking, just looked at her, as if he thought she was kidding and then was shocked that she wasn't. He *should* be shocked, he realized. Julie Jones didn't admit to weakness often. Never, in fact. He was probably as surprised as she was that the first time she did, it would be to him. Her nemesis. Her worst enemy and, right now, her only friend.

13

Sean noticed that Dawn deliberately shoved him ahead of her in the line going into the Landmark Theater, so that when they took their seats in the audience, he was sitting between Dawn and her mother, with Kayla on Dawn's other side. Jones was drawn up as tightly as a violin string. Something had happened between the time she'd left the station to pick Dawn up and the time she'd arrived back at work with her daughter in tow. He didn't know what, and he didn't expect her to tell him. She still didn't trust him, and knowing that gnawed at him, though he wasn't entirely sure why. After all, up until very recently, he'd had less than honorable motives in wanting to find out her secrets.

He'd wanted to get something on her. To have something to hold over her, even if he never did anything but tease her with it.

Now, everything had changed. He wanted her to trust him, so that he could find out what was going on, so that he could help her. And Dawn.

He swallowed and shifted his focus elsewhere when his mind started pondering further reasons. Like the cockeyed theory that he'd never really disliked Jones as much as he'd pretended. That he enjoyed fighting with her so much because of the sparks that flew between them when they fought. Positive charge meets negative charge. It was almost like sex.

That little change in his perception of their relationship

seemed to have thrown the switch on what had always been a grudging but undeniable physical attraction and turned it into full-blown desire. On his part, at least. He'd been thinking about it ever since that moment in the studio earlier, when he'd damn near kissed her.

But this wasn't the time to be thinking about any of those things.

"I'm so excited," Dawn said. "This guy is really good."

"He's phenomenal," Kayla agreed.

"Have you ever seen his show, Sean?" Dawn asked.

Sean shook his head. "Not all the way through. I watched a couple of taped segments that came with his press kit. Seems to me he's like a TV evangelist of the New Age variety. Does a little channeling, a little healing and talks about God's message. But I have to tell you, kid, I'm a skeptic about this psychic stuff."

"Yeah? You just wait. He'll convince you."

Sean gave the girls a doubtful look, then turned to Julie. "How about you, Jones? You believe in this crap?"

"I'm keeping an open mind," she said. "I did notice there were cameras on us the entire time we stood in line. And I think I saw a microphone or two out there, as well."

"Ahh, good call. I should have brought up something obscure out there. My dear insane aunt Aggie with one brown eye and one blue, just to see if he'd mention it in here."

"You have an insane aunt Aggie?" Jones asked.

He frowned at her. "Doesn't everyone?"

She smiled. It was a real smile, this time, full, spontaneous and potent. It hit him where he lived. He'd been missing that smile lately. "You made it up," she accused.

He wiggled his eyebrows, and they took their seats. Then the lights went down and the crowd hushed. Intro music swelled as the spotlight hit the small stage. Then the star walked out from behind heavy purple curtains and applause filled the place to bursting.

Nathan Z smiled, his shiny bald head gleaming in the spotlights. He pressed his palms flat together and bowed toward each section of seats. He wore white robes and sandals.

Kayla and Dawn were awestruck as they gazed up at him, applauding.

Then he held his hands up for silence. "Thank you all for coming. It means the world to me. This room is just bursting with energy tonight, so let me get straight to work."

He lowered his head slightly, closed his eyes. His fingers made small, rapid circles against his temples. The audience went so still, Sean thought it was holding its collective breath. Then the guru's hands fell to his sides and his head came up. His piercing eyes opened, and he turned, then pointed.

"I'm coming to this section." He moved to the edge of the stage and pointed to an area of the audience. "Who has a…dog? Sam His name is Sam. And he's…no, she. A female dog named Sam. She's not well. Does this make sense to anyone?"

A man raised his hand.

"Come up on the stage with me, sir."

Nodding, the audience member hurried onto the stage. Nathan Z clasped the man's hand in both of his own, nodding, sympathy in his eyes. "You have a female dog named Sam, and you're worried about her health, is that right?"

The man, a skinny fellow of sixtysomething with hair the color of orange sherbet, nodded. "She's not acting right. Not eating, whining all the time."

"She's in a lot of pain," Z told the man. "You need to get her to the vet. She's a golden retriever, isn't she?"

The older man's eyes widened. "Yes. How did you know that?"

Z smiled, his face warm. "She has a ragged old teddy bear she's chewed almost to pieces, but you can't throw it away."

"That's right."

"Why haven't you taken her to the vet?"

The old man lowered his head. "I guess—I'm afraid they'll tell me it's something fatal. Or that she has to be put down. She's old, you know."

"I know," Z said. He closed his eyes briefly, then opened them again. "It's not. It's inflammation in her joints. Arthritis. It hurts to move, to put weight on her legs. The cooler weather is making it worse. She can't eat because she's in so much pain."

The man lifted his head. "Will the vet be able to help her?"

"Yes. She has…she has several good years left."

The old man flung his arms around Z and hugged him hard. "Thank you. I can't thank you enough."

"You're welcome," Z said, smiling, blinking his eyes as if they were damp while the man made his way back toward the audience.

Dawn leaned closer. "I told you he was awesome."

Sean nodded, trying to look suitably impressed. But the reporter in him was itching to get behind this guy's veneer, find out what really made him tick. Did they poll the audience when they sold them the tickets, pick a few and interview them ahead of time, have microphones planted in the lobby, or did they just have plants scattered throughout the crowd?

Or was the guy for real? He looked toward Jones to ask what she thought, but she appeared mesmerized by the man on the stage.

The same thing went on for damn near the full hour, with Z picking people out of the crowd and telling them details about their lives that he shouldn't know. Couldn't possibly know, the subjects exclaimed again and again. There were tears, relief. If the people weren't plants, then this guy was helping them. Making them feel better. Giving them closure and positive, logical advice. He never told them to sell all their possessions and move to Tibet, so that was good.

Finally the guru declared that he had finished with his readings and would now proceed on to today's message for all of mankind. He moved to a large, bowl-shaped wicker chair with a thick cushion lining it, which stagehands had brought out moments earlier. He sat down in it, folding his legs and his robes beneath him, and let his head fall limply to his chest. For several tense moments he sat there like that, breathing deeply, and the silence hung in the air. No one in the audience made a peep. Not a whisper. Once again, they almost seemed to be holding their breath.

God, this guy had them enthralled.

When Z's head came up again, his eyes were so intense that Sean wondered if he'd managed to slip some kind of luminescent contacts in while no one was looking. They nearly glowed.

"I am a prophet," he said. His voice was different now, not the soft soothing, nondescript one he'd had before. But rich, full, booming with power and, interestingly, bearing a slightly Southern accent. "I am an exalted soul, so enlightened that I am not safe on the physical plane, for like all exalted souls before me, like Jesus and John and Galileo and Joan of Arc, I will be misunderstood, persecuted...and killed."

"Ow," Sean muttered, glancing down at the pain in his lower arm, then frowning. Jones was clutching his forearm so hard her nails were digging into his flesh. If she squeezed any harder, she would draw blood.

"For this reason, I must share my message with you now, while I can. This is what you need to know to achieve oneness, wholeness and harmony in your lives. In the past, humans offered sacrifice to their gods in order to receive blessin's. They slaughtered cattle, hosses, lambs, then offered them up on the pyre. But all you need to do is to believe in me, believe in my words. They are the same words, no matter what system of belief you hold dear. No man cometh unto the father except by me, for he who believeth in me shall not perish, but have everlastin' life. I am the way, the truth and the light. So sayeth the Lord."

He paused to let that sink in.

Sean leaned close to Julie. "Am I dreaming here, or did he just imply that he was Jesus Christ?"

She didn't answer, so he glanced sideways at her. Her face was pale, her eyes wide and riveted to the man on the stage. She was shaking, physically shaking. He thought she was going to explode out of her seat in a moment.

"Jones?" he whispered. "Hey, what is it?"

She shook her head. "He's done. Let's get the girls out of here."

The man had stopped speaking, and the audience applauded wildly.

"You're not looking so hot right now, Jones," Sean said. "Tell you what. I'll go get the car, since we parked clear at the other end of the lot. I'll pick you three up at the door, all right?"

He started to rise. Jones closed her hand over his on the armrest none too gently. "Take the girls with you."

He frowned at her. Her words fell like hailstones. Cold, quick, hard. He searched her face for an explanation.

She turned to Dawn. "You and Kayla go with Sean. I just need to find a rest room. I'll meet you out front."

"Sure, Mom. Don't get lost on us." Dawn got up, tugging Kayla with her.

Sean leaned closer to Jones. "What the hell is it?" he whispered.

"Just...watch them, Sean. Don't let Dawn out of your sight. I need a few minutes."

He held her eyes, but she wasn't giving away a thing. "If you think I'm leaving you alone..."

"She's in danger, Sean. Please do this for me."

His stomach knotted, but he gave in. "All right. But if you're not in the car in five minutes—"

"Give me ten."

With a nod, he turned and headed up the aisle with Dawn and Kayla on either side of him.

Julie watched them go until the rest of the audience rose to begin filing out of the studio, blocking her view. Then she walked against the flow of traffic, down and closer to the stage. She had already picked out the likeliest way to get backstage, a doorway to the left of those thick curtains, and she headed toward it, only to have a heavy man wearing a tight-fitting "Z" T-shirt and a radio headset step into her path.

"No one's allowed back there, miss."

She conjured a smile, met his eyes, watched the recognition change his expression.

"Wait a minute, aren't you...?"

"Julie Jones, Channel Four News," she said, extending a hand. He took it, shook it warmly. "Mr. Z is going to be interviewed at our station soon. He gave us the tickets tonight, in fact, and I have a few background questions for him in order to prepare for the segment. Do you think he'll see me?''

''I'll find out for you, Ms. Jones. Just wait right here.''

She waited while he walked a few steps away and spoke into his headset. Then he nodded and came back to her. ''Go on back, Ms. Jones. It's the first door on the left.''

''Thank you.'' He stepped aside, opening the stage door for her. She heard it close behind her again as soon as she moved through. The hall was long, but the first door on the left loomed all too soon. It was closed. No star on the door, no name plaque.

She was shaking, deathly cold, when she lifted her fist, paused, clenched her jaw and rapped on the door.

''Come.''

She wrapped her hand around the doorknob. She didn't want to do this, to face this thing head-on. But she thought of Dawnie, and knew she had to. She twisted the knob and pushed the door open; it felt as if she were opening a long-sealed crypt instead.

He sat at a mirrored dressing table, wiping his face with a soft cloth. He didn't turn around, just met her eyes in the mirror.

She held his gaze, knew now why his photo had stirred that odd feeling of recognition in her belly. It was the smile and the dimple in his right cheek. Dawn had that dimple. Dawn had that smile.

''I know who you are,'' she said.

He closed his eyes briefly. ''Close the door, Jewel. This isn't a conversation we need others to overhear.''

If she closed the door, what was to stop him from killing her? she wondered. Just the way he'd probably killed Sirona and Tessa. But she had to do this. She had to face him. For Dawn. She closed the door and went a few degrees colder.

"Now, who is it you think I am?"

"You're Mordecai Young. A madman the world thinks is long dead."

He lowered his head with a sigh. "What gave me away?"

"Your voice," she told him. "When you were… channeling. The things you said. The accent. It was just as if I was back there again, listening to you." She tipped her head to the side. "The way you just called me Jewel, instead of Julie."

He pursed his lips. "Freudian slip, do you think? Maybe deep down I was hoping you'd figure it out."

He wasn't denying it. It seemed so impossible, especially since he looked nothing like Mordecai. Except for the depth of his eyes and that smile. "How is it you look so different than before?"

"I was burned very badly in the fire, you know." He didn't even try to conceal his Southern drawl, not anymore. "I've undergone numerous rounds of reconstructive surgery. The hair on my head will never grow back. Most folks think it's a style choice—or a spiritual one. Humility or something like that." He smiled gently. "I worked on my accent. But it still comes through when I'm in a deep state of trance."

He got to his feet, and she took an instinctive step backward. He only stood there, looking at her. "You don't have to be afraid of me, Jewel. I have never hurt you."

"What about Sirona? Did you hurt her? Or Tessa?"

He lifted his brows. "They survived the raid, as well?"

He was either genuinely surprised or he was a very good actor. "Up until recently, they did. They both died within the past two weeks."

"And you naturally assume I'm responsible. Jewel—" He took a step toward her and she jerked back. "For God's

sake, Jewel, will you relax? I'm not going to harm you."
He waved toward a sitting area, which held a miniature
sofa, a chair and a table laden with dried fruits, muffins,
carafes of juice and fresh flowers. Daisies and black-eyed
Susans. "Sit, relax. We're completely surrounded by security people and staff. You're safe here."

"I didn't come alone," she said. "My partner knows
where I am."

"Even more reason to believe you're safe." He licked
his lips as if he might be nervous. "I've changed, Jewel—"

"Stop calling me that. It's Julie."

He nodded. "Yes. Julie Jones, I understand. You've
changed. You're completely different from the girl I knew.
From Jewel Jordan. That's why you, of all people, should
understand. *I'm* not the same person I was then, either. I've
moved on with my life, Jewel—Julie. I'm trying to do some
good with it. Please, sit down."

Swallowing her fear, Julie moved across the room and
perched on the edge of the chair.

"Help yourself to—"

"Look, this isn't a social call. I just needed to confirm
you were who I thought you were."

"And now that you have?"

She would be stupid to tell him she was going straight
to the police. He would never let her out of there alive.
"Now, I'm telling you to leave me and my family alone.
I want you to get out of town. And don't ever, *ever,* come
back."

He seemed to ponder that for a moment. "And if I refuse?"

She held his steady gaze but said nothing.

"You'll go to the police, reveal my true identity. That's
what you're thinking, isn't it, Jewel? But you won't do that.

You can't do that, not without also telling them how you know.''

"I was one of your victims. I survived. There's no crime in that.''

"Perhaps not. All right, then, I suppose I'm forced to resort to blackmail. Kind of like our dear departed mutual friend, Harry.'' Ignoring her gasp, he went on. ''If you turn me in, Julie Jones, I'll turn something in, as well.''

"What are you talking about?''

He sank onto the sofa, helping himself to a dried apple slice, nibbling it slowly, licking his lips. ''The knife that was used to cut Harry Blackwood's throat. It's got your fingerprints on it, Julie. Oh, it didn't have, originally, but it was easy enough to lift some from the door of your car and plant them on the hilt. Scotch tape, wonderful invention.'' He took another bite. ''The police already suspect you had something to do with it. The murder weapon would clinch it.''

She sat there, stone still. ''You killed Harry.''

"Does it matter? Don't tell me you weren't glad to see him dead.'' He shook his head slowly. ''My plan was to plant the murder weapon at your home, let the police find it, arrest you and get you out of my way. You see, Jewel, you are standing between me and something I want.'' He shrugged. ''But that plan didn't work, and I knew that was a sign from the Almighty that I must proceed differently. Now that you know my little secret, I might as well give you the chance to give me what I want, rather than forcing me to take it from you.''

"I gave all my money to Harry. Everything I took from you, from the compound, is gone. I used it to get an education, a new identity, a home....''

"That's all right, Jewel. I have all the money I need.''

"What do you want, then?''

He smiled very slowly. "Oh, come on, don't tell me you haven't figured it out already. I want the girl," he told her. "I want my daughter."

Julie shot to her feet. My God, he knew about Dawn! "I don't know what you're talking about. She's not—"

"She is. She's my child. Mine and Lizzie's."

"No!" She edged toward the door.

"It's all right, Jewel. I understand you'll need some time. Time to explain to her how you've lied to her all these years. How you stole her from her true father, left both her parents to die in that hell. How you've deceived her, her entire life. And that you need to make it right now."

"You're as insane as you ever were if you think you'll ever lay a hand on my child!"

"I'll give you twenty-four hours. You bring her to me, Jewel, or I will take her from you. And I will see to it you can never try to take her back."

"You stay away from my daughter! I swear to God, Mordecai, if you try to touch her, I'll kill you. I'll *kill* you!"

Jones was a basket case when she came back outside and climbed into the waiting car. She was as white as if she'd just had a conversation with a dead man, so angry that tiny lines he'd never seen before bracketed her lips. She got in, slammed the door, stared straight ahead.

"You all right?" he asked, already knowing the answer.

She nodded. "Let's just go."

He picked up a worried frown from Dawn, returned a "damned if I know" glance and drove the car. "You want to tell me what has you so upset, Jones?"

She shot him a look.

"Come on, Mom, it's not like I didn't notice. And you

can trust Kayla. Her dad's a cop, for God's sake. What happened in there?''

Jones turned in her seat to look at her daughter. She had to make a real effort to ease the tension from her face. "Nothing's wrong, hon. I'm just a little stressed out. It's been a rough week." She faced front again, and Sean saw that her eyes were growing moist.

Dammit.

She refused to talk. Sean felt something—something had changed. Desperation seemed to be wafting from her pores. It stirred an answering desperation in him. Why the hell wouldn't she talk to him?

"Ms. Jones, can Dawnie spend the night at my place?" Kayla asked.

"Yeah, can I, Mom? I know I'm supposed to be grounded and all that, but I promise I'll be good."

She glanced into the back seat at the two girls, sitting so close to each other. Sean saw the stern look that was certain to turn into a "no" slowly change. "Actually, that might not be a bad idea. Kayla, your dad being a policeman and all, I'll bet you have really good security on your house, hmm?"

"You've seen the fence, Ms. Jones."

"Yes, but I've never been inside."

Kayla nodded. "It's like Fort Knox. And you've met Isis and Osiris, right?"

Julie nodded. "I'd forgotten about them."

"Isis and Osiris?" Sean asked, needing clarification.

Kayla grinned. "They're our Rottweilers."

"Ahhh. Remind me not to wander into your yard in the dark, kid."

Jones said, "I need you back early, Dawnie. We need to talk—before school."

"My dad can drop her on his way into work, if you

want,'' Kayla said. ''He leaves at six, and he goes right by your place.''

Julie seemed to think that through. Then, finally, she nodded. ''You're to stay right at Kayla's,'' she warned her daughter. ''Don't go anywhere else. Just hang inside the house and come home in the morning with her dad. Okay?''

''Sure, Mom.'' Dawn squeezed Kayla's hand. Sean felt sorry for the kid. She looked a little scared by her mother's sudden step up on the paranoia ladder.

By the time he'd dropped the girls at Kayla's, watched them all the way inside, and then driven to Julie's place and pulled into her driveway, Sean was determined to get the truth out of her. He was already rehearsing the discussion they would have in his mind. He got out to walk her inside, checking the darkness around the house and seeing no sign of any intruders. When Jones unlocked the front door, he went inside with her, though the looks she was sending him told him she would rather he didn't.

Still, she didn't throw him out, which he took as a positive sign. She turned on the lights, double-checked the security panel near the door to be sure no doors or windows had been opened since she'd left, then licked her lips, rubbed her arms.

''The house just seems so empty without her.''

''I know. But I think she's safe at Kayla's.''

Julie nodded. ''Yeah. For tonight, at least.''

He pressed his lips together. ''I think she, um—I think she knew I'd like some time alone with her mother.''

''You can't put much past her.'' Julie sighed and walked to the sofa, sinking into it as if exhausted.

''So what happened?''

She bit her lower lips. ''I can't—''

''Come on, Jones, don't tell me that.'' He went to the sofa, sat down beside her and studied her face for a moment. Then he lowered his head, shook it slowly. "No, never mind. Don't tell me anything. Just come here."

"Wha—?"

"Shhh. Come here." He slid his arms around her and pulled her taut, trembling body closer. "Let it go, Julie. You're terrified, and so rigid you feel like you're going to break."

She let him hold her but remained as stiff as a board.

"I'm here for you, Jones," he said. "I don't know when it happened, or how, but you've managed to get to be my favorite pain in the ass."

"Yeah?" She relaxed a little. He felt it.

"Yeah. If you can just bring yourself to believe that I'm on your side in this…trust me a little bit…"

"I do trust you."

"Do you?"

She nodded. "I know you want to help, to clear your conscience about the way things happened at that compound sixteen years ago. But—"

"Yeah. I do. But it's more than that now, Jones."

She met his eyes, searched them. "Your motives don't really matter. You can't fix this for me, Sean. No one can."

"I'm not even sure what it is that needs fixing."

She lifted her head, met his eyes. "I'll tell you this much. You're going to have a hell of a scoop tomorrow."

"Am I?"

She nodded.

"You gonna tell me what it is?"

"Not tonight."

He saw the tears pooling in her eyes, and he felt the urge to kiss her.

And this time, dammit, he wasn't going to second-guess himself. He lowered his head, pressed his lips very lightly to hers. She didn't pull away. It was the merest taste, a touch like a breath. He didn't close his eyes, the better to watch every nuance of her reaction. Hers fell closed; her mouth relaxed, and her lips parted slightly. Her breath escaped in a stuttering sigh.

He lifted his head, staring down at her.

Her arms twisted around his neck, and she pulled until he kissed her again. And this time he was a little bolder, partly just to test the limits of this new development, and partly because—well, hell, because he wanted to.

She pulled away suddenly, stared up at him with her eyes full of questions. "I didn't—"

"Neither did I."

"What was—"

"I don't know, Jones." He reached out to touch her hair, but she backed away, so he lowered his hand. "Should I apologize?"

She licked her lips, didn't quite meet his eyes. "No."

"That's good, 'cause I'm not sorry. Surprised. Confused as hell, but…not sorry."

"You should go." She looked him in the eyes when she said it, and he caught the need in hers, saw it clearly. She didn't want him to go home tonight any more than he wanted to.

"You really want me to go?"

She lowered her gaze. "Things are already so complicated."

"That isn't an answer."

She lifted her eyes again, held his. "I don't want you to go," she whispered.

"That's better." He got to his feet. She rose with him, took his hand and led him to the stairs, and up them to her bedroom.

For the life of him, Sean could not believe what was happening, but there it was. He kissed her as she pushed

the bedroom door closed. The kiss grew into something
more, something that felt as desperate and frightened as he
sensed Julie was deep down inside. They yanked and
tugged at each other's clothes, until they landed on the bed,
mouths still locked, him wearing only his jeans, and those
undone and half off him, Julie down to a bra and panties.
He got rid of those in a hurry.

And then he wanted to slow down. He wanted to turn
on a light, to look at her, touch her. But Jones wasn't having any of that. She wrapped her body around his and clung
so tightly he could barely breathe, and when she shoved
his jeans out of the way and moved over him, there wasn't
a hell of a lot he could do to slow things down. She lowered
herself, and he was inside her. She moved over him, and
he stopped thinking about anything at all. There was only
sensation, pleasure, friction and heat. And a silent desperation in her that he didn't begin to understand. He wrapped
his arms around her, rolled her over so he was the one on
top, and gave her all he could give her, as hard and as deep
as he could give it to her. She snapped her hips up to meet
him every time, no matter how powerfully he drove into
her, seeming to want more. Her hands closed on his but-
tocks, nails digging into his flesh, and she pulled him into
her.

She bit his earlobe and in a coarse whisper told him,
"More, Sean. Harder."

He gripped her bottom in both hands, held her to him
for every thrust, slammed into her so hard the head of the
bed banged against the wall.

She screamed his name, wrapped her legs around his
waist and shook all over as he drove her to climax and
beyond.

Then, and only then, did Sean slow down. He rolled
again, pulling her on top, so he could run his hands slowly

over her body, up and down her back, her thighs, between their bodies to touch her breasts and her belly. He kept moving inside her, slowly, gently, while the spasms that rocked her body slowly ebbed, faded. He would build them again.

He caught her face in his hands, kissed her deeply. "Julie," he whispered.

"Shh. Don't talk."

So he didn't talk. He made love to her again, gently this time, slowly, only increasing his pace when he felt her passion begin to build. This time, when she peaked, he was there with her, shuddering deep in his soul and whispering things he wouldn't remember later.

And then he lay in the bed, with her curled up in his arms, and he held her until she slept.

14

Julie had kissed him awake at 5:00 a.m., and told him it was time for him to go home, before Dawn showed up. He hadn't argued with her. He hadn't insisted they "talk about" things, either. He wasn't ready to do that, and he doubted she was, either. He had simply held her for a minute or two before rolling out of her bed, stumbling into his clothes and driving himself all the way back into the city with a dumb-ass grin on his face. He'd showered and changed at his apartment, and then headed in to work, stopping for a supersize Mac-breakfast on the way.

Sean was nervous as hell about what to say and how to act when he saw Jones at work that morning. He wondered if she would act differently toward him. He wondered if a night of mind-blowing passion between enemies changed everything or nothing at all. He wondered what she was feeling and thinking about it—hell, he wondered what *he* was feeling and thinking about it.

He could count on one hand the things he did know. He knew that he didn't dislike Julie Jones as much as he'd always pretended to—or at all. And maybe he'd kind of known that all along. He was more attracted to her than he'd ever been, now that he knew what her mouth tasted like and how her body felt when he pulled it up tight against his. A lot more. He was both eager to see her again and dreading it. The bite of her sarcastic little mouth was more than he wanted to deal with this morning. The idea that she might show up making doe eyes at him made him want to throw up. Maybe it would be better if she kept on hating him.

He couldn't imagine her soft and loving toward him. He couldn't imagine being this turned on by her if she suddenly turned into a girlfriend rather than a nemesis.

He liked her the way she was. He liked their relationship the way it was. Adding sex to what they already had was his notion of perfect. He wondered if she would go for that idea. And then wondered why he had been sitting in the newsroom listening to everyone brainstorm story ideas and pass out assignments for an hour and she hadn't walked in yet.

She was probably tired this morning, probably as worn-out as he had been. It had been a long time since he'd spent such an energetic night. Maybe she was sleeping in.

He'd been at the office since eight. It was nine, and Julie wasn't there.

Where the hell was she?

Allan Westcott must have begun wondering the same thing, because it was at that precise moment that Sean realized the man was leaning over him, finishing a sentence with the words "...the hell is she?"

It wasn't hard to fill in the "where" or to figure out that Jones was the subject in question. "She had to drop the kid off at school. You know that."

"School starts at eight, MacKenzie, and it's only a half hour away. It's 9:02. You telling me you haven't heard from her?"

Sean frowned, shook his head slowly.

Westcott looked around the room, speaking loudly enough to be heard over everyone, in a tone that shut them all up after the first word landed. "Has anyone heard from Julie this morning?"

People looked at each other, shook their heads, muttered. "Someone call her," Westcott barked.

"I've got it," Sean said, and his voice was as firm and insistent as the boss's had been. He left the newsroom, vaguely aware that he hadn't heard anything about a single story he was supposed to be covering today, and, moreover, he didn't care.

He headed into his office, slammed the door closed behind him, grabbed the desk phone and dialed Julie's number without sitting down. He hated that he knew her number by heart. He hated that he was worried about her. He hated that he was pretty sure he had reason to be. He hated that he had left her alone, even for an hour. Goddammit.

While he listened to her phone ring, he booted up his computer. By the time Jones's machine picked up, he had his address book program opened. "Jones, it's MacKenzie. It's after nine, and you're late for work. Call me." He hung up and tried her cell phone. He got her voice mail and left the same message. Then he double clicked on the Cazenovia High School icon on the computer screen, waited for the computer to dial that number and then held on while it rang.

"Cazenovia High School," a cheerful voice said. "How may I direct your call?"

He thought about just asking point-blank but realized Jones had warned the school officials about the man who'd seemed to following Dawn. They weren't likely to give him any information over the phone. "Give me a…" He struggled to recall the name of that teacher Dawn was always talking about—the one who'd promised to keep a special eye on her for Jones. "Ms. Marcum," he said when it came to him.

The phone clicked. He glanced at his chair, shoved it away from the desk to make more room for pacing. Finally a woman's voice said, "This is Ms. Marcum. Can I help you?"

"Ms. Marcum, this is Sean MacKenzie. I'm Julie Jones's coanchor at Channel Four."

"Yes, I know who you are. Dawn speaks very highly of you, Mr. MacKenzie."

He blinked, surprised. "Actually, Dawn is the reason I'm calling. Her mother hasn't shown up for work, and she doesn't answer her phone."

"Oh, no." Her voice changed, those two words emerging as a hoarse whisper that vibrated with dread. Then she cleared her throat, seemed to make an effort to steady her voice. "Dawn hasn't shown up for school this morning, either," she said. "I've called the house several times and was just about to call the station to speak with her mother."

"Do me a favor and call me if you hear from either of them?"

"Only if you'll do the same for me."

"Deal." He quickly rattled off his cell phone number, jotted down hers and hung up. Then he headed for the office door.

"Well?" Westcott asked in the hall.

"No answer. I'm going out there."

"You look worried."

"I *am* worried."

Lieutenant Jackson sipped her third cup of hot coffee and looked again at her desk, where two sets of bank records were laid out side by side. She'd received the files an hour ago. April 20—Julie Jones withdrew twenty thousand in cash. April 21—Harry Blackwood made two ten thousand dollar deposits. June 3, Jones made another withdrawal. On the fourth, fifth and sixth, Harry made three more deposits, totaling the amount of Jones's withdrawal. The pattern repeated in August. Harry had made other large and inexplicable deposits in between those dates—deposits that didn't match up with any withdrawals in Jones's accounts. That had thrown her off at first.

Not for long, though.

The senator's brother had been a blackmailer. He'd taken in better than a million five over the past year. More than two hundred thousand of it had come from Julie Jones. Small potatoes compared to the huge sums he'd been getting from other sources.

"There's her motive," Jax said.

Chief Strong looked over her shoulder at the statements. "It could also have been an even bigger motive for whoever else he was blackmailing," he said, reaching past Jax to run a forefinger along the column listing Blackwood's deposits. "Jones's contributions are relatively small in comparison to some of these others."

"Jones was at the crime scene," Jax said. "Motive plus opportunity makes her look pretty good for this."

Strong shrugged. "Any physical evidence?"

"We got a DNA sample from that mascara tube. I thought I might pay Jones a little visit today, ask her to voluntarily supply a DNA sample for comparison."

"Think she'll do it?"

"Not if she's guilty." She shrugged. "Maybe I should show up armed with a court order, though, just in case. You think we have enough to get one?"

"Barely, considering her status in this town."

She shrugged. "I'd better call a judge." She picked up a phone.

Sean's Porsche roared into Jones's driveway. The house was dark, the garage door closed up tight. No overt signs of trouble, he told himself as he got out of the car. Right. So why was the lump in his throat damn near choking him?

He peered through one of the garage's little windows, cupping his hands around his face to block the glare of the bright morning sun. Dawn's pretty blue Jeep sat inside, but there was no sign of the Mercedes. He continued on to the front door of the house, knowing goddamn well it would be locked and trying it anyway. He could hear the telephone ringing. It stopped, probably when the machine picked up, and within a few seconds was ringing again.

He raced around to the back of the house. God, he could have kicked himself. He'd spent the past several hours worrying about how to act, what to say, how their night of lovemaking would change their relationship, feeling like a teenager with his first bad crush—while she'd been going through God only knew what.

He hit the backyard and hurried over the lawn to the back door. It was cold this morning, crisp and kind of gloomy. Clouds covered the sun.

The glass in the back door was broken.

"Jesus." Sean ran to it, gripped the knob and turned. It wasn't locked. He stepped into the kitchen, and his shoes crunched on the broken glass on the floor. He listened and heard nothing, then damn near jumped out of his shoes when the phone started ringing again.

"Julie?"

He called her name but didn't really expect an answer. Then he yanked up the telephone just to shut it the hell up. It was cordless, so he continued walking, moving into the living room as he said hello. Things were off-kilter. The cushions not quite right on the sofa. The plants in the wrong positions on the stands.

"SafeGuard Home Security, sir. I'm calling for Julie or Dawn Jones."

"They're not here. And I don't have time to talk."

"We've notified the police—"

"Good idea." He hit the cutoff, dropped the phone onto a table and continued through the house. "Be all right," he whispered.

He went from room to room, walking slowly, every sense on high alert for any sound, while his eyes scanned the place. Every time he entered another room, he held his breath, dreading that he might see Julie or, God forbid, Dawn, lying on the floor, injured or worse. Every time he stepped into another room and didn't see that, he felt a little more relieved.

Finding no one, and no real clues as to what had happened here, he ventured upstairs. Dawn's bedroom had that same slightly off feeling that the rest of the house had. He'd never seen it before, so he couldn't say for sure that things had been moved around, but he felt it. That sense of invasion, of contamination. The mattress wasn't perfectly straight on the bed, and the bedspread was rumpled, as if someone had lifted it up to look underneath, then dropped it back into place again, too rushed to be careful. The book she'd been reading—the autographed copy of Nathan Z's book—lay open on the bed. The computer was on. And open to Dawn's e-mail program.

Frowning, he moved closer, reached for the mouse and clicked on the Sent Mail button. Only an empty screen came up. If Dawn had sent anyone an e-mail before vanishing from the face of the earth this morning, it had been deleted. The question was, had it been deleted before or after the intruder had seen it?

Sean backed out of Dawn's bedroom and moved down the hall to check the bathroom, before continuing on to the next bedroom. Julie's. But he only got as far as the slightly open door before memories of the night before came rushing in, trying to distract him from the matter at hand. God, he could still feel her body moving against his, could still smell her hair, hear those soft sounds she made, taste her mouth.

"Where the hell are you, Jones?" he whispered.

He pushed the door open, and the sight of the place chased the memories away like a fist to the stomach would have done. They hadn't been as neat in here, whoever they were. The blankets and sheets lay balled up on the floor; the mattress had been stripped bare. Dresser drawers hung wide-open, some completely removed from the dresser, and their former contents formed mountains of soft fabrics on the floor. The closet door was open, and the clothes inside had been knocked from their rack, hangers still in them. "Where the hell are you?"

"Put your hands on top of your head and turn around. Do it now."

The voice was strong and female and it meant business. Sean thought there were not too many people who would refuse to comply, and he wasn't one of those few. His back itched with the knowledge that there was a gun pointed at it. He lifted his hands to the top of his head, then turned to face the woman, as ordered. "Hello, Jax."

She lifted her eyebrows, lowered her gun. "I figured that was you when I saw your car out front."

"Then why did you point your gun at me?"

"Just making sure. What are you doing here, Mac-Kenzie?"

"Not breaking and entering," he told her. "Somebody beat me to it."

"Yeah? Then you're the one who answered the phone and talked to the security people?"

"Yes."

She nodded, seemed to relax a little. "So what's the deal?"

"I came looking for Jones, she wasn't here, I let myself in." He waved a hand at the mess. "It was like this when I arrived."

"Have you touched anything?"

"Doorknobs on the front and back doors, the telephone downstairs."

"Why were you looking for Jones?"

He shrugged, averting his eyes, wanting nothing more than to get the hell out of here so he could search for her. He didn't have time to play twenty-questions with Jax.

"She didn't come to work this morning?"

He knew Jax could confirm it with a simple phone call, and he knew she would. "No. She didn't come in."

"Did she let anyone know she would be taking the day off?"

He shrugged. "I'm her partner, not her boss. She doesn't answer to me."

"But she didn't let you know."

"No."

"And you couldn't reach her by phone," she said.

"No."

"What about Dawn? Did she show up for school today?"

He glanced at Jax with a puzzled frown. "What makes you think I would know?"

She pursed her lips, scowling at him. "I know goddamn well you know." Turning her head, she shouted toward the stairs, "Have someone call Cazenovia High School and see if Dawn Jones showed up for classes this morning, pronto."

"You got it."

She turned and faced Sean again. "She's skipped, hasn't

she? She knew I was getting close to arresting her, so she skipped town.''

"I hope to God she's skipped on you. Because if she hasn't—" He couldn't even finish the thought, much less speak it. He looked around the room, lifted his hands. "Are you not *seeing* this mess? You think Jones did this herself, just to throw you off? Is it not clear to you yet that someone is after the woman?"

"If someone is, he'd better watch himself. The last guy who messed with her got his throat cut."

"Oh, come on, you know as well as I do that Jones had nothing to do with that."

"He was blackmailing her, MacKenzie. We have the bank records. She's paid him a small fortune over the past six months. What I don't know is what he had on her."

He lifted his brows, played his hunch. "Rumor has it that blackmail was a goddamn vocation with this guy. You telling me she's the only one?"

Jax didn't answer.

"Someone's setting her up, Jax. It ought to be obvious to a cop as good as you are."

"Oh, right, flattery's gonna work."

He rolled his eyes. "Hell, you got here fast. I'll give you that much."

"I was on my way here before we got the call from the security company," she admitted.

"What for?"

"DNA." He must have looked surprised, because she looked smug. "Got a judge to issue an order this morning, in case Jones doesn't want to cooperate. We managed to get a sample off that makeup container we found at the crime scene, and all I need now is a known sample for comparison."

He shrugged, trying her smug look on for size. "Guess you can't get a sample if Jones isn't here to give it."

"Don't be so sure about that. I'm pretty sure I can find a sample around here somewhere."

He pursed his lips, angry and wondering why. "Jones is no killer, Lieutenant. She's in trouble, and if you don't start taking that seriously, she's liable to wind up as your next victim. You'll have to live with that. And it won't be easy, trust me. Especially if her kid ends up getting caught in the cross fire. Believe me, I know."

He thought his final sentence got to her, but he couldn't be sure. She flinched just a little, aimed her penetrating gaze at something besides him.

"I have to go," Sean said. "Do me a favor and let me know if you hear from Jones?"

"Funny, I was just about to say the same thing to you," Jax said. "Not that I expect you to comply."

"Have a little faith."

"Morning, Mr. MacKenzie," a voice called as Sean hurried out the front door, toward his car.

He turned and spotted an old fellow walking toward him, apparently from the house next door, and he frowned. "Have we met?"

"Nah, but Dawnie's told me all about you." The older man smiled, turning his face into a roadmap. "Recognized you by your car."

"You must be Rodney White," Sean said, taking the hand the old fellow extended. "Dawn has told me a lot about you, too."

The man's grip was firm and cool. "You're worried about them, I take it?" He nodded toward the police cars on the side of the road. "They must be, too."

Sean nodded. "Do you know where they might have

gone?'' Please, he thought, tell me they've gone some-where.

He shrugged. ''Julie wouldn't say. Just that it was a va-cation weekend, and that she didn't know when she'd be back.''

Sean's entire body eased in a flood of relief. ''Then you saw her before she left? She definitely went somewhere of her own free will?''

''Yep. About six this morning. She piled a couple of suitcases into the car, then left it running while she came over here. Told me you'd be coming around. Asked me to give you something.''

Sean's heart damn near stopped as the old man reached into his pocket and pulled out a white envelope. When he stretched out his hand to offer it to Sean, Sean noticed his jacket sleeve had been pushed back a little, and he glimpsed the edges of a tattoo. Not a professional one, but the dark blue lines of the homemade variety. The kind you got in prison.

He frowned, wondering just how much Julie knew about her next-door neighbor. But there was no time to quiz the old fellow. Not now. He took the envelope quickly, glanc-ing back toward the house and hoping to God Jax hadn't seen the exchange.

''Thank you, Mr. White.''

''Call me Rodney.'' He pursed his lips, shook his head. ''Tell you the truth, I'm worried about those girls.''

''So am I, Rodney.'' Sean was itching to be away, to be out searching for Julie, to read the note she'd left. ''Did you see anyone near the house after Julie and Dawn left?''

''No. Why, has someone been there?''

''Yeah, there's been a break-in. The police are looking into it.''

The man shook his head slowly, sadly.

Sean looked longingly toward his car. "Look, they'll probably question you when they come out. Can you do me a favor?"

He nodded. "You don't want me to tell them about that note she left you. I don't figure that's anything they need to know, Mr. MacKenzie. That's private, between you and Julie."

Sean thanked the man and got into his car. But he only drove around the block before pulling over, taking out the envelope and reading the letter inside. The handwriting was Jones's.

Sean,

Dawnie and I have left town. I'd tell you it's only for a few days, like I've been telling her and even myself, but the truth is, I don't know when we'll be back. I don't know if we'll be back at all. Don't try to call us. There's no cell phone reception where we're going. Don't feel as if you need to break it to Allan Westcott on my behalf. I'll find a pay phone somewhere and call him later in the morning. Meanwhile, here's that scoop I promised you. Consider it a going-away present. It'll make you famous. Mordecai Young is alive and well and going by the name Nathan Z. I realized it when he slipped into that Southern drawl during the show.

About what else happened—between us, I mean—last night, hell, there's not much point in going there, is there? I don't know what it meant, Sean, if it meant anything at all. I'm sorry I couldn't stick around to find out. I doubt it was anything earth-shattering on your end, but it sure as hell threw me for a loop. And I don't regret a single second of it.

If you care, MacKenzie, I'd really prefer you burn

this note and tell no one about it. But I guess you'll do what you want with it. It's out of my hands.

Thanks—thanks for everything. Believe it or not, I'm going to miss you.

That was it, the end. She'd signed the bottom "Jones." He traced the swirls and loops of the letters with his eyes and then his fingertip. And then he paused, frowning at the tiny blotch on the sheet that suggested a drop of water— or maybe a tear?

Yeah, in your dreams, MacKenzie, he told himself. His throat felt oddly tight, and he found it tough to swallow. He needed some coffee. But not before he'd read the note one more time. Jesus, she shouldn't have taken off on her own like this. Not without telling him just what the hell was going on. Then again, she didn't need to tell him, did she? He could put the pieces together. Jones had been at the Young Believers' compound on the day of the raid. She'd lived to tell the tale, and Mordecai Young—a man wanted on a dozen charges, including unlawful imprisonment, statutory rape, murder and federal drug and weapons violations—stood to lose everything if she talked. She obviously believed he was after her.

He read the letter again, searching for clues as to where she might have gone, but there were none, aside from the obscure remark that there would be no cell phone reception there. Then he stopped on the one line that give him hope. "Don't feel like you have to break it to Allan Westcott yourself. I'll find a pay phone somewhere and call him later in the morning."

"That's it. That's how I find her," he whispered. "If it's not already too late."

15

Julie drove the car along the winding road, twisting under overhanging trees that still held on to their thin layers of brightly colored leaves. The fall foliage was well past its peak, but there was still color to be seen. The trees, she thought, were like old women who applied bright makeup to their crinkle-paper faces just to let the world know in no uncertain terms that there was still life inside. It was a show of defiance against aging and death, the way those few scarlet and yellow leaves clung to the bony arms of the skeletal trees. It was a shout against decay.

"So where are we?" Dawn asked. She had a road atlas open on her lap.

Glancing sideways, Julie said, "Look in the north and find Herkimer County."

Dawn's finger ran along the map, and her eyes followed. "Oh!" She looked through the windshield again. "So these are the Adirondack Mountains?"

"We're in the thick of them."

"Cool. How far are we going?"

Julie shrugged. She'd been racking her brain to figure a way out of this mess, but she was drawing a big fat blank. She could try to find evidence to tie Mordecai to the murders he'd committed. Tessa, Sirona—even Harry Blackwood. But she couldn't do that from here, and if she stayed home, the bastard would try to take Dawn away.

She couldn't risk that.

It had even occurred to her to wonder if she were capable of killing him. She wasn't certain she was, but she hadn't ruled it out. The list of things she wouldn't or couldn't do to protect Dawn was tiny. Microscopic. Maybe blank.

"Mom?"

"Hmm?"

"How far are we going?"

Julie realized she'd already asked the question once. "I don't know. Till we find a place that strikes us as perfect. Maybe we can rent a cabin on one of these lakes. I think it's sort of off-season."

"There sure are a lot of them. Lakes, I mean."

"One after another." She'd told Dawn she wanted a spontaneous getaway. A long mother-daughter weekend. There was so much she had to explain to her daughter. This would be a good time to begin.

"I'm getting kind of hungry," Dawn said. "Can we think about stopping for a hardy northern breakfast soon?"

"You got it." She glanced at her watch. They'd been on the road for several hours already, taking a wildly round-about route, just in case anyone had tried to follow. It was 10:00 a.m., and she hadn't yet called her boss. She would have to do that soon.

She thought about Sean. Was tempted to call him, as well. But the sound of his voice, even over the telephone, might be more than she could handle this morning. After last night—God, what the hell had happened to her and Sean last night? They'd had a perfectly wonderful relationship that worked for both of them—and then everything went crazy.

She felt warm inside when she remembered him. She hadn't known he could be so tender—or so talented. Her lips trembled. She wondered where things might have led if she hadn't had to run for life.

But there was no point in pondering things that would never happen. She honestly didn't think she and Dawn were ever going to be heading back home.

She kept on driving, looking now for a place to stop and eat. Eventually they saw a log cabin with a sign hanging in front advertising Down Home Cookin' At Family Prices and Julie pulled into the driveway-size parking lot and killed the engine.

"I'm thinking pancakes," Dawn said. "Or maybe French toast."

"I'm going for an omelette. Gooey cheese and mushrooms."

"Blueberry syrup—unless they have maple. Real maple, not the phony stuff."

"I'll bet they do. Heck, with all these trees around here, why wouldn't they?" Julie got out of the car and waited for Dawn to unbuckle and do the same. Then she hit the lock button on her key chain.

A car passed on the road behind them as they walked into the diner, and Julie noticed Dawn frowning at it as continued on the road.

"Honey? What's wrong?"

Dawn frowned, gave her head a shake. "Nothing. I've been hanging around my jumpy mom too much, I think." She smiled brightly, even though deep down she had to know something was wrong—that this was more flight than vacation. But she was too good a kid to press her mother on it right then. Instead she hooked her arm through Julie's and tugged. They walked side by side into the diner, where a sign over the counter told them this place had not only real maple syrup but the best real maple syrup to be found.

He didn't want to burn Julie's note, dammit. He wanted to keep it, in case he never saw her again. Besides, it might have more clues to yield. He pursed his lips. Lieutenant Jackson would want to talk to him again. Jones was still a suspect in the Harry Blackwood murder and she had skipped town. For an instant a vision flashed through Sean's mind of Jax and one of her uniformed sidekicks slamming him up against his car the second he stepped out of it, frisking him and finding the note.

He read it one more time, willing himself to commit it to memory. Then he used the cigarette lighter to set it ablaze. He opened the car door, set it on the curb and watched it burn until there was nothing left but ashes. Then he put the car in motion again, grabbing his cell phone as he did, dialing his boss's direct line.

Westcott picked up on the second ring. "Jones?"

"No, it's me," Sean said. "Has she called you yet?"

"Not yet. Have you heard from her?"

"Not a word," Sean said. "But I've got something else. Something solid on the Mordecai Young story."

"Is it true or a hoax?"

"It's true," Sean told him. "He's alive."

"Holy shit." Sean heard the man slam a hand onto his desk. "This is fabulous. Is anyone else on to this?"

"Nope, it'll be an exclusive. And not only can I get proof, I can identify him, if you'll trust me enough to do what I'm about to ask and not ask me any questions."

"You've got it, MacKenzie. Whatever you need, just say the word."

Sean nodded. "You have call forwarding?"

"Come again?"

"Call forwarding. Do you have it?"

"Sure I have it."

"Okay. Then here's what I need. I want you to set your call forwarding so that every call you get today comes straight to my cell phone. Every single call. It should only be for an hour or two. And you have to do it fast. Understand?"

"No. I don't."

"Just think about what will happen when we break this story," Sean told him. "Think of the scoop."

"All right. But I want my phone calls back by the end of the day. And I want constant progress reports. You're to tell no one about this, except maybe Jones once we track her down. We can't risk it leaking out to the other stations."

"Got you. Now don't forget the call forwarding."

Westcott sighed. "I'm doing it now. The second you hang up."

"Got my cell number?"

"Of course I do."

Sean nodded. "Thanks, Allan."

"Just get busy. Go get the proof we need to run with this story."

Sean dropped his cell phone on the seat beside him. And then he drove. He had no idea where to go, where to even begin looking for Julie and Dawn.

His cell phone rang within seconds, and he picked it up fast with his heart in his throat. The panel gave him the number that was calling—a local number. God, could she be that close? He jerked the car to the shoulder, yanked out a pencil and scribbled the number down. Then he answered the phone.

The woman on the other end was not Julie.

"Is this Sean MacKenzie?" she asked.

"Yes."

"Mr. MacKenzie, this is Miss Carter. I work for Nathan Z." Sean lifted his brows but didn't interrupt. "I understand you and he had an appointment for an interview today?"

"Did we?" He had paid so little attention at this morning's meeting, he wouldn't have known if he had.

"Yes, set up by a Mr. Westcott? For 1:00 p.m.?"

"Right," he said.

"I'm afraid I'm going to have to cancel that appointment."

Just as well, Sean thought. Because he didn't have time for it, not until he found Julie, and if he did meet up with the so-called Nathan Z, he would probably beat the man senseless.

"He's been called out of town on an emergency. I'll call your office as soon as I can reschedule."

Sean held the telephone and blinked. "He's left town?"

"Yes."

"When?"

"Early this morning. Why do you ask?"

"If I were you, lady, I'd start looking for another job." He hung up the phone, and wished to God Julie would call. Jesus, what if Nathan Z was the one who'd broken into her house? What if he somehow knew where she'd gone and was even now on her trail?

Julie stood at the pay phone outside the diner, freshly invigorated by three cups of coffee, mentally composing the words she would use to tell her boss that she was gone and probably wouldn't be coming back. There was no other solution she could think of, though it killed her to make this choice. It was going to break Dawn's heart to have to leave her home, her friends, her school, everything she knew, and start life again somewhere else. But it was the only solution. Short of hunting Mordecai Young down and killing him herself, it was the only way out. And Julie didn't think she had it in her to kill a man—not even him.

The phone on the other end rang four times, and she was

beginning to wonder if Allan Westcott would pick up at all, when someone answered. But the voice that said "Hello" was not the voice she'd been expecting.

It was Sean. And just hearing that one word from him evoked an empty feeling deep in her belly. A longing that made no sense to her. It was alien, foreign. She'd always disliked Sean MacKenzie—or she thought she had. But it wasn't dislike that wrapped itself around her vocal chords, refusing to let her speak. It wasn't even close.

"Jones? Is that you? Don't hang up, just—just don't hang up. Please."

She swallowed past the tightness in her throat. "Yeah. It's me."

"Thank God. Jesus, it's good to hear your voice. Where are you? Are you all right?"

She closed her eyes, because his words were full of emotion. She wasn't used to hearing him sound this way— almost desperate, almost pleading. She was used to his sarcasm and his flirting and his politically incorrect nonsense. Not this. This was too raw, too honest.

"Julie?"

"I'm—I'm all right. Dawn is, too. We both are."

"Good. God, I've been worried. Jones, this isn't the answer. Running away isn't going to fix this thing."

"Nothing is going to fix this thing," she said softly. "Nothing can."

He seemed to hesitate before speaking again. Then he said, "If you'd just trust me, tell me what the hell it is you're running from…"

"I can't."

"It's Young, isn't it? Or Z, or whatever the hell he's calling himself these days. But, Julie, he can't hurt you. I won't *let him* hurt you. Just give me a chance—I'll expose him and he'll end up behind bars. He can't hurt you from prison."

"He can hurt me from anywhere."

"How? Jesus, how the hell can he do anything to you? Jones, he's a criminal. You were a victim. You got out alive. Even if he exposed you as having been in that compound, the public would celebrate that, not crucify you. You'd be a hero, for God's sake."

She swallowed hard, looking toward the car where Dawn waited. It was running, and Dawn was leaning forward, probably picking out a radio station for the rest of their drive. Her blond hair hung over her face. She was so beautiful.

"Jones, are you even listening to me?"

She closed her eyes. "I'm listening. But you're wrong. It isn't exposure or public crucifixion that I'm afraid of, Sean. It's not my career or my reputation I stand to lose."

"Then what is it? What else could he take from you?"

Dawn looked up, met her mother's eyes, and sent her a smile and a wave. Julie's heart twisted in her chest. "The only thing that matters," she said. "I could lose my child, Sean. I could lose Dawnie."

Sean didn't answer right away. Then he said, "I was right, then. Mordecai Young is her father."

"I can't—"

"Goddammit, Jones, talk to me! Stop being so freaking stubborn and let me help you."

She shook her head slowly. "I have to go."

"Jones, don't. Don't, please. I have a lot more to say to you. It won't matter that he's her father. He couldn't possibly try to challenge you for custody given what he's done. It's crazy to think any court in the world would—"

"I'd lose her, Sean. Maybe not to him, but I'd lose her. You don't know everything. I do."

"Then tell me. For God's sake, Julie, give me a chance. After what happened between us last night…"

"What happened between us last night…" She choked on tears. "Sean, it was…it meant something to me. But it doesn't change anything."

"You're a lousy liar, Jones."

"You'd be surprised. I've been lying for years."

"And you're lying now. It changed everything. It changed *me*. Us. I'm damned if I understand how just yet, but I'm goddamn determined to find out. I can't do that if you're not here."

She drew a breath, forced down the emotions rising inside. "It's impossible," she said. "I'm sorry, Sean. I'm so sorry."

"I'm not."

"Goodbye, Sean."

"Wait, you have to know some things. There was a break-in at your house this morning. And Z's apparently left town. Julie, I'm worried about you."

She shivered with dread, then shook her head slowly. "There was nothing in the house that could tell him where we are. But I'd better get moving, just in case."

"Julie—"

She hung up the telephone, resting her forehead against it for just a moment, blinking away tears that had no business being there. Finally, pulling herself together, she straightened up and wiped away her tears with the sleeve of her jacket. She plastered a fake smile on her face for Dawn's sake and went back to the car.

Dawn had several flyers on her lap over the seat belt, which she'd dutifully fastened. "Did you look at any of these, Mom?"

"Hmm?"

"Flyers from that rack in the diner. They're rental cabins

and inns and stuff. Right along the lakes. There are tons of them. We can take our pick.''

Julie glanced sideways as she pulled the car out onto the road and started northward again. She was going to have to tell her daughter the truth. She didn't want to, but Dawn was old enough, mature enough, to handle it. And she had a right to know. ''Tell you what,'' she said. ''You pick.''

''Really? Any one I want?''

''Any one you want.''

Dawn smiled. ''Did we bring a camera? If I come back home without pictures, Kayla will kill me!''

''We can pick up some of those disposable ones, once we find the perfect spot,'' Julie said. ''So where will it be?''

''Gosh, the pressure.'' Dawn flipped through flyers one after the other, unfolding them and skimming their contents. Finally she picked one up with a flourish. ''This one. 'Deluxe private cabins with full kitchen and bath, each with its own hot tub and breathtaking view of Blue Mountain Lake.'''

''Sounds perfect. Hot tubs.''

Dawn read on, relaying information. ''They have boat rentals and dinner cruises, hiking trails, horseback riding. It says the cabins are 'widely spaced for maximum privacy.' Not too shabby.''

''Not at all too shabby. How far is it?''

She glanced at the little map on the flyer, then yanked her road atlas from the dashboard. ''Looks like about twenty miles ahead. We go left where Route 28 joins 30, and it's another few miles from there.''

''Then that's the one.'' Julie licked her lips and glanced at her daughter, her Dawn. ''Dawnie?''

''Hmm.''

She had to do this. She had to. ''When we get there and

get settled in…we need to have a long talk. About—about everything that's been going on.''

Dawn looked serious and maybe a little bit frightened. She slid her hand over her mom's on the wheel. ''It's about me, isn't it?''

''About you, but not because of you. It's important to keep that distinction straight in your mind.'' Julie sighed. ''It's way past time for this discussion. I just—I just—I guess I'm scared.''

''I can handle it, Mom. I promise.''

''I know you can. I'm just afraid…it'll change things. Between us.''

''Nothing could do that.''

Julie tried to believe that.

''It's pretty big, this thing you have to tell me. Isn't it?''

Julie nodded. ''Pretty big.''

Dawn nodded. ''You think I won't love you anymore, once you tell me.''

Julie snapped her head around sharply. ''No. I just think you'll be very angry that I didn't tell you a whole lot sooner.''

Dawn nodded slowly. They drove in silence for a long while. Dawn found a radio station she liked and cranked the music up a little. But she seemed pensive and worried.

After ten minutes she reached up and turned the music down again. She looked at Julie, and she said, ''I'm adopted, aren't I?''

16

Sean couldn't remember the last time he'd felt this bad. No, he could remember one time. The day of that raid, when all those innocent kids had burned to death or been shot down at the Young Believers' compound, while he sat safely under cover, taping it all for posterity. The guilt, the horror, the unending nightmare of that day—that was the only place in his memory where he could find this kind of gut-deep ache.

But that had been different. He hadn't known any of those people. With Julie and Dawn, it was personal. And there was one other difference. With them, there was still hope. Because he was good at what he did. He was good, and it really didn't matter whether anyone else in the news biz ever acknowledged that. He knew it. And because of it, he was going to find Julie Jones and her daughter, and he was going to see them safe again.

When his cell phone rang again, he'd been driving back to WSNY. He'd pulled off onto the shoulder of the road. By the second ring, he was yanking a pen from his pocket, and searching for something to write on. It rang a third time, and he gave up the search, picked up the cell phone to read the number that appeared on its tiny screen and scribbled it on his hand. He was in a state of near panic, fearing that the caller was Jones and that she would hang up before he answered. It rang a fourth time, and he hit the button, brought the phone to his ear, said "Hello" and prayed it would be her. And it was.

He'd expected the sound of her voice to get to him, but not quite the way it did. He got choked up, and dammit, he *never* got choked up. But he found himself wishing she was closer, wishing he could touch her, hating that he had to settle instead for a five-minute conversation.

His efforts at talking her down hadn't worked. He didn't think she'd taken his warning about Nathan Z being on the lam seriously at all. When she hung up, the finality of the click felt like a bullet in the chest. But he stiffened his jaw, told himself it was far from over. He couldn't talk her down. Fine. He would just have to fall back on his skills. His ability to track things down, to find the truth in people's garbage, to uncover the lies they told. Jones had been telling lies. She'd admitted as much. And those lies were the key to what was driving her away. He was good at exposing people's lies. Now he was going to expose hers.

He dialed the number back, but there was no answer, so he phoned the most unscrupulous P.I. he knew, one of his many valuable connections. He'd hired Tommy Warren many times in the past, and the man had always come through. His one fault was that he would sell your information to anyone who came along and offered him more money than you'd given him to keep quiet.

In this case, that didn't matter. Time was what mattered.

"I need you to track down a phone number for me," he told Tommy, skipping the usual greetings and smalltalk. "A pay phone, I think. And I need it yesterday."

"Shoot."

Sean read the number from his hand into the phone. Then he drove back to the station and gave his boss the okay to answer his own calls again.

"You heard from Julie, didn't you?" Westcott asked.

"Yeah, I did."

"Where the hell is she?"

Sean pressed his lips together. He wanted Jones back, and his chances were better if he made an effort to see to it she still had a job to come back to. "She's in trouble, Allan. I don't know what kind, exactly, and I don't know where she is…yet. But I promise you, I'm going to find out, and then I'm going to fix it."

Westcott's brows went up. "Fix it?"

Sean nodded.

"You two, uh, have gotten past your animosity, I take it?"

"Right now I'm the best friend she has. I don't know if she knows it yet. But she will."

Westcott smiled and slapped Sean on the shoulder. "Do what you need to. I don't want to lose her."

As he walked away, Sean muttered, "Neither do I." Then he went to his own office and placed a call to Nathan Z's PR person, wheedling and bluffing until he got the make and model of the man's car out of her. He drove a late-model black Jaguar. She flat out refused to give him the plate number.

Black Jag. So Julie had been right. It *had* been him following Dawn that day.

Sean wanted to throttle the son of a bitch. Hell. What to do next? He couldn't go hunting for Jones until he had a starting place, at the very least. Okay, then. He would just wait here for his P.I. friend to call with the address. Until then… He swallowed hard, wishing to Christ he knew where to begin looking for Julie and Dawn.

He was afraid for them. Whoever had been in their house, he realized with a sick feeling in his stomach, might very well already know where they were headed. And he was afraid for himself, because he wasn't sure he could handle it if anything happened to those two.

Dawn's question shocked Julie to the soul, but she should have been expecting it. Dawn was sharp, savvy, too smart to be fooled for very long. She'd hinted that she had an inkling of this in the past. Hell, she would have to be blind not to have had an inkling. She was as pale and blond as Julie was dark and bronze. But she'd never come right out and asked.

Julie didn't answer right away. She pulled the car off the road, killed the engine and fought to control her emotions.

"I've suspected it for a long time now, Mom."

"Why?"

Dawn shrugged. "I don't know. The fact that we look nothing alike. I mean, not even things that should be passed down. And then there were the things you told me about my father. That he was a high school boy who was killed in a car accident before you ever told him you were pregnant. That his family was ultrareligious and telling them about me would only have made them feel worse. That you had no living relatives of your own." She shrugged. "I just started adding it up. I've been trying to work up the courage to come out and ask for a while now."

Licking her lips, Julie met her daughter's eyes. "I didn't give birth to you. But I was there when you were born. I delivered you, Dawnie. I was the first person to hold you. To feed you. To bathe you. Your…mother…" She had to force the word out. It was not easy to refer to another woman as her daughter's mother. "She was my best friend."

"Was?"

"She died when you were only a few months old. The last thing she asked me to do was to take care of you."

"And you agreed."

"It wasn't even a question, Dawn. I loved you as if you were my own already. I did from the moment you opened your little eyes and looked into mine. Lizzie and I, we used to say you were our baby. Both of ours. That's how we thought of you."

"Her name...was Lizzie?" Dawn smiled through gathering tears.

Julie nodded. "She was wonderful, Dawn. A wonderful, smart, beautiful woman. She loved you so much."

"What was her last name?"

Lowering her head, Julie sighed. "We never shared last names. We were both runaways, and...last names were something we avoided using at all."

"You were runaways?"

Julie nodded.

"How old?"

"I was seventeen. I think she was about the same."

Dawn seemed to absorb that slowly, to let it sink in.

"You look like her," Julie said. "Sometimes, when I look at you, I think I'm seeing her again."

"I wish I'd known her." Then she shook her head slowly. "God, seventeen. I'll be seventeen next summer. I can't even imagine having a baby—much less taking care of someone else's."

"You were never someone else's," Julie insisted. "We were like sisters, Lizzie and I. I loved you, Dawn. I would have fought anyone who tried to take you away. No one had to force me to take care of you."

Tears welling in her big eyes, Dawn said, "Oh, Mom, how could you think I would feel differently about you because of this?"

Julie stroked Dawn's hair, then pulled her closer and held

her. "Because I should have told you sooner. Because you had every right to know."

Dawn nodded. "You should have told me sooner." She returned Julie's fierce hug. "And now that you've started, Mom, you have to tell me the rest."

Julie stiffened.

Dawn pulled away and looked her in the eyes. "All of it, Mom. I know there's more. I know all this has something to do with what's been going on. And you have to tell me. No matter what it is, it's about me, and you have to tell me."

Julie nodded, wiping tears from her eyes. A car passed them, a dark car with tinted windows, enough like the car Dawn had described following her before that it reminded Julie how exposed they were out here on the roadside. "I'll tell you all of it, honey." She put her own car into gear and pulled back onto the road, picking up speed as she went. "But let's get to that cabin first, okay?"

"Okay. But as soon as we do…"

She never finished the sentence. The car that had just passed them slammed on its brakes and spun in a complete circle in the road.

"Dawnie?"

"Mom?"

"Honey, did you tell anyone we were leaving before we left this morning?"

The black car was speeding back toward them. God, it was going to hit them head-on!

"Oh, God. I'm sorry, Mom. I did. I e-mailed Kayla. Mom, look out!"

Julie jerked the wheel to avoid the oncoming car and hit the brakes, but the car skidded out of control. And then Julie lost all sense of direction as her world spun around, to the sounds of crushing metal, shattering glass and her daughter's scream.

* * *

Sean felt a full-body shudder ripple through him for no good reason the instant before his desk phone rang and he grabbed it.

"Got that number for you, MacKenzie. It came from a diner called Jenny's, up in the Adirondacks."

"Address?"

"The address will tell you nothing. I got directions instead. Take the thruway to 365 and cut through Rome. From there, take 28 North into the Adirondacks. Start looking once you see Raquette Lake. It'll be on the right-hand side, on the stretch between Raquette and Blue Mountain Lake. It's only a twelve- or thirteen-mile stretch. You should be able to locate it."

Sean yanked one of the maps from his top drawer. He kept a bunch of them, as most reporters did, just in case he had to cover a story in an area unfamiliar to him. He wrestled the map of the Adirondack Region open and traced the route with his fingertip. "That's gotta be over a hundred miles," he said.

"Yeah. Take you two hours."

"The hell it will." Sean hung up the phone, refolded the map incorrectly and headed outside to his Porsche.

Dawn lifted her head and tried to take stock. Everything hurt. Moving hurt more.

She pressed a hand to her forehead, hissed and pulled it away again. Blinking, she looked around her. Her lap was full of tiny bits of shattered glass and coated in powder from the deflated air bag. She seemed to be at an odd angle, as if the nose of the car were pointing downward, while the back was up. Her seat belt was the only thing that kept her from falling forward against the dash.

Then she caught sight of her mom, slumped over the steering wheel, and it all came clear. The car, the wreck. She reached out a hand, touching her mother's shoulder, shaking her gently. "Mom? Are you okay?"

Her mother made no reply. Dawn shook her a little harder, realizing that once again her mother had forgotten to buckle up. Her throat closed up tight. "Mom?" There was still no response, and Dawn gently pushed the hair away from her mother's face, the better to see her. Her head was bleeding.

God, she was hurt—they needed help. Dawn had to find help. She tore her attention from her mother to look beyond the car. It wasn't easy to see through the spiderwebbed windshield, but her own side window was completely demolished, probably thanks to the tree limb sticking in through it. The car was nosedown at a sharp angle. Swallowing hard, Dawn tried to open her door, but the tree was blocking it. She looked again at her mother, tried again to rouse her, and battled the tears and panic that were trying hard to take over. Her mom needed help, and there was no one but Dawn to get it for her.

She freed herself from her seat belt and climbed over the seat, into the back of the car. That door opened without resistance, so she got out, shocked when she took a look around. The car was partway down a steep wooded hillside and could easily have plummeted a lot further if not for the tree that had stopped it. The nose of the car was caved in against the trunk of a giant pine. That tree had probably saved their lives.

Turning, Dawn looked upward, to where the road must be. It surprised her how far away it was, but she almost sagged in relief when she saw someone standing up there, looking down at them.

She cried out, waving her arms. "Help! We need help down here!"

The person—whoever it was—started down the hill, slipping and sliding a lot of the way. As he drew closer, she saw that he was completely bald and dressed all in white. It didn't take him long to reach her, and only then did Dawn gasp in surprise and relief. Nathan Z himself smiled at her, like an angel sent from heaven to rescue her. It was a reassuring smile meant to offer comfort, and it worked.

"Thank God you're all right," he said. "When I saw the accident, I was afraid..." He looked toward the car. "Your mother?"

"She's hurt. Badly. I can't wake her."

He shook his head slowly. "She shouldn't have jerked the wheel and slammed her brakes like that. All she had to do was pull over."

"Please, do you have a cell phone or—"

"In the car," he said. "Come on. Hurry." He took her arm, helped her along as he started back up the hillside.

"I don't want to leave her!"

"We'll call for help and come right back to her," he promised. "They'll want your names and information about your mom, and it'll be faster if you can give it to them yourself."

She looked back toward the car, and the tears flowed this time.

"Trust me, child. She's in the hands of spirit. She'll be all right. As long as we do our part. She needs our help."

"Couldn't you...you know, do something for her. Make sure she'll be all right until we get back?" She blinked through her tears at the man.

His lips pressed tightly together, but then he sighed and nodded. He moved closer to the car, wrenched open the driver's door and put his hands on Julie's head. Then he tipped his own head back and closed his eyes. "Be well," he whispered.

"Please, please, please be okay," Dawn added.

Z backed away from the car, closing the door again; then he returned to Dawn. "She'll be okay. I promise you."

Nodding, Dawn believed him. "I promise, Mom, I'll be right back." Then, with Z's help, she made her way back up the hill, using saplings to help pull herself along. "We have to call the police, too," she told him. "Some maniac ran us off the road." The same maniac who'd been following her the other day. That same black Jag, with the custom chrome wheels. She'd been so sure she was only being paranoid when she had thought she'd seen the same car earlier that day. There were probably lots of black Jags around. But she should have known.

The man clambered up the last few steps to the roadside, turned and reached back down for her. "Come on, you're almost there. Are you sure you're not hurt?"

"A little bump on the head. It's Mom I'm worried about." She let him take her hand, and he pulled her up easily. Dawn brushed the bark and dirt from her hands, took a single step toward the waiting car, then stopped in her tracks.

The black Jag sat there, waiting.

She shot her gaze to Nathan Z, her eyes wide and confused. "It was you?"

"I don't know what you mean. Get in the car, Dawn. Sit down and rest, and we'll place that phone call." He stood near the passenger door, holding it open for her.

She hadn't told him her name! Dawn moved backward, glancing frantically up and down the road, seeing no other traffic, no buildings, no help. "I don't know what's going on here, but I'm not getting in that car with you. You're the one who's been following me. The one who ran us off the road. I don't understand. Are you some kind of maniac or what?''

"Now, Dawn," Z said softly. "That's no way to talk to your father."

Shock hit her like a tidal wave, and Dawn backed away, shaking her head from side to side. "No. No, you aren't…''

Nathan Z calmly pulled a gun from his pocket and pointed it at her. "Get in the car like a good girl. I promise this will all make sense to you once I have the chance to explain.''

Julie felt something stinging her eyes, blinked them open and tried to wipe the sting away. Her hand came away bloody. She lifted her head, blinking her vision into focus, and it all came rushing back. The black car. The accident.

"Dawn!" She scanned the car but didn't see her daughter. The back door was open, though. "Dawnie!" Julie wrenched her own door open and clambered out of the car, but the second she put weight on her left foot, it seemed to crumple underneath her, and she landed hard on the ground. Then she sat there, panting against the pain, realizing something was wrong with her foot, or, more precisely, her ankle. She tugged the leg of her jeans up just a little but couldn't see beyond the cross trainers and ankle socks. Gently, every move causing excruciating pain, she loosened the laces of the shoe and took it off. Then she peeled off the sock. God, it hurt.

The ankle was swollen to twice its normal size and mottled with deep purple. She closed her eyes and wondered how it had swollen up so fast. That thought made her turn her wrist to look at her watch.

God! She must have been lying unconscious in the car for more than an hour.

She looked around as panic set in. "Dawnie! Where are you? Dawn!"

The only replies to her calls were the sudden flapping movement of startled birds and the echo of her own voice from the steep mountains all around her. Beyond that, there was nothing. A hundred feet above her, she saw the guardrails that marked the side of the road. Much further below her, a little stream meandered, vanishing in thick forest, then appearing again.

Where the hell was her daughter?

Swallowing hard, she told herself that Dawn had probably been uninjured. She'd been wearing her seat belt. The air bag had deployed. Julie hadn't fastened her belt, and her own air bag hadn't been reset since her last fender bender. Dawn must have been unable to rouse her mother and gone for help. That must be it.

But deep down, Julie feared something far worse. She'd seen that car, the black car that had run them off the road. The cat that was its hood ornament. A Jaguar. It had to be Mordecai Young. It had to be. He'd promised he would come and take Dawn if Julie didn't hand her over. What if that was exactly what he had done? Run them off the road, stuck around to survey the damage he'd wrought and then taken Dawn away.

Julie looked at her watch again. One hour and ten minutes. The bastard had a head start. But she would catch up. No way was he taking her baby from her.

Julie used the still-open car door to pull herself upright and got back onto the front seat. She found her cell phone on the floor, reached for it and turned it on. And oddly, the only person she could think of to call, besides nine-one-one, was Sean. Even more oddly, there wasn't a doubt in her mind that he would come just as fast as he could. It wasn't even a question.

The phone beeped once, and she looked at the screen. No Signal glowed up at her.

"Dammit!" She threw the phone down, reminding herself that there were no cell towers permitted within the Adirondack Preserve. Too harmful to the wildlife. Which was why she'd used the pay phone to call her boss in the first place.

Fine, she would just find a phone. She would find a phone, and she would get help, and then she would track down Mordecai Young. After that, God help him. She might not have felt capable of murder before, but she felt willing and able now. He'd pushed her too far. And if he hurt Dawnie…

"No. He won't. He won't hurt her. She's his daughter. Why would he hurt her?"

Julie got out of the car, hitting the trunk release as she did, and then hopping on one foot to the rear. She leaned over, tugging open a suitcase and rummaging through it for something to use to wrap her foot. She would never make it up the hillside if she couldn't protect it somehow. Settling on several pairs of nylons, she dropped to the ground again, wrapping them around and around her ankle so tightly that she bit her lip until she tasted blood. Layer upon layer, she built a soft but firm nest for the injured ankle, knotted it off and finally got herself upright again. Gingerly she lowered the foot, put some weight on it. Pain shot up her leg, and she cried out.

"Okay, okay," she told herself, breathless, dizzy with pain. "Just think." She looked around her and spotted a tree limb lying on the ground. It was as tall as she was and a couple of inches in diameter. After hopping over to it, she picked it up. It was solid.

Good. She nodded firmly and turned to face the steep climb. "This is going to hurt like hell, Jones," she told herself, using Sean's name for her without bothering to analyze why. "But losing Dawn would hurt a lot more. Remember that." Grating her teeth, she started forward, distracting herself from the pain by trying to recall the last inhabited building they'd passed on the way up here. Sadly, the last one she remembered was the diner. It had to be at least a few miles back.

Halfway up the hill, she stepped down onto a rock that slid out from under her injured foot, twisting the ankle so hard she screamed in agony. The sound echoed around her, and then dizziness closed in. She clung to the hillside, fighting to stay conscious. She wouldn't give in to the pain. She couldn't. Drumming up every bit of strength, she forced herself to push on, growling with the effort, with the determination, like a mother lion in defense of a cub. Inch by blindingly painful inch, she clawed her way up that hillside, and finally she half climbed, half fell over the broken guardrails onto the road's grassy shoulder. She lay there for a moment, waiting for the pain to ebb, waiting for the strength to return, for her heart to stop pounding and her lungs to catch up with her body's demands for oxygen.

The pain didn't ebb, and her heart didn't slow, and she didn't catch her breath. Precious minutes were ticking by. She clutched her makeshift crutch in her hand, pushed herself upright with it and started limping back toward the diner.

"Where are you taking me?" Dawn asked softly.

Z had a way of looking at her that gave her the absolute creeps. It was almost...adoring. But he was a stranger to her. He had no business looking at her that way.

"To one of my houses," he said. "You're going to love

it there, honey. It's a mansion, really. Pool, hot tub, we even have our own lake.'' He reached across the car as if to stroke her hair, but Dawn ducked away from his touch.

He let his hand hang in the air for a moment, his eyes looking wounded. ''You're not even giving me a chance.''

''A chance to do what? I don't even know you.''

''A chance,'' he said, his voice soft, ''to be your father. I am, you know.''

''No, I don't know. I don't know any such thing.'' She lowered her head. ''You used to be…one of my heroes. Now you're nothing. Less than nothing.''

''I'm your father. We can have blood tests done to confirm it, if it would help you to accept me, Dawn.'' Then he smiled slowly. ''Dawn. That's not your real name, you know.''

Dawn blinked at him. She was afraid, not only for herself, but for her mother, lying back there over that drop-off, unconscious or worse. She wasn't even sure anyone could see the car from the road. What if no one found her? What if…?

''When you were born, your mother named you Sunshine.''

Dawn frowned, looking at him. ''That's not a name.''

''Sure it is. We called you Sunny.'' He smiled softly. ''We were inseparable back then. I spent so much time with you. And when you would look up at me, you had these eyes that seemed so much wiser than they should. Like you knew me.''

She licked her lips, lowered her head. ''How can I believe anything you tell me?''

He frowned, tipping his head sideways. ''I don't—''

''How can I trust a word you say when you kidnapped me at gunpoint after you ran our car over that cliff?''

"That wasn't supposed to happen. She shouldn't have lost control."

"It doesn't matter. What matters is that you left my mother back there, hurt and alone."

"She's not your mother."

Dawn jerked as if he'd slapped her. "She is. To me she is. She's the only mother I've ever known."

He glanced at her. Dawn let the tears come, and he reacted. "Don't cry, Sunny. Please, don't cry. I don't want you to be unhappy."

"Then call someone to help my mother. Please." His lips thinned, and she thought his anger was returning. "If you don't, I'll never see you as anything other than a man who left someone I love to die. I'll never believe you really tried to heal her back there. I'll never believe anything you say to me."

"Sunny—"

"But if you do send help, I'll believe you," she said, her voice softer, calmer. "I'll listen to what you have to say. I'll even try to keep an open mind. I promise, I will."

He glanced her way again, considering.

"I'll know that you really do try to live by the things you write in your books. That you aren't a fake. Things like—you only get good if you give good. And that doing harm to others will draw harmful energy right back to yourself."

His brows went up, and he looked surprised. "You've read them?"

"All of them," she told him. "Every single one. And I watch your show, too."

He smiled. He didn't look at all frightening when he smiled. He had a pleasant face, round eyes that were the deepest darkest brown she'd ever seen, and a shaved head.

He could look solemn or menacing, but right now, he looked kind. He looked like the man she'd once admired.

"All right," he said. "We'll call as soon as we can get reception on the cell." He nodded toward where the cell phone hung from its holder on the panel. "You keep track, let me know when we're in range, okay?"

She forced herself to return his smile. "Thank you."

"Uh-uh. Thank you, what?"

She fought down the sarcastic reply that leaped into her throat and said what she knew he wanted her to say. "Thank you, Father."

He reached toward her, cupped her head with one hand. "I've been waiting so long to hear that. God, you have no idea how it's been. Searching for you. Missing you."

To Dawn's utter surprise, a tear welled up in his eye. He turned away, then focused on the road, dropping his hand away from her.

Dawn reached for the cell phone and waited for a signal to appear.

Julie hobbled back along the road for an amount of time impossible to measure. It seemed endless. Step by agonizing step, weight on the right foot, weight on the branch, drag the left foot ahead. When she stumbled and put pressure on the damaged foot, the pain set off fireworks in her head. She prayed a vehicle would come along and give her a lift, but none did. This place was deserted. The fall foliage was long past its peak, and the hunting season hadn't yet begun. They'd seen almost no traffic on the drive up. Almost. With the exception of one black Jaguar.

The wind was colder than it had been before, stiffer. It smelled of pines and winter. She hadn't tasted winter on the air at home. It came earlier here. She shivered and hugged herself.

She had no idea how long she'd been walking when she spotted a trailhead off the roadside that led down a hill and into the woods. She paused on a hunch, went to the wooden structure that held a map of the trail and saw that it was what she'd hoped it was. A shortcut to the diner. While the road looped out and around, the trail went straight down, through the steep woods, meeting the road again at the far side. It would save a couple of miles.

She took the trail, forcing herself to walk as quickly as she possibly could, blocking out the pain by telling herself that she had to get to Dawn. She had to save her.

When the little diner came into sight way off in the distance, it was like seeing a candle in the darkness. She forced herself to move faster.

17

Sean started looking for the diner five miles before he spotted it, panicking at the thought that he might have passed it. When he finally saw the sign up ahead, swinging in the wind that seemed to be picking up, he sighed in relief. He wouldn't find Julie and Dawn still there, he knew that. It had been hours since Julie's call. But maybe someone there would remember them mentioning where they were going or where they planned to stay, or even so much as what direction they'd gone. Anything, any clue, would help.

He pulled into the driveway and saw a woman standing at—no, leaning against—the pay phone, and the shape of her, the color of the ponytail that was barely holding together, made his heart contract. The hairband had slid low, and there were as many dark locks flying loose in the wind as there were held within its confines.

He stopped the car, got out and started toward her. "Jones?"

She didn't turn. She was leaning against the side of the phone booth as if she could barely stand, holding the telephone to her ear, whispering adamantly into it, though the words were carried away by the wind. He couldn't hear them. She wore jeans that were splattered with dark stains, a denim jacket and a tennis shoe on one foot, but the other was shoeless, wrapped in some kind of bandage. A tall stick leaned near her side.

He moved closer.

"Dammit, MacKenzie, pick up, pick up," she whispered at the phone.

Sean put a hand on her shoulder. "Jones?"

She swung her head around and just stopped, the phone in midair, her eyes fixed to his. He winced at the glistening blood in her hair, the smears of it on one side of her face, and the front of her shirt and jacket.

"Christ, Jones, what happened?"

The telephone fell from her hand, and she sagged against him. He wrapped his arms around her. "All right, easy now. Easy. I've got you."

"You're here."

"Right here, Jones."

"I never thought I'd be so glad to see *you*, MacKenzie."

"Yeah, go figure." Sean gathered her up, carried her back to his car, lowered her gently onto the passenger seat. Then he bent over her, pushing her hair away from her face, better to see the gaping cut on her head. "What happened?"

"Dawn," she said. "We have to get Dawn."

"We will, I promise, we will. But you have to tell me what happened, Jones."

She closed her eyes, licked her lips. "It was Mordecai. It had to be."

"What was Mordecai?"

"The car, the black car. He must have followed us. Oh, God, Dawnie." She started to sob but fought it, and her breath hitched and bucked. It was difficult to make sense of her words. "He...the black car...I tried to swerve...lost control."

He thought the injury to her head must be serious enough to be giving her trouble. Her speech was a little slurred, in addition to being broken, and her head kept starting to nod, as if she were going to pass out, but then she snapped it up again.

"Stay with me, Jones. Come on, tell me what happened. Where is Dawn?"

"The black car...ran us off the road. I hit my head." She shook her head slowly, and he could see her searching her mind. "When I woke up, she was gone. She was gone."

Sean clasped her shoulders, held her firm and tried to bank the horror rising in his own belly. God, if that son of a bitch had Dawn... He shook the thought away. Jones was probably having enough nightmarish thoughts for the both of them. She didn't need him having more. "We'll find her. We'll get her back." He glanced back toward the pay phone. "Did you call the police?"

She lifted her eyes to his. "I called *you*."

"Okay. Okay." She needed to be in a hospital. "Stay here, all right?" He straightened away from her, but she grabbed his hand, looking panicky. It yanked his heart into a knot, and he knelt again, touched her face. "Relax, Jones. I'm not leaving you—especially not with my keys in the switch. I'm just going to the phone to call the police. It'll just be a minute."

"And then we'll go after Dawn?" The tears brimming in her eyes were like white-hot blades driven into his soul. This thing between them—it was way beyond what he'd been thinking it was.

"Yes. Just let me call for help, and then we'll go find her."

She nodded hard. "He—he—he won't hurt her. He's...he's her father."

"I know."

She let go of his hand. He had trouble dragging his eyes away from her, but he forced himself, ran to the pay phone

and dialed 9-1-1, reporting as clearly and concisely as he
could that a car had been deliberately run off the road, and
that one of the passengers, a sixteen-year-old girl, had been
abducted by the other driver. He added a solid description
of Dawn, of the black Jag and of the perpetrator; he told
them where to find the wrecked car, and that he would be
waiting at the nearest hospital if they needed more information. He kept his eyes on Julie the entire time he spoke.
She kept hers riveted to him, though they kept falling
closed. The 9-1-1 operator insisted he stay on the line. He
apologized and hung up on her, then dropped in a few more
quarters, and dialed Lieutenant Cassie Jackson's cell phone
number.

She picked up on the third ring.

"It's MacKenzie," he said. "I've got to make this fast,
so pay attention. I'm with Julie Jones. She's been injured
and her daughter's been kidnapped."

"*What?*"

"Your suspect is Nathan Z."

"The TV guru? Why the hell would *he* want to kidnap
Julie Jones's kid?"

"It's complicated, and we're short on time. He's driving
a late-model black Jaguar. I didn't get the plate number.
He forced Jones off the road, then took Dawn and left."

"Where did this happen?"

"Two hours north of Syracuse." He repeated the same
directions he'd used to get there. "You'll find us at the
nearest hospital, though I have no idea where that will be
yet. We've already notified the local authorities."

"Okay, okay." He got the feeling she was scribbling
notes as he spoke. "Look, this is good. This is enough to
activate the Amber Alert System. If they haven't done it
already, I'll do it myself. You're sure this is an abduction?"

He wasn't. Neither was Julie. But he would gladly take

the consequences if he turned out to be wrong. "I'm sure," he lied.

"Okay, then. I'm on it. How about Julie Jones? How badly is she hurt?"

He looked back at the car, realizing he'd become involved in his conversation and had taken his eyes off Julie. She lay limp in the seat, her head slumped to one side, eyes closed. "Shit," he said, hung up the phone and ran back to the car.

"Jones? Come on now, snap out of it."

She didn't respond, but she did have a pulse, and she was breathing. He heard the creak of a screen door and turned to see someone coming out of the diner, a man in a red-and-black plaid shirt, and worn jeans.

"You, mister," Sean called. "Where's the nearest hospital?"

The man frowned, looked from Sean to Julie, then widened his eyes and dug a set of keys from his pocket. "Follow me," he said. "It'll be faster. She looks in a bad way."

Sean nodded and got behind the wheel as the man in plaid climbed into a pickup truck and made it roar to life. The pickup took off, and Sean followed, his eyes straying from the road to Julie's still face far too often, even while his mind wondered what poor Dawn was going through right now. God, she must be frightened to death.

Ms. Marcum had been patiently answering all of Lieutenant Jackson's questions about Dawn and Julie Jones when Jackson's cell phone rang. The lieutenant frowned and picked it up, then listened as Sean MacKenzie told her the most unlikely tale she'd ever heard in ten years on the force.

Ms. Marcum rose up from her chair behind her desk,

overhearing Cassie's side of the conversation. She pressed a hand to her chest. "Dawn's been kidnapped?"

Cassie gave her a grim nod, then went on with the conversation. It was a damn good thing she knew MacKenzie well enough to doubt he would make any of this up or she never would have believed it. What it did to her case, and her suspicions about Julie Jones, she still wasn't sure. "Where did this happen?" she asked.

As she listened to Sean's reply, she shot a look at the desk that stood between her and the teacher she'd been questioning. Reading that look, Ms. Marcum handed her a pad and a pen, and watched her scribble down a set of driving directions.

Jackson dropped the pen and tore off the top sheet when she finished writing. "This is enough to activate the Amber Alert System. If they haven't done it already, I'll do it myself. You're sure this is an abduction?" Listening to the reply, she nodded rapidly. "Okay, then. I'm on it. How about Julie Jones? How badly is she hurt?" She waited a moment, then she frowned at the phone. "MacKenzie? Hello?" Swearing softly, she disconnected.

"Is there anything I can do to help?" Ms. Marcum asked as Cassie shoved her hair back and turned to go.

"No. I..." She sighed. "Listen, maybe it would be best not to say too much about this just yet. No more than you see released by the press, anyway. Other than that, Ms. Marcum, the only thing you can really do is wait. And...pray."

She walked out of the office, already punching another number onto the keypad of her cell phone, speaking crisply into it as she paused in the hallway outside the door. "I need Amber Alert activated immediately. Here are the details."

From the corner of her mind that wasn't completely distracted, she heard Ms. Marcum on another telephone, saying, "I'm sorry, Principal Slocum, but I need to go home for the rest of the day."

Dawn stared out the side window at the trees and hills that flew past. She didn't dare face the man, because her thoughts were racing faster than the scenery, and she was sure they must show in her face.

She had to get away from him. That much she knew. Sitting quiet and meek and letting him take her where he wanted would only get her into deeper trouble. You didn't get to be sixteen years old with a mom like hers and not learn things like that. Basic survival skills for "just-in-case" scenarios she'd never believed would happen to her in a million years.

First and foremost, get away. Never let them take you to the secondary crime scene.

He was driving too fast for her to jump out of the car without getting herself dead. He'd also locked the doors with the button on his side, and she wasn't sure she could unlock hers. Besides those things, she was so terrified that even thinking about an escape attempt had her nearly paralyzed. For the first time she understood why girls went with their abductors to isolated places. It was so much harder to fight than it was to just go along and hope for the best.

He didn't seem insane, she thought, glancing sideways at him when he wasn't looking. He didn't seem dangerous. He seemed kind of...sad.

She lifted a hand to rub the back of her neck.

He noticed and sent her a searching look. "You're not hurt, are you?"

"My neck's getting a little stiff."

"The accident," he said. He shook his head slowly and

then suddenly slapped his hand against the steering wheel, making her jump. "That wasn't supposed to happen."

Frowning, Dawn glanced at him again. She couldn't seem to resist looking at him when he wasn't looking back, wondering if what he said could possibly be true—that he was her birth father. She searched for some resemblance in his face but failed to see one.

She couldn't seem to meet his eyes at all or to hold his gaze even briefly.

He was staring at her then, intense and apparently worried. "I was only trying to force Jewel onto the shoulder. She was supposed to pull over and stop, not jerk the wheel and lose control."

"I believe you," Dawn said. "Mom's a terrible driver. She always has been."

He lowered his head, shaking it slowly. "I never meant to hurt you. I would never do anything that would hurt you."

That puzzled her, truly puzzled her. "Taking me from my mom hurts me. You must know that."

"Jewel is not your mother."

She bit back the angry, sarcastic reply that leaped automatically to her lips. It wouldn't be a good idea to piss him off.

"Besides," he said, "the pain of leaving her is pain that comes for a reason. For the greater good. And it's in keeping with God's plan for you, Dawn. Jewel…she'll understand that. In time."

She drew a deep breath, forced her words to come out calmly, quietly. "You…keep calling her Jewel."

He looked at her, his lips pulling into a very slight smile, a nostalgic one. "That's the name she used when she came to live with me. Your mother was Lizzie, and your name was Sunshine. I was known as Mordecai back then. Mordecai Young.''

Dawn almost choked. The name Mordecai Young was as well-known as that of David Koresh. She racked her memory, wished she'd paid more attention in social studies class when they'd covered local history. There had been some kind of compound or something, not all that far away. And a raid that ended in disaster. A lot of people had died. She thought Mordecai Young had been one of them.

"Lizzie was so sweet. She never would have taken you away from me without Jewel's influence on her. But then there was the raid…'' He fell silent, shaking his head sadly.

"The raid?'' she asked, just to keep him talking.

He nodded. "We lived on a farm, all together, sharing the wealth and the work.''

"Like a commune?''

"Yes. A spiritual family. The Young Believers. All we wanted was to be left alone, but the government has its own ideas about nonconformists. They sent in soldiers.''

She frowned, certain there had been more to the story. Hadn't there been illegal weapons and drugs involved? And weren't most of the residents underage girls? She thought so. Probably best not to ask, though.

She looked at the cell phone. "We have a signal now. Can I call 9-1-1 for my mom?''

He looked angry, but only briefly—and probably because she'd referred to Julie as her mom again. "Wait just a second, first.'' He flicked on the radio, started changing channels, then paused when he heard a deep voiced anchor in midstory.

…is sixteen years old, five feet eight inches tall, with long, black hair and blue eyes. The suspect is a thirty-nine-year-old white male, with a shaved head and no facial hair, piercing brown eyes, six-two, one hundred seventy pounds.

*The two were last seen in a black late-model Jaguar with
N.Y. plates, traveling in the Adirondack region along Route
28. If you see anything, please call 555-AMBER. Do not
phone tips in to this station. This Amber Alert will be repeated frequently throughout the day and for as often as
necessary until Dawn Jones is found.*

He clicked off the radio. "Well, I guess we don't need
to call anyone. Jewel survived, and she's apparently done
everything but call out the National Guard."

"You must have known she would." She tipped her
head to the side. "You did know, didn't you?"

"Of course I knew."

She licked her lips. "But you didn't kill her. Even
though you had a gun."

He pursed his lips. "No, Sunny, I didn't kill her. I—I
tried to heal her, in fact. It wasn't part of the Higher
Power's plan for her to die. I only act in accordance with
spirit. Don't think that means I would hesitate to kill, or to
die, if that were what the universe wanted of me. I let her
live because our Source told me to."

Dawn tried not to let the chill in her blood cause her to
shiver visibly. She said, "How did God tell you? Did you
hear a voice?"

"No. I saw a sign. When I first looked down at the car,
where it lay, the sun hit the broken glass, and it made a
rainbow that arced right over the car, right over Jewel. I
knew I was supposed to let her live." He closed his eyes.
"I don't know, maybe they're supposed to come after us.
Maybe that's the plan, to complete the cycle that was left
unfinished sixteen years ago."

He looked at her, his eyes sad, but then he smiled gently.
"Don't worry, Sunny. Whatever happens, it will be in
keeping with spirit's plan."

She rubbed her arms, wishing he wouldn't call her by

that strange name, but afraid to tell him so. "You killed the other guy, didn't you? Harry Blackwood? Then planted the knife in our kitchen trash?"

He shot her a look—almost denied it, she thought—then blew air through puckered lips and looked at her again, but said nothing.

"He was a lowlife," Dawn said, to ease the tension from the kidnapper's face. "I think he found out about me. My birth, I mean. He was blackmailing my mother."

"He knew about you because he was there. And he was blackmailing me, too."

She shot him a look.

He shrugged. "He knew I was still alive and who I was. He threatened to expose me unless I paid him off. I was hoping, Sunny—" She must have made a face or something, because he stopped there, tipped his head slightly to one side, and started over. "I was hoping, Dawn, that I could manage to keep my secret *and* get my little girl back. Killing him was necessary to accomplish the former, and every sign from spirit told me to go ahead with that act. He wasn't worthy to live, really. Setting up your mother— well, I acted impulsively on an idea that was solely my own, thinking it would clear my path to you. Spirit disagreed with that decision. Had I taken the time to seek the signs, I'd have known as much. That's why it didn't work."

Dawn listened carefully. She had always believed in this man's powers. She wasn't entirely sure she disbelieved them now, and that made him even more frightening. "Was I the secret you were so determined to keep? The fact that you had an illegitimate daughter? 'Cause I don't really think it's that big a deal."

He drove a little faster. "As Mordecai Young, I was a wanted man—justified or not, there it is. They thought I died in the raid."

"And you let them think it."

He nodded. "Otherwise I'd be sitting in a prison cell right now."

She shook her head. "You've got such a great career going. The talk show, the books. You do so much good for so many people. But this—this is just throwing it all away."

He nodded. "My work is important. But nothing is as important as you are, Sunshine."

She frowned at him. "Why?"

"Are you kidding?" He sent her a loving look. "Because…you're mine."

The words, spoken so gently, so softly, sent a shiver right down her spine, but she wasn't sure why. She shook it off, changed the subject. "So…where is this mansion of yours, anyway?"

His eyes seemed to light up. "You'll love it, Sunny. I bought it before you were born, but it needed so much work. I've spent the past sixteen years getting it ready for you. It's perfect."

"And south," she said. He shot her a look. "We're going south."

He nodded. "It's in Virginia, and not just a mansion, an entire plantation. Not a working one, of course."

She blinked and felt as if the bottom had fallen out of her stomach. "Virginia."

"Blue Ridge Mountains. A crystal blue lake right at our feet." His smile grew. "It's a dream your mother and I shared. To live there, with you, together."

Virginia. That was a long, long way from home. She no longer thought he would kill her—not when she was the center of this intricate fantasy he'd been building in his mind for the past sixteen years. Not unless she threatened to blow it to bits on him.

Play along, she told herself. Just play along.

Sean pulled into the Emergency entrance of the hospital right behind the man in the pickup, who gave him a wave and kept on going around the looped driveway and back out onto the road. Sean stopped in front of the double entry doors, got out of the car and ran around to Julie's side, then scooped her into his arms and carried her inside.

He was almost dizzy from the force of so many unfamiliar feelings flooding his brain all at once. Holding her this way, limp and pale, scared the hell out of him, and he hurt down deep—not just for her. For himself. For Dawn. For all of them. Panic was like a windstorm in his mind. What if she didn't make it? What if she were hurt far more seriously than he knew?

God, what if he lost her?

He forced the thought from his mind as he carried her into the E.R. and people in white surged toward him. A nurse grabbed his shoulder. "This way, bring her in here. What happened?"

"Car accident," he said as she led him into a room. He lowered Julie carefully onto the narrow bed that stood in its center. "She has a head injury. Ankle, too. I don't know what else."

The woman was leaning over Julie, prying open her eyes and shining a light into them, then pressing a stethoscope to her chest. "You saw the accident?"

"No. She crawled out of the wreck and made her way to a phone. That's where I found her."

"So she was conscious." She was taking Julie's blood pressure now.

"She was unconscious right after the wreck, came to and made her way to a phone. Then she passed out again in my car." He'd moved to the other side of the table, so he could be close to Julie without getting in the way. "Is she gonna be all right?"

"We need to get some X rays. But her vitals are good." She was pushing the hair aside to look at the cut in Julie's head. "She'll need a few stitches." Then she moved to the foot of the bed and unwrapped the bundled ankle, shaking her head slowly as she did. "She was a quick thinker. Nylons. Must have been damned determined to get where she needed to go."

"The man who ran her off the road abducted her teenage daughter."

The nurse's head snapped up fast. "Jesus. The police have been notified?"

He nodded. The woman shook her head, returning her attention to the ankle. She crossed the room to a phone on the wall, spoke to someone in the X-ray department, then came back to Julie.

"You won't be able to keep her here long, once she comes around," Sean told the woman. "Whatever you need to do, do it fast."

"Can't say that I blame her. I have a daughter myself." Her lips thinned. Then others came in and wheeled the bed right out of the room with Julie on board.

Sean closed his eyes. "Be all right, Jones. You'd damn well better be all right."

18

A feeling of panic surged through Julie as she opened her eyes wide, sat bolt upright and shouted, "Dawn!"

"It's okay. Easy. Easy now."

A jackhammer was pounding inside her head, and she squeezed her eyes shut against it, even as MacKenzie leaned over, his hands gentle on her shoulders.

Julie opened her eyes, facing him. "Sean." God, the relief that flooded through her at the sight of him was utterly ridiculous. Then she took in the room beyond him. "What happened? What are we doing here?"

"You passed out in my car, Jones. I had to bring you to a hospital. I was afraid you might die on me."

She shook her head, flinging aside the sheet that covered her, intending to get to her feet, then pausing to stare down at her thickly wrapped left ankle.

"You have a bad sprain in that ankle. They thought it was a break but couldn't find one. You have a concussion, and you took five stitches in the head. They want to keep you overnight."

"That's not going to happen." She looked down at the pillow, spotted the call button lying beside it, pressed it down and held it.

"That's what I thought you'd say."

"We have to find Dawn." She kept her thumb on the button until a nurse came running into the room. She looked as if she expected to find an emergency, then looked irritated. Julie didn't even miss a beat. "Find me a pair of crutches. I have to leave, immediately, and it'll be faster if I don't have to walk on this thing."

The woman's eyebrows went up, and she exchanged a look with Sean.

"I told you. There's no point in arguing with her," he said.

"No, I don't suppose there is." The nurse crossed the room to where a pair of crutches leaned in the corner. She brought them closer to the bed and left them there, hurrying back to her duties elsewhere.

Julie shot a look at Sean. "Why didn't you tell me those were there?"

"You didn't give me a chance. Listen, we're supposed to wait here for Lieutenant Jackson. She should be here any—"

"She's here now," a woman said from the doorway. Cassie Jackson walked in, eyeing Julie, who sent her a glance and went right on with what she was doing, getting upright and onto the crutches.

"Not leaving so soon, are you, Ms. Jones?"

"Damn right I am. I have to find my daughter."

Jackson had the good manners to wipe the smug expression off her face. "Look, we have every agency in the state looking for Dawn."

"Glad to hear it." She looked down at her bare legs, bare feet and hospital gown, then looked up at Sean. "Where are my clothes?"

"Not much left of them," Sean said. "They cut the jeans off, and the blouse was all bloody."

"I, uh, keep a spare set of clothes in my car, if you're interested," Jackson said.

Julie didn't try to hide her surprise. "You'd do that for me?"

"In exchange for a little of your time, yes."

Pursing her lips, Julie shook her head. "No deal. I don't have any time to spare, I'll just go as I am."

"Julie, we've activated the Amber Alert System. Signs on every highway are flashing descriptions of Dawn and Z and the black Jag. Every media outlet is running this, including your station. Someone is going to see them and call in. Until then, there's not a hell of a lot we can do but wait."

Julie didn't feel reassured. Glad, but not reassured. Reassurance wouldn't come until she was holding Dawn tight in her arms again—safe.

"She must be so afraid," she whispered.

"She's a tough kid. Tough, and smart. We'll get her back," Sean promised.

Julie sat back down on the edge of the bed and looked up at the lieutenant. "What else is being done?"

"We have people tracing every piece of property Nathan Z has ever owned. We'll have cops watching in case he shows up at any of them."

Julie glanced at Sean, licking her lips. She was going to have to tell this cop—and dammit, she didn't want to. How much, though? How much to tell her? Sean gave her a very slight nod. She looked at Jackson.

"What?" the cop asked.

Julie licked her lips.

"Give us a second, would you, Jax?" Sean said.

The lieutenant frowned, clearly not liking this, but finally nodded and stepped out of the room. Sean closed the door and went back to the bed, sitting down on the edge of it, beside Julie. "You're going to have to tell her who he really is. You know that."

"I know."

"They need to be checking out property that he owned when he was Mordecai Young."

She met his eyes. "Dawnie isn't my biological daughter."

He went very still, just staring at her. "But—"

"She was my best friend's. The other girl you saw on the tape. The one who was carrying her. Lizzie died in the fire. She wanted me to raise her daughter, and that's what I've done."

He sighed deeply, lowered his head. "Now I get it."

"I could lose her, Sean. I have no legal right to keep her."

"Who are they going to give her to? Young?"

"What if he has relatives? Or what if Lizzie's are still living? God, she had a bad enough time at home that she ran away. I don't want Dawn in a place like that. Even for the two years she has left as a minor. And I don't want her to end up a ward of the state." She bit her lip. "I can't lose Dawnie. God, Sean, she's all I have."

His hand cupped her face, tipped it until she looked at him. He started to say something, then seemed to change his mind, dropped his hand, turned to paced the room. "Look, you don't need to tell Jax that part," he said. "Just that Young is her father, that you thought he was dead, and that he's tracked you down to take her from you."

She stared hard at him. "And you won't tell her?"

His eyes widened a little; then he lowered his gaze, hiding whatever was in it. "If you were thinking straight right now, you'd know better than to even ask. At least, I hope you would."

She frowned at him, and he met her eyes again.

"Just how hard is that head of yours, anyway? No, Jones. I'm not gonna tell her anything."

She swallowed hard and wondered what was going on

with him, why he suddenly seemed so much more intense than he ever had before.

"How did you know to come up here?" she asked him slowly.

"My cell phone has caller ID. I had a P.I. friend tell me where the phone with that number was located."

She nodded. "And why did you answer when I dialed Allan's number?"

"I knew you'd call him. So I arranged to have all his calls forwarded to my cell."

"So you had it all planned—so you could track me down and come charging up here when I got into trouble."

"I was charging up here before I knew you were in trouble."

She held his gaze, probed it. "Why?"

He stared into her eyes, not saying a word. But there was something there, in that look. She broke eye contact first, her head spinning.

"Can I call Jax back in now?" he asked.

"I'm afraid of that cop, Sean. She thinks I killed Harry, you know that. If she decides to arrest me, I won't be able to help Dawn."

"You think she's going to arrest you with me here?"

She looked at him, frowning.

"It's two against one, Jones. I've got your back. She tries to arrest you, then you and I will be making a fast exit, and I can tell you right now, that Crown Victoria she's driving isn't going to get close enough to my Porsche to smell the exhaust."

Staring at him, she shook her head slowly in blatant amazement. "I don't know what to say to you, Mac-Kenzie."

"Say you'd have done the same for me."

"I'm not sure I would have. Not until recently, at least."

He lifted his brows. "Well, you get points for honesty. You ready?"

She nodded. Sean went to the door, opened it, and a second later, Lieutenant Jackson came back inside. She had a pair of jeans and a polo shirt in one hand, and she dropped them on the bed.

Julie lifted her chin, swallowed her fear. "We have to go through this quickly. I don't feel good about sitting still while my daughter is out there, in danger. The only reason I'm even willing to do this at all is that I have no clue where to begin looking for her. But the minute I get one, I'm out of here."

Jackson nodded, taking out a pen and pad. "Maybe we can start with the night of Harry Blackwood's murder."

"I had nothing to do with Harry's murder. So let's start with something relevant."

Jackson's brows arched. "Such as?"

"Such as the fact that Nathan Z used to be known by the name Mordecai Young."

Jackson's jaw dropped. She clapped it shut again. "*The* Mordecai Young?"

"Yes. I was one of the girls at the Young Believers' compound when the raid happened."

"I thought there were no survivors."

"There were five survivors—that I know of. Two other girls by the names of Sirona and Tessa, me, Dawn and Mordecai."

"The full names of the other two girls? I'll need to verify this with them."

"They used false names, ended up married and taking their husbands' names. Sharon Beckwith and Teresa Sinclair. But you won't be able to check anything out with them. They're both dead, both within the past two weeks.

Supposedly suicides by hanging, but I think it was Mordecai.''

"Jesus, Jones, you should have freaking told me this,'' MacKenzie said. "No wonder you've been so freaked out.''

"I think Mordecai knew we survived, and he tracked them down, tried to make them tell him where Dawn and I were, and killed them, either because they wouldn't talk or to keep them from warning us that they had.''

Jackson frowned hard. "I'm not sure I'm following. Why would Mordecai Young, assuming he is alive, be so determined to track you and Dawn down?''

"Because he's Dawn's father. And yes, Harry Blackwood knew it. He'd been blackmailing me for months. I was there, in the hotel room, where we had agreed to meet for the latest payoff. I went to the bathroom, and when I came out, Harry was dead. I believe Mordecai killed him.''

"Did you see it?''

"No, but he admitted it to me.''

"That's hearsay.''

"Do you really think I give a shit if you believe me? I'm telling you what I know so you can use it to track down my daughter before that maniac does something to her.''

"Okay, okay.'' She held up a hand. "So Nathan Z is really Mordecai Young, and he murdered Harry Blackwood.''

"Yes. He has the murder weapon. And he says he managed to put my prints on it. Something about Scotch tape. He said that unless I brought Dawn to him, he would turn it in so I would be arrested for the murder, and he'd end up with a clear path to Dawn anyway. I didn't like either of those options, so I decided to run, instead. But he was watching us. He knew when we left. He broke into the house. Dawn said she'd e-mailed her friend before we left, mentioning we were heading north, though we hadn't decided exactly where we were going. He must have found that e-mail, and he followed us. And now he has my daughter.''

Jackson glanced at Sean. "And you knew all this?"

"I—"

"He's hearing it for the first time, same as you." Julie picked up the jeans. "When I ran into MacKenzie at the hotel that night, I acted as if I had just arrived. He thought he was telling you the truth when he said I was with him the whole time. He had no way of knowing I'd already been there for more than a half hour." Legs over the side of the bed, she tried to pull the jeans over her wounded ankle but winced when moving the leg brought pain.

Sean took the jeans away from her, then dropped to one knee on the floor and gently worked them over the bandaged ankle, pulling them slowly up her leg. Julie stared down at him, surprised.

He was still holding the jeans for her, so she slid her good leg into them.

Jackson frowned, lips pursed, then looked at Julie again. "And what about you? How long have you known Z's true identity?"

"I'd never seen Z face-to-face until we attended a taping of his show yesterday."

"Surely you'd seen him on television. In the papers."

"Yeah. But it's not the same. *He's* not the same." She got up, and Sean did, too, bracing her so she could pull the jeans up and fasten them under the hospital gown. Not a bad fit. "I knew him as soon as he slipped into his old Southern drawl. He's had quite a bit of reconstructive surgery or I'd have recognized him sooner."

"He deliberately altered his appearance?"

"He was badly burned in the fire the day of the raid."
Julie picked up the shirt, put it over her head, then pulled
her arms out of the hospital gown and thrust them into the
shirtsleeves. Then she tugged the gown out from underneath, and tossed it onto the bed. "That's everything I
know, Lieutenant. Everything. I'd like to go look for my
daughter now."

Jackson cleared her throat. "Ms. Jones, you've admitted
to being in the room when Harry Blackwood was murdered,
that he was blackmailing you, and that the murder weapon
might by now have your fingerprints on it. I can't just let
you walk out of here."

"You can't stop me, either."

Jackson stood between her and the door. She didn't pull
her gun, but she thought about it; Julie read it in her eyes.
The detective shot a glance toward Sean, wordlessly asking
him to choose sides.

"She's not going to skip on you, Jax," Sean said. "She's
not going anywhere until her kid is safe and sound. You
know that."

"I can't just let her walk."

"I can't let you take her in. Not yet."

"I could arrest you for obstruction."

"You're going to want some backup before you try."
He nodded at the gun. "Unless you're willing to shoot me
over this."

"Goddammit, MacKenzie!"

He put an arm around Julie, shocking the hell out of her.
Jackson looked angry enough to take him up on his challenge to use her gun on him, but she didn't. She stepped
aside and let them pass, Julie hobbling on her crutches,
surprised that she wasn't already in handcuffs.

"I'm going to need to know where you're staying. How
to reach you."

Julie was almost grateful to the cop. Jackson didn't have to let them walk out of there, not really. She had a gun, handcuffs and plenty of reasons not to let them go. Maybe she wasn't the bitch Julie had wanted to think she was.

"Back home, Jones?" Sean asked.

"Yeah. As fast as you can get me there."

Sean nodded and helped her to the exit, even while a nurse came running after them with a form for Julie to sign.

"Once you're back home, don't leave the area. Stay local," Jackson called after them.

Julie didn't even look back. She let Sean help her out to his car, got in the passenger side and sat there stiff with tension until he'd cleared the parking lot and hit the open road. Only then did she lean back and close her eyes. "Thanks for that," she said when he got in.

"You're a slow learner, you know that?"

"What?"

"Buckle your seat belt, for chrissakes."

She did so, giving herself a lecture for not having done it right away. He was right; she *was* a slow learner. "Guess I'm still trying to figure out what's in this for you."

"Like I said, you're a slow learner."

She shrugged, tipping her head to one side. "It's a lot to wrap my mind around, MacKenzie. I never expected that when my entire life went to hell, my worst enemy would turn out to be…"

He looked at her, waiting. "Go on. To be what?"

"The only person in the universe on my side."

He smiled a little. "I'm not the only one."

"No? I didn't see anyone else sitting by my bedside when I woke up in that hospital. Much less facing down that bulldog of a cop to get me out of there." She shook her head slowly. "So how many times have you saved my ass now?"

"More than you've saved mine. Guess you owe me."

"Guess I do."

He looked sideways at her. "So are you ready to pay up?"

"How?"

"Tell me. Tell me about that day. The raid. How you survived."

She lowered her eyes.

"Jones, that day has been replaying in my mind for sixteen years. I have to have the television or radio on all the time—even when I'm asleep, which isn't often—because if it gets too quiet, I live it again. It haunts me. I need to know. I need to hear it. All of it. And we've got a couple of hours on the road ahead of us. So tell me."

Sean drove, but he found it difficult to keep his attention on traffic while Jones tried to begin her story.

"The compound wasn't such a bad place—at least, not at first."

"Back up a little," he said.

She blinked, looking across the car at him. "I don't—"

"What were you doing there? How did you end up there in the first place?"

She frowned a little—maybe as surprised as he was that he wanted to know those things. Things about her. Shrugging, she said, "It's not a pretty story. And it's not all that relevant."

"It is to me."

Jones turned her head, pretending to look at the passing scenery, giving a shrug that he thought was probably supposed to seem careless. "My father was a drunk. One day he hit my mother a little too hard. She died. He went to prison."

"Hell."

She shrugged. "It was only a matter of time. I think Mom knew it. I know I did. I used to sit up nights, planning to kill him myself before he could kill her, but it took me too long to work up the courage to actually do it. I still blame myself for that."

He frowned hard. "How old were you?"

"When she died? Sixteen, same age Dawn is now."

"Did it—" He almost couldn't force the question out. "Did it happen in front of you?"

"I was in my room. That was the drill, you know? We had it down to a science. When he came home drunk, I went to my room, locked the door and didn't come out until after he'd gone to work the next morning. Then I'd go wake Mom, clean her up, drive her to the clinic sometimes for stitches or a cast, or whatever." She shrugged. "That last time, though, when I went to check on her in the morning, she wouldn't wake up."

"And your father?"

"He'd gone to work as usual. Probably didn't even realize he'd killed her. He didn't like looking at her on those mornings—probably couldn't stomach seeing his handiwork once the booze wore off."

"Jesus." He pictured her at sixteen, trying to wake her dead mother. His throat got tight, and he had to blink his eyes clear. "What did you do?"

"I called the police. Then I went to my room and packed my things, and I was gone before they got there. All I could think was that I didn't want to be there when my father came back, if he came back at all. It was only later that it occurred to me that if I went back, I'd be a ward of the state, probably get stuck in a foster home somewhere." She shook her head. "I didn't want that."

"How did you live?"

"On the streets. Shelters. Took odd jobs when I could

get them. Stole when I couldn't.'' She shrugged. ''That's where I met Lizzie. She was a runaway, like me.'' Lowering her head, she said, ''I really loved her. She was my family, you know?''

He nodded.

''She met another girl who told her about this haven for runaways that was run by a New Age guru, and she was bound and determined to go there. Hell, I wasn't going to let her go without me. She was all I had.''

He shook his head slowly. ''But when you saw the place—the fences, the guards...''

''Wendy, the girl who took us there, made it all sound perfectly reasonable. Most of the girls there were underage. The authorities might come and try to take them. The fences were to keep people out, to protect us, not to keep us in.''

He nodded.

''We were kids, what the hell did we know?'' She sighed, looking at him again. ''We moved into a bunkhouse with a bunch of other girls, shared all the work—cooking, cleaning, the gardens and greenhouses where Mordecai was growing opium and marijuana. We had campfires and sing-alongs at night. And every day started with a sermon from Mordecai. He talked about love and light and healing.'' She shook her head slowly. ''The kicker is, he's good. He was so good. Had such a positive message, and some of the things he could do—'' She shook her head slowly. ''And hell, what he gave us was a lot better than what we'd had in our pasts. For a while it seemed like paradise.''

''And then?''

Her lips thinned. ''He was drugging our meals. He started out with real mild stuff, so we wouldn't catch on. But we did. I did, anyway. We were supposed to feel happy and calm all the time, and it worked. It did. We lived in a numb-brained state of bliss. But I knew something was wrong. Lizzie didn't believe me. So I started sneaking food from the kitchens and gardens, hiding it around the place, and I convinced her to stop eating the meals we were given and eat the stolen food instead. It didn't take long for the chemicals to wear off.'' She ran a hand slowly along the dashboard. ''It was about that time that another girl told us she thought we were being held prisoner. She said she'd told Mordecai that she wanted to leave, and he told her that wasn't allowed, so she was planning to sneak out. One night she disappeared. We didn't see her for several days, and we figured she'd made it. But then one of the guards came carrying her body in through the gates.'' Her hand stilled; she licked her lips.

Sean's stomach clenched a little, her words bringing vivid visual images into his mind.

''The story we got was that she'd run away and been killed by some maniac on the outside. That it was a lesson to all of us, a message from the Creator warning us that it wasn't safe out there. That the outside world was dangerous, and that we were only safe in our haven, under the protection of Mordecai. Everyone bought it.'' She shrugged. ''Maybe it was the drugs. I only know that Lizzie and I knew better. We knew they'd killed her, and we knew the same thing would happen to us if we tried to get out. We also knew we couldn't stay there.''

He reached out a hand, touched her hair. The white bandage was stark, with her dark hair spilling around it.

She looked at him. He bit his lip and drew his hand back to the steering wheel. ''So what did you do?''

''We came up with a plan. It wasn't all that complicated, but if we had kept on eating the drug-laced food, we never could have pulled it off. It was simple, and pretty obvious.

Get close to Mordecai. Become his favorites. His ego worked in our favor. He bought it from the beginning.''

Sean didn't like what he was thinking. He didn't like it at all.

"We volunteered for every job that put us close to him. We flattered and flirted and fawned over him. Within three months, he'd moved us both into the house.''

"You had sex with him?'' He took his eyes off the road to look at her as he asked the question.

She returned his gaze, not flinching. "I didn't have a choice. Neither of us did.''

"I wasn't judging you, Jones.''

She hesitated, then went on. "Lizzie—I don't know, something happened to her. Mordecai was handsome, charming, very attentive. She forgot it was a game. She fell for him for real. He started spending more and more time with her and less with me, which was fine by me. Except…I could see her changing toward him. Softening, you know? I was worried she'd change sides on me. And then, the next thing we knew, she was pregnant.''

"It's lucky you both weren't.''

She shot him a look. "Not so lucky. Turns out I can't have kids. Of course, I didn't know that at the time.''

He could have kicked himself for the callous remark. "I'm sorry.''

"Don't be. I've got Dawn. She's all I need.''

He winced at the reminder of how much the girl meant to her.

"I delivered her, you know. Mordecai brought in books and film strips on natural childbirth, made me study them until I was damn near brain-dead.'' She shrugged. "He may have even stopped drugging our food—hers for the sake of the baby and mine so I wouldn't screw up the delivery. Though neither of us dared put that to the test.''

"And the delivery went all right?"

"For Dawn and me. Lizzie—she was weak after. She'd lost a lot of blood, and it didn't seem to me as if she was recovering as fast as she should. I begged Mordecai to take her to a hospital. He refused, and she wouldn't even argue with him. She was convinced by then that Mordecai loved her, loved the baby, wouldn't let any harm come to either of them."

"And did he? Love them?"

She tipped her head to one side. "I think he did, in his own twisted way. Kind of like a duck hunter loves his favorite Lab, you know? He saw all of us as his property, but especially Dawnie and Lizzie and me. We belonged to him. At the end I thought Tessa and Sirona were gaining favor over us, but he adored us as long as we showed him absolute, unflinching devotion. So that was what we did. Lizzie really felt it. Until the day of the raid."

"And what happened that day?" he asked, half afraid to hear her describe it, afraid it would increase the burden of guilt he'd lived with all this time.

"When the soldiers came, he left us. He left us locked in our room, took the baby with him. There was gunfire, and then there was all this smoke, and we realized the house was on fire."

"My God."

"Lizzie knew things by then that I didn't. We both knew about his escape tunnel in the basement. But she knew about the money he kept down there—lots of lots of money. Duffel bags full of it. He'd been making plans with her, promising crazy things. Like how he was going to find good homes for every girl in the compound, and take her and Dawnie away to some make-believe mansion in the sky. How he was going to marry her and give her everything she had ever dreamed of."

She lifted her eyes to Sean's. "How did it start? The raid, I mean. You were outside, you must have had a clearer picture of it than I did."

He shook his head slowly. "The soldiers had the place surrounded and under surveillance for hours before they moved in. They waited until the middle of the night, thinking there would be less resistance. They knew Young had weapons stashed. They took the dogs out first. Tranquilizer darts, dead silent. Then they moved in on the guards he had posted at the gates, but the guards fought back. When the first shots were fired, the house just came alive. Guns poking out every window, firing at the troops. A couple of soldiers went down. The Young Believers poked a sleeping dragon when they shot those soldiers. All hell broke loose after that. The troops started launching tear gas, rolling tanks."

"Didn't they know that house was full of innocent girls?"

"I don't think they much cared. I thought the girls in the bunkhouses would surrender, but instead they fled into the main house. When I saw the fire—flames licking up from the house and no one coming out—God, I wanted to die. All I could think was that I had been there. I could have warned them before the soldiers attacked. They could have had a chance."

Her hand slid over his on the steering wheel. "It wouldn't have mattered. Most of them would have stayed anyway. He had them so brainwashed, they'd have followed him into hell if he'd asked it."

"Not all of you."

She nodded. "There might have been a few of us who would have heeded your warning, Sean. But Mordecai wouldn't have let us leave anyway."

"I'll never know that, because I didn't try."

"You didn't know it would go down the way it did. You expected those troops would walk in there, and walk out again with Mordecai in handcuffs. You expected them to free all those girls. You had no way of knowing."

"I should have tried." He turned his hand over, lacing his fingers with hers. "I'd seen you there. You and Lizzie and Dawn. The thought of that little baby haunted my dreams for months after that raid. I thought—I thought she'd died in the fire."

She frowned so deeply that he thought he might have angered her. "Is that why you're helping us now? Out of some sense of guilt for what happened that day?"

He pulled the car to a stop at a red light, turned to stare into her eyes. "Partly. Does it matter?"

She shifted her eyes, a sure sign of a lie. "No. Of course not. It's just that you don't need to perform an act of penitence, Sean. We survived."

"Thank God."

"And even if we hadn't, none of it was your fault."

He looked down at their joined hands. "How did you get out of that hell alive, Jones?"

"We broke our locked door open and headed down to the tunnel in the basement. We could hear Dawnie crying from down there. Lizzie had been shot, but she never let on. On the way downstairs, we found two other girls alive and we took them with us." She shook her head slowly. "We ran into Mordecai down there, too. Lizzie yanked the keys from the chain on his neck, and I took the baby from him. Then he was buried underneath a mountain of flaming debris when the ceiling collapsed. I would have sworn he was dead."

"But he wasn't."

She shook her head slowly. "Just before the tunnel, Lizzie sank to the floor. She begged me to take care of

Dawnie. She told me to take the money I would find hidden in the tunnel and use it to start a new life for her baby. And then she died. I dragged her body into the tunnel and left her there, so she wouldn't burn with Mordecai.''

Tears flowed down her cheeks now.

"We made our way out," she said. "Tessa and Sirona and Dawn and me. We split up the money, and we went our separate ways, each of us vowing never to breathe a word of what had happened there that night. We picked new names right then and there, and we picked cities in which to hide. We promised to keep our phone numbers listed, under our new names, in case we ever needed to get in touch."

"I can't even believe…you were what? Sixteen?"

"Seventeen by then."

"How did you get by?"

"It's amazing what you can do when you have the money, Sean. And there was a lot of money in those duffel bags. I hired a P.I. to create a new identity for me and for Dawn. Forged birth certificates and Social Security numbers. I bought the house and hired a nanny and enrolled in journalism classes." She shrugged. "The rest, you pretty much know."

He was stunned. "What—what was your name, Julie? Your real name?"

She smiled just a little. "Jewel Jordan."

"And Dawnie?"

"Lizzie named her Sunshine. Called her Sunny for short."

He nodded. "You said Mordecai loved her, in his way. Do you think he would hurt her?"

She met his probing eyes. "I don't want to think it, but…yes, I know he would. If she doesn't fall into line with his expectations, I'm afraid that's exactly what he'll do.''

Sean wasn't going to let that happen. Something, some unrecognizable being he'd never met before, seemed to emerge from inside him, growing until it filled his entire body. It stiffened his spine and swelled his chest. He was going to get Dawn back. He was going to make her mother's life all right again. He didn't know how, and he was afraid to examine why. He only knew he would. He *must.*

19

"This is it," the kidnapper said, his voice little more than a whisper, his eyes a little moist as he stared through the windshield and brought the car to a stop.

Dawn looked, too. The house stood in the darkness like a jewel nestled in a crown of crystal mountains, emerald pines and a glittering diamond lake all drenched in moonlight. It was a redbrick mansion, with curving white balconies and towering white pillars. The driveway was lined in red gravel.

"Well?"

He was looking at her, she realized, waiting for her to say...something. "It's...really beautiful."

"Wait until you see inside." He opened his door. "Come on."

Dawn frowned as he got out of the car. He wasn't menacing or frightening now. Not that he really had been—since he'd put the gun away, at least. He was more like an excited child, eager to show off his newly made clay ashtray. She got out and looked around, wondering if she should run. But there was nothing. Just woods, and that gorgeous lake. The winding road they'd taken to this place had been narrow and unpaved. She couldn't remember the last sign of intelligent life they'd passed. It had to be a long way back.

"Come on," he called, halfway to the front door now, looking back at her, smiling.

Sighing, Dawn went to him. He would only come after her if she ran—and he still had that gun. Best not to give him a reason to use it.

He walked her to a big wooden door with a huge stained-glass oval inset and a brass knocker with a lion's head, digging a key ring from his pocket on the way. Then he opened the door with a flourish, and stood aside. "Your castle awaits."

"*My* castle?"

His smile faltered. He lifted a hand, ran it over her hair, and she forced herself not to shiver at his touch. "All this is for you, baby. Don't you realize that? I bought it before you were born, and I've been fixing it up all this time—just for you. Getting ready for the day we'd be together again. I knew they couldn't keep us apart forever. You're—you're mine." He smiled again, but it was shaky. "My only child. Heir to all I have—all I *am*."

She licked her lips, tried to return his smile.

"You don't even know what that means yet, do you, Sunny?"

"N-no."

"It's all right. You will. Come on, come inside."

Nodding, Dawn walked past him into a foyer that arched to the sky. Tall windows glittered with starlight from outside, until he flipped on a switch and flooded the room with light from a giant crystal chandelier. Ahead of her, a broad staircase rose and split into two staircases that rose even higher and curved in opposite directions.

"What do you think?" he asked. "Ready for the grand tour, or would you rather see your rooms first?"

"I…" She searched her brain, praying she would say the right thing—the thing that would preserve his tender mood and not anger him. "I *am* a little tired," she said. "And I'd like to clean up."

"Your rooms, then. You'll find everything you need there."

"If you're sure that's okay with you. We can do the tour after."

"Of course it's okay. I want you to be happy here, Sunny. Please believe that."

"I do. I...I do."

His smile was back, full and firm, as he turned and led the way up the stairs. He took the left flight, which ended at a stretch of open hall with a railing. She could look down into the foyer for part of the way; then they entered an enclosed hallway, with numerous doors. At the far end, he opened a set of double doors and ushered her into what she could only guess he saw as "her rooms."

The floor was lined in deep plush carpet of pale pink. The walls were papered in pink roses, and the tooled woodwork was ivory toned. A small round table seemed set for high tea, with a gleaming silver service and delicate china cups. Further inside, there was an overstuffed love seat, a matching chair and a wooden rocker with a giant teddy bear sitting on it. An entertainment center covered one entire wall, with a wide-screen TV, DVD player, VCR, video-game console and stereo system lining its shelves, alongside delicate knickknacks and china dolls in elaborate gowns and feathered hats.

He opened a door, leading the way through it into a second room, where there was a pink canopy bed that was loaded with so many pillows and stuffed animals she could barely see the comforter. There were dressers and lamps, far too much to take in. He opened a sliding door to reveal a closet full of clothes and another door to reveal a bathroom straight out of a fantasy, with a tub as big as a small pool.

"This is...all this is for me?"

"All this...and so much more. But we'll get to that."
He pointed to the French doors at the far end of the bedroom. "Those lead onto your private balcony. There's a
hot tub out there. And a beautiful view of the lake."

She moved closer, then looked past him as he held the
curtains open, toward the lake below, moonlight gleaming
on its surface. She swallowed hard, wondering why such a
beautiful sight should make her feel like crying. She had
to look away, toward the bookshelves. Then she frowned,
noting the titles. All of his own books were there, along
with copies of the Torah, the Que'ran, the Bible, the Ti-
betan Book of the Dead and many others.

"Don't worry," he said. "I don't expect you to study
tonight. There will be plenty of time for that after you're
rested and feeling more comfortable here."

She faced him, lifting her brows. "Study?"

He nodded. "I'm not an ordinary man, Sunny. I'm...far
more—but you already know that, don't you?" She nodded. He paced across the floor, never taking his eyes from
her. "And because I'm more than ordinary, so are you. We
were put on this earth for a reason, Sunny. We have a
mission, you and I."

A little shiver danced along her spine. "A...a mission?"

"Yes. A mission from God." He smiled gently. "It's all
right if you don't understand just yet. You will. For now,
why don't you clean up, and get some rest, hmm? We'll
talk more in the morning."

Swallowing hard, certain now that he was insane, she
nodded and forced a smile.

He turned as if to leave but stopped at the bedroom door.
"Now, I know you might be tempted, Sunny, but please,
don't try to run away from me."

"I wasn't—"

"Of course you were thinking about it. You wouldn't be

your mother's daughter if you weren't. She tried to run away from me. That's…that's why she died, you see? She went against spirit's plan, tried to thwart me in my mission." He gazed at her lovingly. "It would kill me if something like that were to happen to you, too."

He blew her a kiss, then walked out of the room.

Dawn backed up until her back hit the wall, then slowly sank to the floor and, hugging her knees to her chest, cried.

It was late by the time Sean pulled his Porsche into Julie's driveway, killed the engine, and turned to look at her. His former sparring partner sat there staring blankly at the dark, empty house. Not a trace of life lingered in her usually sparkling eyes. She'd stopped talking around the time night fell. He understood that. It was worse, somehow, to think of Dawn in the hands of a madman in the dark.

Impulsively he put a hand on her shoulder.

She blinked, but didn't turn to face him. "It looks so empty."

"I know."

"I thought we'd have her back by now."

"We'll get her back soon, Jones. Don't doubt it."

She turned her face toward him, and her eyes were wet, red rimmed, puffy. Her hair was a mess. She looked like hell, and yet he couldn't take his eyes off her. He wanted to pull her close. He wanted to kiss her. He wanted to tell her about this new feeling that was suddenly infecting his every thought. But he couldn't. Not now, not until Dawn was safe and home. He was ashamed of himself for thinking about his own feelings at a time like this. And yet he couldn't stop himself. His brain had picked up a virus, and no matter what program he tried to run, the symptoms remained. He was sick about Dawnie. He would willingly saw off a limb with a dull blade to get her back. And even

while he was cutting, he thought, he would be looking at
Julie Jones, wanting to hold her, to taste her, to save her.

He was looking at her now.

And she was looking back, her haunted eyes getting
damp before she lowered them. "We should go inside."

He didn't reply, because he was stuck where he was,
aching with her pain, searching for a way to ease it and
knowing he couldn't. Then something tapped the window
beside him, and he damn near jumped out of his seat.

"Rodney!" Jones cried. She opened her door, jumped
out awkwardly and, dragging her crutches with her, hobbled around the car to the old man from next door.

Sean got out, too, then felt an irrational rush of jealousy
when the fellow wrapped Julie up in his arms. "I heard
about Dawnie," he told her. "It's been all over the television. God, Julie, I'm so sorry."

He was holding her, rocking her in his arms. Julie even
hugged him back a little, without letting go of her crutches,
and let some of the tears she'd been holding in check spill
onto her cheeks. Sean could only stand there wondering
what to do with himself. He felt like an outsider, all of the
sudden. But then Julie extricated herself gently from the
older man's embrace, hopped a step or two back. "We're
going to get her back," she told him. And when she said
it, she looked toward Sean, as if for reassurance.

"Damn straight we'll get her back," Sean confirmed for
her. "This Z character doesn't know what a hornets' nest
he's stirred up."

Rodney nodded hard. "If I were a younger man—"

He met Sean's eyes and let the rest go unsaid. Sean only
nodded his understanding. Julie turned toward the front
door, then paused. "My keys…" Then she closed her eyes.
"Hell, they're still in the car, over that cliff up north."

"I still have the one you gave me after the new locks

were put in,'' Rodney said. He took the key out of his pocket.

Sean took it from him, helped Julie up the front steps and then started unlocking the door. ''The place is a mess, Jones. Like I told you, someone was here before the police, and then—''

''I cleaned it up, best I could,'' Rodney said. When Sean frowned at him, he went on. ''I hope that's okay. I was too damn worried to sit home, and I got to thinking Dawnie might try to call home if she could get to a telephone, so I came over here.''

''Of course I don't mind,'' Julie said. ''That was a good idea, Rodney.''

Sean swung the door wide, and Julie went into the house, leaving it open for the two men to enter behind her. The entire place smelled of chocolate. Sean sniffed and watched Julie's reaction. She paused, inhaled, then went very still.

''I baked some peanut butter chocolate chip cookies,'' the old man explained. ''Just to pass the time. Besides, they're Dawnie's favorites.''

Julie didn't move. She just stood there on her crutches, so stiff and so tense that Sean was afraid she might shatter.

''We baked them together, last winter. Remember, Julie? Surprised you when you came home from work.''

She nodded, the motion jerky. ''When I smelled them, I thought maybe…she was here.''

''Aw, dammit, Julie, I'm sorry.'' Rodney pushed a palm across his thin, powder-white hair. ''I didn't mean…''

She held up a hand to stop him, tried to say something, then just gave up and, turning, thumped away from him.

''I made things worse.''

''No, you didn't,'' Sean said. ''Honestly, nothing could make this worse for her. She's been holding everything in all afternoon. It had to come out. It was inevitable.''

The old man met Sean's eyes, nodded. "You're right. Still, I'm sorry."

Sean nodded.

"Do they know anything about this Z character? Any reason he'd do this?"

Sean pursed his lips, thought about playing it close to the vest, but decided against it. This old neighbor was close to Julie and Dawn. The nearest thing they had to family. It would harm nothing to tell him. "This stays between us for now, okay?"

"Of course."

"Nathan Z is really Mordecai Young."

The old man's eyebrows went up. "*The* Mordecai Young? I thought he died in that botched government raid, what, fifteen, sixteen years ago or so?"

"So did everyone else. But he didn't." Sean drew a breath.

"Well, I'll be. And what would a lunatic cult leader want with our Dawnie?"

Sean shook his head, unwilling to reveal that secret. It wasn't his to tell.

"Ah, hell, you're right. Julie will tell me herself, when she's able. Or ready. I should go," the old man said, still shaking his head at Sean's revelation. "Please, please let me know if you hear anything. Anything at all. Those two girls—" He glanced toward the stairs. "They're like my own. They mean that much to me."

"I know the feeling, Mr. White."

The older man pinned Sean's gaze with his pale blue one. "Now, I told you once, it's Rodney to you, son. You're practically family yourself." He clapped Sean on the shoulder. "Take care of her. And don't forget to let me know—"

"I will. I promise. The second we hear anything."

Rodney nodded and headed out of the house.

Sean pursed his lips, unsure he was equal to the task of comforting Julie Jones. He knew he had to try, though. He took time to place a fast call to Jax's cell phone to ask for any new information, and then he went up the stairs to Dawn's bedroom, stood in the doorway and looked inside.

Julie was sitting on the floor, hugging one of her daughter's sweaters to her chest, rocking back and forth slowly, rhythmically, tear tracks burned into her cheeks.

He tried to speak, not even sure what he was going to say—her name, maybe. It didn't matter; no sound came out. His throat had closed off. Talking wasn't going to help, anyway. What the hell could he say that could free her from the nightmare she was living through tonight? It was real. Nothing could change that—not until they found Dawn.

No, words just weren't going to do it. He shook off the stillness and walked into the room. She didn't look up, maybe didn't even know he was there. He crouched beside her, slid one arm around her back and the other beneath her folded legs, and rose again, lifting her with him as if she were a small child.

Julie wasn't paying a lot of attention to what was going on outside her. There was pain, throbbing insistently. It was centered in the left ankle but radiated outward, encompassing the entire foot and half of her lower leg, as well. It was nothing, though, compared to the pain of not knowing what was happening to her precious daughter. She'd gone to Dawn's room on sheer instinct and the need to be as close to her as possible. But once there, Dawn's absence was so powerful that Julie had gone weak and limp, and ended up huddled on the floor in the corner.

She wasn't there now.

As she forced herself to focus on the real world, she

knew she was resting in her own bed. She heard water running somewhere, and she smelled something that made her stomach rumble. She felt cold and shaky, and she sat up, looked around, thought she ought to get on her feet and find out why she was alone. She didn't want to be alone. She wanted...

"Sean?"

He appeared the second she called his name, almost before she had a chance to wonder why the hell it was his name on her lips at a time like this. But she didn't need to wonder about that. She knew. There was no one else. God, she'd probably even alienated dear old Rodney, the way she'd barked at him a while ago. How long? God, how long ago was that now?

Sean was leaning over her. The water had stopped running.

"Hey. How are you doing?"

She stared into his eyes and wondered why the hell he was on her side. Why him?

"Here, take these." He opened a palm, where two coated tablets rested. "Strongest pain reliever I could find in your medicine cabinet, and this is a double dose. It ought to ease the pain in that ankle."

She took the pills from him, popped them into her mouth. He handed her a dewy water glass, and she drank, washing the tablets down.

"Good girl. Now, come on." He scooped her up and carried her into the bathroom.

"What are you doing, Sean? What—"

"You're a mess. Chilled to the bone, bruised to hell and gone, and you still have weeds in your hair and God knows what else, from your little Adirondack adventure. I ran you a nice hot bath with epsom salts." He set her down on the toilet seat, knelt in front of her, untied her running shoe and pulled it off, then peeled off the sock. "I've been on the phone with Jackson. She's agreed to contact us the second they get a hit on where the bastard might be. I have everyone at the newsroom working on it, as well as every source I've ever used. They're all under instructions to call us here with any information. Until they do, there's not much we can do."

She sat there, searching for words, while he gently unwound the Ace bandage from her sprained ankle.

"Can you get up, just for a sec?"

She nodded and, bracing her hands on his shoulders, stood on one foot. Then she just held on to him as he undid her jeans and slid them down her hips. There was nothing salacious in his eyes, not a single smart-ass comment on his lips. He just pushed the jeans down, then lowered her until she was sitting again and knelt to pull the jeans off, careful not to jar her sore ankle.

"Why are you doing this?"

He had set the jeans aside and was unbuttoning her borrowed shirt this time. She wasn't wearing a bra underneath it. Lieutenant Jackson hadn't offered her one, and she hadn't asked.

"Because you need me to do this."

She frowned, staring at him, puzzled, until he met her eyes. "Sean, I can't even think about—about—anything but Dawnie. Not now."

"You think I can?" He'd finished unbuttoning the blouse, but he didn't take it off. He left it hanging, kept his eyes on hers. "Look, you're a mess. It's only a matter of time before we get a lead, I promise you that, and you need to be ready when we do. You need to get cleaned up, take the edge off the pain, get some food into your belly and rest, so you can come up swinging once we find out where that bastard took our girl."

"Oh." Our girl. It reminded her of the way she and Lizzie used to refer to Dawn when she was just a little baby.

She studied him.

"I just...don't know why."

He looked right into her eyes, and for a second her belly tightened into a knot of yearning so powerful she almost gasped. "I think you do," he said. "But this isn't the time."

He started to push the blouse off her shoulders, but she clutched it in front of her. "I...I can do the rest."

"Yeah?"

She nodded.

"And how are you going to get into the tub on one foot?"

She thought about that, frowning, realizing he was right. She couldn't very well hop on one foot and then leap over the side of the tub one-footed, as well.

"This is no time for shyness, Jones. I promise, I'll be a perfect gentleman."

Thinning her lips, she sighed and lowered her arms. Sean pushed the blouse down off her shoulders, off her arms. She sat there in nothing but her panties, and he knelt in front of her. His eyes lowered, maybe against his will. He looked at her, and she saw his Adam's apple swell and recede before he forced his eyes level with hers again.

"Sean?"

"Yeah?"

"What if the phone rings?"

"What?" He looked confused for a moment, then blinked it away. "I mean, I thought of that." He nodded toward the counter, where she saw a cordless phone resting. "Even double-checked to be sure it was working. Good strong dial tone. The ringer's set to 'loud.'"

"Oh."

He put his hands on her waist. "Up you go." His voice seemed a little hoarse.

She held to his shoulders and got up on one foot again. Sean slid his hands lower, pushing her panties down as he did, letting them fall to the floor, off her injured foot, which she held up. They pooled around the foot on which she stood.

He stared for a moment, and her body stirred down deep. Then he rose again, lifted her up and lowered her gently into the bathtub. "How's the water? Too hot?"

"Just right," she told him, and he lowered her farther. The heat wrapped around her, soothed her. She felt guilty as hell for the relief. The pain eased bit by bit. That she should be feeling physical relief while her daughter was still in danger seemed wrong, somehow.

"Relax, will you? Dawn wouldn't want you torturing yourself. She'd prefer you strong enough to come and get her."

She closed her eyes and knew he was right. Sighing heavily, releasing the pain as she did, she lay back in the water, let it do its work. Around her there was only silence, but she knew Sean was kneeling there beside the bathtub, staring at her. She opened her eyes to see that she was right. He was staring, and his face was odd.

"I lied before. When I said I'd be a gentleman. I'd have to be six months dead not to have a few impure thoughts running through my head right now."

She felt her face heat and wondered how long it had been since she'd blushed. She couldn't remember the last time. She wasn't the blushing type.

"Is that a compliment?"

"To put it mildly." He was kneeling beside the tub, her loofah in his hand, and he dipped it into the water, squeezed

it, and then ran it over her neck and shoulders. He lifted
her right arm and ran the sponge along it to the very tips
of her fingers.

She sighed in pleasure. "I can do this myself, you
know."

"Yeah, but you don't really want to. Do you?" He
dipped the sponge, ran it down her other arm. He moved
it over her palm, washing finger by finger, then back up
the sensitive underside.

"No."

He had her lean forward, washed her back, his touch
utterly magical. It seemed every stroke of the sponge eased
some of the pain, some of the tension, even while creating
tension of a different sort. When she leaned back again, he
put a dollop of her scented body wash on the sponge,
rubbed up a lather, then began moving the sponge over her
chest. He ran it over her breasts, lathering them, using slow,
deliberately arousing strokes over her nipples, and he was
probably very pleased with himself to see them stiffening
in response. He spent a lot of time there before rinsing the
suds away and moving the sponge lower, running it in small
circles over her belly, her abdomen, her thighs.

He lathered the sponge again and ran it between her legs,
and for some reason she couldn't have named, she just
relaxed her thighs open and let him. It felt good, the rough
texture of the loofah, softened by the suds, rubbing back
and forth beneath the steady pressure of his hand. She let
her thighs fall wider, let her head fall back against the tub,
let her eyes close, let the sighs of pleasure escape her lips.

His touch changed. The sponge, she realized, had fallen
away, and there was only his hand now. His fingers spreading her, exposing her and finding the sensitive places—the
places no hand but her own had touched in a very long
time. Up until last night, at least. He touched those places.

His fingers were not like her own. They were bigger, rougher at the tips. They were foreign, and yet they seemed to know just where to move, how deeply to probe, how hard to pinch, how fast to rub.

Her breath came faster, and the tightening began. God, he was going to get her off, right there in the tub. What the hell was she thinking?

She opened her eyes, clamped her thighs tight around his invading hand. "Sean…"

"*Shhhhh.*" He pinched gently, and waves of pleasure rolled through her body. "Relax, Julie. Lay your head back, close your eyes. Let me make it better. Let me do this for you. Come on, relax. Open for me, Julie. Just let it go."

She relaxed. Her legs fell open. Her eyes fell closed.

"Good girl." He rewarded her obedience by sliding his free hand to her breast to knead her nipple, tugging it and letting it snap, pulling and pinching. His other hand continued exploring every recess of her core, two fingers sliding inside her, moving in and out and wriggling around in her depths, while his thumb pressed and rolled her clitoris harder and faster.

The orgasm came like a hurricane, and when it hit, he increased the pressure of his touch to the very edge of pain, intensifying it. She shivered and trembled, and his mouth moved very close to her ear, whispering things to her that made it even stronger. Sexy, forbidden things, promises of what he would do the next time.

She cried out, his name perhaps, several times over, and he kept moving his fingers inside her, squeezing her nipple, pushing her further and further into mindless pleasure. And finally, when the waves began to subside, he eased his touch, reading her body and its signals as clearly as if it were printing them out in his mind. His touch became a caress, and then a massage, and then he was moving on and the sponge was back, and he was washing her legs and her feet as if nothing at all unusual had happened. He moved to her head, while she was still trembling with aftershocks, and began working shampoo into her wet hair, his touch on her scalp as erotic and arousing as it had been before. He washed and rinsed and conditioned her hair, and she lay there in the water like putty in his hands.

Finally he scooped her up out of the water, wrapped her in a towel and carried her back into her bedroom. He lowered her to the bed and returned to the bathroom. Her head was clearing now. The pain meds were kicking in. The throbbing in her ankle had eased, and her blood was reaching her brain again. Part of her wanted to lie back and pull him to her. But the rest was back in control. She remained sitting up, fixing the towel around her sarong-style. Then she took a towel from the stack he'd placed on the bed beside her and used it to rub her hair dry.

He came in again, the telephone in his hand, his jeans poking out in front. He saw her noticing, met her eyes, swallowed hard. "I'm not expecting anything, Jones. I wouldn't take it if you offered. Not now."

"But—you just—"

"I just gave you a little release. You were like a pressure cooker, woman. Something had to give."

She lowered her eyes. She didn't know what the hell to think, what the hell to make of any of this. She'd thought…she didn't know what she'd thought. It didn't matter. Only Dawn mattered.

He was at her dresser now, rummaging in an open drawer, taking out underwear, then jeans from another drawer.

"I…I can dress myself."

He went still, his back to her. "Are you sure?"

"I'm sure." She didn't tell him to get out and give her

a minute to pull herself together, but she thought he heard it in her voice.

He sighed, nodded. "Okay, then. I put some leftovers in the oven to warm. Why don't you come down when you're ready, get something to eat? Can you manage the stairs?"

"I managed them on the way up."

"Okay." He turned, sent her a searching look. "Your crutches are there, beside the bed."

She returned his gaze but kept all expression out of hers. "Okay."

He lingered in the doorway for a moment, but when he turned and started to leave, she said, "Sean?"

He turned back.

"I—I'm glad you're here. I'm not sure I could get through this alone."

He smiled a little crookedly, gave her a nod and turned to head down the stairs.

20

She cursed herself for foolish pride every time she banged her tender ankle or lost her balance as she awkwardly put her clothes on. She repeated those curses as she learned, by trial and error and damn near hurling herself to a painful death, the correct way to go down stairs on crutches.

Finally she arrived in the kitchen, breathless and probably red in the face from exertion, which she supposed was better than from embarrassment, both over what had transpired between them upstairs and over allowing herself to become so dependent on him during the past several hours.

Sean was removing a tinfoil-covered casserole dish from the oven, so she hobbled to a chair and sat down, leaning the detestable crutches against the table. They promptly fell over.

"Not exactly at pro status with those things yet, are you, Jones?"

"No, and I hope never to get there."

He set the dish on the table, using a folded towel instead of a trivet. There were plates and forks for each of them, and he'd even brewed fresh coffee. She peeled the tinfoil off the dish to see her own leftover macaroni and cheese, with two fried chicken legs lying on top of it. She lifted her brows and looked at him.

He shrugged. "Why dirty two dishes when one will do?" He helped himself to a piece of chicken, dropped the second one onto her plate, then used a large spoon to scoop enough macaroni and cheese onto his plate to feed three of him. Then he handed her the spoon.

"That's very efficient of you." She added a scoop of the macaroni to her plate.

"You want coffee?"

"I can get it."

He sent a disparaging glance at the crutches on the floor, then at her, and quickly got up and filled a mug with coffee. He went to the fridge to add a splash of half-and-half, then spooned in some sugar, without being told, then set the cup down in front of her.

"Thanks."

She took a sip, amazed that the coffee was good. Then again, she supposed a man living alone would have to learn to make decent coffee or die of caffeine deprivation. Her hands moved on autopilot, picking up the fork and scooping up some of the food, but she stopped halfway to her mouth, her stomach going queasy at the thought of eating.

"I know it's hard," Sean said. "And it seems like the coldest thing in the world to do something as self-involved as eating when we still don't know where Dawn is. But you have to try."

She took a breath, knowing he was right, and forced the food into her mouth, chewed without tasting and swallowed. Her stomach lurched, and she pressed a hand to it until the spasm passed.

"Okay?"

She met Sean's eyes, shook her head. "No. I can't eat, not now. I'll throw up."

"It's okay. Can you at least manage the coffee?"

"I think so."

He reached across the table, pushing the sugar bowl toward her. "Add some more of this, then. It'll help."

She did as he suggested and slugged back the coffee. "I

should call Rodney. I was short with him before. He didn't deserve that.''

"I apologized for you.''

"I ought to do it myself, though. He adores Dawnie. I should tell him he's welcome to wait it out with us.''

"We won't be here long. We'll have a lead to follow soon.''

"You think?''

He nodded. "Jax got the feds to send her their list of every piece of real estate ever owned, rented or borrowed by Mordecai Young and his closest cohorts, a handful of whom are still alive and doing time. Most of the property was confiscated by the government and sold at auction after the raid. But some had been sold just prior. Those are the ones she's most interested in.''

"And what is she doing about that interest?''

"Right now they're just going over the lists, prioritizing. As soon as they've got the most likely sites, they'll have local authorities drive out to those places and report back on what they see.''

She went stiff in her chair. "If they alarm him…''

"I know. I mentioned that. She assures me they'll be under instructions to use unmarked cars and to do very careful drive-by recon. Nothing that might tip him off.''

She pursed her lips. "What about when they figure out where he is? What then?''

"I don't know.''

"Sean, he won't give her up without a fight. My God, it could turn into the raid on the Young Believers all over again.''

He licked his lips. "Don't think I haven't thought of that.''

"I want that list. I want to find out where he is before they do.''

He nodded slowly. "I asked for it, but Jax wouldn't budge. I could go over there, try to lift a copy."

"And get yourself arrested."

"It wouldn't be the first time."

She pursed her lips. "I don't know. I have to think." Leaning down, she picked up her crutches, got to her feet. "Let's go talk to Rodney, then we'll head into the newsroom, work from there."

"You need some sleep."

"I need my daughter."

He bit his lip, nodded. "Okay. However you want to do it. You're calling the shots on this." He got to his feet, leaving his food barely touched, and headed for the front door ahead of her. Taking her jacket from the coatrack, he draped it over her shoulders, then opened the door for her.

"Bring the cordless phone. My cell's still in the car."

"It'll ring that far from the base?"

"Halfway. Leave it at the edge of the lawn. We'll hear it if it rings."

He nodded and went back in for the phone, giving her a head start. Not that it mattered. She moved at the speed of a tortoise, she thought. Still, she was nearly at Rodney's front stoop by the time he caught up. She could see the old man, sitting there on his screened-in front porch, in his wicker rocking chair. Odd, this late in the fall. It was chilly enough that he had to wear a jacket. His back was toward her, but she could hear him clearly as she drew near. Being hard of hearing himself, Rodney tended to speak more loudly than was necessary.

"I told you everything I know," he was saying into the telephone. "Julie is home now. She's with that MacKenzie fellow."

Julie stopped in her tracks, frowning. She felt Sean come

up beside her and sent him a quelling look. He went silent and listened.

"No, her injuries aren't serious enough to stop her. She's on crutches. Left ankle's all wrapped. And she must have hit her head, too. It's been patched up."

Sean looked down at Julie, his brows drawn together.

"Lieutenant Cassandra Jackson, she's the one in charge," he said. "Yes. Yes, I'll call you the second anyone makes a move. I *will* stay by the phone. Call me back as soon as you know what I should do next."

Nodding at something the other person said, he lowered the telephone into its cradle. Julie sent Sean a look, then started forward. He dashed ahead of her up the two steps, opened the porch's screen door and held it for her. At the creak of its hinges, Rodney swung his head around fast, then surged to his feet, looking guilty as hell.

"Rodney," Julie said slowly. "I hope to God that conversation wasn't what it sounded like. Because it sounded as if you were keeping someone informed of my every move. And I can only think of one person who'd be interested in that kind of information."

Rodney blinked. "I don't under—"

"Dawnie's kidnapper," she said. "Are you working for him, Rodney? Have you been keeping him apprised of our situation this whole time?"

The old man's brows shot upward, and his jaw dropped.

"Don't look so wounded!" she shouted. "It's obvious you've been reporting to someone. Who the hell else could it be?"

Rodney licked his lips and shot a look toward Sean as if seeking assistance, but Sean only returned a firm, steady stare. "Tell us, Rodney. Tell us the truth."

Sighing as if from the very depths of his being, Rodney

nodded. "Yes, I suppose it's time. You're not going to like it, Julie. But…well, maybe you'd better sit down."

"I'm not sitting, and this isn't going to be a long conversation. If you know where my baby is, just tell me. Just tell me, for the love of God!"

He shook his head slowly. "I don't know where she is, child. Lordy, if I did, I'd be on my way there myself. I might know, though. In a little while." He glanced at the telephone. "When he calls back."

"When *who* calls back?" Sean asked, his voice so sharp it was almost frightening.

Rodney said, "Sit down, listen, and I'll tell you."

"Rodney…" Julie began.

He sighed. "Fine. Fine, I'll just blurt it out, though this isn't the way I would have preferred to tell you. Julie, the man on the phone just now—it was Larry Jordan. It was your father."

He didn't need to tell her to sit down again. Her one good leg dissolved, and she was just lucky Sean was close enough to catch her as she lost her balance and began going over backward. He gripped her around the waist, then took the crutches away. He leaned them against the wall, then helped her to a chair and lowered her into it, taking another one close beside her.

"I think you'd better explain yourself," Sean said. He was looking at Jones, his expression worried, searching. "Julie told me her father went to prison for murdering her mother."

"She told you the truth," Rodney said. "And there he'll remain, most likely for the rest of his days. But he's not the same man he was when he did what he did. I can attest to that. He's changed."

Julie dragged her eyes upward to focus on his pale blue ones. "I don't give a damn how much he's changed," she whispered. "But I would like to know just how you know so much about him, and why the hell you're keeping him posted on my life."

Rodney licked his lips. "I was his cell mate for twelve years, Julie."

She blinked, stunned. "You were in prison?"

Rodney nodded. "Armed robbery. I did twenty-two years. Every last day of my sentence. For the last twelve, Larry and I were cell mates. More than that, we were friends. He saved my life once, when I got on the wrong side of a thug with a shiv. I owed him and swore I'd pay him back one day. He called me on it when I was about to be released. Asked me to find his little girl, to watch over her the way he would do if he were able, and to let him know, sometimes, how she was doing."

Sean licked his lips, looked at Julie. She sat there, trembling all over. "How dare he ask about me? How dare you tell him anything about my life? About my daughter? He killed my mother!"

"I know. And it haunts him. He makes no excuses. The man was a drunk—a mean drunk—and he knows it. He knows he deserves the time he's doing. He knows you have every reason to hate him forever, and he doesn't expect any less. But, Julie, that's between you and him. What's between him and me is that he saved my life. I owed him. I used every cent I could get my hands on to pay a private eye to help me track you down."

"So you found me, and then you moved in next door and pretended to be my friend?"

He shook his head. "Pretended? Now, you know better. You're angry and overwhelmed and worried, and I don't blame you. But you know better, Julie. I love you and that girl of yours as if you were my very own. You know that." Tears welled in his eyes.

She was furious. She wanted to lash out at him, to rage at him. But she couldn't. Sniffling, she said, "We loved you, too, Rodney. And we trusted you. But you betrayed us."

He lowered his head. "I gave my word. The man is paying for his crime, Julie. His heart is broken. And you can't possibly hate him for what he did as much as he hates himself."

"Don't even think of asking me to forgive him."

He shook his head slowly. "I wasn't. He knows that's never going to happen."

Sean placed a hand on Julie's shoulder, quieting her for a moment. "Rodney, when we came in, you said you might know where Dawnie is when someone called you back. How is that possible?"

He nodded rapidly. "Yes, yes, that. Well, you told me it was Mordecai Young who took Dawnie. And of course you know every one of his associates didn't burn with him in that raid wound up in prison. Turns out one of them, a fellow by the name of Gray, was the no-account who called himself Young's lawyer back then. He was taking a portion of the drug money for his services and covering Young's ass in court. For a while, anyway. He's in Attica. Same prison where I was. Same prison where Larry still is."

Sean blinked, sending Julie a look that told her this was Very Good News. But before she could search his eyes for clarification, he was focused on Rodney again. "So he's going to question Gray?"

Rodney licked his lips. "If Gray knows anything, he'll give it up. Larry's been in that prison a long time. He's respected, has a lot of men loyal to him. Gray will talk."

"And then he's going to call you back? Are you sure? Isn't his phone time limited?"

"He said he'd bribe a guard. It's not all that tough to

arrange. If he can't get out, he'll pay someone else to use his own phone time to get a message to us.''

"How long do you think it'll take?"

Before Sean finished the question, the telephone rang.

"Not long," Rodney said. "Not long at all."

The map lay unfolded on the seat beside her, held open by an English Eleven textbook and an attendance folder, illuminated only by the dashboard lights. Ms. Marcum ran a finger along the narrow twisting line as she maneuvered the car over the road it represented, her eyes darting between the two. She'd heard all about this place from Mordecai, over and over and over again. But she'd never been there, outside of the lush, vivid descriptions he had painted in her mind's eye with his words. And she knew the address. Number One Pine Tree Lane, Heaven, Virginia. He'd told her the mansion was the only house on the road that wound around an unnamed peak in the Blue Ridge Mountains.

Pine Tree Lane turned out to be little more than a worn dirt track cut into the mountainside by years of use. No pavement, not even any gravel, and not a streetlight for miles and miles. Her headlights didn't seem to penetrate very far ahead of her, and she had to drive slowly, even though everything in her was urging her to hurry. It had been a long time. Too long.

Finally the house came into view. "Oh, my God," she whispered as she guided the car into the driveway, and its headlights illuminated the front of the place. "It's incredible."

Her hands trembled on the wheel as she braked to a stop. Then, reluctantly, she put the car in Park and turned it off. She had to draw on every ounce of courage she possessed to make herself turn off the headlights, get out and walk along the flagstone path through the moonlit night. She stood outside the car for a moment after closing the door as soundlessly as she could manage and just listened. Insects whirred and chirped and buzzed, and somewhere a bullfrog croaked. She heard the soft breeze in the pines, whispering a thousand secrets to the night. She heard a splash and recalled Mordecai mentioning a crystal mountain lake. So many memories. Shards like shattered pieces of a fallen mirror, some so sharp they drew blood when she touched them.

She forced herself to move forward, walking slowly, hearing the echo of her own steps on the flagstones, wondering if he could hear them. Mordecai was a careful man. She imagined him inside, watching her approach, and so she walked slowly, keeping her hands out to her sides, so he could see she was carrying no weapons.

She reached the front steps, which marched upward between giant columns to the massive front door, and hesitated before mounting them. She strained her eyes toward the windows but could see nothing beyond them. Nothing moved. She heard no sounds coming from within.

Swallowing hard, lifting her chin, she mounted the steps and walked slowly up them. At the top, she kept going across the porch to the beautiful door with its stained-glass oval and its lion-headed knocker. Trembling like a dry leaf in an autumn wind, she reached toward the knocker.

A light came on, glaring down on her from above, blinding her, and the door flew open. She tried to shield her eyes from the glare and to see who stood there in the open doorway, but she could only make out a dark silhouette.

"Who are you?" a man's voice asked. "What do you want here? Are you lost?"

Blinking still, she held one hand over her brow, like a

salute, and that shadowed her face enough so she could stop blinking. "Mordecai?" she asked.

He said nothing. "How do you know that name?"

"Don't you recognize me?" She swallowed her fear and took a single step closer to him. It was as far as she could go without crossing the threshold.

"I thought you were dead, Mordecai," she whispered. "For the longest time, I thought you were dead."

A hand shot out, gripping her upper arm. He drew her inside, closing the door after her. She blinked in the dimness, willing her eyes to adjust, and as they did, she saw him standing there, staring at her in dawning wonder. He stared for a long time, and, finally, he cupped her face between his palms and leaned even closer. "My Lizzie? My God, is it really you?"

She nodded. "I came as soon as I knew you were alive, Mordecai. God, you don't know how long I've dreamed of this. Prayed for it. I thought I'd die without you." Closing her eyes, she moved mere millimeters closer and pressed her mouth to his. He was stiff, but he didn't pull away. It was only as her tears ran over her cheek, onto her lips and his, that he shivered and closed his arms around her and returned the kiss. When he finally lifted his head, he was smiling, his eyes were damp.

"I have Sunny here."

"I know."

"You know?" Suspicion clouded his eyes immediately.

"I've been watching over her, you know, from a distance. I teach at her high school."

"And yet you never let on?"

She shook her head. "No. There—there was so much going on. It's…it's a long and complicated story." She let her eyes roam his face. "You must have one of your own. God, Mordecai, you look so different."

"I was badly burned." He lowered his head. "You...I thought you were dead, but you and those others, you left me there. Left me to die."

"No, Mordecai. Not me. I never left you. I never would."

"But—"

She pressed a forefinger to his lips. "I was shot, bleeding. I was dying. I knew I was. I wanted to get Sunny out of there, but I knew I wouldn't be going with her. My destiny was to die there, with you. When that ceiling collapsed on you, I knew I wouldn't leave, even if I could. As it turned out, Fate agreed with me. I passed out just a few yards away from you. I thought the next time I saw you we'd both be in heaven."

He smiled slowly, no longer suspicious of her, and stroked her hair. "And so we are."

"And we have our Sunny back again?" she asked, her voice a breathy whisper.

"We do." He leaned down to kiss her again. "She's fine. Upstairs in her rooms."

"Have you told her—who she really is?"

"She knows I'm her father. And that Julie Jones is not her birth mother. I told her about you. But like me, she thinks you died." He sighed, smiling. "God, it's a miracle. She's going to be so happy."

Lowering her head to his strong shoulder, she let him stroke her hair. "I want to see her. Can I see her, Mordecai?"

"In a little while," he said. His hand felt good in her hair. Good and tender and loving. She'd loved him so much once.

She still did. Despite everything.

"I love you, Mordecai," she whispered.

"Come, then. Come with me. Let me be with you again,

the way we used to be. God, I've missed you so much, Lizzie.''

He scooped her into his arms and started up a broad, curving staircase. She kissed him enthusiastically, let him run his hands over her as he took her along a hallway and through a set of double doors into a darkened room. She felt the bed beneath her back as he lowered her onto it, felt the cool air on her skin as he began to undress her.

Sean kept his hands on Julie's shoulders. She'd surged to her feet when the old man picked up the phone and was probably battling the urge to shout at him to hurry up while he listened. Finally he nodded and repeated an address. ''Number One, Pine Tree Lane, Heaven, Virginia,'' he said.

Sean scrambled for a pen, found one on a nearby table and scribbled the address. But then he realized Rodney was talking again. ''I've told her everything, Larry,'' he was saying to the man on the phone. ''Yes, in fact, she's here right now.'' He paused, looking intently at Julie, and then he said, ''I don't know. I'll try.'' Then he slowly moved the telephone toward Julie, holding it out to her. ''Will you talk to him?''

Sean dropped the pen, seeing the stark-white color of Julie's face as she stared at the telephone. She backed away, knocking over a chair in the process, and shook her head rapidly from side to side.

Rodney drew the phone back to his own ear. ''Sorry, Larry. It's too sudden. All right. Yes, I'll let you know as soon as Dawn is safe.'' Nodding, he said, ''Yes, I'll tell her.'' He looked at Julie again. ''He loves you, and he's sorry for what he did. He's praying for Dawnie.''

''I don't want his love, *or* his apologies,'' she said, lunging forward again, shaking off Sean's grip on her shoulders. ''And I don't need his prayers.'' She yanked the telephone out of Rodney's hand and shouted into it. "Do you hear me? I don't need anything from you! Not ever!" Then she tugged the phone away from her ear, staring at it, and Sean moved closer, took it from her and heard the dial tone that told him her father had already hung up. He replaced it in its cradle, wishing to God he could do something to ease the pain in Julie's eyes.

"At least we have a lead now. We know where she might be."

"Larry was pretty sure," Rodney said. "He said that according to Young's former lawyer, that's the place where he always planned to go one day, and he transferred ownership to one of his aliases before the raid."

Sean nodded. "We should phone Jax, let her know where they—"

"No!" Julie slapped him with the word.

"But, Jones, they're going through a list of more than a hundred possible locations. This would speed things up."

"Just exactly what do you think it would speed up, Sean? The moment when a couple of hundred soldiers with machine guns and explosives surround my innocent child and her insane father? Jesus, if the cops get to them before we do, history will repeat itself. He won't let them take her alive. I have to get to her first. I have to."

He nodded slowly, then shot a look at Rodney.

The old man held up his hands. "I won't say a word to anyone if you don't want me to."

Sean pursed his lips, looking again at Julie. "If we leave, they're going to be after us. You know Jax is keeping an eye on you."

She nodded. "How far is it?"

"By car, nine to twelve hours, depending on where it is in the state. I can give you a better idea with a map."

"Then let's go get one."

"We could fly down there. Save time."

She nodded. "Jax will check the airlines the second I'm missing. And as soon as she knows where we went, she'll be that much closer to setting loose the hounds of hell on my kid."

"She's going to figure it out anyway, just by the process of elimination, Jones."

Julie sighed, and he knew she was wrestling with the weight of the decision.

"Come on. Let's get this show on the road." Sean handed her the crutches. She'd been putting weight on the bad ankle and barely aware of it, he thought. "We'll have you call Jax to check on things just before we leave. That way she shouldn't think to check on your whereabouts for a while." He glanced at Rodney. "Can we use your car? That way ours will still be in the driveway and they may not realize we've skipped out quite as soon."

"I'll do better than that," he said, getting to his feet as if it were an effort. "I'll drive you to the airport. That way they won't know you're gone or notice my car missing, either."

"Then it sounds like we have a plan." Sean looked at Julie. "Okay?"

"We should have weapons. We should have a gun."

"We'd never get it on the plane, Julie," Sean said.

She lowered her head. "Then I'm going to have to find a way to kill him without one. Because one way or the other, I swear to Christ, Mordecai Young is not going to live to torment me or my daughter again."

The scary part was, Sean didn't doubt for one second that she meant it.

21

Dawn didn't sleep. She lay awake in the bedroom with the lights blazing brightly. She'd never been afraid of the dark before, but here, in this strange place, with this insane man—her birth father—she was terrified. God, she still couldn't believe it was true. That Mordecai Young, one of the most famous cult leaders she'd ever heard of, was her father. It might be. She supposed it made some kind of sense. But she didn't want to believe she was genetically related to a lunatic. Didn't that make her part lunatic, as well? She'd never *felt* crazy.

Maybe he didn't feel crazy, either. Maybe crazy people never felt as if there was anything wrong with them.

She wanted her mom. She wanted her nice house and her own room and some of Rodney's chocolate chip cookies. She wanted Kayla.

There was no telephone here, no computer and Internet. She'd kept her eyes peeled for any way to get a message out, but she'd found none. There must be at least a telephone somewhere in this house, though. She'd planned to slip out of her room and search the mansion for it, but her so-called father had locked her in.

She closed her eyes against a new rush of tears as she wondered if she would ever see her mom again. Then she dashed those tears away with an angry swipe of her hand. Julie Jones was her mom, no matter what biology or insane kidnappers might say. And she was the most aggressively protective mom on the planet. She was probably doing a house-to-house search right now. She would kick this man's ass all the way back to Cazenovia when she caught up to him. She would never stop searching until she found her. Never.

Poor Mom, she thought, aching for the pain and terror her mother must be suffering right now. Thank God she had Sean around to help her through this.

There were footsteps outside the bedroom door, and Dawn sat up straight in the bed. It was 3:00 a.m. God, what could he want at this hour? She fixed her eyes on the door, her mind racing, her heart pounding, as the knob moved. Slowly the door opened.

But the woman who stood there was the last person she expected to see. "Ms. Marcum?" Dawn leaped from the bed and ran across the room, flinging her arms around her favorite teacher. "Oh, God, how did you find me? I'm so glad to see you! Did you bring the police?"

"Easy, easy, Dawn." Her teacher hugged her hard. Behind her, Dawn saw Mordecai Young, looking at the two of them, his eyes damp, his smile unsteady.

"You two have a lot to talk about," he said. "I'll leave you alone." He pulled the door closed.

Dawn pulled out of her teacher's embrace all at once and stared up at her as she backed away. "What *is* this? Do you *know* him?"

The woman nodded slowly; then she looked around the room, spotted the French doors. "Let's sit outside, shall we? It's a beautiful night."

"I don't want to go outside, I want to know what the hell is going on! That man kidnapped me! I want to go home."

"I know. Everything's going to be all right, Dawn. You just have to trust me." She crossed the room, opened the doors and stepped out onto the balcony, then turned, waiting for Dawn to join her there.

Dawn couldn't remember ever being more confused in her life, but she went outside. Ms. Marcum closed the doors after her.

"Why don't we sit?" she asked, nodding toward the patio chairs. "It's so much warmer here than at home, isn't it?"

"I guess." Dawn sat down, tried not to shiver. It wasn't cold, and she was still fully dressed in a pair of jeans and a sweater she'd found among the clothes in the closets and drawers. There were tons of them, in a wide range of sizes. He must have been stocking up for years.

"Dawn, I know that you're already aware of that fact that your mom didn't give birth to you. I, um—I was there, with her. At the Young Believers' compound all those years ago."

Dawn shook her head. "Mom never said she knew you."

"She doesn't know who I am." Ms. Marcum shrugged. "I always manage to be absent when she's coming in for a school event or open house. Haven't you noticed that?"

She waited for a response, but Dawn didn't give one. She was busy recalling all the times Ms. Marcum had vanished just as her mom arrived at the school and the way her mom had just said the other day how badly she felt for never having met Dawn's favorite teacher.

And then she remembered something else. "Mom said everyone who was with her there was dead."

"She thought I was. I was shot, and I collapsed. She dragged my body into the escape tunnel and left me there. I guess she just couldn't bring herself to leave me behind in the burning building. I was found there, still alive, though barely. I spent months in a coma, and when I woke, I had no memory of who I was."

"That's awful!"

She nodded. "Yes, it was awful. But gradually, things started coming back to me. Bits and pieces of my life before. It took years, and my memory is still very sketchy in some areas, but I do remember my time at the Young Believers' compound. I remember your mom. And I remember you, Dawn." She smiled a little, and Dawn went stiff in anticipation of what was coming next. "My name is Elizabeth, Dawn. Lizzie, back then. I was your mother's best friend. I'm the one who gave birth to you, and who begged Jewel to take care of you because I thought I was dying."

Dawn shot to her feet. "No!"

"I know it sounds crazy, Dawn, but it's true. I'm your mother."

"No!" Dawn shouted the word. "Stop it, stop all of this. I don't want to hear any more!" She pressed her hands to her ears, turning away from the woman who was suddenly just another threat to her.

"Please, Dawn. Don't be childish. You have to be strong, be brave. You have to face the truth."

"Truth?" Dawn whirled to face her again. "What do you know about truth? I've known you since seventh grade! Why wouldn't you have said anything before now?"

Ms. Marcum lowered her head. "Years went by before I remembered enough to even begin searching for you. By then I'd gone back to school, earned a degree in English. Then I found you—quite by accident. Your mother was covering a freak storm, a tornado in central New York, and it was picked up by the wire services. I saw it, saw her byline. Julie Jones, WSNY in Syracuse N.Y. It was like…it was like kismet. Like fate wanted me to know where you were."

"Now you sound like *him.*"

She shrugged. "He's not entirely wrong, you know."

"Not everything is a sign from above, Ms. Marcum. It's like Mr. Bonwell in psychology says. 'Sometimes a cigar is just a cigar.'"

She smiled. "This time, it was a sign. So I moved to Syracuse, looked you up. You were so happy. I decided the best thing to do would be to just stay out of your life. But I couldn't bring myself to do that, not entirely. So I got a job as a substitute teacher in your district while I worked on my teaching certification. I never planned to tell you the truth, Dawnie. Just to watch over you from a distance. As long you were happy, I saw no need to disrupt your life." She lowered her eyes. "But now...things are different now."

Dawn felt her eyes widen, but Ms. Marcum went on. "Now that I know Mordecai is alive, we can be together, as a family. Just like we always planned."

Her hand came out to stroke Dawn's hair, and Dawn closed her eyes and wondered if the entire world had gone insane.

Lieutenant Jackson waited while Julie Jones's telephone rang and rang, and then she heard the unmistakable clicking sound on the line, and a new ring, sounding slightly different, began. She pursed her lips. Jones had her call forwarding activated. That meant she wasn't at her house.

The new ring sounded several times before voice mail picked up and asked her to leave a message. It sounded like the cellular voice mail message she used herself. Jax hung up the phone, got to her feet and pulled her coat from the back of her chair.

"Where you going?" Chief Strong asked. "We're still waiting to rule out eighteen sites!"

"Gotta check on Jones," she said. "She's not at Channel

Four, and there's no answer at MacKenzie's place, or at Jones's, either. She's got the call forwarding on.''

"To where?''

"Her cell, I'm guessing. But she's either out of range or turned off.''

The chief pursed his lips. "Your case, your call. How do you want to handle it? I can have a warrant issued. Just say the word.''

Jax hesitated. She would hate like hell to put out a warrant for Julie Jones's arrest while the woman's daughter was still missing. It seemed heartless, and despite popular opinion, Jax was far from heartless. She did have feelings; she just didn't indulge them the way some did. She wasn't a sap. She was fairly certain Jones had murdered Harry Blackwood. She was equally certain the bastard had it coming. But it wasn't her job to justify crimes, just to solve them. She was going to have to lock Julie Jones up, sooner or later. She wasn't going to like it, but she damn well was going to do it. It was her job.

She pursed her lips. "You know, I doubt she'd skip town without a good reason,'' she said. "She knew I'd come after her the second she did, and she seemed to want to avoid a jail cell as long as possible.''

The chief lifted his heavy brows. "You think she may be going after the girl?''

"Maybe. Why don't you have someone check the airlines for me while I drive out to her place?''

"Done. Call in when you get there.''

She nodded once and headed out the door. Within twenty minutes, she was at Julie Jones's place, because she'd done eighty most of the way, even though she hadn't bothered with lights and noise. No one bothered her. When she pulled in, MacKenzie's car was parked in the driveway. A palm to the hood told her the engine was cold. She peered into the garage, saw the Jeep parked there. No damp tire marks behind it, so she didn't think it had been moved lately. The roads were wet this morning. Jones's Mercedes was either still over a ravine up in the mountains or sitting at some roadside garage waiting for her to come and claim it. She hadn't driven that. She hadn't driven anything, by the looks of the place. But it was locked up tight and looked empty, despite the lights Jones had left on to make it look occupied.

Jax pulled her cell phone from her pocket and called in, asked for the chief and waited while she was put through. He picked up. "Well?"

"Nothing. They're not here, either of them. All vehicles are accounted for."

"Someone drove them, then."

"Drove them where? Did you get a hit for me, Chief?"

"Yeah. They're in Virginia. Hopped an American Airlines flight from Hancock to Norfolk that left around 4:00 a.m."

"Hell."

"We're already on the horn to Norfolk. Wait a sec." His voice became muffled as he yelled to someone else in the room; then he came back a moment later. "Yeah, they rented a car when they arrived at Norfolk. We have the make, model and plate number, but where they're going is anyone's guess."

Jax narrowed her eyes. "Check the list."

"What's that?"

"Check the list of properties associated with Mordecai Young, the one we've been going over. See if any of the ones we haven't checked out yet are in the state of Virginia. Or anywhere close to it. Maryland, D.C., maybe West Virginia." She heard papers rustling. "I mean, maybe they got a lead we didn't know about, though why the hell they would take off like a couple of vigilantes instead of letting us handle it is beyond—''

"Bingo."

She stopped speaking. "You found it?"

"Number One, Pine Tree Lane. Someplace called Heaven, Virginia. It changed hands just before the raid. Ten to one the new owner is just another alias."

"I'm hopping a flight to Norfolk."

"I'll let the locals know you're coming. He's crossed state lines, now, Jax. The feds will be there in droves."

She swallowed hard. "We don't know that he's crossed state lines. We're guessing. Why not let me confirm it before we notify them, huh?"

"Jax—"

"I'm thinking about the raid, Chief. I'm thinking about what happened the last time the feds got involved with this maniac. We want the kid back, don't we?"

He was silent for a long moment. Then, finally, he sighed. "Get down there, find the place, and stay in freaking touch. You're bound and determined to cost me my job, aren't you?"

"Only if I get to replace you, Chief."

He told her to do something that would require a marital aid and hung up.

Jax clicked the cutoff button and drove north, past the city and toward the airport.

Julie was tense and stiff, her ankle aching as much as her head did. Sean, she thought, looked like hell as he drove the rented car, and he kept rubbing the back of his neck with one hand as if his muscles ached.

"You didn't have to come with me, you know," she told him.

He glanced sideways at her, his eyes tired. "Yes, I did."

"Why do you say so?"

"You telling me you don't know? Think about it, Jones."

Pursing her lips, she tipped her head as she thought. "Oh," she said at length. "You're still trying to make up for what you think you did wrong sixteen years ago, the day of the raid."

He frowned. "Funny. I hadn't thought about that in quite a while." He shrugged. "But it's not why I came."

"Why, then?"

He sent her a searching look, then finally just shook his head. "Not now. It's not the time."

"Come on, Sean. You must have an angle."

He looked a little sad for a moment, but then he sent her a wink. "Always. Besides, I promised the kid she could take her driver's test on my car. And she needs a lot more practice."

Julie swallowed hard and wondered. For a while last night, when he'd touched her the way he had, she'd started to think he might have something long-term in mind for the two of them. But she didn't know who the hell she was kidding. He wanted her sexually. She wanted him that way, too. She supposed there wasn't going to be anything more than that.

It was a good way to pass the time, wondering if she would give in and have a brief, sexual affair with him, turning it over in her mind. It didn't keep her from worrying about Dawn, didn't even calm her roiling stomach or sooth her frayed nerves. But it passed the time.

"What's the name of that road again?"

"Pine Tree Lane," she said, glancing down at the map that was open on her thighs. "We should get off in about two more exits."

"Great. We'll be there before you know it." He nodded

at her bag on the floor. "How about the cell phone? You have a signal yet?"

She pulled the phone out of her bag. "Nope. Not even a weak one."

"It's the mountains," he said.

He drove a little farther, and she saw the next exit sign, confirmed the number against her map and nodded hard. "Should be the next one. Off the ramp, straight about ten miles, then hang a left onto Pine Tree. It winds its way up a mountainside."

"It's up ahead, I can see the sign from here."

She nodded, glancing at the dashboard clock. It was early morning, the sun was barely up. But she would be with her daughter soon, she told herself. Soon. What the hell was she going to do when she got there?

All too soon, she found out.

Sean took the exit, and the next ten miles seemed more like a hundred. But finally they were turning onto Pine Tree Lane and making their way along its winding length. Steep mountain stone rose up on her left, and there was a seemingly bottomless drop-off on her right. She felt like a spider walking up a wall.

"That must be it," Sean said at last, pointing at the roof that was just coming into view up ahead. "We should park down here, walk the rest of the way."

"Element of surprise and all that?"

He nodded. "Yeah, but you can ride piggyback."

"I can walk."

"Crush a guy's fantasies, why don't you?"

She smiled at that, because he sounded almost normal. As if every crazy thing that had happened in the past few days didn't exist. As if things were the way they were supposed to be, with the two of them exchanging killer barbs that cut to the quick and loving every minute of it.

He pulled the car onto the shoulder, got out. She got out her door, and when Sean leaned in from his side, reaching into the back seat for her crutches, she told him, "Leave them."

"Jones…"

"Leave them. It barely hurts to walk on it."

"You're a freaking liar." But he left the crutches where they were and came around the car. "Come on, then. It's either the crutches or piggyback."

"You don't have to—"

"Jones, will you stop arguing and wrap your goddamn thighs around my waist, already?" He turned his back to her and bent low. Sighing, she mounted his back, legs hugging his waist, arms hugging his neck.

"Not exactly what I have in mind when I mutter that line in my daydreams," Sean said, "but what the hell."

"Your rapier wit is killing me."

He straightened easily and started hiking up the road.

She stared down at his head as he carried her. "Gee, is your hair starting to thin back here?"

"Don't even joke about something like that." He glanced up at her, smiled a little. "Good to have you back, Jones."

"Good to *be* back, MacKenzie."

He gripped her thighs in his hands for added support as he marched along. Then the house came into view, and he veered off to the side, walking to a large boulder and lowering her to the ground so that it blocked her view of the house.

"You stay here," he said. "I'll sneak up and get a closer look."

"No."

"You're impaired. I'm not. I'll be quicker, quieter and less likely to get caught."

"If he sees you, he'll kill you."

She looked around the ground, snatched up a short limb and marched out from behind the boulder toward the house. Every step sent pain shooting through her ankle, and she wished to God she'd listened to Sean. She was approaching the house from the side, and she veered at an angle across the meadow beside it, toward the rear, rather than walking at it head on.

Sean, of course, was right beside her. "Goddammit, woman, why won't you listen to me? You think you have less chance of pissing him off than I do?"

"He could have killed me after the accident, but he didn't. I have to believe he had a reason. Mordecai *always* has a reason. He'd have no qualms about putting a bullet in you, though." She limped faster. "Stay put, and let me be the one to take a look."

"No way, lady. I'm not letting you go in there alone."

"Afraid I'll scoop you? Get the big story all for my-self?"

"We're partners. When are you going to get that through your head?"

She stopped hobbling and glared at him. He stood close to her and glared back.

"I didn't come down here for the story, Jones. I came down here for you and for Dawnie. And you goddamn well know it."

She lowered her eyes slowly. "I really...wasn't sure."

"Then you're an idiot." He snapped his arms around her waist without warning, yanked her hard against him and covered her mouth with his, kissing her hard and fast and thoroughly. When he let her go again, she was breathless.

"Sean, I can't—"

"Shut up, Jones." He scooped her up and carried her back to the shelter of the boulder, set her down, and then made his way slowly to the house, moving from one tree to another, completely exposed in between.

She held her breath as he darted ever closer to the house. When she thought she saw something move beyond one of the heavily curtained windows, she almost shouted a warning that would have been heard by anyone inside.

Finally he got all the way to the rear of the house and the back door, and peered through the glass—just one quick peek; then he ducked again. She wondered if he'd seen anything, wondered if he'd *been* seen.

But she didn't have to wonder long. Something icy cold and hard pressed into the hollow beneath her ear, and a voice, laced with just the merest hint of the familiar Southern drawl, said, "Jewel, my precious. I'm so glad you could join us. It's gonna be just like old times, honey. You and me, Sunny and Lizzie, all together again. Come on, now. Come on with me, and not a peep now, or I'll have to put a bullet in your nosy boyfriend."

He tugged her, and she went with him around to the front of the house and up onto the porch. He made her move far more quickly than she'd been moving before, and her foot was screeching with anguish every single step of the way. She couldn't see Sean anymore, and, dammit, she was longing to.

Then he was there, peering from around the corner of the house as Mordecai tugged her onto the front porch, then pulling back quickly.

But it was too late. Mordecai had seen him. He tightened his hold on her and said, "No, no, no, you don't. I don't think so. You just step on out here or I'll kill her."

"Let her go," Sean said.

"Don't delay—MacKenzie, isn't it? Didn't we have an appointment yesterday? You step on out now. It's her or you." He thumbed the hammer back, pressed the gun to her chin.

"Don't do it, Sean!" Julie shouted.

Sean poked his head around the corner, met her eyes, held them.

"Good. Now, step all the way out, where I can see you. Come on, move it."

"Don't, Sean. Run. For the love of God, run!" Julie cried.

But instead of listening to her, Sean stepped around the corner of the house, hands out at his sides.

"Thank you for making this so easy, my friend." Mordecai jerked his gun away from Julie's head, aiming it instead at Sean. It exploded in Mordecai's hand, splitting her eardrums. She shrieked, but never heard the sound. Sean crumpled, landing in a heap in the grass. Mordecai opened the front door and dragged her inside, slamming the door closed behind them.

22

Dawn sat across the pretty hardwood table from Ms. Marcum, finishing her breakfast of cold cereal and toast, even though she had very little appetite for it. They'd moved the table closer to the French doors of her bedroom, so they sat in a pool of morning sunlight. It would have been almost pleasant if she wasn't being held prisoner.

"Thanks for staying with me, Ms. Marcum. It's better when I'm not alone." She needed to win her teacher over to her side, but it was extremely difficult to hide her increasing anger and frustration.

The woman smiled gently at her. "You can call me Lizzie, you know."

Dawn nodded, decided to try to force it, even though it felt strange to call her teacher by her first name. Especially a first name that belonged to a teenager. She was Ms. Marcum. She'd been Ms. Marcum for three years. And now she wanted Dawn to suddenly stop thinking of her that way, to think of her as…what? Her mother? She supposed she should be grateful Ms. Marcum wasn't asking Dawn to call her "Mom." Mordecai or Nathan or whoever the maniac was, insisted she call him "Father." She had managed to address him that way once or twice, sensing he would go postal on her if she disobeyed, no matter how sweet and loving he was trying to act. Sweet, loving men didn't kidnap their offspring.

"At least when you're in here, he doesn't keep the doors locked," Dawn said at length. "I hate being locked in."

"Once he's convinced that you won't try to run away, he'll stop locking you in. But he won't stop watching over you. Mordecai is always watching...over you." She glanced toward the front door as she spoke, making Dawn frown, but then she went on. "It's really for your own safety, you know. If you took off in this terrain—well, anything could happen."

"Yeah. I could be kidnapped by a maniac, for example. Oh, wait, I forgot. That already happened."

Ms. Marcum pursed her lips. "He wouldn't appreciate your sarcasm, Dawnie."

"I don't appreciate being held against my will."

"I know." The woman slid her hand over Dawn's on the table. "It's going to be all right. I promise."

Dawn snatched her hand away. "I want to get out of here, Ms. Marcum. I want to go home. My mother was hurt in that accident, God only knows how badly. And besides that, she's got to be going out of her mind worrying about me by now."

"I know. I know."

"Maybe he'd let me call her. You could talk him into it, I know you could. He...he likes you. I mean, loves you, right?"

She smiled softly. "Not enough to risk losing you again, I'm afraid."

"You have to at least try. Please, Ms. Marcum? Lizzie? Please? Just get him to let me talk to her. So I can tell her I'm all right and she can stop worrying herself sick over me. Please?"

She lowered her head. "I'll try."

"Now?"

"As soon as he comes back inside."

Dawn blinked, and her pulse seemed to skip. "He's not in the house?" She jumped to her feet.

"He thought he saw something outside," Ms. Marcum said, following Dawn to the bedroom door. "He only went out to look. He didn't go far, Dawnie."

She stopped there, her words cut off by a sharp explosive sound. Dawn swung her eyes to Ms. Marcum's. "Was that a gunshot?"

"I don't know. Dawnie, wait!"

But Dawn was off, racing into the hall and down the wide staircase. She heard a woman's voice cry out, and she ran into the foyer, where she saw Mordecai dragging her mom into the house, slamming and locking the door even as Julie tried to rip it open again. He turned and shoved her away from him, and she stumbled backward a few steps, then landed on her backside on the floor.

"Mom!" Dawn raced to her, falling to her knees beside her and into her arms.

"Dawnie. Oh, God, oh, God, you're all right." Her mother hugged her hard, and Dawn hugged back, unable to stop the tears from running down her face.

"Sunny, get back to your room." Mordecai's voice wasn't loud, just very firm and insistent.

Dawn lifted her head to glare at him. "Go to hell. You touch my mother again and I'll kill you myself! Look at her! Look at what you did to her!"

He stared at her and at Julie for a long moment, and Dawn expected him to explode. But he didn't. He noted the bandage on Julie's head, the wrapped ankle, the exhaustion and pain etched on her face, Dawn thought. Then he drew a breath, closed his eyes briefly. "I didn't mean for you to get hurt, Jewel. I was only trying to force you to pull the car over and stop."

Julie leveled a furious glare on the man. "You could

have killed us both. Dawn and me. But you risked it anyway. That's not love, Mordecai. That's not what a man who loves a child does.''

"You know nothing about what I feel for my daughter. Nothing." He pushed a hand over his shaved head and paced a few steps away before facing her again. "How many came with you? Who else knows?"

"No one."

He stared at her as if trying to decide whether to believe her; then his eyes shifted to Dawn's again. "It really was an accident, what happened on that road, Sunny. I would never do anything to hurt you."

Dawn wanted to swear at him, but she sensed he was near the end of his patience.

"And what about Sean?" Julie asked. "Was that an accident, too?"

"Sean?" Dawn looked at her mother. "What happened to Sean?"

Mordecai sent a look across the room, toward where Ms. Marcum waited at the bottom of the stairs. "Take them both up to Sunny's room. Stay there until I tell you differently."

Ms. Marcum hurried forward, while Dawn helped her mom to her feet. Julie rose and, leaning on Dawn, began to limp toward the other woman, but halfway there she stopped and just stared. She blinked back tears. "Oh, my God. Lizzie?"

"Hi, Jewel. It's been a long time."

"But—but how? I don't understand." Julie frowned then, her arm closing protectively around Dawn's waist. "Are you a part of this?"

"Mom, let's get upstairs." Dawn sent her mom a look, and when Julie met her eyes, Dawn knew she'd gotten the message. It was one of those exchanges they shared so often, when they didn't need words to tell each other the really important things. Dawn knew better than to push Mordecai much further. And she thought she might be starting to get through to Ms. Marcum.

With an imperceptible nod, Julie continued limping across the room, and she let Dawn and Ms. Marcum help her up the stairs. Below them, once he saw they were following his orders, Mordecai began running from room to room, looking out windows, checking the locks.

"What happened to Sean?" Dawn whispered when she was sure they were out of earshot.

"Mordecai shot him," Julie said softly.

"Is he…?"

"I don't know." She looked to the other woman. "Is there a window where we can see the front lawn? He was lying there, in the grass just off the end of the porch. I have to look. I have to see."

"No. I shouldn't. Mordecai said—"

"Please?" Dawn asked. "It'll only take a minute."

After a nervous glance down the stairs, Ms. Marcum nodded and led them to one of the rooms on the opposite side of the house from Dawn's. "He gave me the grand tour last night," she explained to Dawn. "After you went to sleep. I think you'll be able to see from here…."

Julie broke away, limping rapidly to the window at the far end of the lushly furnished but unoccupied bedroom. She pushed the lace curtains wide and stared down at the ground, and Dawn hurried to stand beside her, looking all around, but seeing nothing. "Where is he?" Dawn asked.

"I don't know. He was…he was right there." She pointed.

"Then he's not dead," Dawn said, and she said it emphatically. "He must have been able to get away."

"Not away. Maybe undercover, but not away. He's still out there somewhere. And Mordecai will find him and—"

"Mom, how can you be sure? He was hurt, but he probably made his way back to the car—you guys must have had a car, right? So he probably managed to get back to it, and he's gone for help."

Julie shook her head slowly. "He won't leave us here. He won't." She licked her lips. "He knew Mordecai would shoot him—he just stood there and let it happen. To protect me."

"Oh, God, Mom." Dawn embraced her mother again, burying her head on her mom's shoulder. "He'll be okay. He has to be. I can't believe this is happening." She lifted her head, then rested her forehead against Julie's, blinking away her tears. "At least you know he loves you."

Julie frowned, turning away, blinking rapidly. "Don't be silly, Dawn."

"We should get to the bedroom, as Mordecai told us," Ms. Marcum said in a harsh whisper.

That seemed to distract Julie, because she looked up at Ms. Marcum, and her face darkened. "What are you doing here, Lizzie? Why in the name of heaven would you have stayed involved with a lunatic like him all this time?"

Lizzie looked stricken, but Dawn spoke before she could. "I don't think it's like that, Mom."

"She's right, it's not."

"Maybe you'd better tell me what exactly it *is* like," Julie said.

Lizzie nodded. "Jewel, I was barely alive when they pulled me out of the wreckage of that compound. I was in a coma for months, and when I woke, I didn't know who I was or what had happened to me. It took years to regain my memory. As soon as I did, I started searching for the two of you. But it was a long time before I finally found you.''

''And when was that?'' Julie asked.

''Four years ago. Dawnie was only twelve. Seventh grade. And she was so happy. You were— God, Jewel, you were a better mom than I ever could have been. I could see that. Anyone could see that.''

Frowning, Julie sat down on the bed. It seemed as if she'd just run out of energy to stand. ''You've known where we were for four years?'' She shook her head slowly. ''And you didn't say anything? You didn't try to see Dawn, or...''

''Oh, I saw her. I saw her every single day.''

Julie looked blank. Dawn closed a hand on her shoulder. ''Mom, Lizzie is Ms. Marcum.''

Her mother looked stunned. ''You? You're her teacher?''

She nodded. ''I wasn't trying to meddle in your lives, and I never even thought of trying to take her back. God, Jewel, I was the weak one. Don't you remember? You were the one always protecting me, looking out for me. You were the one who figured out that Mordecai was drugging us. You were the one who figured out a way to smuggle untainted food in from the gardens so that we could get our minds back, and you were the one who came up with the plan to get us close to Mordecai so we could find a way to escape. Dawnie wouldn't have survived to be born if not for you. And none of us would have survived that raid.'' She lowered her head. ''I knew you were the best mom my Sunny could ask for. She was so happy, and she loved you so much. I could see it. I couldn't even think about disrupting the life you had built for her.''

Julie blinked slowly. ''And every parent-teacher day, every open house, every time I set foot in that school, you managed to be absent or called away on some assignment or something.''

Ms. Marcum nodded. ''I just wanted to be where I could see her from time to time. Watch over her. And also protect her. Because I was sure Mordecai hadn't died in that fire, either. I was convinced of it, even though sometimes I questioned my own sanity.'' She bit her lip. ''I saw those obituaries. Sirona and Tessa. I recognized them. And I knew—I knew he was back, and I knew he was coming.''

Julie blinked. ''You're the one who sent me the obituaries,'' she whispered.

''And I was the anonymous caller. I was trying to warn you. So you could protect Dawn. Not that he would ever hurt her—he wouldn't. You have to know he wouldn't.''

''Who are Sirona and Tessa?'' Dawn asked, having lost the thread of the story.

Julie looked at her. ''Two other girls who escaped the compound with you and me that day.''

''And you think Mordecai…killed them?'' Dawn asked. Her voice shook a little, even though she tried not to let it.

''No, of course he didn't,'' Ms. Marcum said with a quick glance back toward the door. ''He wouldn't have hurt them. I think they killed themselves when they were forced to face how deeply they'd betrayed him.''

''You're still as deluded as you ever were, aren't you, Lizzie?'' Julie asked.

She shook her head. ''You never understood him, Jewel. But I did. I knew, when I got the news that Dawn had been taken, that it had to be Mordecai. And I remembered all the promises he made to me about how he was going to establish a new church, with himself as the head of it. The new Messiah. And how he had this plantation house in Virginia that he'd bought and was having renovated. We would be a family, the three of us, Mordecai and me and our baby girl, and we'd live in our home at the highest point in Heaven, the only house on Pine Tree Lane. Number one. He said it was fitting. I remembered it all.''

In the distance, Dawn heard a sound. A siren. No, more than one. And as they grew louder, she saw Ms. Marcum and her mom exchange a look that chilled her to the bone.

"Oh, God," Julie whispered. "God, not this, not again." She gripped Ms. Marcum's arm hard. "We have to get Dawn out of here, Lizzie. We have to do it now!"

"Lizzie! Sunny!" Mordecai's voice rang through the hall as his feet pounded closer.

Mordecai burst into the room just as Lizzie slammed the back of her hand across Julie's face. Dawn yelped in horror as Julie tumbled backward onto the bed. "I told you to get Sunny back to her bedroom, and I meant it!" Lizzie shouted. "Don't cross me, Jewel."

"You'll pay for this, Lizzie. I was your friend once. I raised your child for you. God, how could you turn on me like this? Much less on her? Your own flesh and blood?" Julie's words seethed with anger. Dawn trembled with the force of it. She'd never seen her mother this angry.

"You *stole* my child," Ms. Marcum corrected. "But that's over now." She gripped Julie's arm, and pulled her to her feet. "Come on."

They all turned, and Ms. Marcum saw Mordecai, in the doorway, came up short, as if in surprise, then spoke to him. "I'm sorry I didn't take them straight to the bedroom. It's not a mistake I'll make again."

He stared at her, searching her eyes. "For a moment I thought you'd decided to run out on me. Leave me to die at the hands of the soldiers. Like last time."

She went to him, pressed herself close to his body and slid her hands around his neck. The tears that rolled down her face were thick, and they left red streaks. "I didn't mean to leave you, Mordecai, but to die with you. Just as I will now, today, if that's what it takes to prove my love to you.''

He seemed to hesitate, then, finally, closed one arm around her waist and let her lips find his. She kissed him almost desperately. "I love you, Mordecai. I know you better than anyone else, I know the man you are inside, the man no one else can see. I've always known that man. I've always loved him.''

He ran a hand over her hair, clasped her nape, kissed her forehead. "No one ever loved me the way you do, Lizzie. God, I need you.''

"And I'm here.''

He nodded, gently pushing her aside, and that was when Dawn saw the gun in his other hand, as he waved it toward her mother. "Come on, you two. You need to go into the safe room, downstairs. It's bulletproof, fireproof. You'll be safe there. I promise.''

Dawn clung close to her mother and walked ahead of Lizzie and the madman, as sirens screamed and brakes squealed outside the house.

Sean felt as if he were reliving the nightmare that had haunted him all his life, only instead of crouching in the bushes outside a compound with a camera, he was crouching behind a boulder with a sizable bullethole in his chest. And instead of agents from the bureau of alcohol, tobacco and firearms piling out of vehicles and taking up positions behind them, it was a selection of police. County Sheriff's Department vehicles and Virginia State Police cruisers came to cockeyed stops alongside unmarked sedans that could have belonged to federal agents. No trucks full of soldiers in full body armor. Not this time. But the results probably wouldn't be any different. The arrival of two ambulances on the fringes of the action confirmed his theory that they were expecting the worst.

He struggled out of his shirt, leaving on the ribbed tank style undershirt he wore beneath it, better to examine the bullet wound. He'd fully expected to be dead in short order when he'd felt the impact—like a sledgehammer to the chest. It hit him so hard his feet left the ground several heartbeats before his back slammed into it. Now, though, he saw that it wasn't as bad as it could have been.

He tore a strip off his shirt and used it to dab away the blood until he could locate the hole, two inches below the collarbone on the right side of his chest. Far from the heart, thank God, and he didn't think it had impacted a lung, either. At least, he seemed to be breathing okay. The pain was intense, but nothing like he would have imagined a bullet wound would feel. It burned, as if someone had taken a cattle brand to his chest. It had bled quite a lot, but he was still conscious, so he didn't figure it was a life threatening loss. He wadded up another piece of his shirt and pressed it to the hole, wincing at the increased pain the pressure brought. Almost as an afterthought, he leaned forward, craning his neck to try to see his own back. He couldn't see any blood back there. Then he picked up his shirt, wincing when he moved his right arm to do so, but forcing it. He held the shirt up and saw no blood anywhere on the back of it. No exit wound, then.

He told himself that was a good thing. He'd covered a lot of shootings, and he knew exit wounds tended to be bigger and bloodier than the neat round holes bullets made when they entered a human body. But part of his brain argued that only meant a sizzling hot bullet was still smoldering inside his chest somewhere, waiting to cause trouble.

He didn't suppose it mattered much which part of his

brain he listened to. There wasn't a hell of a lot he could do about it either way.

He pressed his back to the boulder and levered himself to his feet, still holding the patch to his chest. Off to his right, in front of the sprawling mansion, the cars were lined up now. They'd shut off their infernal sirens, and most of the officers were standing on the driver's sides of their vehicles, aiming weapons over the roofs in the general direction of the house. A man in a dark blue suit got a bullhorn out of a trunk. A blond woman gripped his arm and spoke emphatically. And then Sean recognized her. Cassie Jackson. All the way down here.

He drew a big breath and yelled, "Jax! Jax, over here!"

She frowned, turning and searching until she spotted him, and then her jaw dropped. She shot the suit a look, said something, pointed, and when the other guy nodded, she jumped into one of the cars, slammed it into Reverse and backed up, off the road and right up to the boulder. When she got out, she kept low and ran to the cover of the oversize rock.

"Jesus, what happened to you?"

"Mordecai Young happened. He has Julie inside, and probably Dawn, as well."

"Let me see that." She reached for the hand he held over the wound, but he backed away.

"Just get me over there where the action is, before it's too late."

"It's already too late," she told him. "I made the locals promise to let me verify Dawn was up here before they put out the word, but they only kept that promise as long as it took me to leave the room. They had the entire freaking cavalry on my tail, feds included, before I ever got here." She pushed his hand aside and winced. "That's a bullet wound."

"No shit? I thought it was a beesting." He got to his feet and ran to her car, got in the driver's side. "You coming or not?"

She got in, and he shifted into gear and drove back to the crowd of vehicles and cops. He got out, and so did she.

"Who's in charge here?" Sean asked.

"I am," the guy in the suit said. "Special Agent Ken Phelps, FBI."

"Congratulations. Listen, you've got two hostages in there, and a man who'd rather die than give up. If you push him, he'll push back, and those hostages will end up dead."

Phelps frowned at him. "And just who the hell are you?"

"MacKenzie. The only journalist who witnessed this the first time you feds botched it, at the Young Believers' compound, sixteen years ago."

"We have protocol in these kinds of situations, MacKenzie. We know what we're doing."

"Yeah, as you demonstrated so aptly back then." He saw the man getting impatient, turning away, picking up his bullhorn. Sean put a hand on his arm. "Please, just listen to what I have to say. I know this guy."

"Listen to him, Phelps. He's trying to tell you the same thing I've been trying to tell you from the second you showed up," Jax said. "This guy doesn't respond to protocol, or to threats or to force. He'll shoot back, and he'll use those hostages in whatever way he has to."

"It's more than that," Sean said. "He thinks he's some kind of messiah. Probably believes dying in a hail of gunfire would fulfill his mission in life. And he would far rather let Dawn Jones die with him than let her go."

Phelps frowned. "And just how do you know all this?"

"Because the woman who's in there with him, Julie

Jones, told me. And she knows because she was one of the girls with him at that compound during the raid."

"Bullshit. No one survived that raid."

"That's what I thought, too. I've spent the sixteen years since believing it. Living with it. I was there, I could have done something to stop it, and instead I just kept quiet, crouched in the bushes to get a story, and let everyone in that compound die. But they didn't. Julie Jones survived. And so did her daughter. And I'm not going to stand by quietly and let them get killed—not this time."

The cop blinked, clearly stunned. Slowly he lowered the megaphone. "Okay. Okay. So you have some kind of insight into this guy's mental state, I'll grant you that. But we have limited options here. Do you know how many ATF agents died in that raid? Just what do you suggest we do?"

Sean lowered his head, shaking it slowly. "It's too late for stealth." Lifting his gaze, he locked it with Jax's. "We have to get them out. Make sure they're safe before a single shot is fired."

"Someone has to go inside," she said.

Sean nodded.

"Impossible," Phelps argued. "We don't even know where they are. The house is huge. Probably booby-trapped. We have no idea how many guns he has inside, how many people are in there. It's too risky. Whoever we sent in would be a walking target, and we know from past experience, he won't hesitate to take our people out."

Sean nodded slowly. "I'll go."

"You're wounded."

He glanced down, saw the blood flowing from his wound. He'd eased off on the pressure. Again he looked to Jax. "You got a first aid kit or anything like that around here?"

She nodded, leaned into her car and pulled out a handset microphone, spoke into it. "I need a paramedic over here. Tell them to stay low."

A second later, a man came running from one of the ambulances, carrying a white box in one hand. "Sit down, MacKenzie," Jax said, then she nodded at the new arrival. "See if you can patch him up a little."

"Make it quick." Sean peeled off the bloody undershirt. The medic made a sympathetic face and opened his kit. While he worked to clean the wound with alcohol, which stung like hell, Sean stiffened against the pain and tried to think logically. "If you can get him talking, I might be able to slip in from the back," he told Phelps.

"And get picked off by whatever sniper he has watching the perimeter? I don't think so."

"Better me than Julie or her daughter."

The guy finished his work, taping a heavy patch over the gauze he'd packed into the bullet hole. It hurt like hell, but it had stopped bleeding. "Thanks," Sean said. "Anyone got a shirt?"

"You're not going in there, MacKenzie," Phelps said.

"You wanna stop me, you're gonna have to shoot me."

"And I'm going with him," Jax said.

Phelps stared at them for a long moment. Finally the agent turned and signaled a nearby uniform. "Get me an extra vest and a spare shirt if you can find one." Then he faced Lieutenant Jackson again. "You get yourself killed, I'm gonna deny I ever approved this."

"Understood," Jax said. She reached into her car, pulled out a shotgun, handed it to Sean. "You might need this."

23

Julie had spotted something in Lizzie's eyes, or thought she had, just before Lizzie had hit her. It had seemed almost...apologetic. Now she was confused. Just whose side was Lizzie really on?

"Don't. Don't lock us in any room, Lizzie," Julie said as Lizzie led them down the stairs and toward the rear of the house.

Lizzie looked at her sharply. "It will be safer there."

"I don't want to be trapped in another house that's under siege. Not again. We have to get out."

Lizzie looked behind them, fear in her eyes. "Don't be ridiculous," she whispered. "If he saw you trying to leave..."

"What's back here? Is there a back door?" Julie hurried ahead, not waiting for an answer, and found her way to a kitchen that seemed to be at the very back of the house. There was a door, and she ran for it, reached for the knob.

"No, Jewel, the alarms!"

Julie froze with her hand inches from the door, for the first time noticing the lighted digital panel mounted on the wall beside it.

"He'll know if you open the door. Jewel, there's nothing out there but open lawn and the lake. He'll never let you leave."

Julie searched Lizzie's face, not sure whether to believe her or not. Her hands trembling, Julie pushed the curtain aside and stared out at the rolling back lawn. It was a vast green expanse of open area between the house and the distant woods, which were the only hope of cover. Lizzie had been honest about that much, at least.

Then she saw something move in the trees and, squinting, stared harder. "Someone's out there," she whispered.

Dawn and Lizzie crowded close to her, staring out the window as four figures emerged from the trees and came running toward the house.

"My God, is that…?" Julie prayed she was seeing what she thought she was. But it couldn't be. It couldn't be.

"It is, Mom. It's Sean!"

Julie sagged in relief. "He's all right," she whispered. He wasn't. She could see as he ran closer that he wasn't. He held one arm oddly, bent at the elbow with the forearm clutched protectively across his chest, and his gait was uneven. Closer still, she noticed his color—stark and pale— and the lines of strain around his eyes. And then she couldn't see details anymore through the veil of her tears. God, the power of what she felt when she saw him—it was irrational.

Three gunshots, short and rapid, shattered the stillness and tension, and the men outside hit the ground, facedown, halfway across the lawn.

She tried to see if they were hit or if they'd just hit the ground in an effort to avoid being shot. They didn't seem to have fallen but to have flung themselves down, and they were now clinging to the skimpy cover of a tiny slope in the nearly flat lawn—which was barely any cover at all. She noticed long blond hair and realized they weren't all men. One of them was Lieutenant Jackson.

One of the men raised his head, and immediately another shot was fired.

"They're pinned down," Julie whispered. Then she

moved away from the door and hurried through the house, her ankle so swollen by now that it was starting to go numb. It felt as if she were walking on a stump that wasn't a part of her body. At least the pain had lessened. Dawn and Lizzie followed, both speaking at once, but Julie only ignored them and kept on going until she met Mordecai at the foot of the stairs with a rifle in his arms. He'd been about to go up, but he stopped when he saw her and shot a look at Lizzie.

"I told you—"

"I tried, Mordecai. There are two of them and only one of me. Give me a weapon, for God's sake, so I can make them obey."

He frowned deeply at her, shook his head side to side, just once, then started up the stairs. Julie grabbed his arm when he took the first step and yanked him around to face her as forcefully as she could.

"Just what are you going to do?" she demanded.

He lifted his brows. "I'm going to go upstairs, where I can get a better angle on those men cringing in the grass out there, so that I can send them to their maker."

"Mordecai, don't. My God, can't you see it's a lost cause? You're surrounded by police, just like before. You're outgunned and outnumbered, and you have innocent people who are going to die—again—unless you do the right thing."

He stared at Julie and, slowly, lifted a hand to cup her face. "You never did get it, did you, Jewel? Death is nothing to fear. How many times did I tell you that? It's paradise." He smiled gently, shifting his gaze to Dawn. "You'll understand everything soon," he said. "When we cross over together, the veils will be lifted from your mind, and you'll see that everything I did was for you."

"Mordecai, you're confused," Julie said.

He shook his head slowly, smiling. "No, my Jewel. I'm the only one in this room who isn't confused. I understand everything so clearly. I always have. It's everyone else who's mixed up, misled, on the wrong path. This life is nothing, Jewel. We're spirit beings. Our time in these bodies is just a blip on the radar screen of the Universe." He glanced past her. "Tell her, Lizzie. Tell her how it will be."

Lizzie smiled softly, moving closer to Mordecai, putting one hand and then her head upon his shoulder. "We're surrounded," she said. "We're not going to survive this, are we?"

"Not in the physical world, no. But we will survive."

Nodding slowly, she lowered her eyes. "And we'll re-unite with our Source, and then we'll understand why all this was necessary."

He nodded. "And we'll be together. All of us, together."

"Yes."

A bullhorn-enhanced voice came through the walls. "Mr. Young, I implore you. Talk to us. We can't give you what you want if you don't tell us what your demands are. Tell us your demands."

"My demands?" he said softly. Then he sighed. "I have to go upstairs now," he said. "Our blood cannot be the only blood spilled here today. We have to make our point. We have to make sure they remember."

Again Lizzie nodded. "We have to go down fighting," she said. "But I have to die fighting by your side, Mordecai. Please, don't deny me that. I can't bear to survive if you don't. I don't want to live another sixteen years grieving you."

Julie couldn't believe what she was hearing. She held Dawn to her side, edging away from the two lunatics one millimeter at a time.

Mordecai stared at Lizzie for a long moment. "All right." Reaching to his side, he removed a handgun from the holster that hung there, pressed it into her hands.

Mordecai started up the stairs again, but stopped when a high-pitched alarm screamed through the house. "Damn! They're trying to get in the back door!"

Julie grabbed Dawn and pushed her to the floor, then lay down on top of her, certain they were about to be caught in the cross fire. Mordecai came off the staircase, leaping over them, lifting his rifle.

Lizzie flung her arms around him. "Mordecai, I'm so afraid!"

He embraced her. "I know. But I have to go before they get inside."

"One kiss," she whispered. "One last kiss before we face them and death."

His face softened, and he lowered his mouth to hers, kissing her deeply, passionately. And then a deafening shot exploded between them.

Mordecai went stiff, his eyes flying wide, still clutching her. "Lizzie?" he whispered.

"I love you, Mordecai. I'm sorry."

He fell backward. Julie scrambled to her feet as the weapon fell from the other woman's hands. Lizzie stood there, staring unseeingly at the fallen man, tears flowing silently down her face.

"I had to make him believe in me," she said, her voice strained. "I'm sorry I hit you, Jewel."

Julie tugged Dawn with her, wrapping her free arm around Lizzie, and running for the kitchen and the back door. As they rounded the final corner into the kitchen, the back door burst open and Sean lunged inside, wide-eyed.

Then he saw her, and the relief in his eyes was palpable. He moved toward her, pulled her and Dawn into his arms.

"Thank God, thank God, when I heard that shot, I thought—"

"Where is he, where's Young?" Lieutenant Jackson, crowding past them with her gun drawn, sounded fierce.

"I shot him," Lizzie whispered. "I killed him. I had to."

Jackson's taut stance eased, her weapon lowered just a little. "And who are you?"

"I'm…Elizabeth Marcum. I'm Dawn's…" Her eyes rose, locked with Julie's. "I'm Dawn's English teacher."

Julie held Lizzie's eyes, thanking her without a word.

Jackson frowned. "What the hell are *you* doing here?"

Lizzie closed her eyes. "I knew Mordecai once. A long time ago. I knew about this place, and when I heard he was alive and that he'd taken Dawn, I suspected he might have brought her here. So I came…."

"Naturally. Rather than notifying the authorities. Makes perfect sense." Jackson turned to the men who'd entered with her. "Where's the body?"

"At the foot of the stairs," Lizzie whispered, pointing the way. She was starting to shake.

Jackson nodded to the other two men. "Go get him. Search the place for anyone else while you're at it." They hurried out of the kitchen to obey. Then the lieutenant picked up her radio, spoke into it. "Phelps? The suspect is dead, the hostages safe. We're coming out." She replaced the radio in its holder at her side and turned to the back door. "Let's get you all out of here, hmm?"

Dawn put an arm around Lizzie. "You were only pretending the whole time," Dawn said. "You saved me," she whispered. "You saved us all."

"I love you," Lizzie said. "I always have."

Sean stumbled a little as the four of them followed Jackson out the back door. Julie pulled his arm around her shoulders, tried to help him as much as she could, limping along on her wounded ankle. "He didn't miss when he shot at you, did he?"

"No. I was kind of surprised that I wasn't dead."

She closed her eyes. "I thought you were." Her voice broke when she said it.

"And you cared?"

She looked up at him. "To put it mildly."

He smiled, though she could see he was in considerable pain.

"Are you going to be okay?"

"I have to be. No way do I plan to die and let you have this story all to yourself." He stopped their progress. They'd circled the house and were nearing the front, where all the police were parked. Julie was relieved to see a pair of ambulances waiting, lights ablaze. But he caught her chin in his hand, turned her face to his. "Besides—and I hate like hell to be the first one to say it, trust me on that— but I'm pretty sure I'm in love with you, Jones."

"I kind of figured that out when you stood there and let Mordecai shoot you to protect me. You jerk."

"Well, you know, I figured a grand gesture is always good in these situations, and I didn't have a ring handy, so—"

"Shut up, MacKenzie." She leaned up and pressed her mouth to his. He kissed her softly, lifted his head away, searching her eyes.

"Am I supposed to interpret that as reciprocation?"

"Dawnie says I'm slow to pick up on these things. I didn't know it until you were lying there in the grass, bleeding. But, yeah. I'm probably in love with you, too."

"Well, hell, I should have gotten shot a long time ago." His knees bent a little. He sagged, then forced himself upright again. "So what does Dawn think about it?"

"Let's get you to that ambulance, Sean. You can ask her yourself."

He walked with her, but she could tell he was getting weaker. They reached the ambulance, and he sat on its rear bumper as the medics crowded around him. "Back off, guys, just let me get out of this gear."

Julie knelt in front of him, helping him peel away the shirt and the Kevlar vest he wore. She saw the bandage on his chest and felt her heart skip a beat as her eyes shot to his.

"Stop looking at me like that. I'm fine. I think the adrenaline rush is just wearing off, that's all."

"Sean?" Dawn asked. She'd been standing with Lizzie, talking to Jackson, and from the look on the lieutenant's face, Julie thought she knew a lot more than she had before. Dawn ran to them when she saw them at the ambulance. "Oh, God, Sean, are you okay?"

"Come on, kid, no man dies before putting fifty thousand miles on his Porsche. It's just not done."

One of the paramedics moved in to peel the bandage from the wound, and Sean winced. "Listen, Dawnie, come here."

She came closer, and Julie rose to encircle her daughter with one arm. The medic plucked the gauze wad from the wound, then leaned over to look at Sean's back and shook his head. "You shouldn't even have been moving, much less running around like that. The bullet's still in there." He turned his head. "Bring that stretcher over here."

Someone did, and Sean got to his feet so they could open the ambulance doors. But he didn't get on the stretcher. "Not yet," he said. Then he turned to Dawn again.

But before he could say anything, her face crumpled and she moved closer to him, hugged him gently. "Don't die, okay? I really want to keep you around."

"Yeah?"

"Yeah. Besides, my mom's nuts about you, in case she didn't get around to telling you so when you were kissing her back there."

He grinned. "She did. So are you okay with that?"

"I've been okay with it longer than either one of you have. God, you adults can be so slow to see the obvious."

"We need to transport you, now," the paramedic said.

Sean nodded. "Okay." Ignoring the gurney, he turned and climbed into the back of the ambulance.

"We'll be right behind you," Julie promised. Then she turned, finally curious about the increasing activity of the police. Frowning, she called out to Lieutenant Jackson, who was talking animatedly to Lizzie. "What's going on?"

Jackson looked at her. "There's no body."

"What?"

"Young isn't there. He's gone." She walked closer, holding up a vest like the one Sean had been wearing. "We found this. And I imagine the bullet in it will match the gun Lizzie fired."

"He's not dead?" Lizzie whispered. "Mordecai isn't dead?"

"We've got men going through the house. We'll find him. If you shot him from as close as you told us, he'll at least have a couple of broken ribs, and he'll be hurting bad. He won't be moving fast."

Lizzie shook her head very slowly. "You won't find him," she whispered. "You'll never find him." She looked toward Julie. "But you can bet he'll find me." She looked at Dawn. "And you," she said softly.

"Jax!" Sean called. "She'll need protection. They all will."

"I know. Look, Ms. Marcum, we're going to keep you safe, I promise you that. Besides, there's no need to panic.

They'll probably have him in custody within a few minutes. But I'd like to take you out of here now, get you somewhere safe, just in case. All right?''

Lizzie looked at her blankly. ''There is nowhere safe. Not for me. I betrayed him. There's nothing Mordecai hates more than a traitor.''

A team of men came out of the house, approaching Phelps and shaking their heads. They hadn't found Mordecai in the house. Julie's heart went cold.

Lizzie wrapped Dawn up in a fierce hug, kissed her cheek, then turned and let Jackson put her into the back seat of her unmarked car. Julie looked at her, held her eyes for a long moment before the door closed; then she turned to Sean.

''Come in the ambulance with me,'' Sean said. ''I don't want you two out of my sight again until this bastard is in custody.''

Julie didn't argue. She didn't want to be away from him anyway. Taking Dawn's hand, she let her daughter help her into the back of the ambulance, then Dawn climbed in with her. One medic joined them, making it crowded. The other closed the doors, then got into the front. A police officer joined him there to ride along.

Detective Jackson's car pulled into motion right behind the ambulance. Julie saw Dawn staring intently out the rear window, her eyes locked with Lizzie's, in the other car. The vehicle bounced over the dirt road, and Sean winced with every bump. Julie held his hand, stroked his arm, wished she could make it better.

When they got to the bottom of the mountain, they took the narrow road that led to the highway, but when the ambulance turned north, the car that followed it turned south.

Dawn pressed her palm to the glass in the rear doors. Julie leaned closer and saw Lizzie's hand pressed to the glass of the vehicle in which she rode in the opposite direction. Julie stroked Dawn's hair. "She's gonna be all right, baby."

Dawn shook her head slowly. "I don't know, Mom. I...I don't think I'm ever going to see her again." She turned into her mother's arms and finally gave way to the tears.

Sean reached out, ran a hand over Dawn's shoulder, then Julie's hair. "What a pair," he said softly. "I think I'm gonna have my hands full with the two of you." He met Julie's eyes, held them. "Making the hurt go away. Making you smile again, after all this. It's gonna be one hell of a challenge. But I think I'm up for it."

"You've already made up for whatever mistakes you think you made in the past, Sean. My God, you saved my daughter for me. You saved me while you were at it. You got that redemption you've been looking for."

"This has nothing to do with the past, Jones." Leaning closer, he wrapped them both in his arms. "It's all about the future, from here on in. Our future, the three of us. If that's okay with the two of you?"

Julie just stared at him.

Dawn elbowed her. "Mom, I think the guy just asked you to marry him."

"He did?" Dawn nodded. Sean nodded, too. Julie swallowed hard. Then she shrugged. "Well, you do realize I'm going to insist on top billing on the invitations."

"Is that a yes, Jones?"

She smiled. "That's a yes, MacKenzie. You lucky son of a gun."

He kissed her, while Dawn and the paramedic grinned from ear to ear.

Epilogue

Mordecai sat on the pew in the very back of the church, aching deep in his soul as his only child walked down the aisle. She was serving as maid of honor at her adoptive mother's wedding, and she looked beautiful, in a lemon-yellow gown, carrying a bouquet of black-eyed Susans.

Beautiful. Yes.

But Dawn wasn't what he'd hoped for. She wasn't what he'd believed she was. The signs had made that clear to him. He'd had plenty of time to meditate and commune with spirit since that dark day in Virginia. In fact, he'd gone into the mountains, fasted and denied himself water for four days while he waited for guidance to come.

And it did. It always did. And he understood now. Dawn wasn't the one. She wasn't heir to his legacy. The child who was would not be his biological offspring but someone chosen by God. He would find the heir. He would—just as the holy monks of Tibet always found the reincarnation of the Dalai Lama. He would find the heir. All he had to do was watch the signs.

It troubled him that Dawn would live in fear of him, never knowing the things he knew. He didn't want her to be afraid. So he'd decided to visit her one last time. When her mother opened his wedding gift, she would know. She would understand.

The bride came down the aisle next, and everyone rose to their feet. At the altar, Sean MacKenzie turned to watch her approach in a slender, figure-hugging gown of vanilla-tinted satin. She didn't wear a veil, just a red rosebud in her hair. She looked lovely, Mordecai thought. She really did. And the man who awaited her seemed unable to wipe the happy smile from his face.

Dawn had wet eyes as she watched Jewel coming to the altar. When she got there, and they all turned to face the minister, Mordecai slid from his pew and moved silently to the door. His gift was simple. A packet of legal documents, relinquishing all parental rights to Dawn Jones, formerly known as Sunshine Young.

He thought it would probably be the most memorable gift the couple received.

As he exited the church, stepping into the bright sunshine, he pushed the ridiculous toupee from his head, shoving it into his coat pocket, but left the sunglasses in place.

He'd rather hoped Lizzie might show her face at the happy event. But no. She was safely relocated in some faraway place, living under an assumed name, thanks to a helping hand from the federal government.

But nothing could stand between him and Lizzie. Nothing. She had been his only real love. She was the mother of his child. She had lulled him, won his trust, and then put a bullet into his heart, or tried her best to. She'd betrayed him in the most hateful way he could imagine. With a kiss.

Just like Judas.

He had a gift that could not be denied, even by those who might question his sanity. And he had a powerful connection to his Lizzie, his Judas.

He would find her.

And when he did, she would learn the true price of betraying the Son of the Father.

"Amen," he whispered, and he walked down the church steps to his car.

Turn the page for an excerpt from

EDGE OF TWILIGHT

the newest WINGS IN THE NIGHT
*title from Maggie Shayne coming in
March 2004 from MIRA Books*

1

There was no way the woman could have known he was waiting in her apartment when she walked in that night. She couldn't hear him, because he made no sound. She couldn't detect his body heat, because he didn't emit any. He had all the advantages. He could see her just as well in the dark as he could have in full light. Maybe better. He could hear every sound she made, right down to the steady beat of her heart and the rush of blood through her veins. He could smell her. Strawberry shampoo, baby-powder–scented deodorant, aging nail polish, a hint of perfume, even the fabric softener scent that lingered on her clothes.

She stepped into the dark apartment, closed the door behind her and turned the locks, all without reaching for a light switch. She leaned back against the door and heeled off her shoes, shrugged the heavy-looking handbag from her shoulder, along with her coat, and draped them both over a hook on the tree near the door. Still no light switch.

She sighed and padded across the carpet, sank onto the sofa, let her head fall backward. She worked as a nurse at an elementary school in rural Pennsylvania, spent her days wiping bloody noses and checking heads for nits. A far cry from her former career.

He waited until she'd closed her hand unerringly on the remote control and aimed it at the television before he spoke. ''Don't turn that on.''

The remote dropped to the floor, and she shot to her feet

with a broken cry, her hands pressing to her chest as she searched the darkness with wide, frightened eyes.

"No need to be afraid," he said, stepping from the darker shadows near the door into the slightly lighter ones that surrounded her. She could see him now, just barely. A black silhouette in the darkness. To help her out, he shook a cigarette from his pack, put it to his lips, fired it up. He watched her fear deepen as the flame briefly lit his face. He took a long pull and released the smoke while she stood there with her heart pounding like a rabbit's. "I didn't come here to hurt you. I will, of course, if you make me. I'd probably enjoy it. But ultimately, it's up to you."

"Who—who are you? What do you want?"

He rolled his eyes at the utter predictability of the questions. "Sit down. Relax. I only want to talk to you." He held out the pack. "You want a smoke?"

"N-no." She sat down, just barely perching on the very edge of the sofa, shaking from head to toe. "B-but..."

"But what? Go on, ask. The worst I can do is say no. What do you want?"

"Could you t-t-turn on a light?"

"No." He smiled, amused by his own little joke. "See? That wasn't so bad, was it?"

She let her head fall forward, catching her face in her palms. Crying now. God, he hated crying women. He reached out for a handful of the blond hair on the very top of her head, and tugged her head upward. It didn't cause her any pain, but she whimpered anyway. "Come on, now. I'm going to need your full attention for this."

She sniffled, wiped her eyes, squinted through the darkness at him. If she could see him at all, he supposed she could probably see his hair. He didn't really care. He'd only refused to turn on the lights because she wanted them on. He needed her uncomfortable, afraid and off balance.

"So here's the thing," he said. "I've been hunting for this man for…oh, years now. And during the course of my search, I found that he had a connection with you. So here I am."

"What man?" Her voice was only a whisper now.

"Frank Stiles." He saw the way she jerked in reaction, then tried to hide it.

"Why is it you're looking for this…Stiles?"

He didn't have to answer. But he answered anyway. "He's a vampire hunter. I'm a vampire, you see. Thought it might be fun. Turn the tables, hunter becomes the hunted and all that."

"Oh God, oh God…"

"I understand you worked for Stiles five years ago or thereabouts." He took another drag, blew a few smoke rings. "That true?"

"No. I…I never heard of him."

He moved his hand too fast for her to follow it, gripped her throat and squeezed. He kept the pressure light, just enough to cut off the air supply and reduce the blood flowing to her brain, enough to make her panic. Not enough to crush her larynx. She would be no good to him dead. Then he let her go. She fell sideways onto the sofa, and her hands shot to her throat as she gasped for breath.

"You're going to tell me what I want to know before this night ends." He sat down on the easy chair near the sofa, smoking and giving her time to catch her breath.

"Your name is Kelsey Quinlan," he said at length. "You are a registered nurse. You work at Remsen Elementary. Is all of this correct?"

Dragging herself upright again, still pressing a hand to her throat, she nodded.

"And five years ago, you worked for Frank W. Stiles as a research assistant. Is *that* correct?"

"Yes. I did. B-but—"

"Shhh. Just answer my questions. What I need to know from you is just what kind of research he was doing when you worked for him."

Her eyes shot wider. He smelled her fear.

"I didn't do anything to the girl! It wasn't me. It was all Stiles. I swear it."

"What girl would that be?"

She blinked slowly. "The captive. The half-breed vampire."

He nodded. "Did this…half-breed have a name? Or did you just assign her a number?"

"She called herself Amber Lily Bryant. In the files she was Subject X-1."

Amber Lily. The Child of Promise. Then she *did* exist. He'd heard stories, of course. What vampire hadn't? But he'd pretty much dismissed them as legends. He needed to test his witness, to make sure.

"This child—she was a half-breed vampire, you say?"

The woman nodded. "But she was hardly a child."

"No?"

She shook her head. "Eighteen." Her eyes shifted downward. "I did my best to protect her while he kept her. And she was still alive when the vampires came and broke her out."

"Stiles held the girl for how long?"

"I…don't remember exactly. A few days. No more."

"And he performed experiments on her?"

She lowered her head. "Yes."

"In all the experiments, did Stiles ever find the girl's weakness? Did he ever find out what would kill her?"

She closed her eyes. "Not to my knowledge, no. If he had, she wouldn't have been alive to escape."

It didn't matter, Edge thought. He would. He would find

Amber Lily Bryant, and when he did, he would find her vulnerability. Her poison. Her kryptonite. Because whatever it was, it would be the weapon he needed to kill Frank Stiles.

No half-breed vampiress was going to stand in his way. Not even the so-called Child of Promise.

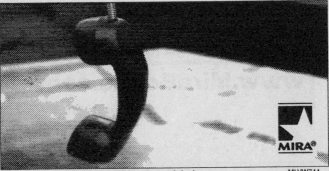

If you enjoyed what you just read,
then we've got an offer you can't resist!

Take 2
bestselling novels FREE!
Plus get a FREE surprise gift!